A TIME-TR

Discover the joy of C

these four time-travel ~~historical~~

MEGAN DANIEL
"The Christmas Portrait"

When lonely Cassie Douglass plunges into a turn-of-the-century window scene suddenly come to life, she is swept into a giddy waltz by the most handsome man she's ever met.

VIVIAN KNIGHT-JENKINS
"The Spirit of Things to Come"

Taylor Kendall dreads Christmas Day until an accident sends her back to Colonial Massachusetts. Jailed there for defying the puritanical laws, Taylor would be left to rot in the stocks if not for Jared Branlyn and his timeless gift of selfless love.

EUGENIA RILEY
"The Ghost of Christmas Past"

A hard-core reporter, Jason Burke has no interest in writing a series of articles on English Christmas traditions...not until he is drawn back to Dickens's London and comes face-to-face with hauntingly lovely Annie Simmons.

FLORA SPEER
"Twelfth Night"

Gazing into a medieval Book of Hours, Aline Bennett never dreams that she herself will travel back to the Yuletide scene before her—and find love with the lord of the castle.

A Time-Travel Christmas

MEGAN DANIEL
VIVIAN KNIGHT-JENKINS
EUGENIA RILEY
FLORA SPEER

LOVE SPELL ✦ NEW YORK CITY

LOVE SPELL®

October 1999

Published by

Dorchester Publishing Co., Inc.
276 Fifth Avenue
New York, NY 10001

MEGAN DANIEL
"The Christmas Portrait"

Chapter One

"God rest ye merry gentlemen, let nothing you dismay. . . ." The Salvation Army band blared in Cass's ears.

Yeah, sure, she thought, I'll let nothing me dismay. After all, it's only Christmastime in New York City; I've got nowhere to go and no one to care if I show up there; the only one expecting me at home is my cat, George; and my hot date for tomorrow is dinner with Stu, my gay-as-a-blade downstairs neighbor who's available because his lover went home to Boise for the holidays and Stuey wasn't invited.

"Remember Christ our savior was born on Christmas Day. . . ."

Christmas was for family, but the only family Cass had left was an aunt and a couple of cousins in California who had sent her a gold-embossed card last week with a gift certificate from Waldenbooks tucked inside. Even they, who she hadn't seen in five years, seemed to know she had no one better than a romance novel hero to snuggle up to at Christmas.

The music clanged on, competing with the incessant *ding-ding* of a sidewalk Santa, the blaring horns of taxis shoveling their way down Fifth Avenue through the slush from that morning's snowfall, wheezing buses belching diesel and holiday revelers, and the occasional wail of a siren. Cass wanted to shut it all out, turn it off and tune in to the lilting notes of the Strauss waltz coming from the speaker over her head. She wanted to fall under the spell of the lovely room and the sparkling people behind the lighted glass.

She had the right. After all, she'd created that world inside the store window. As senior window display artist at Deems & Brown, known far and wide for its intricate and evocative Christmas windows, she'd had full responsibility for designing and executing this one window. By now she was as familiar with the glittering ballroom and the miniature mechanized people waltzing in it as she was with her apartment on Morton Street two miles to the south.

She felt she knew not only the re-creation in the window but the actual, historical room. She'd lost track of the hours she'd spent in the research library at 42nd Street, memorizing every detail of this room, these people, this very night—the famous and wealthy VanderVeens' first Christmas Ball in 1882, one of the highlights of New York's fabled "Gilded Age."

Cass knew that the VanderVeen's fabulous mansion had stood on this very spot at 35th and Fifth.

She knew who had designed the wallpaper for that room, what part of France the silk damask draperies had come from, how many types of wood had been used in the parquet floor gleaming under the feet of the dancing figures. She knew who had designed Helena VanderVeen's ball gown and how much it had cost—six months' worth of Cass's 1993 salary! She knew there really had been a 25-foot-high Christmas tree in the ballroom that night, just as there was in her window, and that it had glittered with diamond-crusted ornaments to be given away as favors later in the evening to all the ladies present.

The room was peopled with the cream of the Upper 400—Vanderbilts and Astors, Sloanes and Fricks and Lenoxes, Goelets and Carnegies. Miss Emmeline Hawthorne waltzed with James Whittington, just as she had done that night 111 years ago, wearing now an authentic copy of the robin's-egg blue satin gown studded with pearls she'd worn then, an ivory fan dangling from her slender bejeweled wrist.

Cass had banked the corners with clouds of white orchids, red roses, and thick bunches of pine boughs in golden baskets, just as they had been that night, though hers were silk and didn't smell "like Christmas in Heaven," as one newspaper had reported. Her orchestra had the requisite number of violins and cellos and flutes. With artistic license, she had added the two kids peeking through the stairway railing and the spaniel wagging its tail, but Nicholas Wright, the artist making sketches for his newspaper's society page, was real. In fact, it was Wright's drawing of the ball in the *New York Sun* that had given Cass many of the details for the window.

"Oh-ohh, tidings of comfort and joy, comfort and joy, oh-ohh, tidings of comfort and joy."

Fat chance, Cass told herself, hugging her parka closer and shoving her gloved hands deeper into her pockets. Her best shot at comfort and joy tonight was a hot buttered rum and a TV Christmas special beside a happily crackling radiator—if the steam came up, which it had failed to do twice in the last week. If it didn't, tough, because the super had gone to Poughkeepsie for Christmas with his daughter.

She leaned closer, her nose practically touching the cold glass. She wanted to fade right through it, ease into that happy room full of smiling, wealthy, contented people. That seemed like comfort and joy to her.

Beyond the ballroom's miniature Plexiglas windows, the warm yellow glow of gaslights lit the street. It had taken Cass days to get just the right effect. She thought she saw a vague movement beyond that miniature window, but that was impossible. The world she'd created didn't extend beyond the window except for the gaslight, an iron railing, and a tree limb just visible above it. It must have been a reflection in the store window.

A hand light as a snowfall touched her arm. "You shouldn't oughta be unhappy, honey."

Cass turned and smiled down into the face of a tiny woman, bundled in layer upon layer of clothing: ragged sweater, torn shirt, filthy skirt, and blankets, shawls, and scarves. Stiff wisps of gray hair stuck out from a moth-eaten wool knit cap. "Merry Christmas, Olga," Cass said to the homeless woman she had befriended over the past year. Olga lived in the 40th Street subway station. Cass often brought her coffee or a sandwich, sometimes on cold days a cup of soup. Sometimes, she gave her a ten dollar bill with instructions to eat a decent meal, but she never knew if the old woman did. Cass had tried to get Olga into a shelter or some sort of program that could get her off the street, but Olga always smiled and said, "No thanks, honey," adding mysteriously, "You're a good child, but I'm where I need to be. My lessons are here, and my job."

"What job?" Cass had asked, but Olga would say no more. Finally, Cass gave up trying and decided to simply be the crazy old woman's friend.

Now, though she smiled, Olga scowled back. "You look like Cinderella, sitting by the ashes and wishing you could go to the ball."

Cass laughed. "Yeah, I'd say a fairy godmother wouldn't come amiss right about now."

"What you need, honey, is someplace where you're needed, someplace where you'll be loved."

Cass laughed again, though it wasn't a happy sound. "In the words of the immortal Charlie Brown, 'wouldn't that be nice'," she said, then she shrugged. "Don't mind me, Olga. I'm just feeling sorry for myself. I tend to get maudlin when the holidays strike. Christmas is a real below-the-belter. I'll be fine once the damn season of comfort and joy is over and done with." She reached into her pocket for a five dollar bill.

But the old woman didn't take her money this time. Instead, she put her arthritic hand covered in a torn glove on Cass's cheek and muttered, "Yes, yes, another place, another time. You should go."

"And you should go inside where it's warm," Cass said with a smile. She had come to genuinely

11

care about the crazy old bag lady. "It looks like the snow's about to start up again." She smiled. "Why don't we go up to the Chock-Full-O'-Nuts on the corner? I could use some coffee and some company. I'll buy you a Christmas Eve feast."

For once, Olga ignored the offer. "Look into the window, honey," she said. With a gentle pressure on Cass's cheek, she forced her to turn until she was gazing back into the 111-year-old Christmas party. "It's pretty there, isn't it?" Olga said, her voice sounding almost hypnotic. "It's warm and alive. People are laughing there. There is love there."

Cass looked. Yes, love, warmth, laughter—most likely. Money and security certainly. The beautiful people in the window knew they'd never have to worry about a thing. Their backgrounds, their breeding, their families, and their money saw to that.

"Look at them," Olga went on, her usually cackly voice a soft drone, and Cass felt drawn into the window's magic. "See how happy they are. Let the music wrap itself around you, honey. Wouldn't you love to be dancing there now?"

The chandeliers sparkled, the music lilted, the couples spun on the little mechanical axles Cass had created for them. The dog wagged his tail and the artist moved his knowing hand over his sketchpad. It all seemed so real to Cass. She shivered and wrapped her arms tighter around herself, burrowing into her parka.

A movement at the ballroom's window drew her eye and she gave a startled cry. For there, beyond the Plexiglas window, surrounded by amber light, stood a shadowy figure she certainly hadn't put there. As she looked, it seemed to grow more distinct—a young woman in a red parka, her arms wrapped around her, brown hair peeking from under a black wool beret. Behind her, snow had begun to fall softly, snow Cass hadn't put there because it hadn't snowed that night. And beside the figure in the parka stood another, an old bag lady with spiky gray hair who seemed to shimmer with light. Cass couldn't take her eyes off the phantom figures beyond the ballroom window, even though she knew she had to be imagining them.

"Go on, honey," Olga said softly, right beside Cass's ear. "You need to go. You're needed there."

Without conscious thought, Cass raised her hand toward the glass.

"Take off your glove, honey," Olga whispered. Cass did.

When her fingers touched the glass, they threw off sparks, but Cass didn't even flinch. She laid her whole hand on the surface of the window. It was remarkably warm. Then suddenly she couldn't feel it at all, as though it wasn't there anymore.

Her fingertips began to tingle. She felt dizzy, like she was falling but not falling. The lilting Strauss waltz grew louder. As she watched, mesmerized, her hand seemed to move right through the impenetrable glass barrier. She yanked it back as though she'd been burned.

"Olga?" she called, her voice frightened and small.

"Go on, honey," whispered the bag lady, gently nudging her hand back toward the glass. "Go on."

Cass reached out again.

13

Suddenly, there was a terrific flash of light behind her eyes and a ringing sound inside her head, and she instinctively squeezed her eyes shut. She felt like she was spinning, or flying, or falling, or all of them at the same time. The Strauss waltz grew louder and louder, swirling around her like the cyclone winds in *The Wizard of Oz,* and always, beneath the mounting racket, she could hear Olga's whisper. "Go on, honey," it urged. "Go on. It's where you need to be. It's where you belong."

Then, as suddenly as it had begun, the dizziness left her, the swirling stopped, and she could feel the ground beneath her again. The only sound was the Strauss waltz, which still played, but more gently now.

Cass opened her eyes.

Chapter Two

Olga was gone. The store window was gone. In fact, the whole big, impressive Deems & Brown facade was gone. Fifth Avenue was gone! Cass looked around at the room where she stood.

She didn't have to ask where she was. She had been living with the image of the VanderVeen's ballroom for months; she would have recognized it anywhere. She glanced at the pine boughs over the door, caught up with great bows of shimmering crimson satin. They were so familiar, she almost cried out. How she had fretted over those bows in miniature!

Yes, she knew perfectly well where she was. The how of the whole thing was a bit harder.

Had she fallen, or slipped on the icy sidewalk, and bumped her head? Had she tripped, perhaps, and hit hard against the glass of the window? For surely she was only imagining that she had passed through the barrier of the window—and the barrier of 111 years—and that she was now standing in the great Adamesque archway gazing into the big, bright ballroom decorated for a high society Christmas party on a December night in 1882. This simply could not be real.

She turned to look for Olga. All she saw were people in exquisite gowns and tailcoats and jewels, servants passing trays of champagne, and the architectural details of this room she had researched so thoroughly and knew so well. More people were arriving, bringing with them the smell of winter and expensive French perfume, leaving their fur-lined capes and muffs with servants at the door before glittering their way into the ballroom, kissing the air around each other's cheeks in greeting, wishing each other Happy Holidays. It looked exactly like the opening scene of the New York City Ballet's annual production of *The Nutcracker*.

She realized how out of place she must look—unless she was invisible?—in a parka and blue jeans and a pair of high-top Reeboks. She glanced down at herself—and froze.

Her feet were encased in green silk slippers with dainty heels and topped with rosettes of ecru lace. Moving up from there, she discovered she wore a gown of forest green *peau de soie*, low cut and intricately draped, foaming with ecru lace trim. She twisted to peer over one shoulder and could just see the protrusion of a bustle, green draperies pulled up and puffed and falling like a waterfall to the floor.

She reached up a hand, hoping against hope that the black wool beret she'd pulled on for warmth had gone the way of her jeans and sneakers and was relieved to discover it had. Her hair was pulled up into a topknot with a few feathery wisps curling around her face.

She wondered how on earth they'd managed that when she had tried every trick in Christendom to get her hair to curl with no luck. But maybe she wasn't *she* anymore. Maybe she was no longer Cassandra Douglass, New York window dresser, born 1965. What if her trip through the window had dumped her into someone else's body and life as well as another time?

She knew the ballroom was lined with large gilt-framed mirrors. Trying not to call attention to herself—she was crashing this party, after all— she edged through the archway, smiling at two or three people who, luckily, did not immediately point their fingers at her and shout, *Imposter! Throw her out!*

She got a clear view of one of the mirrors and relief whooshed through her. The face was hers, though she looked more than a little startled and a brilliant flush colored her high cheekbones. It was her own chestnut hair atop her head, adorned with a perfect white rose held on with a diamond clip. She had been transformed, but at least she was still herself.

The Cinderella metaphor was inescapable. Cass had wanted to go to the ball and Olga had obliged. Automatically, she glanced down at her wrist to see how long she had until midnight. But her super-duper time/date/stopwatch Swatch had been replaced by a pair of thin gold bangle bracelets studded with diamonds.

This was all very intriguing, but it was also more than a little confusing and frightening to be standing there in a room full of strangers in a time she knew nothing about and afraid she'd be tossed out into the street at any moment. Thanks but no thanks seemed to be the operative emotion. She was ready to wake up, say good night to Olga, hop a cab to the Village, feed George, and crawl under her very own patchwork quilt on her very own bed in her very own apartment—no matter how lonely it might be. She turned in the direction she knew would take her to the front door. Surely the snow outside would wake her up or snap her out of this fantasy or whatever it was. . . .

"You must be Cassandra," said a woman sailing toward her like the *U.S.S. Enterprise*. Cass recognized her at once—Helena VanderVeen herself, social lioness, arbiter of fashion, dreaded maker and breaker of would-be socialites, and owner of this fabulous mansion and hostess of this equally fabulous party. "Welcome, my dear," the tall and very imposing woman said, taking Cass's hand. "I had hoped you would arrive before the ball began so we could get you comfortably settled and have a nice chat, but Olga wasn't certain when your train would get in. Of course I would have sent the car for you had I known. Did you have a pleasant journey?"

"I . . . I don't think . . ."

"I must say you don't look exhausted. I always find train travel so tiring, myself. Thank God for private cars, I say. Did Olga send you in her Pullman? Well, look at you; of course, she must have, since you've already changed. One could hardly dress for a ball in a public car, now could one? Are your trunks in the hall? I shall just have Roberts fetch them upstairs and then I shall introduce you to all the eligible young men. We shall have you waltzing in no time."

Cass didn't know what to say, but obviously it didn't matter anyway, since this wasn't really happening and it was all going to go *poof* any minute and she'd be back in the snow in her parka. She heard Helena VanderVeen say something to a servant about the Lilac Room, then felt herself being led around the ballroom. She was introduced to people—oddly enough, by her right name—and she tried her best to smile and nod acknowledgments. Several gentlemen kissed the air over her hand, which was sheathed in an elbow-length glove of pale green kid. Several ladies let their eyes stray briefly to her décolletage. When she raised a hand there, she felt something and glanced down to find that her throat was encircled by a gorgeous necklace of what she would have sworn were real diamonds and emeralds.

"And this," said Helena, leading her to a man of about thirty, "is my son, Richard." She made a formal introduction, then added, "Cassandra has not waltzed yet, Richard. Perhaps you will rectify that fact."

"Gladly, Mother," he said with a smile that dimpled his cheeks. Cass looked into his remarkably handsome—and remarkably familiar—face, like a young Robert Redford, she thought, all blond hair and crystal blue eyes and a boyish grin that was totally charming. She felt she already knew him. Richard VanderVeen had always been her favorite character in the window, the one she had long fantasized about waltzing with. And now she was going to do it! She chuckled silently. Olga, you old witch, or guardian angel, or fairy godmother, or whatever you are, Cass said to herself; when you decide to pull a trick, you do it right, don't you, complete with Prince Charming to dance with Cinderella at the ball.

He took her hand. As he swung her into a lilting, swooping waltz, Cass silently sent up a prayer of thanks to her late, charming father. He'd never had much talent for making a living, but he sure knew how to waltz, and he had taught Cass well. Waltzing with her dad was one of her fondest memories of that engaging scamp, and the young man now holding her lightly within the circle of his arms and swinging her in graceful circles about the large and grand room even resembled him a bit. She'd never danced in a floor-length gown with a bustle and a train, and twice she almost tripped; but she soon learned the trick of kicking the excess fabric out of her way as she turned.

It felt so lovely to dance exactly as the people in her window danced. It might last only a few minutes until she was back in the snow in sneakers instead of dancing slippers, so she decided to give herself up to the pleasure of the waltz and the joy of being held in the arms of a gorgeous man.

She couldn't help but compare the sweet sounds of Strauss to the knife-edge hardness of modern rap, or the elegant swaying of the waltzing couples with the frenetic gyrations of a '90s disco. Her own era did not come out on top in that particular comparison.

She let her eyes take in the room and was proud to note that every detail was exactly as she had recreated it in her store window, right down to the real diamonds glittering on the Christmas tree ornaments. Well, of course they were the same, she told herself, since this could only be a fantasy or a dream or something. Her imagination would work with what it had. It had even given the room a fresh, piney smell from the huge tree mixed with the scents of roses and perfume, and it had created a shimmer of heat rising from the gaslight globes on the walls.

Richard VanderVeen smiled and cast his blue eyes down at her. She'd never had a fantasy that talked before, but this one set up a regular chatter. "You dance divinely, Miss Douglass," he said, "but then, of course any protégé of Olga's would."

"Do . . . do you know her well?" she asked, almost afraid to trust her voice.

"Oh, everyone knows Olga. She's an institution in our world. Of course, it's been years since she's been to the city. Keeps herself locked away up there in Saratoga year-round. I can't imagine how she stands it once the season is past."

"Does she have many protégés?" she asked weakly. Was that, in fact, what she was?

"Oh, yes, famous for them, and all of them well-born, well-bred, charming, and accomplished." His eyes twinkled smilingly into hers. "But you are by far the prettiest."

Cass felt herself blush, wondering if her face had changed to match her clothes. She knew she wasn't precisely a dog. Her mother had even told her once that she had the kind of bone structure that would one day make her beautiful. But she'd never been called pretty before. It seemed such a nice word, especially the way Richard VanderVeen said it.

"How is it we've never met, Cassandra? May I call you Cassandra? I can't see myself 'Miss Douglass'-ing you forever when we're living in the same house, can you?"

Living here? He thought she was going to be living here? Before she could deal with that intriguing thought, he went on. "I was in Saratoga most of the summer, but I'm sure we weren't introduced. I would have remembered."

"So would I," she replied, flipping her mind into high gear. "But I'm not from Saratoga. I'm from Illinois." That much was true, anyway, as far as it went. She had been born in Springfield one summer while her dad was playing in summer stock there with her mom resentfully sitting out the season. It was hard to get yourself cast in musicals when your stomach was swollen with a baby about to be born. And she had been to Saratoga once, for part of a season when she was twelve; her parents did *Showboat* and *The Apple Tree* that year, she remembered.

"Illinois," he said with a laugh. "That's somewhere to the west, isn't it?"

She laughed back. Obviously New York chauvinism was not a recent phenomenon. "Yes, definitely west," she said.

"Well, now we must show you the real world. My mother says this is your first visit to the city."

"Uh . . . no, not exactly," she said, though it was true she'd never seen New York in 1882.

"No matter. Until you've seen it with a native, you haven't seen it at all. Tomorrow, I'll show you some of the sights if you like."

"Thank you. I'd like that," she said, even though she assumed there wasn't likely to be a tomorrow for them. This . . . this . . . dream, fantasy, glitch in time, karmic learning experience—whatever it was—surely wouldn't last that long.

The music swept to a finale and he spun her into a series of dizzying turns. Then the dance ended and even before he bowed over her hand, another partner appeared to claim her. Then another. And another. Then Richard once more. She waltzed and waltzed, growing more comfortable with her train and bustle, with the movement and the music and the champagne, and with the idea that she really was in a 19th-century ballroom.

Chapter Three

As yet another handsome fellow in a cutaway and wing collar thanked Cass for the dance, Helena VanderVeen reappeared. "Come, my dear," she said, taking Cass's elbow. "We must have the occasion of your first New York ball immortalized." Then she led her across the room toward the artist sketching the guests and the room for the morning edition of the *New York Sun*.

"Mr. Wright," Helena said, causing him to look up from the large sketchpad over which his fingers moved so easily, "you must be sure to include Miss Douglass in your drawings."

He turned toward Cassie and she felt a jolt as striking as the surge of electricity she'd felt when she touched the store window. It came from the intensity of his dark eyes, which looked as though they were about to eat her. Did he look at everybody like that? she wondered.

He was nothing like she had imagined he would be, and that fact confused her. Why, if this whole episode was merely her fantasy, didn't he look the way he was supposed to look? Of course, he hadn't included himself in the sketches she'd used for her research, but still . . . Why wasn't she fantasizing him as a pallid, blond young man in a flowing bow tie, thin and aesthetic looking, as she had made him in her window? Why was she imagining this gorgeous thing, all six feet of him, in his mid-30s, looking casual despite his so-correct evening attire, with strong hands, the fingers almost blunt, and with a thick head of nearly black curls that fell over one eye? Why was she seeing dark eyes that seemed to smolder with incredibly intense emotion held barely in check?

"Of course," he said to Helena, his eyes not leaving Cass's. "We wouldn't want the *Sun*'s readers to miss out on a single detail of the VanderVeen ball, would we?"

Helena seemed not to notice any sarcasm in the remark, but Cass knew she wasn't imagining the bitter edge to the man's voice. Nor did she have trouble recognizing the lines of a cynic that creased his face—she saw them every day in her own, modern New York. She knew instantly that Nicholas Wright had lost whatever faith he once had in the world.

Helena went off to see to her other guests, and Nick Wright's blunt, sure fingers began to capture Cass's likeness on his sketchpad. His eyes fastened on her face; he seemed barely to glance down at the page as the pencil moved across it with bold, sure strokes. Cass found it strangely exciting to have his gaze studying her; she couldn't remember the last time a man had looked at her so intently.

Feeling the need to say something, anything, to break the intensity of that silent scrutiny, she said, "I admire your work, Mr. Wright."

"No, you don't," he said curtly, his hand never stopping.

"I beg your pardon?"

"You've never seen my work."

"Of course I have, many times, in the *Sun*." She didn't have to tell him that she'd seen it on microfilm in the Reading Room of the New York Public Library more than a hundred years from now.

"That's not my work," he said. "That's what I do for a living."

She smiled, understanding. How could she not, when she had heard her mother and father use almost exactly the same words whenever they were reduced to doing temporary office work, waiting tables, or, in her dad's case, painting sets for productions he couldn't get a job acting in. "Well, you do it well, just the same," she said. "There's reason for pride in that, as well as in your 'real work'."

He had glanced down, but his head snapped up. "Pride in being a hack?"

"There are a lot of people who wish they had the talent to be such a hack."

He merely shrugged, and she thought she heard a soft *hummph* come from his throat. He turned back to his sketchpad. "Turn your head," he said a moment later.

"Yes, sir," she said sharply.

"Please," he added, a bit sheepishly she thought, though she might have imagined that. He reached up and touched her chin, pushing it gently to the profile angle he wanted, and his touch was the most real thing she'd felt since falling through the window.

Looking away from him, her eyes on the dancers spinning around the room, or on the orchestra sawing away at their strings, or on the candles twinkling among the branches of the giant Christmas tree, she was still intensely aware of his eyes on her face. It was almost as if she could feel him, as if he touched her with his gaze, stroked whatever part of her those sure fingers were recreating on the page. When he asked her to turn back, the feeling only increased. As his hand delineated the arch of her cheekbone, she could feel a tingle there, a warmth, as if the contact had been skin to skin instead of eye to animate shape. When, with a feathery touch, he outlined the delicate curve of her lips, she felt sure she had just been kissed. Involuntarily, her tongue came out to lick the spot, to see if she could taste his essence there.

When his hand moved lower to sketch the line of her long neck, the angle of a collarbone, the hollow at the base of her throat, her whole body shivered and she felt a flush creep up from the neckline of her gown. He noticed her reaction and grinned, a look that lightened his face miraculously. She wanted to drop from embarrassment.

"You'd do better without the rocks," he said with a suddenness that made her start.

"What?"

"The stones." He nodded toward the string of diamonds and emeralds around her throat. "Other women in this room need dazzle like that to cover up for what they don't have. But with you

27

they just take away from the purity of your bone structure."

She looked at him a moment, a small smile lifting her mouth. "Thank you, I think."

"You think? You don't strike me as the coy type, Miss Douglass. I imagine you know very well that you are an extraordinarily beautiful woman."

Cass felt her face grow even warmer and hated knowing that she was now a furious red. Did he really think her beautiful? A man with the eye of an artist? Earlier, Richard VanderVeen had called her pretty and she had liked it. But her reaction had been nothing compared to the pleasure she felt hearing Nicholas Wright call her beautiful.

To cover her fluster, her hand went to the necklace and she said again, "Thank you, but I think I'll keep them just the same."

"I thought you would."

She couldn't pretend not to hear the sarcasm in his voice, and she hated it. She wanted to defend herself, to explain that the necklace wasn't hers, that she wasn't a rich, vain New York society member. She didn't know why it seemed so important that he think well of her, this man who was really a stranger, but it did.

Just then, Helena motioned the orchestra to stop, sailed across the room, and threw open a pair of high French doors. Music drifted in from the street and Cass went to the window.

A group of carolers stood on the sidewalk of Fifth Avenue, the women in bonnets with big bows tied beneath their ears and their hands tucked inside muffs, the men in long coats and high hats and mufflers—looking for all the world like a Currier & Ives print come to life, and in living color.

"God rest ye merry gentlemen, let nothing you dismay . . . ," they began, and Cass heard herself chuckle.

"Is that a funny song?" Nicholas Wright asked just behind her.

"Only tonight," she said, remembering how depressed she'd been just an hour ago, listening to that same song played by an off-key Salvation Army band. She smiled, enjoying her private joke and singing along with special pleasure when the carolers got to "Oh-oh tidings of comfort and joy." She'd been right. Here, indeed, was comfort and joy. She might as well enjoy it while it lasted.

When the carolers finished, Helena invited them in for cider. Within minutes, the orchestra had struck up another waltz. Impulsively, Cass turned to Nick. "Dance with me?"

He gave her a look that was almost a sneer. "The *help* doesn't dance, Miss Douglass."

"But you're not . . ." She stopped. She supposed that to a woman like Helena VanderVeen a sketch artist from the local newspaper, no matter how useful for publicity purposes, would scarcely rank higher than her servants. Cass was afraid she'd offended him, and she wanted to make amends. She laid a hand on his arm. "I'm sorry. I didn't mean . . ."

"Besides," he cut her off, "I've got to get out of here. It's nearly midnight."

"I thought I was the only Cinderella here."

She was pleased when that brought out a smile, and the awkward moment seemed to have passed. His face looked entirely different when he smiled, younger, almost boyish, and eminently appealing. "What do you turn into at the witching hour?" he asked.

"I'm not sure," she answered truthfully, since she didn't know how she'd got here, how long she'd be allowed to stay, or how she'd get back home again. "How about you?"

"Unemployed, if this isn't on my editor's desk in time to make the morning edition. We can't have New Yorkers forced to finish their breakfasts without a picture of the ball, can we, Cinderella?"

"No, we can't have that." As he gathered his sketchpads and pencils, she said, "May I see?" And even as she asked, she realized that she was the only one in the room, aside from Nick himself, who already *had* seen his sketch of the party.

He shrugged and handed her the pad.

It was exactly as she remembered it; this was the exact picture she had studied for hours, becoming so immersed in it that once, before she could stop herself, she had actually asked one of the waltzing women to turn around so she could see the draping at the back of her gown. But there was something different. . . .

"But you've put me in it!" she exclaimed.

"Of course. You're here."

"But . . ." How to explain to him that she wasn't really? That she didn't belong in the picture, that if he put her there, then her window more than a century in the future would be inaccurate? But she wanted to be in it. She had always wanted to be in it.

He had put her in the very center of the picture, dancing with Richard. They made a handsome couple though little of Richard's face showed. The depiction of her was quite detailed; clearly, he'd started it long before Helena brought her to his attention. He had sketched her in three-quarter profile and put a faraway look on her face, as though she were seeing beyond the walls.

And he had made her beautiful.

She flipped to another page. It was covered with dozens of small, thumbnail sketches of the room, the Christmas tree, the dancing couples.

And Cass was all over the page: dancing, standing still, talking, laughing, nibbling caviar, sipping a flute of champagne. There were quick sketches that caught only a long-lashed eye and the curve of a cheekbone, and others done in detail, the shadows cross-hatched below her chin, diamonds sparkling at her ears.

None of the other women at the ball had merited more than one or two quick studies before being added to the overall tableau. Why, then, had he drawn Cassie over and over again? Even as she wondered, she felt a thrill that it was so. He had told her she was beautiful. He had made her beautiful in his drawings. Tonight perhaps she was, in fact, beautiful. Maybe it was all part of Olga's magic.

Her hand was shaking as she gave him back the sketches. She wished with sudden intensity that he didn't have to leave. She hadn't had nearly enough of studying his great-looking face, hearing his smooth voice with its edge of sarcasm, watching his competent fingers doing what they did so well. She was surprised to realize that she wanted those fingers to trace the bone structure he had so admired and to skim over the curves he had sketched so fluidly on the page. Cass had been lonely for a long time, and had wished for someone to care about, but it had been even longer since she had yearned for a specific man's touch.

She felt a touch on her shoulder, and for a moment she thought he had reached out to her. But then Richard's voice sounded beside her ear. "Cassandra? I hope you've saved me another dance?"

"Oh, yes, of course." She turned back to Nick Wright and offered him her hand. "It was a pleasure meeting you, Mr. Wright."

He took it; she could feel his warmth through the kid of her glove. His strength sent a chill up her arm. His gaze, locked again on hers, made her want him not to go. "A pleasure, Miss Douglass," he said, still with that sardonic smile on his face. "And welcome to New York. I'm sure you will enjoy the gilded cage." He gave Richard the briefest of nods. "VanderVeen."

Then he turned and disappeared through the crowd.

Chapter Four

Sunshine streaming through the window woke Cass and she wiggled her toes. But she couldn't feel the familiar weight of a 20-pound tabby cat curled up on her ankles where George always slept. Where had he got to? She hoped he wasn't killing yet another mouse in her bathroom.

She stretched and opened her eyes—and sat up with a start. Good God, she thought, I'm still here. Like someone in a corny cartoon, she pinched herself and said "Ouch!" It wasn't just a Cinderella dream. Midnight had long since come and gone and here she still was, tucked up beneath a down quilt in a huge, four-poster bed in Helena VanderVeen's Lilac Room on Fifth Avenue on a December morning in 1882.

The first thought that crossed her mind was, how wonderful! How truly marvelous, and what a great adventure! Then she laughed. It sounded

just like something her mother would have said,
and Cass was nothing like her mother. She went
to great pains to be nothing like her mother, or
her father. She had dearly loved them both, but
a more irresponsible pair never walked the earth.
Norman and Blair Douglass had lived entirely for
the moment—and the next acting role. Experience
was all. Do it now! her mother used to shout whenever Cass hesitated to take a chance on anything.
Go for it!

And it had killed them. They had gone for it—
in a helicopter ride over Niagara Falls (they were
playing Rochester that week)—and went down in
a ball of fire. Cass was 18 then—a very old 18. The
next day she felt like 100, and she hadn't gotten
any younger since then.

But now she felt the most remarkable feeling
of freedom. She felt young for the first time in
years, and very much alive. She was having her
very own adventure. Mom would be proud.

A horse whinnied outside and she went to the
window, grabbing a lilac silk wrapper from a
nearby chair. She threw open the French doors
and stepped onto a balcony overlooking Fifth
Avenue. She shivered in the crisp morning air
but breathed it in deeply all the same. It smelled
so fresh and clean—no car exhaust or bus fumes,
no smog drifting across the river from the factories
in Jersey. The cold even seemed to have damped
down the smell of the horses crisscrossing the
streets below—though she shuddered to think
what it must smell like during the dog days of
a New York August.

The city below was familiar and not familiar.
Even with no skyscrapers and buses, or taxis
crawling down the avenue like so many yellow

cockroaches, it still looked and felt like New York.

She leaned out and peered up the avenue. She could just make out the slanted granite wall of the Croton Reservoir at 42nd Street, where the Public Library would one day stand. A block downtown from where she now stood, the Empire State Building would rise in a little less than fifty years.

It was early, but the street was already full of people, and all of them looked to be in a tearing hurry. New Yorkers hadn't changed, she realized with a smile. On the corner was one figure, however, that wasn't running off in all directions. He wore a tweed jacket and a bowler hat, and he was leaning against a lamppost, his hands busy with something.

It was Nick Wright, she realized with a shiver that had nothing to do with the December chill. He had a sketchpad and a pencil in his hands.

Just as she noticed him, he looked up, not seeming surprised to see her standing there on her balcony, barefoot and dressed only in a silk wrapper (which she was sure was not proper public attire for 1882). He looked at her for a long moment, that look on his face that was an odd combination of a grin and a sneer. Slowly, he reached up one finger and tipped up the brim of his hat in a little mock salute. Then he turned and walked off up 35th Street.

What was he doing there? Was it just a coincidence that one of the few people she knew in this world—and the best-looking man she'd seen in donkey's years—should be standing outside her window at eight in the morning? And why did simply seeing him there make her feel like Christmas?

Anticipation bubbled up inside her. She didn't know what was going to happen to her in this world, but she had the clear, strong feeling that it was going to be wonderful. She could almost hear her mother's voice. "Go for it, Cassie," she'd say. "Seize the moment!" And her father's voice, too, chiming in with his favorite phrase. "Yes, by George!"

George! Responsibility came crashing back over her. Who was going to feed George? If Cass had had any warning, she could have asked Stu to do it, just as she looked after his toy poodle when Stu was away. But she couldn't have guessed she was going to be gone, zapped into the past. She didn't even know if, in fact, she *was* gone in 1993. Maybe this was just time out of time. But she still worried about her cat.

At that moment, Helena VanderVeen sailed into the room. Layers of silk chiffon and lace swathed her ample figure and trailed behind her, and a piece of yellow paper fluttered from her hand.

"Oh, good, you're up. I hope you slept well?"

"Very, thank you," Cass said, coming back inside and closing the French doors.

"Wonderful. We've had a telegram from Olga; she wanted to know if you arrived safely. I wired her back that you did."

"How kind of her. And thank you."

"Oh, yes, and something else. She said to tell you that George also arrived safely and is being looked after. Does that mean anything to you, dear?"

"Yes! It certainly does," Cass answered with a great sigh of relief. Apparently Olga, in true fairy godmother style, had thought of everything.

"Well, good, then. I'll leave you to dress. Something appropriate for morning callers. Later, you can change into a walking dress and we'll go shopping. 'Tis the season, you know. I'll send Mary up to dress your hair, shall I?" And she breezed out again before Cass could say anything more.

Something appropriate for morning callers. What on earth did that mean? Cass wondered. She knew as much about 1880s high society fashion as she did about 1990s high society fashion, which was to say very little indeed. And besides, where was she to get this "appropriate" ensemble?

A huge armoire stood in one corner of the room. Had Olga truly thought of everything? Tentatively, she opened it. Dresses and skirts and cloaks and shoes filled its depth. Petticoats, too, long and flat in front but with rows and rows of ruffles spilling down the back to create the soft bustle look of the period. A dozen hats, bedecked with feathers and flowers and ruchings and ruffles of tulle and lace and satin ribbon, graced a shelf.

She laughed to think of her closet at home. A stock of jeans and tees, three good wool skirts, a few silk blouses, some sweaters, and a DKNY coat that had been a splurge even with her store discount.

A drawer revealed neatly folded piles of silken underthings, including the corset she'd needed help getting out of last night—and which she didn't plan on wearing again if she could avoid it.

Well, it was fortunate Olga had sent some clothes with her, since she didn't have money to buy any. Almost as if the thought turned on a light over the bureau, her eye fell on a velvet handbag that lay there. She was almost certain it hadn't been there a minute ago. She opened it; it bulged with bills and a few coins and a very generous letter of credit drawn on the Bank of New York made out in the name of Miss Cassandra Douglass.

She shivered. This was getting too weird.

By her third day in 1882, Cass was starting to believe—fear? hope?—that she was in the past to stay. She felt like she was holding her breath, waiting for the other shoe to drop, for the universe to realize that she was out of place and push her right back where she belonged with a cosmic "tsk, tsk."

She was having the time of her life, but she was also exhausted and her feet were sore from so much dancing every night. Helena had filled her days with Christmas shopping, visiting, more shopping, receiving callers, sight-seeing with Richard, and shopping some more. And every night they went to yet another Christmas ball to dance until the small hours.

Cass loved the shopping outings, especially at the great department stores along the famous "Ladies' Mile" of Sixth Avenue. How many times she had walked up the avenue, looking at the great leftover buildings that lined the blocks between 14th and 23rd Streets, the once-famous department stores, forlorn now that they were inhabited by warehouses and sweatshops and offices, all but the faintest traces of their former glory gone. How often she had tried to imagine what they must have looked like when the cream of New York society passed through the doors, bowing to the doormen, examining the goods from all over the world, spending their money.

And Cass could not believe the way these people spent money. Yesterday, Helena had bought her sister a cashmere shawl that cost $1,000. One thousand 1882 dollars! Richard had purchased a silver and mother-of-pearl humidor for his father that cost more than Cass made in a week in 1993.

She had read that this was an age of excess, of conspicuous consumption with a vengeance, but Good Lord! It was the 1980s Decade of Greed magnified tenfold. The spectacle both intrigued and sickened her. She wondered what it must feel like to live all the time with that sort of money—and to never have to worry about paying income tax on it because there wasn't any income tax yet!

And then she discovered that, in fact, she *had* that sort of money, more or less. The president of the Bank of New York, when she went to draw on her letter of credit, told her an account had been opened in her name, and the sum he mentioned as having been deposited in it staggered her.

It seemed she had only to wish for something to have it magically appear, or worry about some potential problem to have it just as magically disappear. When she hoped they would have a white Christmas, the snow started falling within the hour, fat, soft flakes that clung to the bare branches of the planer trees and turned them to lace. And once the snow started and she realized she had no warm boots, she looked in her wardrobe. There they were. She was certain they had not been there the day before.

Then there was Richard VanderVeen. She was not so naive that she didn't know he was "giving her the rush." And she couldn't help but be terribly flattered. It wasn't every girl born in Springfield, Illinois, brought up on the summer stock circuit, then left on her own to make her living who could say she had a drop-dead handsome Gilded Age millionaire hanging out after her.

She liked Richard immensely. He was handsome, he was rich, he was charming. And he seemed besotted by her. From his first "good morning" at the breakfast table each morning to his final "good night" at her bedroom door each night, he was rarely away from her. He was constantly telling her how pretty she was, how charming, how clever. Heady stuff.

Then last night he had kissed her. Standing in the hallway outside her bedroom, he ran his long-fingered, patrician hands up her bare arms to her shoulders, to her neck, to twine in her hair. He had whispered her name with a groan. He had bored his blue eyes into hers and pulled her close and kissed her deep and long.

And it had been . . . very pleasant. Yes, very pleasant, indeed.

It had been a long time since any man had touched Cass in that way. Oh, she had had dates in New York, her empty Christmas calendar notwithstanding. But there was no one she wanted to get that close to . . . though a few of them were willing. None of them lit any spark, and sex—or even the prelude to sex—just seemed lifeless and empty to her without *something* else going on.

And something *was* going on with her and Richard, though she wasn't sure yet what it was.

But there was also something going on between her and Nicholas Wright . . . and it was even harder to understand.

It seemed that everywhere that Cass went, Nick Wright was sure to show up. Of course, the season was in full swing in this last week before

The Christmas Portrait

Christmas, and Nick's job put him in the middle of it all, armed with his sketchpad and pencils. In an age when the best part of having vast amounts of money was letting the world know you had it, Nick was a valuable ally to the wealthy. As a part of the Fourth Estate, he could visually portray the splendor of their parties and clothes and carriages. And he looked good in evening dress. He was always welcome among them.

Despite all the attention Cass got from everyone, all the handsome and eligible young men who danced with her and brought her champagne and generally paid her court, and the attraction Richard felt for her, which grew more apparent by the hour, it was Nick she found herself gravitating toward whenever he was present.

Her feelings about Nick were a jumble she couldn't begin to understand (but then, she hadn't understood anything since she fell through her store window!). Oddly enough, she felt she could relax with him. Odd because he wasn't at all a relaxing sort of guy—too prickly, too intense, as though some mad genie was bottled up inside him unable to get out. Yet, around him Cass found herself breathing easier, not always on guard. He made her laugh with his sarcastic but funny remarks about the world she now inhabited. And she sensed that he wouldn't care if she said something stupid or came out with some mystifying anachronism.

But just as strong was the way he made her breathless when she caught him staring at her with his artist's intensity—which seemed to be more and more often. And when she settled into her lilac bedroom each night, even while Richard's kisses were still fresh on her lips, it was Nick's face she remembered, Nick's smile that warmed her, Nick's confident hands she imagined on her skin.

She hadn't been sleeping well.

As she began to dress for yet another ball of which she was sure to be the belle—she'd come to accept that now as an integral part of the fantasy; Olga was nothing if not a perfectionist as far as being a fairy godmother went—she realized it was Nick she was dressing to please.

She pulled one gown after another from the wardrobe, tossing them all on the bed. Lace and tulle, crepe and gauze piled up in a heap. She remembered all the disparaging remarks she'd heard Nick make about the gowns other women had worn to the balls she'd attended. Gaudy was not his style, nor frilly, nor grand; and nothing in her wardrobe was going to work.

She stood a moment in the middle of her room, thinking. Then she smiled. From nowhere, it seemed, a memory had popped into her mind, a clear image of a favorite painting, and she knew exactly how she wanted to look, even though she suspected it would be very daring. "OK, Olga, do your stuff," she said to the walls. She waited a minute, her eyes closed, mentally crossing her fingers and holding her breath, then went to the wardrobe.

There it hung. The dress. It was made of velvet in a deep wine red so rich it seemed alive. She put it on just as Marcy, the maid, conveniently came in to hook her up. She turned to the mirror.

Yes! She looked exactly like John Singer Sargent's *Portrait of Mme. Gautreau,* which hung in the Metropolitan Museum (or would hang there one day; she realized it wouldn't even be painted for another two years yet).

The dress, perfectly cut, was totally without adornment. It dipped into a deep heart-shape in the front and left her arms, shoulders, and neck completely bare. Against the rich color of the velvet, they looked as white as the snow that had fallen all afternoon. She decided to wear no jewelry at all, though her drawers were positively bursting with diamonds, pearls, and other gems. Instead, she pinned a sprig of shiny green holly in her upswept hair. She was ready.

Chapter Five

Just before she left her room, Cass threw on a kimono-cut velvet wrap, so it wasn't until they reached the Whitneys' mansion and were leaving their wraps with a liveried servant that Richard, and everyone else, got the full impact of the dress.

"My God," he breathed when she slipped the wrap from her shoulders.

"Do you like it?" she asked, nervous that perhaps the Sargent gown went a bit too far. She did not, after all, know anything about what sort of woman Mme. Gautreau had been. Had she modeled herself on a famous courtesan, perhaps?

"It's . . . I . . . you're magnificent, the most desirable woman here. . . ." His words petered out.

"But?"

He took a deep breath, as though gathering his courage. "No buts, my dear," he said. He offered

44

her his arm. "Shall we?" She laid a hand on it and he led her into the ballroom.

The music didn't stop or anything; nobody dropped a champagne glass; the room did not fall into shocked silence. But she could feel the reaction nonetheless. It was definitely a mixed review.

From the men, she felt stares of gratifying admiration; the women standing beside them were less than pleased. A couple of lorgnettes went up; a couple of heads bobbed together in harsh whispers. She felt a strange stew of shock, envy, surprise, jealousy, disapproval, and I-wish-I-had-the-nerve/the looks/the figure wash toward her in a wave. In a sea of pleats and ruchings, of beading and silver-shot silk, of overfrilled and undertasteful gowns, Cass stood out like some exotic, perfect quetzal bird.

She hated being the center of so much attention; obviously she'd blown it. "Hey, Olga, could you help me out here?" she muttered under her breath. "I think I have screwed up royally."

Cass thought she heard a voice, very soft, and it seemed to come from inside her head. It sounded vaguely annoyed. "Well, it worked, didn't it?"

"Huh?"

"Turn around, silly," the voice whispered sharply.

She did. Nick Wright was standing not ten feet away. He was leaning against a pillar, and he was looking at her the way a hunger striker looks at a banquet. She felt devoured.

Yes! The word shot through her body, taking her by surprise, and she was glad she'd worn the dress, stares and all. She stood there as his eyes moved over her, sweeping across her milky shoulders, admiring her smooth arms, pausing at the low dip of the neckline between her breasts. And then he looked up into her eyes—and gave a slow grin. Cass let out her breath.

"Cassandra?" Richard said beside her, and she remembered where she was and who she was with. "Shall we?" he asked, and led her into a waltz. Other couples began waltzing around them, and the worst seemed to be over.

As usual, Cass danced and danced. Not with Nick, of course, but she could feel his eyes on her wherever she moved, literally *feel* them, brushing across her sensitized skin. It was as though whenever she was within thirty feet of him her nerves all came right to the surface and lay in wait just below her skin, anticipating his attention. This supercharged awareness she felt whenever she was in his presence both thrilled and frightened her.

Despite that, when she finally had a moment alone with him, she relaxed for the first time since walking into the room.

"You're a brave woman, Cass Douglass," he said as he picked up his sketchpad and proceeded to do his job, finally. She liked it that he called her Cass—he was the only person in this world who didn't use the more formal Cassandra, which she had always hated.

"Brave or stupid?" she asked.

He grinned at her. "Maybe a little of both." His fingers flew over the page.

"I don't imagine I've increased my quota of female friends tonight."

"Probably not."

"I feel like Bette Davis in *Jezebel*—a bloodred rose in a sea of pure white daisies."

"Who?" he asked, capturing the curve of her shoulder.

She shook her head. "That's one I'm not going to be able to explain."

He delineated an elbow. "They'll get over it. This time next week, half of them will own gowns exactly like that one—God forbid."

She chuckled. "Maybe Mme. Gautereau will hear about it and decide to order one."

"Who?" he asked again, and she laughed.

"Never mind."

He sketched her silently for several minutes; then his hand stopped moving and he stared at her. His eyes seemed to have gotten caught.

"I could paint you like that," he said, the words barely audible, as though he was talking to himself, or merely wishing out loud.

"Would you like to?" she asked, almost as softly.

A look of pain crossed his face, and she wondered what she had said wrong. He let out a sharp sigh and threw down his sketchpad. "I've had about as much of the Four Hundred as I can take for one night. Have you either impressed or shocked everyone here you need to?"

"What do you mean?"

"I mean, what do you say we get out of here?"

"To where?" she asked, both stunned and exhilarated at the invitation.

"Someplace real. Someplace where people know how to have fun and aren't afraid to do it."

Oh God, she wanted to, but . . . "I can't. The VanderVeens . . ."

"Are they your keepers?"

"No, of course not! But they are my hosts."

"Is that what Richard VanderVeen is to you?"

She felt herself blush and hated herself for her reaction. What the hell made him think it was any of his business what Richard VanderVeen was to her anyway? "Richard has been very kind to me," she said, her voice cool.

"So I've noticed." He picked up a leather bag from the floor behind him and began stuffing his pads and pencils into it. "You coming?" he asked as he turned toward the door.

Yes, she was. She knew it the minute she saw him walking away. The idea of him leaving without her was insupportable. "Well, I'm already in for a penny with the dress," she muttered. "I don't suppose the whole pound will make much difference now."

"Nope," he answered over his shoulder.

She glanced around. Helena was nowhere to be seen; probably she was already perusing the banquet tables in the dining room, preparing her taste buds. Richard had gone into the card room with some other gentlemen a while ago.

She hurried to catch up with Nick. "Just let me leave them a note." She grabbed paper and pen from a desk in the hall, dipped the pen in the ink pot, and scribbled, "I've been asked to join some friends for Christmas caroling. They will see me safely home. Don't worry and please don't wait up." Well, it was the best she could do on the spur of the moment. She added her name, sprinkled it hastily with sand to blot it, and gave it to a servant with instructions to see that Helena got it. Then she retrieved her wrap and hurried out into the frigid night after Nick.

He hailed a hansom cab and in minutes they were rolling down Fifth Avenue.

It was cold and Cass's wrap, though velvet, was also lined with icy satin. She shivered and Nick instantly pulled off his own coat and tucked it about her. Then he added his arm to the mix, wrapping it around her shoulders. She gave a deep sigh and felt her whole soul relaxing, as though Marcy, the maid, had just unlaced her corset. The thought made her giggle. She felt like herself for the first time all day.

"Christmas caroling, huh?" he asked with a grin.

"Well, I had to say something. I—"

He cut her off with a tune. "God rest ye merry gentlemen . . ." he sang softly, a note of teasing laughter in his voice.

"Could we maybe try an 'Adeste Fidelis' or even a 'Jingle Bells'?" she said, chuckling softly. "This 'God rest ye . . .' business is starting to feel too much like a metaphor."

"For what?"

"That would be even harder to explain than Bette Davis in *Jezebel.*" She shook her head at the absurdity of this situation. "Maybe when I know you better."

"That can be arranged," he said, laying a hand on her bare arm where it stuck out from the layered wraps.

What was it with him? Every time he touched her, even lightly, even when it was only with his eyes, she felt as she had when she touched the store window—a tingling, a burning, as if she could actually see sparks flying from her skin and like scary magic was about to happen.

And then it did happen: the magic. One minute she was looking out the carriage window at the soft glow of the gas lamps pooling circles of golden light on the fresh snow and the next Nick's hand was at her chin, turning her face toward his, staring into her eyes. Kissing her. And it was not at all like Richard VanderVeen's kiss. It was not . . . pleasant. It was devastating.

Softly at first, then more insistently, he investigated her lips with his. His tongue traced the line where her lips joined, and they opened at once, giving entrance to his probing tongue. It poured into her like hot honey, filling her mouth, and she welcomed it eagerly, gladly returning the kiss. Her hand moved up to mingle in his hair, that glorious inky hair curling at the back of his neck, and she realized her fingers had been yearning to feel it ever since she first laid eyes on him. She heard a moan and didn't know if it came from her or from him. She didn't care.

As demanding as his lips were, his fingertips were just as gentle. With almost feathery strokes, they smoothed over her cheek, her chin, her eyebrow, as though he were sketching her with the lightest of pencil strokes. They snaked their way up into her hair, loosening the elaborate Victorian coiffure. With his tongue still exploring her mouth so that she was hardly aware of what he was doing, his fingers pulled out the big tortoiseshell pins and her hair fell in soft waves to her shoulders. She felt it fall, and the softness of it on her bare skin was incredibly sensuous.

Grabbing a handful of the luxuriant chestnut mass, he pulled his mouth from hers and rubbed his face in her hair, breathing deeply of its scent. "Like lilacs," he murmured. "You smell like lilacs in spring. I knew you would."

Wanting to make him feel the same electricity she was feeling, she turned her face and kissed his ear, nibbling at the lobe. She heard his gasp. Almost roughly, he pulled her mouth back toward his and plunged into it once more. She thought she was drowning.

As his mouth laid claim to every inch of hers, his hand did some prospecting of its own. Leaving her chin, it moved to her throat and stroked the soft, sensitive hollow just above her collarbone. Involuntarily, she stretched her neck to give him better access, and she thought she heard him chuckle lightly. Slowly, leaving a trail of fire on her flesh, his fingers moved lower, pushing aside her wrap and his own jacket. She didn't need them anymore, anyway. She was on fire.

She silently blessed the velvet gown; such an accommodating dress, so accessible to his so-welcome hand. How easily it slid past the heart-shaped neckline, down and inside to enfold one breast, cup it, stroke it. She felt herself expanding like a flower, wanting to offer him more, more flesh for him to touch, to kiss, to turn to volcanic fire. Gently, he began to caress her breast . . . and then less gently. How surely his fingers found the pert nipple, already erect and begging for his touch. And when he granted that wish, how exquisite was the sensation that shot through her.

"Yes," she moaned, not sure if she'd actually said the word or only thought it, but he seemed to hear it nonetheless, for he easily lifted the breast from its velvet nest and lowered his mouth to take the place of his fingers, sucking the little strawberry bud of flesh into his mouth and licking it, savoring it, worshiping it with his teeth and tongue. For a moment, she forgot where she was—and when she was. It didn't seem to matter, as long as Nick went on doing what he was doing.

My God, she thought, I never knew. It had never felt like this before. As sensation flooded her, sweeping from the point where his teeth nibbled and his lips feasted to the very core of her, one thought consumed her. More, she wanted more. And Nick seemed perfectly willing to supply it . . . as much as she could hope for.

His lips returned to hers—leaving the poor nipple momentarily bereft. His hand was pushing up the heavy velvet skirts of her gown, sliding along the thin barrier of her silk stockings, approaching a part of her sensitized body that fairly shouted for him to hurry, when the cab jolted to a stop.

Chapter Six

They broke apart, breathless and staring at each other.

Nick managed to speak first, one soft but intense word—"Damn!"—a muted explosion of frustration.

"Where are we?" Cass asked, struggling to sit up. She seemed to have slid down a bit on the leather seat.

"The *Sun*. I've got to turn in tonight's work. We'll have to delay the rest of this for a bit." He leaned over and kissed her again, briefly but quite thoroughly. "But not for long." His voice was husky, as she imagined her own was, too.

As Nick climbed out, Cass tucked her breast back where it belonged—she could hardly stand to touch herself, so exquisitely sensitive was her flesh now—and pulled her wrap about her. He helped her down from the carriage.

While he paid the driver, Cass tried to clear her head. She looked around. They were standing in front of a large building that had obviously been electrified; it blazed with light from almost every window even though it was now nearly midnight. Other buildings all around them glowed with light as well.

With her senses so heightened, Cass seemed to see everything in stark relief: the pools of amber light cast by the gas lamps lining the curb, the dark silhouettes of the trees across the street, a reflection on the wheel of the hansom cab as it drove away. She fancied she could hear the very hum of the electricity coming from the buildings, and she could smell the snow that would probably start to fall during the night.

She gave herself a mental shake and tried to think where they were. She recognized the small park across the way and the dome of City Hall, the building's illuminated clock glowing in the dark night. Park Row, that's where this was. She'd once heard the area referred to as Printing House Square, and now she knew why. All around her, brilliant signs on the buildings burned into the night—The *Evening Mail*, The *Herald*, The *World*, The *New York Times*, and The *Tribune*, with its steepled tower like something on a fairy-tale castle.

Men passed in and out of the buildings, clearly in a hurry. Newsboys sat on the steps, a few of them curled into sleeping balls, waiting for the morning papers to come off the presses. A rumble vibrated up from the pavement beneath Cass's feet, like a subway train passing, but she knew that was impossible. They hadn't built the subway yet.

Before she could ask Nick what caused that ominous rumble, he took her elbow, his touch causing yet another electric jolt to shoot through her. "Let's get this over with," he said. "We have better things to do." Boy did they ever, she thought. She lifted her heavy skirts and followed him through the doors of the *Sun* building.

A sleepy man at a high desk in the lobby woke up enough to wave Nick in. He seemed to be the only sleepy thing in the building. As they went up a stairway, scurrying copy boys and reporters and telegraph deliverers passed them, all of them seeming to be in a tearing hurry. Still, whenever Nick and Cass were alone on the stairs for even a second, he stopped, pulled her roughly against his body, and gave her a solid kiss that made her toes tingle.

Several floors, and several kisses, later, they reached the newspaper's editorial room.

It was a wide-open and low-ceilinged space. Smoke from innumerable cigars and pipes swirled up to form intricate cloud layers. More than a dozen men sat at small desks, scribbling madly on long sheets of paper. Young boys ran from desk to desk, collecting the pages as they came from the reporters' pens, rolling them up, and sticking them into small tin boxes, then taking them to a large pillar in the center of the room. Cass realized as they shoved the boxes in and took others out, pulling long, still-moist page proofs from them, that the pillar was a hollow shaft, a sort of communication system with the typesetters elsewhere in the building, maybe hydraulic, maybe using ropes and pulleys; she couldn't tell.

She chuckled, wondering what this crew—and Nick—would make of computers, faxes, cellular phones, and satellite transmissions.

A small man in an ink-stained linen duster, with a huge cigar dripping ashes onto his chest to add to the inky mess, roamed from desk to desk, shouting past the soggy stick of tobacco in his mouth. "Put a minion cap head on the General," he yelled to one reporter. "Cut down Mallory, and double-lead the pope," he said to another. "Boil down the Evangelicals," he said to a third, pounding the desk for emphasis. "I want no more than four on 'em."

He spied Nick and hurried toward him. "Nick, what have you got for us?" he asked around his cigar.

Nick pulled out the sketches of the Whitney ball and introduced Cass to Joe Carper, the *Sun*'s night editor and despot of the hour. He nodded a greeting and glanced at the sketches. "Good, good," he muttered, jotting a couple of notes on the edges before handing them to a copy boy who popped them into a tin box, shoved them into the communication shaft, and sent them off into some unknown newspaper limbo. "Jim brought in copy on it an hour ago," Joe said. "Anything happen since then we should know about?"

Nick grinned down at Cass. Had anything important happened in the last hour? his smile seemed to ask. She felt herself blush, afraid she was as red as her wine-red gown. Nick grinned at Joe. "Naw, same old society flash," he said, "and I'm done here."

Joe looked at Cass and gave her a grin that seemed awfully knowing. With her hair down around her shoulders—which she realized was not done in this Victorian age—and her lips undoubtedly bruised and puffy till she looked like Geena Davis, she must look absolutely wanton. She certainly felt wanton, and that made her blush even harder. "Can't say as I blame you," said Joe, transferring his cigar from one side of his mouth to the other. She was sure she saw him wink at Nick before he turned to a scurrying copy boy and started shouting orders again.

"C'mon," Nick said, and led her back to the stairs.

With each floor they descended, the rumbling Cass had felt and heard earlier grew stronger and louder. The whole building seemed to be throbbing. "What *is* that?" she finally asked Nick as they neared the ground floor.

"What?"

"That noise, like there's a giant heart beating somewhere in the basement."

He chuckled. "You should be a reporter. That's not a half-bad metaphor." He took her hand. "C'mon, I'll show you."

As he led her down another flight, the noise grew to deafening proportions. He pushed open a door and there were the huge presses, twice the height of her head, rolling, stamping, churning out the first pages of the morning edition. The noise was so loud she could feel it; it moved the very air around it. The air was thick with paper dust and smelled heavily of ink.

"Oh, Nick," she shouted over the roar, "it's wonderful!"

He grinned down at her. "So are you," he said. She could barely hear him, but she read his lips and they sent a quiver through her even stronger than the vibration of the giant presses.

As he stared at her, his grin changed to something altogether more interesting, more sensuous, a look that promised that he was eager to continue what he had begun in the hansom cab.

The throbbing vibrations coming up from the floor and ringing through her whole body, the pulsing sound, her awareness of Nick's nearness so that every tiny move he made seemed like an exquisite touch on her skin, were affecting Cass strangely. Her whole body felt as though it were primed, coiled, tuned as tight as a guitar string, simply waiting to be plucked.

Nick grabbed her hand and pulled her, almost roughly, toward the door. She didn't argue. They were both in a hurry now.

Just as they were crossing the lobby to the front door, Joe Carper exploded from the stairwell, ashes flying from his ever-present cigar. "Nick! Glad I caught you," he cried, puffing up to them. "Big warehouse fire over at South Street; I need an artist over there pronto."

"No way, Joe. I'm done for the night."

"'S what you think. Get your butt over there." He glanced at Cass in a quick apology, then glared back at Nick. "Now!" Then he turned and scurried back up the stairs.

Nick groaned. Cass felt herself deflating like a balloon. God, talk about bad timing! But she knew he had to go. It was his job. She laid a hand on his arm. "It's all right," she said.

"It's a damn long way from all right!" He ran his fingers through his hair, the same hair she had fingered so eagerly in the carriage. She wanted to do it again, but she knew it wouldn't be a great move just now. "I only meant that I understand." She did, really, but that didn't make her like it. "It's your job. If my boss told me to go, I'd have to, too."

He eyed her strangely for a minute and she realized he didn't know she had a job. Society women in this world didn't work. But she couldn't explain that now. She wondered if she ever could—or if she'd ever need to.

He gave a defeated sigh and nodded. "Yeah, it's my job." He ushered her out the door and hailed another hansom cab. As it pulled up beside them, he grabbed her again and kissed her silly, his hands roaming under her cloak to wrap around her rib cage, his thumbs just touching the outside swell of her breast. Oh, God, she thought, if he keeps doing that he'll never get to that fire. He'll be too busy putting one out right here. "I'll see you soon," he whispered into her ear before he gave her a last kiss. "Soon." It was a promise she prayed he would keep.

She was dizzy as she climbed up into the cab.

All the way back uptown, Cass felt like she was floating. She hadn't felt this way in years. Hell, she'd never felt this way, like she wanted to take Nick Wright off to some very private place and devour him and be devoured by him—but also like she wanted to talk to him, laugh with him, know him in every way a woman could know a man.

And she'd only just met the man a few days ago!

It frightened her, this feeling. She didn't trust it. How could it happen so quickly and so completely?

The answer, of course, was Olga. Obviously, Nick was all part of the fairy godmother trip, the Cinderella fantasy come to life. She needed a Prince Charming to make the picture complete, so along came Nick. But the problem with Cinderella stories was simple: eventually midnight had to come. She didn't know when that would be, but there was no doubt in her mind that any time now she'd find herself back in the snow in 1993 staring in a department store window, wishing the Salvation Army band would pack it in with the Christmas carols. Or sitting in her solitary studio apartment, stroking George's fur just so she'd have something warm and alive to touch. She realized she didn't want to go back at all. And she was sure she'd have to—for that was real life.

Suddenly this fantasy stuff didn't seem like quite so much fun, not when the potential for pain was so great.

Cass's well-developed sense of self-protection sprang to life, and she wondered where it had been all week—and particularly during the last hour! Had she checked it at the door of Helena VanderVeen's house, along with the last vestige of her common sense, on the night she first appeared there?

Whatever, it was back now, taking away the glow Nick's hands and lips had bestowed upon her, replacing it with the chill of hurt she knew would soon come.

She decided she'd be a hell of a lot better off if she never saw Nicholas Wright again.

Chapter Seven

Cass woke with a headache, which wasn't helped by Helena VanderVeen's cheerful face and even more cheerful plans.

"Today is Christmas basket day," Helena announced while Cass was still sitting up in bed sipping a cup of hot chocolate. "We do it every year. It's the least we can do, we who have so much, for those who have so little. You'll want to come, of course."

"Of course," Cass muttered into her cup, wishing she could have just one morning—even one hour—totally alone. As an only child, saddled with a childhood in which she had constantly moved from place to place as her parents' theatrical fortunes waxed and waned (and waned and waned), Cass was something of a loner by nature. But now the only times she had to herself seemed to be when she was changing clothes—

up to five times a day!—and then only when she didn't need a maid to hook, button, or lace her into her clothes. She'd always dreamed of having a big, demanding family, and now she more or less had one—since Helena insisted on treating her like family . . . "just as Olga would expect."

"Be careful what you wish for . . . ," she muttered half to herself as she put down her cup and swung herself reluctantly out of bed.

"What, dear?"

"I just said I can hardly wait to do Christmas baskets with you," she said, pasting on a bright face.

"Good. Come down to the kitchen, then, as soon as you're dressed. We'll be preparing them."

It turned out that to Helena, preparing the Christmas baskets meant standing in the kitchen and watching the servants sort, count, fill, wrap, and tie. Cass was sure the shopping had also not been done by the benefactress. She did condescend to fluff up the red tissue paper bow on one or two offerings.

The servants went about the preparations in assembly-line fashion, the baskets in a pile on the floor and the goods lined up on the long table where the staff took their meals. Daisy, a scullery maid, picked up a basket and moved along the table putting items into it, while Margaret, the cook, ticked them off the list in her hand: "Flour, beans, bacon, lard, dried milk, matches, salt, oatmeal, turnips, salt cod. . . ." When the last item went in, Margaret put down her list. "And the eggs," she said last, carefully adding half a dozen of them on top of the pile before Clara, the parlor maid, wrapped the whole thing in white paper and added the bow, the single note of festivity in the whole package.

Cass appreciated the generosity the baskets represented, and she knew the recipients needed such staples—they would be able to feed themselves and their families for some time—but she did think Helena might have included one item that was totally unnecessary and even frivolous: a chocolate bar, a pretty hair ribbon for a little girl, a tin of scented powder—something that would feel like a Christmas present instead of just a charity basket.

Soon some three dozen baskets were finished and carried out to the carriage and Cass was heading downtown to help play Lady Bountiful.

They were not alone in the carriage. Richard had decided to join them. "And I can imagine why," Helena said with a twinkle. "I've been trying for years to get Richard to do the baskets with me, Cassandra, but he always manages to find an excuse to beg off . . . until this year. I wonder what the appeal could be?" Her tone was arch and her expression teasing.

Cass tried to smile at Richard, who sat facing her, his back to the driver—ever the gallant. He was staring at her mouth. She wondered if she still had Geena Davis lips, puffy from Nick's demanding kisses. Her fingers went up to touch them. They were still there, but she couldn't tell in what state without a mirror.

"I missed you after you left last night," he said softly, his face washed with more than a touch of hurt. "Did you have a good time?"

A good time? Had she had a good time last night? Boy, he didn't know what he was asking! "I . . . uh . . ." Not exactly a glib answer, she thought.

"Who did you go caroling with?"

"Huh?" Her eloquence was really quite stunning. "Oh! Caroling! Oh, it was . . . there was a large group. I . . . I didn't know them all."

"Where did you go?" He was a regular Grand Inquisitor today.

"Uh . . ." Her mind raced. "Downtown!" Well, at least it had the virtue of truth. Since she was lying her eyeballs out, she thought it best to stick to the truth where she could.

"Cassandra," he said, leaning forward and taking one of her hands in both of his, "last night, when you . . ."

"Oh, look!" she exclaimed, pulling her hand away and pointing to a complete nonentity of a building. Anything to get him off the subject. She didn't want to talk about last night. She didn't want to think about it. She'd thought of little else for most of the night, tossing in her bed, her skin itchy with need, her insides achy with longing, her mind edgy with inevitable pain, until at last she'd fallen into a sleep less relaxing than her tossing had been, studded as it was with disturbing dreams, dreams in which Nick Wright was touching her and setting her on fire, then leaving her to burn to a cinder as he walked away, laughing.

Luckily, before Richard could ask any more awkward questions, they rolled to a stop before a big, grimy redbrick building in Hester Street.

Cass felt like she'd stepped into a colorized version of all the photos of old New York she'd ever seen. The streets throbbed with humanity: women in shawls and kerchiefs, men in caps, Italians talking with their hands, Orthodox Jews with earlocks swinging, newsboys hawking papers in half a dozen languages. Pushcarts lined the curbs, offering a bounty of fruits and vegetables, pots and pans, pins and needles, and anything else needed in a poor and crowded neighborhood. Laundry flapped from lines stretched between buildings. The entire street positively buzzed with life.

She would have stood there for an hour simply drinking in the scene, but Helena bustled her into the building with Richard trailing close behind. Though dirty on the outside, the Hester Street Mission was spotless inside. Old, worn, tired, and overworked, but spotless.

They were met just inside the door with effusive greetings of gratitude. The director of the mission, a large woman in black bombazine, practically bowed them in as if the queen herself, accompanied by the heir apparent, had descended upon the serfs to hand out alms.

Cass thought she might be sick.

But Helena positively reveled in it, clearly taking all the attention as no more than her due, smiling benevolently on all about her as she swept past the poor people waiting patiently in line—looking well-worn but not well-fed. Her skirts of cashmere wool trailed across the cracked tiling of the floor; the seal fur of the muff that warmed her hands glistened in the pale winter light coming through the windows; the coq feathers on the hat that had cost more than many of the people waiting for her would earn this year bobbed them a Christmas greeting.

Be fair, Cass admonished herself. It isn't Helena's fault she is rich and they are poor. She's doing what she can to help.

She stole a glance at Richard to see how he was dealing with the situation. To his credit, he looked uncomfortable, refusing to meet the eyes of those who awaited his bounty. But on closer inspection, Cass knew it was something else in his expression, in the way he pulled his shoulders into his body as if recoiling, that told her it was not the inequity of the circumstances that bothered him; it was having to associate with such people at all.

The line inched forward and Cass watched Helena hand out the baskets with unmistakable pride and disgusting condescension. She behaved as though she'd grown the wheat and ground the flour herself, collected the eggs and slaughtered the pig for the bacon. Yet at the same time, Cass couldn't help noticing that Helena went to great lengths not to have to actually *touch* the people on whom she was bestowing her charity. Her arm seemed to have grown a foot, so far did she stretch it when she thrust a basket toward its recipient.

And though there were softly muttered thank yous and many of the women curtsied briefly, the recipients were not pleased. Their faces were not grateful; they were sullen, or hurt, or ashamed.

They know. The thought popped unbidden into Cass's mind. They know she despises them, and it hurts their pride to have to accept her charity nonetheless.

The people scarcely spoke as the line moved slowly forward. But when they were finished and Helena turned to sweep out again, Cass did overhear bits and pieces of conversation. But she couldn't understand it and, as they stepped up into the waiting carriage, she realized why. It was Yiddish.

"Helena," she exclaimed as the horses began to move, "they were Jews!"

"Well, yes, but we don't let that stop us, dear. They are in need."

"We do try," Richard added, clearly relieved to be back in the carriage, "not to be prejudiced."

"I don't mean that," Cass said, flapping at the air in indignation. "You brought them bacon!"

"And why not?" Helena seemed genuinely confused.

"It isn't kosher. They can't eat it."

Helena shrugged and tossed her head, setting her coq feathers bobbing again. Richard answered, "They will if they are hungry."

And that seemed to be that. The horses headed north.

By the time they crossed Houston Street, Cass was fuming. How could they be both so blind and so sure of themselves? How could they despise someone simply because they were poor? Was that what having obscene amounts of money did to a person?

By the time they neared Bleecker Street, she was desperate to get out of the coach. She needed fresh air and fresh sights, and she needed some time to herself.

"You can drop me at the corner," she said suddenly, gathering her cloak about her.

"Drop you . . . ?" Helena began.

"I . . . I have some shopping to do."

"Surely not in this neighborhood," said Helena, peering out the window at Greenwich Village with a moue of distaste. Cass almost laughed. This was her neighborhood, where she had lived for the past five years.

"I hear there are some of the most cunning little shops down here," she said, her voice like honey.

"But . . . ," Helena began.

"Don't worry about me; I know my way around the Village and I can find my way home."

"Cassandra," said Richard, frowning, "we have the Thomases coming to lunch, remember?"

She bit her tongue so she wouldn't spit out her opinion of the Thomases. "Please make my excuses to them." She reached up and pulled the check string to signal the driver to stop, something she had seen Helena and Richard do enough times for it to sink in. "I will see you later at home," she added as she grabbed her reticule and opened the carriage door. She hopped down to the street before Richard could help her, a severe breach of Victorian etiquette, she was sure, but she couldn't seem to make herself care at the moment. She closed the door and waved them off. She could see both of their faces frowning out the carriage window as they rolled off.

Chapter Eight

She was standing alone on Bleecker Street. She sucked the cold, glass-hard air into her lungs and one word filled her mind. Free!

She caught herself up short. Free from what? Wasn't she living her fantasy? A life she had always envied, in a time she had always admired? She had all the money she could want, beautiful clothes, people who cared for her. She moved in the highest society in the land. And she had Richard VanderVeen. She was sure she could get him to propose if she wanted him to. Olga had truly done her work well. Cinderella had turned into the princess.

Of course, this being out of time business could be tiring. She was always afraid she was going to make some horrible faux pas and embarrass everyone. There was so much she didn't know. And, too, there was the insecurity of her position in this world, the very real prospect that it would all disappear in a puff of smoke, plopping her back into her own world. But she no longer thought that was about to happen; she didn't *feel* it. She felt that this was now her place, whether she wanted it to be or not—and she honestly didn't know if she did.

She shook her head. She wouldn't think about all that now, not when it was a gloriously sunny and crisp winter day, she was free to go wherever she wanted, and she was in her own neighborhood. She had missed the Village more than she would have expected.

She headed north, knowing she'd soon come to Washington Square. She felt at home here, even with the differences made by a century less living. The tree-lined streets edged with brownstone houses hadn't changed. Nor had the oasis of Washington Square, though Fifth Avenue still bisected it and the white marble arch hadn't been built yet. The planer trees were bare of leaves, their branches black against the hard blue sky, just as they had been a few days ago—and 111 years from now—when she'd walked through the Square. The first Gothic-style building of New York University already reigned over the east side of the square, but its latter-day architectural monstrosities hadn't yet been allowed to spoil its scale and symmetry. It looked just as she had always tried to imagine it looking, the way it must have looked when Henry James wrote *Washington Square*—she looked at "The Row" edging the north side of the park—right *there*. He had lived in that house—and not so many years ago now.

A wind had come up, and she pulled her elaborately caped coat closer about her. She needed to walk. And she knew where she wanted to go. She wanted to see her building, the brownstone turned into apartments where she lived on the top floor. She knew it had been built in the 1870s. Why, it would be practically new!

She turned south, walking briskly down Mac-Dougal Street, passing the twin houses Aaron Burr had built in the 1830s; they looked just the same. And there was the house where Louisa May Alcott had lived. It, too, would be there a hundred years from now.

Along Bleecker she went, where the small mom-and-pop shops didn't look all that different, except that in her time, interspersed among the green-grocer, the fishmonger, and the place where she bought homemade Italian pasta, would be shops featuring pricey antiques, pricey leather clothes, and pricey greeting cards.

But it was home! And so eerily familiar. As she turned onto Morton Street, she felt almost as though she would run into Stuey at any moment, hurrying off to an audition somewhere.

She didn't, of course. Instead, she ran into Nicholas Wright. Well, not actually ran into him. She saw him nearly half a block away and was so startled she stopped dead in her tracks. He was strolling up Morton Street, his hands thrust into the pockets of his overcoat, a bright red muffler tossed lightly around his neck. Coincidence? Or was Olga up to her tricks again?

Whatever, he was the most beautiful thing she'd ever seen.

All the sensations she had felt last night poured back over and through her like a *tsunami*.

He looked up then and saw her, too. He didn't stop, or even slow his step before he headed

71

straight in her direction. He didn't seem surprised to see her. It was almost as though he expected her to come along. She stood and waited for him.

When he reached her, he simply offered his elbow; she took it. He tucked her arm more firmly through his, covered her gloved hand with his, and headed back down Bleecker.

"Where . . ." Her voice sounded funny in her own ears and she cleared her throat and started again. "Where are we going?"

"Shopping."

That made her laugh. "Great! I'm not a liar after all." He looked questioningly at her. "Never mind," she said with a last chuckle. "Who are we shopping for?"

"Some friends of mine." That seemed enough of an answer.

And shop they did, and it was many times more fun than shopping with Helena in the Gilded Age department stores and high-society modistes had been. They bought a turkey and a ham, potatoes and yams, beans, rice, and flour, a jar of marmalade and a jar of honey, a tub of sweet butter, a tin of tea and a bag of coffee. They added several bottles of wine and one of brandy. Then they chose bags of fresh vegetables, bunches of herbs, a half-dozen precious lemons, even a rare and unbelievably expensive pineapple. When she saw the price, Cass realized how precious the tropical fruit was. It must have traveled from the Caribbean by ship. No quick cargo flights in 1882 to bring in any out-of-season fruit a jaded New Yorker could want. How she had taken her life for granted!

After buying what seemed like enough food for a very large family for a month, they went in search of scarlet hair ribbons, a doll, knitting yarn, a baseball, and notebooks full of blank paper accompanied by drawing pencils.

Nick constantly solicited her opinion. "Would you like this if you were a sixteen-year-old girl?" he asked of a pretty and demure lace collar. She thought of the sixteen-year-olds she knew—admittedly few of them—and the tank tops and jeans or miniskirts they tended to wear. "I would love it," she said honestly, and he had the collar wrapped into a pretty Christmas package.

"Do you think it's pretty?" he asked a while later of a pearl-backed mirror.

"Beautiful," she answered, her voice more curt than she meant it to be. It was the kind of gift a man bought for a woman he cared about, and it bugged Cass to realize that she didn't want Nick caring that much about any other woman.

Soon, they were staggering under their loads, which jutted from boxes and poked from string bags weighing them both down. Seemingly as an afterthought, he bought a box of chocolate bonbons, the largest one in the candy store. And finally, just before stuffing themselves and all their burdens into a hansom, he bought a Christmas tree. It was small, but perfectly shaped, and it smelled of pine woods and Christmas.

Nick had spent a considerable amount of money, and she knew his salary from the newspaper couldn't be all that great. These must be very special friends, she thought.

The ride was a short one—and Cass didn't know whether to be glad or annoyed. The mere fact of being in a carriage together seemed to trigger a memory of last night in both of them. He gave her a look that fairly smoldered, and she thought he was going to kiss her again, but within three minutes the cab stopped and they were back on the street.

She looked around and realized they were back on the Lower East Side, not more than a block or two from where Helena had bestowed her Christmas baskets on the poor. Grimy brick tenement buildings scaffolded with fire escapes rose all around them.

Nick stepped clear back to the curb, then looking up at the nearest building, he leaned his head way back, stuck two fingers between his teeth, and let out a piercing whistle. Several people on the street stopped and turned; one old woman frowned. But Nick didn't seem at all bothered.

"Nicholas!" The sound floated down to them from a top-floor window, in a feminine voice and an accent that Cass thought sounded French. It came out as "Neek-o-lahhhs!" She looked up to where a pretty, dark-haired woman leaned out the window. Her face was wreathed with smiles as she called down again, "Neek-o-lahhhs!"

"Send down reinforcements, Marie." He waved to the pile of bags and boxes and packages and the Christmas tree littering the sidewalk. "We need a.ms."

The woman's pretty eyes widened, her hand flew to her mouth, and she disappeared back inside. A moment later the street door burst open and two boys and a girl, the oldest no more than twelve, exploded out of it. "Uncle Nick! Uncle Nick!" they called as they ran toward Nick and Cass.

A beautiful young blonde—the sixteen-year-old?—appeared at the top of the stoop, smiling shyly at Nick. He was too busy loading up the younger kids to notice the look of adoration on her face, but Cass certainly did.

They caravanned up five flights of dark, dingy stairs, along hallways heavy with the smells of sauerkraut and sweat and too many people living too close together. The children, laden with packages, chattered all the way. Clearly, Nick was a favorite with them. They had called him "Uncle Nick," and Cass wondered if they were truly family, or if it was just a sign of affection. The smile that the pretty blonde girl gave him didn't seem the least bit niecelike. More like calf's eyes, Cass thought.

As they panted their way around the last turning to reach the top floor, Cass could see the dark-haired woman from the window standing in an open doorway. She was tiny—she barely reached Cass's shoulder—but her smile was as wide as the Atlantic she must once have crossed, if her accent was any clue.

"Oh, Neek-o-lahhhs, what ees all thees?" she asked, gesturing at the booty. Definitely French, Cass decided.

"Merry Christmas, Marie," said Nick, sweeping the tiny woman into a crushing embrace that pulled her right off her feet and into the apartment. Cass couldn't help but notice that the woman wore a slim gold wedding ring, and she couldn't help but be pleased that it was so. Nick turned to the children.

"This is Jean-Claude," he said of the older boy, by way of introducing him to Cass, adding, "but we call him Johnny now."

Marie gave him a fierce frown. "No *we* do not," she said, ushering the smaller boy forward. "And thees ees Henri."

Megan Daniel

"Hank," Nick explained with a grin, causing Marie to frown even more and hit him on the shoulder.

"You, you corrupt my cheeldren's beautiful names to ugliness."

"Uncle Nick," piped up the little girl, eager not to be forgotten. Cass thought she looked about six.

"Oui, ma petite. Je ne t'oublie pas." He scooped her up in his arms and swung her around the room, as if they were dancing an elegant waltz together.

"That ees Babette," Marie said to Cass.

"Babs," Nick said over his shoulder.

"Oh! You Americans," Marie said with a snort, "you have no poetry een your souls."

"True, not a bit," he cheerfully agreed as he put Babette down.

"But some of you, at least, paint like angels," Marie added.

His reaction was amazing, to Cass at least. His bright smile faded like snow in July and his whole body stiffened. Immediately, Marie laid one tiny hand on his arm and said softly, *"Pardonne—moi, mon ami. Je suis stupide. Je le regrette."*

He smiled at her, but Cass thought it was a sad smile, and some of the electric happiness had faded from the room. But he turned to the pretty blonde. "And this is Mademoiselle Dominique duPlessis," he said, putting an arm around her shoulders.

"And, *merci a Dieu*, even you cannot make *her* name ugly," said Marie.

"Nothing about Dominique will ever be ugly."

The girl blushed furiously as Nick gave her a hug and kissed her on the forehead. Nick seemed

76

oblivious, but to Cass it was as clear as the doily on the sofa that the girl wanted that kiss to be on her lips and much less unclelike than it was.

Cass frowned to realize that she was pleased at the girl's disappointment. She didn't want Nick Wright kissing pretty blonde sixteen-year-olds, and the knowledge that she cared so much did not please her at all. She positively sighed with relief when Nick removed his arm from around the girl's shoulders and lifted the first bag onto a scarred but spotless table.

Cass looked around. The whole apartment, though incredibly cramped, was neat and tidy and sparkling clean, the doilies snowy white, the scarred wood gleaming. From the tiny living room, crowded with a bed and a sofa facing each other in one corner and the table and six chairs taking up another, she could see into an even tinier bedroom, where a double bed and a cot barely left room to walk around them.

Paint was peeling from the ceiling and the walls were water-stained. The blue cotton curtain covering a window that Cass would bet opened onto an air shaft was faded almost to white. No matter how clean, nothing could disguise the meanness of the tenement apartment. Marie and her family were poor in a way Cass had never really seen for herself before.

Despite that, her welcome to Cass was at least as warm as Helena's had been. "You are so welcome een our home," Marie said, adding in a whisper, "You are the first woman Neek-o-lahhhs has brought here. I have hope! You must come back alone and we will drink tea and tell the truth to one another, *n'est-ce pas?*"

Megan Daniel

Cass laughed, very much liking Marie DuPlessis. "Of course, until we discover it's sometimes more fun to lie."

"Oh, Neek-o-lahhhs, I like her, your friend."

He grinned at Cass. "So do I," he said, and the words were like hot water on cold skin, painfully wonderful.

Marie turned to the bags. "Oh, Neek-o-lahhhs. Eet ees too much," she said, staring wide-eyed. "Too much. Much too much." She repeated it softly, like a litany, as she reverently lifted each package from the bags, as though they were precious beyond compare—jeweled Fabergé eggs or gold-leafed bibelots instead of flour and potatoes. She lifted out the bag of lemons. "Oh!" she exclaimed, almost beside herself, "Oh, Neek-o-lahhhs, I will make madeleines!"

Nick grinned. "Why do you think I bought them? You know I die for your madeleines, Marie."

She smiled at him. "I theenk you bought them because you are a very good and a very kind man." She kissed his cheek. "I theenk I must call you 'Saint Neek.' Ees that not the American *Père Noel?*"

Cass watched this interplay with interest. What a contrast between Nicholas Wright's charity and that of Helena VanderVeen! Nick gave his with love and an attempt to make it seem not like charity at all. Helena gave hers because it was expected, and assumed a properly appreciative audience of recipients whom she would, thank goodness, never have to see or speak to from one Christmas to the next. Helena gave the bare necessities. Nick gave them, too, because they were needed, but he spiced them with the kinds of frivolities Marie could obviously never hope to afford for her children, no matter how she scraped and saved.

She was seeing a whole new side to Nick Wright, and she liked what she saw.

The visit turned into a party—a tree-trimming party. They made paper chains from strips of newspaper glued together with paste made from water mixed into a bit of the flour Nick brought. Cass remembered that she had some sheets of silver paper in her bag that she had intended to use as Christmas wrapping and set the boys to cutting out stars of various sizes. Dominique tied some hair ribbons into pretty bows on the tips of the branches, and Marie hung her one pair of earrings toward the top of the miniature tree.

As they worked, the adults sipped coffee and wine, while the children dipped into the bon-bons. They were sternly told that the other treats must wait for Christmas, including the packages with their names on them. They moaned but acquiesced.

By the time they finished with the tree, it was the most beautiful Cass had ever seen—because it was decorated with that most exquisite of ornaments: love.

It was beginning to grow dark outside by the time Babette put her little hand on her tummy and moaned.

"*Qu'est-ce que tu as, Babette?*" asked Nick.

"*J'ai mal*," said the little girl.

"Too many chocolates," Marie said, picking her up and carrying her into the bedroom.

"I think that is our cue," Nick whispered to Cass, reaching for the coat she had laid over a chair near the door.

"Definitely."

"Do you have to go, Nick?" asked Dominique. The slight emphasis on the "you" made it clear that she was hoping Cassandra would disappear and leave her a clear field with Nick. She gave him the sort of coquettish smile it seemed to Cass only a Frenchwoman could ever truly master. They seemed to be born with it.

"Sure do, honey," he said, chucking her on the chin. She winced and Cass felt sorry for her. The girl wanted to seem so grown up in Nick's eyes, and he clearly thought of her as a child still. Thank God!

A few good-byes and promises from Nick to return on Christmas Day, and they were climbing back down the long, dingy stairs to the street.

And Cass wondered what was going to happen next.

Chapter Nine

"Are you cold?" Nick asked. "Shall we walk?"

"Yes and yes," she said, tucking her hand through his arm. It *was* cold, but she could feel his warmth right through the wool of his coat and her own.

He stopped, pulled the red muffler from around his neck, and wrapped it around hers. "No, I couldn't," she protested, but he went on as if she hadn't spoken. His movements were slow and tender, the movements of a lover. She was afraid to move as he gently tucked the ends into her coat. Then he put his hands on either side of her face and kissed her.

His hands were cold, but his lips were warm against her winter-chilled skin. It was a brief kiss, soft and sweet rather than passionate, though she felt the usual jolt at his touch.

"Thank you," he said softly, looking down into

her eyes in the glow of a gas lamp.

"For what?" she whispered back.

"For coming with me today. I was glad you were there."

Somehow, it felt like the most extravagant compliment she had ever received.

"That was a lovely thing you did today," she said as they began walking back toward Greenwich Village. "She hides it well, but she's really desperate, isn't she?"

"She's hardly found any work since Jacques died."

"Her husband?"

"And my friend," he said with a nod. "We met in Paris. He was a portraitist, a good one. I was the one who convinced him to come to New York. I knew his style would be in demand here." A look of acute pain crossed his face. "He never even got his first commission; he was hit by a carriage before he was two months off the boat."

"I'm sorry," she said, instinctively pulling closer to him as they turned into Houston Street. He seemed to welcome it.

They walked a while in silence, and then he asked, "Have you about had enough?" She didn't understand the abrupt change of subject.

"Enough what?"

"Of the Four Hundred. Enough of the Vander-Veens and the Waldorfs and the Astors and company. You don't belong there."

"How do you know that?" He'd startled her; did he know about her? Had Olga told him?

"Because I know them. Remember, I stare at them practically every night. I study their faces— and that tells me more about them than their waltzing partners will ever learn. You're not one of them. You don't belong there."

She smiled. "And I suppose you know where I do belong?"

He smiled back. "For tonight, I do."

There was no mistaking his meaning. And she wanted to agree. For tonight, at least, she wanted to belong with him, to him. But could it possibly be worth the pain that would come tomorrow? He had said "for tonight." Obviously, he wasn't interested in anything beyond that.

Of course, it was silly of her to want more; she didn't even know if it was possible. Perhaps a one-night stand with Nicholas Wright was part of Olga's plan for her. If so, she didn't think she liked the plan.

"I've got to go home."

"Another ball?" There was a slight sneer in his voice.

"The opera. Then Delmonico's." She'd been looking forward to the evening. She had always dreamed of experiencing the golden days of the great Delmonico's, where Lillian Russell and Diamond Jim Brady might well be holding court at the next table—sort of the Elaine's of Gilded Age New York, she figured. But now the prospect seemed pretty bland. Weighed against a night with Nick Wright, Cass imagined anything short of a flight to the moon would seem bland.

He nodded but said nothing and they walked for several blocks in silence. Finally, as they neared Morton Street, he stopped. The wind had picked up. People scurried past, their coat collars turned up, hurrying to get home before it grew truly frigid. Ignoring them and the scandalized stares they sent his way (along with a few envious smiles), he pulled her into his arms and kissed her again. And it was not a soft, sweet kiss. It was not without passion. It was a thumb-your-nose-at-the-world kiss, an I-don't-give-a-damn-who's-watching-or-what-they-think kiss. It was a kiss she felt all the way to the toes that wriggled inside her fur-lined boots.

"Skip it," he finally said, his voice thick.

"Skip what?"

"The opera. Delmonico's. The VanderVeens. Most of all, skip Richard VanderVeen."

"Okay," was all she could manage before he kissed her again.

"Come home with me," he said when the kiss was over.

"Okay," she said again. She felt stupid and didn't give a damn. She wanted to go home with him. She was *going* to go home with him. She'd worry about tomorrow, tomorrow. (And hope Olga was still in her corner; she had a feeling she'd need her.)

They walked faster now. Cass hardly paid any attention to where they were going. But she did stop short when he reached to open a gate.

"What's wrong, sweetheart?" he asked.

"Why are we stopping here?"

"Because this is where I live."

A very strange feeling skittered up her spine. "On the top floor?"

"How did you know that?"

"With a north-facing skylight? And an arched opening between the two parts of the room? And a view of the back garden, where a dogwood tree blooms outside your window in spring and when the petals fall it looks like it's been snowing pink snow?"

The Christmas Portrait

He gave a nervous little laugh. "Are you a witch?"

"No," she said with a smile, "but someone is." So, it hadn't been coincidence, running into him earlier on Morton Street. Probably none of this had been coincidence, not meeting him, liking, or maybe even loving him a little bit. How could it be when Nick lived in her apartment?

The gate made an achingly familiar creaking sound when he swung it open. The entryway was different—apparently this was still a one-family home except for the top floor—but the stairway and its railing were the same, except that now the beautiful wood was stained and highly polished instead of being painted the fairly disgusting shade of yellow she'd never been able to get used to.

As they passed the door one floor below the top, she had to bite her tongue to keep from calling out, "Stuey, you home?" As they reached the top floor and Cass found herself staring at her own front door, she laughed. "I don't suppose you've got a cat named George."

He froze, his key in the lock. "You are a witch."

"Don't tell me you do!"

"Georgina," he said with a nod, finally opening the door. "I thought she was a male when I first got her. By the time I found out otherwise, she was stuck with George." He nudged her through the door.

Cass started to laugh. She couldn't help herself. This was too bizarre; it had to be meant as a comedy. She laughed harder; she was afraid she was getting hysterical. She laughed until he stopped her in the most effective way possible.

He kissed her mouth shut. Then he kissed it open. Then he filled it so she couldn't laugh even if she wanted to. She didn't want to.

She wanted to swallow him. She took his tongue into her mouth and tasted it, savored it, bit it till he grunted. Nick kicked the door shut, and half-pushed, half-led her the few feet toward the bed.

Cass knew they had been working their way toward this moment ever since she first metamorphosed through the window and showed up in Helena's ballroom. He'd been touching her with his eyes whenever he saw her, heating her skin, triggering her pulse, learning the feel of her, making her want him. Then there was that business in the cab downtown last night. What was happening now was merely a logical extension of what they'd been doing to and with each other for days with their eyes and their hands and their minds.

With so much visual and mental foreplay behind them, they neither needed nor wanted to draw out the anticipation. Fingers flew over buttons and hooks and laces. Cass thought probably no Victorian lady had ever shed her multiple layers of protective clothing quite so quickly. Her gown fell away, her petticoats disappeared, her corset evaporated. Nick's shirt was stripped off, his trousers melted. Accessories vaporized.

Soon, though not soon enough, they were bare to each other. The bed received them.

It was not slow and it was not gentle, but Cass didn't want it to be. She wanted him to do exactly what he was doing to her. It seemed like his hands were everywhere at once, on her, around her, and his mouth followed them wherever they went. Never had she been so keenly aware of every part of her body. Every place he touched sang, every piece of skin he kissed danced for joy. And their major key chorus was a single word—more!

He obliged. Teeth and tongue, fingers and lips, he obliged.

More!

Nibbling, probing, demanding, he obliged.

More!

And then he was inside her, huge and hard and oh so demanding. She didn't mind that it was happening so quickly; she wanted him there, she was ready, as ready as she'd ever been in her life, as ready as she would ever be.

It was short and intense, so intense she wondered if she just might die. Within seconds, it seemed, she was soaring, as though all she needed was his presence to turn her into a single nerve cell. And then she was over the top and flying, and he was flying with her.

More, yes, more than she'd ever known, more than she'd believed was possible; that was what Nick Wright gave her.

Over the peak they climbed; then slowly they began the slide down again. Enough, her mind whispered as his body unjoined from hers.

The clouds had made a hole for an almost-full moon, and it poured its blue-white glow through the skylight to cover their heated skin. Nick raised himself up on one elbow and stared down at her. "My God," he said in a whisper so soft she wondered if she'd actually heard it.

But she could certainly agree with the sentiment. My God. She felt like a shattered Christmas tree ornament. Was this what she'd wanted, this . . . coupling . . . with a passion that was almost violent? This out-of-control, hysterical physicality?

Cass had always been honest with herself, and yes, it was what she had wanted, what she had asked for, what she had gotten. But it would have been impossible with anyone other than Nick Wright, she was dead certain of that. The kind of chemistry that existed between them demanded its due, but it willingly gave up its rewards, too.

Chemistry. Yes, there certainly was that. But was there anything more? More. The word seemed to have taken over her vocabulary. She shivered.

"You're cold," he said quickly. He jumped up and struck a match to the fire that was already laid in the grate. She smiled. It had been that very fireplace, together with the skylight that glowed over her head, that had convinced her to take the apartment, even though it was both smaller and more expensive than what she'd been looking for.

She looked around. Certainly there had been changes in over a century. For one thing, there was no electricity yet. A pair of gas globes, dark now, were mounted on either side of the arch that led to the back half of the apartment. And where the door to her bathroom stood there was nothing—just a solid wall. Was there a toilet in the hall? A privy in the garden? A collection of chamber pots? Helena had indoor plumbing in her mansion on Fifth Avenue, but it might not have spread to Village brownstones yet, Cass guessed.

She could see that her open-counter kitchen had yet to be installed. Where her stove would one day stand was a cupboard; beside the galvanized sink in the corner was a pump. So there was plumbing of some sort. On a table stood what looked like a single-burner gas hot plate. That was it. Nick was probably not much of a cook, she thought.

In the front part of the big open space, there beneath the skylight, was where Nick had his studio. An easel stood almost exactly where Cass had placed her drafting table—where she worked out her window display designs during solitary evenings. There was no canvas on the easel, no palette on the nearby table. There were no tubes of paint (making her wonder if paint came in tubes yet), and no smell of turpentine and linseed oil. Nick hadn't been painting lately.

The bed, too, was placed approximately where she would one day place hers, and the thought made her nervous. She felt like she had just made love in her own bed.

The fire was crackling nicely now, casting a lovely yellow glow over the room. In the shadowed light, it seemed more familiar than ever. Cass pulled the chenille bedspread from the bed, wrapped it around herself, and curled into a wing chair beside the fireplace. From out of nowhere, it seemed, a huge tabby cat jumped up onto her lap and stretched.

"Hello, George," she said, stroking the fur that was as familiar as if this really were her George. The cat flexed its claws in pleasure, catching the chenille and reaching through to her bare skin, just as her George had a bad habit of doing. She shifted it into a better position and it settled down for a nap.

Nick lit an oil lamp, set it on the mantel, then sat across from Cass. Idly, almost automatically it seemed, he picked up a sketchpad and a piece of charcoal and began to delineate the lines of her sated body, her curves lush with firelight and moonlight, her shadows that no longer held quite as many secrets for him.

"You're beautiful like that," he said softly, his hand still moving. "I'd like to paint you like that." There was a sad, wistful quality to his voice.

"Go ahead," she said, feeling loose and lazy and yes, beautiful. "I won't mind. I'll just sit here with George."

His hand faltered a moment, then he started drawing her again. "I don't paint. Not anymore."

"Why not?"

He shrugged. "It stopped amusing me." He tried to make it light, but she heard bitterness in his voice. Bitterness and anger and resignation all mixed into a powerfully negative stew.

Abruptly he stood up. "Would you like some coffee?"

"I'd love some coffee."

"I'm out. I'll have to go get some."

"Oh, no, don't bother, I don't really need it."

"I do." In a flash, he had pulled on his pants and shoes, thrown a coat over his bare chest, jammed a cap on his head, and left the room.

Chapter Ten

"Well," Cass said to the walls when the sound of his footsteps faded down the stairs. "What have you got me into here, Olga?"

"Nothing you can't handle, honey." Cass would have sworn she heard the words, out loud, right in this room. And it was definitely Olga's voice.

"Olga?" She looked around, peering into the shadowy corners. "Where are you, dammit?"

"Tsk-tsk. Nick wouldn't like to hear you swearing, honey."

"Is this real? Are you really here in this room?" She stood, dropping George unceremoniously to the floor. "And if you are, why can't I see you?" She felt genuinely foolish talking to the walls of an empty room with a fat tabby cat for an audience. Was she imagining Olga's voice? Was she simply giving Olga the script that was running in her own mind?

"Okay, if you're really here, answer me a question. Why did Nick stop painting? And why does it cause him so much pain?"

Silence. She looked around the room, as if she would see the old bag lady perched on the windowsill or curled up on the bed, or burrowing into the chair. Then she heard the voice again, soft as a whisper. "Look in the closet."

"The closet? How will that help?" But Olga was gone. Message delivered, she'd gone as quickly as she'd come.

Cass picked up the lamp and went to the closet. A robe of maroon wool hung from a hook on the door and she put it on, then she opened the door, almost afraid of what she would find.

Though she'd always hated the dinky little thing, she had realized by now that by Victorian standards it was large. There were no clothes hanging or folded on the shelf, though. Instead, here were the paints and brushes, the oil-soaked rags and palette knives in a jar. And leaning against the walls were canvases, dozens of them, all turned inward toward the walls.

She picked up the one nearest her, turned it around, and kneeled to see it better. Then she gasped. The painting was slashed, a vicious knife cut diagonally across the center. She looked at another; it was slashed too. And another and another. Every canvas Nick had painted had been vandalized. She was sure it was by his own hand.

She pulled one of the least damaged ones closer to the light and studied it. It was a view of the garden behind this very brownstone—Cass recognized it at once. A woman in a pink gown sat on a bench reading a book, the sun painting reddish glints in her blonde hair. It was the sort of scene Renoir would have painted.

And it wasn't bad. In fact, it was charming and technically extremely well done. But it had no spark to it; even Cass could see that. The girl was just a generic girl in a garden, not an individual with secrets the viewer hoped to share.

She looked at a dozen paintings, seeing beyond the violent slashes. They all suffered from the same lack of a spark. They were proficient, even pretty. And they were dull.

There was one picture, larger than the others, propped on a higher shelf and covered with a piece of black flannel. Setting aside her lamp, Cass lifted it down and pulled off its cover.

It took her breath away.

It was a painting of a woman, blonde hair rippling to her shoulders and wearing the sort of white gown the Pre-Raphaelites were so fond of—all drapey muslin tied with a ribbon at the waist. She had thrown her head back and she was laughing—not the genteel titter so favored by most Victorian women but a full-bellied, wide-mouthed laugh. Cass could almost hear the sound of it echoing through the tiny closet.

Now this was a painting! Even by her poor lamplight, she could see that the colors were luminous, with a richness and depth that made the paint seem alive. There was a Monet quality to the colors, a van Gogh feeling to some of the brushwork, but it was not at all a derivative work. It was wholly original. It was the sort of painting Cass could imagine an auctioneer at Sotheby's knocking down for a million and change.

Pulling the lamp closer yet, she looked at the signature in the bottom left corner. "Nicholas—1880."

Now she knew why he was so unhappy about his work. He had had it—the magic that comes only to a very few chosen at birth. And somewhere along the way in the last two years, he had lost it.

Why? What had gone wrong? She had to know.

She closed the closet on both the triumph of the blonde and the failure of all the slashed canvases. Coming back into the room, she picked up the sketchpad where he had committed her face to posterity.

As always, he had made her beautiful, far more beautiful than she could ever believe she was, but tonight she did feel like this exquisite creature he had drawn.

She looked closer. Was she imagining it? No, it was there, that spark. Even with just a rough piece of charcoal on newsprint, he had managed to catch a trace of the magic that so filled the painting in the closet. He had captured the sated quality of her body, the total relaxation of every muscle, and he had caught the expression in her eyes that said she had just been well loved. So real was the quality that she was almost embarrassed looking at it.

She felt like she was truly looking at herself, at the real Cass Douglass, for the first time in her life.

She heard footsteps on the stairs and she dropped the sketchpad with a guilty start. Somehow, she didn't think Nick would appreciate her analyzing his work tonight.

He swept through the door, bringing the winter freshness in with him. He walked to the fireplace and opened his coat to let the heat warm his bare chest. The flames flickering over the smooth, broad stretch of his skin was the most beautiful thing she'd ever seen.

He looked back at her, grinning at the sight of her with his wool bathrobe flapping around her feet. "That suits you," he said.

"I thought so." She gave a model's turn.

"But not as well as nothing at all suits you."

"Maybe, but goose bumps are definitely not my style."

"Goose bumps, huh? Maybe we can fix that." He reached out and pulled her closer, slid his hands inside the maroon wool, and ran his fingers around her waist.

"Eeek!" she squealed. "Not like that, we won't. Your hands are like ice."

He laughed. "Sorry. Here, why don't you get this started." He reached into his pocket, pulled out a small brown bag of coffee, and tossed it to her. Instinct helped her catch it. "Pot's on the shelf." He gestured toward the back of the apartment, then thrust his hands toward the fire once more.

Start the coffee. Hmmmmm. The pot was easy enough, a pretty standard spatter-ware enamel stove-top perk job. She could handle that. The pump—well, she'd seen them in movies. You just pumped the handle up and down, right? She tried it. Nothing happened except that it made an awful scraping sound. She tried again.

"You've got to prime it, silly," he said, walking over to pick up a large pitcher of water and pour it into the top of the pump. Within seconds the water was flowing into the coffeepot. Then she faced the "stove." She hadn't the slightest idea how to use it. It didn't seem to have the sort of knob she was used to. Some wooden matches sat on the table beside it, so she assumed it had to be lit. Great, she'd probably blow the building off the map. Or blow herself back into 1993, which she really didn't want to do right now.

As she stared at it helplessly, Nick came and took the pot out of her hand. "Haven't you ever made coffee before?"

"Yeah," she muttered, "in a microwave."

"A what?" He reached for a match, turned a valve, and lit the burner.

She shook her head. "It's a kind of oven."

"Well, whoever heard of making coffee in an oven?" He set the pot over the fire. "You rich girls. Never get your fingers dirty in a kitchen, do you?"

"I'll have you know I can make a perfect soufflé, boil a perfect three-minute egg, and flip a perfect crepe without a wrinkle. And what makes you think I'm rich?"

"You certainly move with a rich crowd, probably the richest the world has ever known. And don't forget, I've seen you when you've got the rocks on. Poor girls don't go to balls at the VanderVeens with a hundred thousand dollars worth of emeralds draped around their necks."

"Actually, they do," she said, but in a soft voice, more or less to herself—and to Olga.

He opened a cupboard and took out a sugar bowl. Then he opened the back window, reached out onto the fire escape, and brought in a half-frozen bottle of milk.

While they waited for the coffee to do its thing, Cass wondered. Should she say anything about the slashed paintings? Or about the one brilliant piece of work? Did she even have the right? She wanted to help him get past the pain, wherever it came from. But what, exactly, did Nick Wright need to hear from her?

Perhaps he would give up his secret if she let him in on hers.

"Why did you stop?" she asked as the coffee began to bubble.

"Stop what?"

"Painting. You said you used to paint. Now you don't. I just wondered why."

"I've told you why. It ceased to amuse me." He tried to make his voice light, mocking, but the pain came through just the same.

"You don't paint, yet you leave your easel set up in the one spot in the room that gets the best morning light."

"How do you know that?"

She chuckled. "There are a number of things about this apartment I know. You'd be amazed." She took a deep breath. "I can even tell you who will live in this apartment, look out at that back garden, sleep under this very skylight more than a century from now."

As she had hoped, that got a smile from him. "You've been trying all day to convince me you're a witch, haven't you? All right then, who will live here, look out at my garden, and sleep under my skylight?"

She poured two cups of coffee, added milk to hers, and took a sip. It was delicious and wonderfully fortifying. She looked him straight in the eye. "I will," she said.

Well, it was out, for good or ill, and she was glad. It had been such a burden, carrying around this earth-shaking event in her life and not being able to tell anyone because she was sure no one would believe her. She didn't know if Nick would believe her. But she figured she had her best shot with him.

"You will," he said matter-of-factly, sipping his coffee.

"That's right. In the year 1993, I will live in this apartment. I will put my bed right where you've put yours. I will own a tabby cat named George—a male. I will get up every morning and walk to the bagel shop on the corner— it's where that little mom-and-pop grocery store is now. Then I'll get on the subway—they're going to put the trains underground in a few years. If I'm late, maybe I'll take a cab. Not a horse-drawn hansom, but a car with an engine. I'll ride to my job as a window display artist at a department store that will stand on the very spot where I first saw you—where Helena VanderVeen's ballroom now stands, the very spot where I "—how to put it?—"where I fell through time that night and ended up 111 years in the past."

In the flickering light of the fire and the more even glow of the oil lamp, she watched his face carefully as she talked. As she added more detail, his grin faded to something else, but she couldn't be sure what it was. Did he think she was being fanciful? Lying? Joking? Did he think she was crazy?

He sipped his coffee and stared at her for a long moment. Then he said softly, "I always knew there was something different about you."

"You believe me?" She knew she sounded surprised.

"Are you lying to me?"

"No."

"No, I don't think you're capable of lying. Or if you did, you'd give yourself away. You have the most wonderfully expressive face."

"Th-thank you, I guess."

"Besides, that first moment you showed up in that ballroom you had the most incredible look of surprise and wonder on your face, like a child who's just been presented with the world's biggest birthday cake."

She chuckled. "That's pretty much how I felt, and like maybe I'd slipped a cog or two. One minute I was standing in the snow on Fifth Avenue feeling sorry for myself and the next there I was, wearing diamonds and emeralds."

He refilled their cups, added just the right amount of milk to hers, and led her back to the fire. When they were sitting across from each other, Cass with her feet tucked up beneath her and George snuggled into her lap, he said, "Okay, now tell me the whole thing."

And so she did, or at least as much of it as she knew. She told him about the window she had designed, how she had used his drawings from the *Sun* to recreate it in perfect detail. He smiled at that and said, "Well, at least they turned out to be good for something besides wrapping yesterday's fish."

"I couldn't have done it without them."

She told him about the Salvation Army band and the Strauss waltzes she'd chosen to play on the loudspeakers (which needed a brief explanation, too).

He took it all in, fascinated, asking questions and constantly interrupting the flow of the narrative, but Cass didn't mind. He believed her!

And then she told him about Olga, not only how she had sent Cass through the window but how she'd kept up the magic since her arrival.

He nodded. "Cinderella." She nodded too. "You said that night you were Cinderella. Does that mean that midnight will eventually come and you'll turn back into a modern miss sitting in the ashes?"

"I don't know," she said honestly.

He stood, drew her up out of her chair, sending George tumbling to the floor again, and held her close. He ran one hand over her hair. "I hope not."

"Me too." And she realized as she said it that it was true. She couldn't think of a single thing in 1993 that she wanted to go back to, not if she could stay right here in Nick Wright's arms.

He kissed her then, a deep, warm kiss that told her he wanted her to stay, too. And this time, when his hands slid past the maroon wool and around her waist, they weren't cold. They were warm and welcoming.

When he finally pulled his mouth reluctantly from hers, he looked down into her eyes and said, "I'm starving."

"I noticed."

"For food."

"Oh."

"Aren't you hungry? I deprived you of Delmonico's."

"Starving."

"Well, let's see what we've got." He took her hand, as though afraid to lose physical contact, and led her to the kitchen, such as it was. "Bread, cheese, a hothouse tomato," he said, picking it up from the counter and tossing it into the air like a baseball. "A rather nice one, too." He opened the window and reached out onto the fire escape. "And ham!"

"That's quite a refrigerator you've got there. What do you do in August?"

"Eat out."

"Ah."

He set her to slicing bread and tomatoes while he dealt with the ham and cheese. He found a bottle of wine in the cupboard. Soon they were perched on his bed, feasting on the finest food Cass had ever tasted, scattering crumbs all over the sheets, and talking, talking, talking.

He had questions about everything. She tried to answer them as best she could. He was fascinated when she described movies and television, cars and stereos and escalators. She just about lost him when she tried to explain her computer. Maybe that was because she had absolutely no idea how it worked; part of her suspected that dozens of little genies lived inside her CPU awaiting her commands.

Soon she reached for a sketchpad and began drawing what she felt she was inadequately describing with words—airplanes and buses and even her Mr. Coffee.

"You draw well," he said, looking at the quick, sure sketches she'd done.

"I had a lot of drawing classes at F.I.T."

"F.I.T?"

"Fashion Institute of Technology. That's where I went to school. I originally planned to be a designer, and they required a lot of life-drawing and fashion illustration." Her hand moved idly across the page and she realized she was sketching the Mme. Gautreau gown she'd worn last night. Good Lord, was that only last night?

"Why didn't you become a designer then?" he asked as the dress emerged beneath her fingers.

"There didn't seem to be much security in it."

"Security." He spit the word out as if it were laced with cyanide.

"What's wrong with security?" She stopped and looked up at him. "What's wrong with wanting to have nice things and a few dollars in the bank or with knowing you can pay your rent on time?"

"Nothing, but—"

"That's right, nothing. And if you'd grown up without any of that, like I did, never knowing where you were going to be living next month, or where you'd go to school, or who your friends would be, if you even had time to make any, you'd know it."

"But as a designer, you would have had the chance to create, to make something no one's ever made before." He gestured at the gown on the page.

"Yeah, well, believe me, designing yet another leather miniskirt or tweed power suit is hardly the most original thing in the world. And my work is creative." She smiled. "I even recreated you."

"True." He kissed her nose, leaving a trace of mustard behind. "And for that I am grateful."

"Me too." She kissed him back. "Me too."

And he took her in his arms and that very special magic between them started all over again. He made love to her among the bread crumbs, and this time it was not hurried or frenzied. It was slow and sweet with time for each of them to learn the contours and hollows and soft, secret places of the other.

They explored, they teased, they tensed when tension was required, and softened when that was what brought the sweetest pleasure. They gave and they took in equal measure. And when that final, exquisite moment came, they were together, joined body and soul, their timing in perfect sync, as the world exploded within and without.

They lay then, every appetite appeased, comfortable in each other's arms. Her head was nestled on his broad chest; his arm was around her, the other idly stroking her hair.

The clock on the mantel chimed one. "I have to go," Cass said softly into his chest.

"I know."

She was pleased he hadn't argued. "They'll be worried, and they've done nothing to deserve it."

"You'll come back tomorrow." It wasn't a question. "It's Christmas Eve."

"Yes." She didn't know what she'd say to Helena and Richard, how she'd explain, but she knew she would be here. There was no place else in the world she could possibly be.

He helped her with her hooks and laces. It was incredibly sexy to have him dressing her instead of undressing her. Soon, they were both decent again. Outside on the street, he gave her one more long, sweet kiss before he put her in the hansom that would take her back uptown.

"Tomorrow," he said just before he closed the carriage door.

"Tomorrow," she agreed.

Chapter Eleven

The big house on Fifth Avenue was quiet. She tiptoed up the stairs and down the hall toward her room. But she must have made some sound, because the door to Richard's room opened as soon as she passed it.

"Cassandra?" She heard his voice behind her and stopped. "We were worried about you." She turned. He was still dressed in his evening clothes, but he'd discarded his coat, and his black silk cravat hung loosely about his neck. His hair was disheveled, as though he'd been running his fingers through it. It was the only time she had seen Richard VanderVeen other than perfectly dressed.

"I'm sorry. I . . ." She what? What could she say?

"*I* was worried about you." He smiled down at her in the dim light of the single lamp that burned in the hall. Then he kissed her, a light, feathery kiss.

But it was brief. He pulled away suddenly, as though he could taste another man's kisses on her lips. He stared at her mouth, then reached up a finger and ran it lightly across lips that were swollen from Nick's kisses. He looked at her hair, flowing wantonly around her shoulders. He looked at the brightness of her eyes.

"I see," he said softly, pulling away from her.

"I'm sorry."

"Good night, Cassandra."

"Richard, I . . ."

"Good night," he repeated. He stepped into his bedroom and shut the door.

"Oh dear," she said on a sigh as she went into her own room. But she was smiling as she fell asleep on the silken sheets, remembering cotton sheets full of bread crumbs, sheets where magic had happened.

Christmas Eve morning was bright, crisp, the air crackling with promise. Cass was humming as she went into the breakfast room. She was glad to see that only Helena was there.

"Good morning," the older woman said brightly, but she looked troubled. Cass greeted her and helped herself to a cup of coffee and some toast. "Are you all right, dear?"

Cass looked up, surprised. "Perfectly, why?"

"Because Richard told me this morning that you are leaving us. He said you were going back to Olga today. Is that true?"

"Oh, well, I . . . I hadn't really decided." Was this Richard's way of tossing her out? She guessed it was. But where was she going to go?

"Have you not been happy here, my dear? We have tried to make you so."

"Oh, yes, Helena, you have been unbelievably kind. It's just that . . ." Just that what? That I've fallen in love with a man who is not your son, Cass thought, and he can't stand to have me in the same house with him?

The thought caught her up short. Fallen in love. That's what she had just said to herself. Was it true? Had she fallen in love with Nick Wright? Was it even possible, when she knew so little about him? She remembered a line from Shakespeare: "E'en so quickly can one catch the plague?" It seemed people had been falling in love at first sight for eons. Had she?

"Well," Helena interrupted her thoughts. "I imagine you're homesick, what with the holidays and all. But I had so hoped to have you for Christmas. Still, if it's what you want . . . Shall I have Marcy pack your trunks?"

Yes, she should go. It was only fair to Richard. "Yes, please." She supposed she could go to a hotel for a few nights until she figured out what to do. She'd have to ask Olga.

She excused herself from the table, saying she had some shopping to do. That much was true. She also had another very important errand to run today, a call to make.

It was after noon when she climbed out of a cab in front of Marie DuPlessis' tenement building. There were some things she needed to know about Nicholas Wright, and she didn't know who else to ask.

Marie didn't seemed surprised to see her, only genuinely pleased. "For you will be good for Neek-o-lahhhs, I can see it."

"I want to be," said Cass, realizing that it was true. "I want to help him, Marie."

The Frenchwoman made tea and chattered lightly until it was ready. Then she sat across from Cass and looked into her face. "Ah, *oui*, Eet ees so. You are the one, I see."

"I hope so," she said sincerely. "Why did he stop painting, Marie?"

"He didn't. At least not right away. He didn't leave the painting. The painting, eet left him."

"I don't understand."

"But you will. I will tell you. Eet ees time he put this behind him and got on with his life, as all of us must do."

And then Marie told Cass the story. There had been a girl, a woman. Laura was her name. She was French, too, an artist's model. Nick had met her in Paris, and he was totally enchanted with her.

"Me, I never understood," said Marie. "Oh, she was very beautiful, our Laura, and she could be sweet and funny and charming. She loved to laugh and she made everybody else laugh, too." Cass remembered the painting in Nick's closet, the beautiful girl caught in the midst of a full-throated laugh. Laura? "But here,"— Marie touched her heart—"inside herself, no one really existed for Laura but Laura. Neek-o-lahhhs would have discovered that for himself een time. I am sure of that. I think maybe eet was that uncatchable quality that made him want her een the first place. And eet was his painting that made her want him. He was a brilliant painter, you know. Jacques said he was a genius, better than Monet. Laura knew he could make her immortal."

"Did he?"

"He didn't have time. She died, and Neek-o-lahhhs, he blamed himself."

"Oh no. Why? What happened?" But even as she asked and as Marie started to recount the story, the whole scene burst into full color in her brain, as though it had been sitting there all along, merely waiting for her to look at it.

It had happened two years ago this very night, Christmas Eve in Paris. He had been doing a painting of Laura, a languorous nude, as she lounged on the bed, lit only by the candles clipped to the branches of the Christmas tree. And it hadn't been working. He couldn't seem to catch the special quality of the light on her golden skin, the dewy look in her eyes that would tell the world he had made love to her before taking up his paints. Most of all, he wanted to paint her with a look on her face that said she loved him.

"But he could never paint that," said Marie, "because eet wasn't there, you see. Eet never would be; Laura didn't know how to love anyone but herself. But Neek, he would not admit that."

In his frustration, he'd thrown his brush across the room. It hit a pot of turpentine and sent it flying into the Christmas tree. The candles' flames caught it and the tree exploded in a ball of fire.

Though Nick reacted immediately, Laura had been horribly burned. Three days later she died. And Nick hadn't painted a thing worth looking at since that night.

"Oh, my God," Cass breathed when Marie finished the story and the screen in Cass's brain clicked off. "No wonder he can't paint. How much pain he has been living with!"

"*Oui*, but now eet ees time he put eet away. Will you help him, Cass?"

"Yes. I'll do anything. But what, Marie? What can I do?"

Marie smiled. "Well." She cocked her head in that terribly French coquettish way. "I do have an idea."

"Please," Cass begged Nick's landlady four hours later. "It's a surprise, you see." She nodded toward the packages piled on the sidewalk and the Christmas tree that stood beside them. "A Christmas surprise. You've got to let me in."

Mrs. O'Neill was a romantic at heart. It wasn't the packages or the tree that did the trick. It was the look of excitement and love in Cass's eyes. And she'd been worried about her young man upstairs. Bit of a brooder, he seemed to be. This slip of a girl was likely to be just what the doctor ordered. She pulled a ring of keys from her capacious pocket and led Cass up the stairs, ordering the carriage driver who'd brought her to haul up the tree and the packages, "and to be right quick about it, too."

Nick had told Cass that he wouldn't be home until after seven. He had three afternoon parties he had to cover for the *Sun* that day. So she had plenty of time to prepare.

She'd had a busy afternoon. After going back to the VanderVeen house to make her formal thank-yous and good-byes to Helena and ask her to pass the same on to Richard—who fortunately was out at his club—she'd gone shopping. She covered more of the city than she'd covered in years, uptown and down, East River to the Hudson, in search of everything she needed to carry out the plan she had concocted together with Marie.

Now she began unloading. George rubbed up against her ankles and gave a demanding *meow*.

"Give me a minute, pal," she said, twining her fingers into the fur at the back of his neck, just the way he liked it. Wait a minute! That was *her* George. This was Georgina. But the cat didn't seem to care. She just purred and wriggled so Cass's fingers could dig deeper.

Cass began unpacking the overflowing bags. As she arranged things around the room, she muttered, "Olga, don't you dare desert me now. I need you on this one." Then, for good measure, she sent up a prayer in the more traditional direction. She needed all the help she could get tonight.

Such cooking as she'd planned was a nightmare on the single, unfamiliar burner, but she attacked it with determination. First she chopped up some raw chicken hearts for George. They'd always been her George's favorite, and Georgina seemed just as taken with them—and with Cass.

She set a bottle of champagne on the fire escape to chill. She shucked the oysters, which Marie had insisted upon. "You cannot have Christmas Eve without the oysters," she'd insisted. She set aside the fresh crusty bread and the crock of sweet butter. She washed the endive and lettuce for the salad and made the Roquefort dressing, muttering, "Never dirtied my fingers in the kitchen, huh?"

She made the crepes, light as air and a perfect golden brown (she only had to throw out four of them before she got the temperature on the little burner right). She peeled and washed the hothouse strawberries it had taken her an hour and four stores to find—all the time wishing Balducci's, that 1993 gourmet's heaven of a store on Sixth Avenue, would appear for just fifteen minutes. She whipped the cream, pouring in just a touch of brandy.

When everything was ready in the kitchen, she attacked the other end of the apartment. She set up and decorated the tree, humming the "Hallelujah Chorus" as she worked. Then she set out the other things she'd bought, things she hoped would start a new chapter for Nick Wright—and maybe for her, too.

By seven, everything was ready. She wished she had a CD player—or even an old Edison phonograph. She would have loved some music to set the scene—some Carly Simon, maybe, or a little soft jazz, even Christmas carols. She would have settled for Andy Williams. But that seemed to be beyond even Olga's powers. Okay, no music. Still, the fire in the fireplace added a festive touch and the room smelled of fresh pine. It felt like Christmas.

As the final touch, she opened a package and reverently lifted out a beautiful silk kimono in the softest shade of peach, hand-embroidered with huge, multicolored flowers. It had cost the earth, and she didn't care. She undressed and wrapped it about her, tying it with a wide sash of crimson silk. Then she settled into the chair with George to wait.

It wasn't long. She heard him bounding up the stairs, clearly taking them two at a time. He was whistling. She grinned when she recognized the tune: "God Rest Ye Merry Gentlemen."

He was startled to see her there, but only for a moment. Then he charged across the room, swept her into his arms, and welcomed her thoroughly.

"Merry Christmas," she said when he finally released her lips.

"The merriest yet," he agreed, and Cass felt her whole body smile. "How'd you get in?"

"I think your landlady decided a woman's touch was just what this place needed."

"She thought right." He released her and looked around, smiling.

But his smile faded when he saw the Christmas tree. She had clipped candles to every branch and they were lit, making the tree look like something from a fairyland.

He charged over and immediately started putting our candles as quickly as he could, blowing at some, pinching others, heedless of the burning sensations in his fingertips.

"Wait, Nick. Please." She tried to stop him.

"You stupid little idiot! Don't you know how dangerous they are?" It was the reaction she'd expected, even the one she wanted, but she winced anyway.

"Olga?" she whispered. The voice in her ear was apologetic.

"Sorry, honey, this one's yours," came the tiny voice in her head. "If it's going to be real, you've got to do this yourself."

"Right." She sighed.

When the last candle was out, he collapsed into a chair, breathless, his face white in the yellow lamplight. "Do you have any idea what could have happened with those candles burning?" he asked.

"Yes. There could have been a fire, and I could have been killed." She took a deep breath and added, "Just like Laura. But it would not have been your fault, Nick. It would have been an accident."

He stared at her. "You've been talking to Marie."

Cass nodded.

"You had no right! She had no right to tell you."

"She loves you, Nick."

"If that were true, she'd stay out of my business. And so would you."

"In this time and place, I don't seem to have any business but you."

"Is that supposed to please me?" He was being deliberately cruel, and she knew why. It was too painful otherwise.

"I don't think it matters whether it pleases you or not. It's just the truth. I suspected all along that there was a reason I was zapped back here, or maybe more than one. You seem to be it."

He gave a bitter laugh. "Oh, I see, I'm your latest charity case? The lady from the future comes to reclaim the murderer and failed painter?"

She was out of her chair, kneeling at his feet. "No, Nick. No. You are neither of those things. It was an accident."

"I was the one who threw the brush."

"But you meant no harm. You couldn't have known." She looked up into his face, willing him to see the truth.

"If I hadn't been angry, it wouldn't have happened! I was mad because I couldn't capture her on canvas."

"And because she didn't love you."

He sat up straight. "What?"

"You were frustrated because you wanted her to love you and she couldn't."

"How do you know that? Marie couldn't have told you that!"

"She knows you better than you think, Nick. And I do, too. Don't ask me how I know, I just do. Maybe it was programmed into me when I came through that window. But I do know. I know you never cried for her, Nick, or for yourself. You never mourned Laura's death; you never mourned the loss of your ability to paint. And you never stopped being bitter about it all."

He stared at her, his eyes bright, and she could see that he had heard. "How do you do that? How do you stop hurting?"

Her voice was very soft. She took hold of both his hands in hers. "You stop blaming yourself. You acknowledge that a terrible thing happened, that you were partly responsible but that you didn't mean it to happen. You let yourself cry— for Laura and for you." She saw a shudder pass through him at the idea. "Then you forgive yourself, Nick. You forgive yourself and you go on with your life."

She felt a pain in her fingers and realized he was squeezing them, hard. Like they were a lifeline that was barely keeping him afloat.

"Feel it, Nick. It's okay. You won't sink." She was whispering. "Feel it."

"Aaahhh!" The sound burst out of him, a wail of pain pent up for two years. As if a dam had burst, it poured out of him with the power of Niagara Falls, rushing through his eyes whether he wanted it to or not.

Cass got up and squeezed into the chair beside him to hold him tight, her arms around his quaking shoulders, one hand moving reassuringly across flesh while she made soothing little sounds. "Yes, Nick. Let yourself feel it. Let it go. Let it be finished."

He cried and she held him. His anguish came out in sobs that took his breath away and left him gasping for air. "I didn't mean it," he cried. "I didn't mean for her to die."

"Of course you didn't. She knew that."

"I'm sorry, I'm sorry, I'm sorry." The words were a chant, a litany of repentance and forgiveness. The only thing Cass could do was to be there for him and let the pain run its course.

Chapter Twelve

It was almost fifteen minutes before Nick's tears slowed and his gasping stopped. "Don't leave me, Cass. Please don't leave me," he said, his arms tight about her waist, his head on her breast.

"I'm here," she reassured him, running her fingers through his thick, dark hair.

"Cass," he whispered, like a prayer. "Cass, Cass." His head moved gently back and forth, and in a minute she realized he had parted the silk of her kimono. He laid his cheek on the curve of her warm breast. She could feel its heat; she could feel his tears on her skin.

It was but an inch for his lips to reach the nipple that sprang to instant life when they touched it. Her hand tightened on the back of his head, and he interpreted the signal correctly. With the smallest movement of his head, the nipple disappeared entirely into his mouth and he sucked it like a hungry baby.

Now she was the one gasping, but not from pain. Her body reacted with such instant intensity to this man that it took her breath away. She pulled his head from her breast and brought it up. She wanted, needed, to taste his lips.

He indulged the wish, establishing dominion over her mouth with astonishing possessiveness, plunging into it like a diver, exploring its every corner, tasting it, owning it. And she gladly gave him possession. But not without making a claim of her own.

Suddenly he stood, lifting her with him. He pulled the kimono from her shoulders so she was naked before him. Then he scooped her up into his arms, carried her the short distance to the bed, and laid her on it as tenderly as if she were a piece of fine Venetian glass. As she lay there, staring up at him, he slowly removed his own clothes, his eyes never leaving hers.

"You are the most beautiful woman I've ever seen," he said as his shirt hit the floor. "And the kindest." His trousers slid from his hips. "And I am going to make love to you all night and maybe all day tomorrow and all night again after that."

"Yes, please," she said in a very small voice.

He laughed. Soon he was as naked as she, tall and golden, magnificent in his maleness, the evidence of his desire for her standing huge and proud and hungry. He kneeled at the foot of the bed, lifted one of her feet and kissed it, leaving no toe unloved. He caressed her instep, stroked her ankle, kissed his way up her calf. She let out a yip when he gently bit the flesh of her calf and he chuckled. Then he began his upward progress again. He licked the backs of her knees, and she was amazed to discover that was an erogenous zone. But then, where Nick Wright was concerned, every inch of Cass's body seemed to fall into that category.

He nibbled his way up the outside of one thigh, his hand mimicking the movements up the other side. Then his fingers brushed light as sunlight across the curly hair that covered her most private and special place.

Up, up he moved, mapping her body with his lips, kissing his way past the depression of her waist, tasting her navel, tickling her ribs with his tongue. Finally, he found his way back to his starting place, that responsive nipple that reached out for him.

"Nick," she breathed as he bit into it just hard enough, taking the other one between his fingers for the same treatment. As though a wire connected those pink tips with the core of her, a jolt of pleasure shot straight up from her thighs to her brain, and she said his name again, her voice growing more ragged.

"I'm here," he whispered. "I'm here."

"I know," she said, and he chuckled.

His hands roamed as his lips adored her breasts. His touch was different from the two times they'd made love last night. It was gentler, more tender, but also surer. It felt as if they'd been lovers forever, as if they knew everything about each other, and loved everything they knew.

He left her breasts then, but instead of moving up to her lips once more as she expected, he retraced his route, back down across her stomach, across that curling hair, until his lips were doing to her core of desire what they had earlier done to her mouth.

She felt her body arch against his mouth, wanting him closer still, as close as her heartbeat. As his hands reached up to enfold and own her breasts, squeezing the tips until that mysterious connection of above and below was buzzing like an electric wire, his mouth collected her honey and asked for more. And he got it.

It arose within her, that magic that was so easy with Nick. Layer on layer of feeling, building up until it toppled of its own weight. It peaked and pushed her over, as her body arched even more. He put his arms around her waist and held her tight, riding it with her. It seemed to go on a long time, rippling out of her like waves undulating through her whole body. Then it began slowly to subside.

Quickly, Nick moved up onto his elbows, poised one second above her, smiling, then plunged into her. And instantly, it began again. She didn't know if she could take any more, but she also knew she couldn't stop it, didn't want to. She opened her eyes to look at him, and the look of absolute triumph and love on his face was better than a kiss; it sent her spiraling. It was building again, it was rising, it was flowering.

"Come with me, Cass," he whispered in her ear, and the love in his voice was the final caress.

Now! It hit her like a full-speed train, almost lifting her off the bed. "Nick!" she screamed, and he silenced her with a kiss, held only until he had to break free to call out her name as the train hit him, too.

"Cass!" he cried out, then more gently, "Cass," and finally a whisper, "Cass."

They fell asleep like that, still joined, but not for long. Hunger woke them, for food if not yet again for each other. They ate the oysters and salad and strawberry-filled crepes. They tore at the French bread, slathering it with butter. They drank the icy champagne, licking it from each other's lips between sips.

And they talked. For hours, they talked, about his childhood and hers, about his time and hers. They talked about their hopes and dreams and sorrows. They talked about George and Georgina and laughed over how much fun it would be to get them together across a century of time to make a bunch of little Georgettes.

She told him what she knew about Olga, though she still didn't understand much of what had happened to her. She answered more of his questions about the 20th century, smiling at his exclamations of "Amazing!", "Incredible!", and, "You're making that up!"

Finally, as they sat on the rug in front of the dying fire, drinking the last of the champagne, he said, "I have a present for you, a Christmas present." He brought her a large package, beautifully wrapped. She had to think hard to remember the last time anyone had bought her a real Christmas present, one chosen with caring and put in her hand. It had been from her mother, and that had been so long ago.

She untied the blue ribbon and peeled off the silver paper. She opened the box and dug around in the nest of tissue paper. Finally, she lifted out the treasure. And she smiled.

It was an hourglass, a big one, at least a foot high. The stand was of beautiful carved mahogany, the corners reinforced with polished brass. He reached out and turned it over so that the sand began trickling through.

"What do we do when the sand runs out?" she asked, not wanting to think of that moment.

"We turn it over again. Time is not going to run out for us, Cass."

"How can we know that?"

"Because I need it not to."

She sighed. How she hoped he was right. "I have a present for you, too." She got up and went to his easel, sitting to one side of the room. She pulled off the large piece of fabric she'd draped over it earlier.

On the easel sat a blank canvas, glowing pristine white in the dim light. Beside it, on a table, stood a clean palette, his jar of brushes, his paints, arrayed in perfect order. The only thing missing from the scene was the artist.

She heard him sigh; she was afraid to look at him. She heard him get up.

He walked over to the canvas. He stroked it gently with one finger, ran a hand over the paints and brushes, then picked up a palette knife. Would he slash the canvas before it could stand testimony to his lost talent? Would he even be willing to try?

"Thank you," he said softly and turned back to her. "Thank you for everything."

Then he took her back to bed. They were both exhausted, but they couldn't stop touching each other, kissing each other, loving each other. Within minutes, they were fully ready for each other again. And this time when he gave her the essence of his love, then relaxed against her, waiting for their pulses to return to normal, she felt him shudder and felt his tears on her chest.

"I'm here," she said, as she had done before. And she stroked his hair.

"I love you, Cass. Don't leave me."

"Never," she promised, hoping it was a promise she could keep. Please, Olga, she begged, let me keep it. "I love you too."

When Cass awoke, the winter light was just beginning to paint the sky outside the window. It had snowed in the night and the skylight over her head was a solid sheet of white.

But the light she saw came from inside the room. She turned her head. Every candle on the Christmas tree was lit, twinkling beside the bed. Near the easel, a pair of oil lamps glowed softly.

And there was Nick, standing at the easel. Beautiful as a lion, his whole body tense and glistening, his face was lit with the fiercest expression Cass had ever seen, a mixture of concentration, passion, and triumph. His right hand flew between the canvas and the palette. He was painting with the frenzied passion of a van Gogh, as though he couldn't get the pigment onto the canvas fast enough to satisfy his vision.

She started to rise.

"Don't move!" he commanded. "I'm almost done." She moved back into the position she'd been in when she first woke up. "Just turn your eyes so you're looking at me."

Brush and palette knife flew. His concentration was so intense she was afraid to breathe. She thought he had probably taken up all the air in the room.

Half an hour later, he put down his palette and collapsed into a chair. He was breathing hard, and he was sweating. He looked like he'd just run a footrace—or made energetic love.

"Now you can move," he finally said.

She got up. "Can I look?"

He nodded, and she went to the painting.

The Christmas Portrait

She looked long before she could speak. He'd painted her there on the bed, lit by the candles on the Christmas tree. Her body looked sated and warm, all its hard edges and angles dissolved by his loving. And the look on her face said clearly that she adored the man who had made her feel this way—and that she wanted him to do it again. "Oh, Nick," she finally got out. "Is that me?"

He nodded again, but now she could see that there was fear on his face. He was afraid to know what she thought.

He didn't have to worry. She thought—no, she *knew*—that she was looking at a masterpiece. It was glorious, fantastic, perfect. It breathed life; it glowed with a kind of incandescence, a light that seemed to come from inside the paint itself. This was a painting people would be talking about a hundred years from now. She smiled to think that in 1993, people might line up at the Met to look at this painting of Cassandra Douglass.

And she knew what they would think. The men who saw it would want her, they would pine for a woman who wasn't afraid to love and be loved, for a woman who looked at them that way. And the women would wish they were her, that they had a man who could do to them what someone had just done to this woman.

She turned to him, her whole face lit with a radiant smile. "Nick, it's exquisite."

"It's yours."

"But it should be in a gallery! It would sell in a day."

He nodded. "I think so too. It's the finest thing I've ever done. But I'll paint other pictures of you if you'll let me, dozens of them, hundreds of them. You will make us both rich and famous;

123

I'm counting on that. But this one is yours, Cass. No one will ever see this picture unless you want them to."

She laid her hand on his arm. "Thank you."

"You're welcome, and Merry Christmas." He gave her a tender, melting kiss.

"But Nick," she said, looking up into his eyes. "What if we can't? What if I have to go back?"

"Olga wouldn't be so cruel. I need you, Cass, for always. Not just as a model or an inspiration. I need you because you make me complete. Because I love you."

"I love you too. For now, let's just let that be enough."

"Enough," he agreed, and kissed her again.

It was while he was making coffee a few minutes later that there was a knock at the door.

"Who the devil . . . ?" he began. "It's six-thirty on Christmas morning!"

Cass pulled on her peach kimono and went to the door.

"Delivery boy, ma'am," said a young man with a basket in his hand. "You wanna sign for this?"

She did and carried the basket inside. It was heavy. She set it on the table and unhooked the hinged top.

A cat leapt from the bag and started stalking the apartment, angry at having been cooped up for so long.

"George!" Cass exclaimed. He turned and gave an accusatory *meow*; then he discovered Georgina curled up in a chair, which he apparently thought was *his* chair. He ordered her out.

The two of them hissed and arched their backs and stuck their fur up on end for a few minutes, and then the strangest thing happened. It was as though they recognized each other. One minute they were braced for the cat fight of the century, and the next they were curled up before the fire licking each other's tabby fur and purring for all the world to hear.

Nick grinned. "I think we'd better make room for the Georgettes."

"I think you're right."

"There's something else here," Nick said, reaching into the basket. It was a note, handwritten in elegant script on expensive hot-pressed notepaper. "Shall I read it to you?"

"Please," Cass said, suddenly very nervous.

> *My dear Cass,*
> *And now you know why you've come here. You were needed, and you have completed your task. Now it is time to go back.*

"No!" Cass exclaimed. "Please, no." She sank into a chair, her head in her hands.

"Wait, there's more." He read on.

> *However, the choice is yours. Actually, the choice has always been yours. You could have gone back the moment you arrived if you had wished for it hard enough. Now you must decide—to stay in this world you know so little about or to return to your own time and place.*
> *One thing you should know before you decide. My time here is finished; my work is done. If you choose to stay, you'll be on your own. I will no longer be in a position to help you. You'll have to do that for yourself— with the help of Nick.*

125

In other words, honey: no more magic.
Choose wisely. All the best,
Olga
P.S. If you want my advice, you'll stay. Per-
sonally, I think I outdid myself when I picked
Mr. Wright. A Prince Charming indeed!"

Cass laughed, a sound of pure happiness and delight. "Oh, Nick, I can stay. I can stay!"

"And you'd damn well better," he said, pulling her into his arms for a crushing kiss. Then he gave her a pleading look. "You will, won't you? Forever?"

"Forever."

"You won't mind that there will be no more magic?"

She laughed again. "Who says so? We don't need Olga's magic, Nick. I don't think we ever did. We'll make our own magic."

Nick smiled; then he leaned past her and turned over the giant hourglass. Slowly, the sand started trickling through anew, visible evidence of all the time that stretched ahead of them—together.

"Merry Christmas, Cass. Merry Christmas, my love."

"Merry Christmas."

VIVIAN KNIGHT-JENKINS
"The Spirit of Things to Come"

For my sons,
hearts of my heart.

Prologue

Massachusetts, December 25, 1993

Twenty miles from home the weather turned ugly.

No, Taylor Kendall silently amended as she glanced at the gray, cloud-laden sky. Ugly wasn't the right word. Winter in New England might be termed breathtaking, or invigorating, perhaps even treacherous as it seemed intent on becoming now. But never, ever ugly. Not while icicles dangled from the silver birch trees like glistening ornaments, and a pristine coverlet of white blanketed every rolling hill and gently sloping valley. Not when she could almost smell the pungent aroma of the towering evergreens through the glass of her driver's-side window.

Taylor peered beyond the snowflakes playing baseball with her windshield wipers, stretched in her seat, and gripped the steering wheel more tightly. She absently listened to the *thump thump* of the wiper blades keeping metronomic time with Miss Piggy's rendition of "The Twelve Days of Christmas."

What had possessed her? Why had she waited until the last minute to drive to her parents' house when she could have spent the entire holiday season with them?

Taylor swallowed and tugged at the turtleneck of her lamb's wool sweater as she settled more deeply into the bucket seat. The answer was easy. She would rather have avoided the family scene altogether this year.

Without taking her eyes from the road, Taylor reached down and ejected the cassette tape—a gift from a child in her kindergarten class. If someone had told her she would come to dread Christmas, she would have called them a liar. But then again, that was before her 30th birthday.

Taylor sighed and reached beneath her collar to knead the back of her neck.

She wanted to visit her family—she just didn't feel up to parrying their inevitable questions. Her father, a retired pediatrician, would ask if she'd met any eligible bachelors lately. Her mother would peer at her with wise, searching eyes, and ply her with yet another heaping helping of rum-laced fruitcake because she seemed "far too thin."

Placing her booted foot on the brake, Taylor expertly shifted the transmission into four-wheel drive. The Jeep slowed to a crawl as she flipped on her turn signal and made a sharp right onto the desolate rural road that snaked through a sugar maple grove to the doorsteps of her parents' restored lean-to colonial. She'd grown up in the suburbs of Boston and driving in the snow didn't bother her; what awaited her at the end of her mandatory jaunt did.

Her three younger sisters would unwittingly taunt her with updated news on a woman's biological clock while they threatened to hang their own offspring up by their pinkies if they misbehaved. Her brothers-in-law would play checkers or chess, and watch the television version of *A Christmas Carol* with the kids . . . and kiss their wives beneath the traditional mistletoe ball.

And then her well-meaning parents—innate matchmakers—would move in for the kill and introduce a not-so-surprising dinner guest. He'd be some respectable, unsuspecting guy who for unfortunate reasons couldn't make it home for the holidays. To quote her mother, "A poor lost soul in dire need of a substitute family during the season of expectation."

Last year their guest had been an up-and-coming resident doctor from Massachusetts General, the year before a Harvard law student her mother met in the offices where she worked as a paraprofessional. Maybe this time someone would dig up an Indian chief. But not just any old Indian chief would do. Only kind, unattached, moderately prosperous Indian chiefs interested in relieving the burden of spinsterhood from their eldest daughter's shoulders need apply.

Christmas at home could be heaven . . . or it could be hell, Taylor mused.

In a vain attempt to redirect her thoughts, she shoved the cassette back into the tape player. To a chorus of "five golden rings," Taylor adjusted the heater fan, then unbuckled her seat belt and thumbed open the buttons of her bulky suede parka.

She often reminded her busybody family that America was a democratic nation. That as a woman of the '90s she had a choice, a right to remain single—even if she found herself lonely on occasion. To be honest, she doubted the existence of a man capable of loving an idealistic tomboy with cropped flaxen curls and whiskey-brown eyes who preferred hard-boiled eggs over omelettes, wild mayflowers over cultivated orchids, and a chickadee's warble to the symphony orchestra.

Experience had taught her that in a world where almost anything could be bought for a price, wowing a woman enamored of the simple things in life took the pizazz out of most guys. The mention of a firm commitment sent them ducking into shadowed doorways when they saw her coming their way—it seemed commitment was a thing of the past.

At least for a woman with top-shelf expectations.

Taylor chuckled aloud as she weighed the pros and cons of her complex personality.

Everyone knew that thanks to her father, an avid Red Sox fan, she pitched a mean curveball. That she cooked only when cornered. And that even though she owned a perfectly functional washer and dryer, she sent most of her laundry out to the cleaners. Few men ever discovered her passionate nature. Fewer still learned that beneath her no-nonsense attire she wore sexy silk teddies and pearl-enhanced dusting powder. And that she talked in her sleep.

Rarely did a man get that far.

Taylor acknowledged that her lackluster personal life was partially her own fault. She had been waging a boxing match against love—waiting . . . wanting . . . hoping for someone extra-special with whom to share her life. She owed herself that much. Besides, she had plenty of time remaining on her biological clock.

Didn't she?

Steeped in thought, Taylor belatedly noticed the deer stripping bark from a sapling growing along the roadside. She swiftly tooted her horn in warning.

Startled by the man-made sound echoing through the stillness of the forest, the animal sprang into action. But instead of disappearing into the safety of the trees as Taylor anticipated, the deer bounded out across the road as if catapulted from a giant slingshot.

"Not that way!" Taylor cried, instinctively turning the wheel.

The Jeep swerved off the snow-covered asphalt and successfully missed the deer, only to jounce down a short embankment and collide with the broad trunk of a sugar maple tree. The impact propelled Taylor forward. Before she could throw up her hands to ward off the blow, the padded arch of the steering wheel clipped her neatly on the chin.

Like a prizefighter with a glass jaw, Taylor went down for the count.

"Thus times do shift . . ."

Chapter One

Bay Colony, New England, December 25, 1692

Strange, Taylor thought.

From her head to her heels, she felt numb, but only on the back side of her body. She hesitantly opened her eyes, squinting at the clear blue sky through a break in the leafless boughs of the trees.

Taylor wiggled her fingers. Her arms. Her legs. Rolled her head on the stem of her neck. Tentatively testing.

No, nothing seems broken. Thank goodness.

She pushed herself up on her elbows. Gaining her feet, Taylor glanced down at the impression her prone body had sculpted in the pristine ground covering—a snow angel, just like the ones she had fashioned as a child.

With an exhaled breath that vaporized around

her like a puff of cigarette smoke, Taylor pivoted in a tight circle and attempted to recover her bearings. For a moment, she couldn't think where she was. It looked familiar; and then again it didn't. Something was missing. Finally it dawned on her.

My Jeep!

Stomping her feet to jump-start the circulation in her legs, she strolled the perimeter of the meager clearing. Tree stumps, tree stumps everywhere, almost as if someone had hacked up the woods to build a house, Taylor mused. But no sign of a Jeep with its front bumper hugging the trunk of a sugar maple.

Could it have been towed away without her? she wondered. No, that didn't make sense. Why would someone take the Jeep, and leave her to freeze to death in the snow? Even a knothead would realize the Jeep didn't wreck itself, that the driver was obviously missing. They'd check the tag numbers and call them in to the state patrol.

Wouldn't they?

She'd heard of people with head injuries wandering up and down the highway after an accident. Confused by the blow to her chin, had she wandered away from her Jeep? Had someone mistakenly believed it abandoned? Surely not— there would be footprints leading away from it, and therefore footprints to follow back to it.

Only there were no footprints in the clearing. Just the ones she was now making. Perhaps the falling snow had covered them up? No, once again Taylor hit a dead end. She'd been lying on top of snow, not beneath it.

The afternoon took on a surreal quality as Taylor touched her chin with the back of her hand.

It didn't feel bruised. As a matter of fact, except for the cold, she felt great. Just confused . . . and worried . . . and perhaps the least bit frightened.

Taylor fumbled to secure the concealed buttons of her parka all the way to her throat, then flipped up and tied her insulated hood. Diving her fingers into her coat pockets, she found her mittens and slipped them on her trembling hands.

"Where the heck is my Jeep?" she muttered aloud. "More importantly, where am I?"

Her parents' home couldn't be too far away, Taylor surmised. She'd once run in the Boston Marathon; there was no reason she couldn't jog the rest of the way to their house. But in which direction? From here, she couldn't see the road to make an accurate decision, and the last thing she wanted was to be lost in a New England forest on Christmas Day.

Taylor paced one way, then the other, trying to decide which was the better course. Should she remain in the clearing and hope someone stumbled across her, or jog for help? Take fate in her hands, or wait for fate to visit her? Go for help or stay put?

Fate finally made the decision for her.

Filtering through the trees, Taylor heard the faint yet welcome sound of children's voices raised in a somewhat discordant rendition of "The Twelve Days of Christmas." She stilled, straining her ears in an attempt to get a fix on the Christmas carol. After a moment, with a smile of relief and a renewed sense of hope, she struck out toward civilization and the promise of a telephone.

Taylor came upon the community all of a sudden. One moment she was traipsing through the forest kicking up snow with the toes of her boots, the next . . .

The next, Taylor stood transfixed on the edge of a village. Wood smoke from the chimneys of the clapboard houses spiraled into the cloudless sky, while around the commons area a dozen children perched on stools batted a ball to each other in a game reminiscent of cricket. The scene appeared to have been scooped from the pages of a book on colonial history and plopped intact onto the face of the Massachusetts countryside—like a dollop of ice cream on a wedge of apple pie.

One of the younger children spied Taylor almost immediately. She quit singing and rose from her stool, pointing her cornhusk doll in Taylor's direction.

"See over yonder, everyone! A newcomer!"

Eyes widening, Taylor stared at the child. She resembled a miniature adult, dressed as she was in a cloth cap, tan jacket, ankle-length skirt, and white apron. A short woolen cape, tied at the throat, hugged her tiny shoulders.

Taylor recalled visiting a 17th-century village near Plymouth where children dressed such as these—like pilgrim boys and girls. But no such living museum existed near her parents' home. So what . . .

"Perchance there is a newly arrived sailing ship anchored in the harbor," the child continued, dancing in a circle. "That would mean special treats from abroad, would it not? And missives! Oh, how Mother longs for written word from her family in England. She has been exceedingly disheartened with the New World since Father died."

Sailing ship? Missives? The New World!

Stiff with consternation, Taylor swallowed hard and squeezed her eyes shut. Taking a deep breath, she silently counted to ten, exhaled, and opened her eyes, fully expecting her world to have righted itself. To her acute astonishment, the same scene awaited her perusal. The same little girl danced like a pixie around the same three-legged stool, while the same absorbed group of children sang "The Twelve Days of Christmas" off-key.

Taylor blinked. But blinking didn't help. Neither did rubbing her eyes.

Or pinching herself.

Or biting her lip until she tasted blood.

Nothing helped because she realized with a jolt that what she was experiencing was real, as real as the sudden ringing in her ears, the tightness in her chest, and the weakness in her knees.

Impossible! her brain retaliated indignantly. People didn't stroll into the past at the drop of a hat. Or the wreck of a Jeep.

Improbable, but not impossible, her senses argued. The child was pointing at her again. Waving. Calling to her with enthusiastic determination. In a minute, every kid in the commons area would see her! Then what? Taylor asked herself.

Heart galloping and mind awhirl with conundrums, she reluctantly acknowledged that in her search for assistance she had somehow miraculously transcended time. And with that acknowledgment, she panicked.

Spurred by a deep-seated need for time to gather her wits, Taylor managed to surmount her shock. Quickly assessing the surrounding area, she forced her legs to move beneath her and vaulted the railed fence of a nearby paddock. Slipping and sliding, she raced across the empty enclosure, through a gate, circled around behind a building, and finally ducked into the shadows of a blacksmith shop's yawning doorway.

The Christmas carol petered out as one by one the other children stopped singing at the insistence of the little girl.

"'Tis a peculiar time of year for a ship," a boy twice the girl's age said. He cast a quick look down the street. "Besides, I see nothing. Thee must be imagining things again, Sarah," Taylor heard him say from her hidden vantage point directly across the unpaved street.

"I am not, John Edward Nash," Sarah said. "A young man with a hooded waistcoat appeared out of nowhere and stood yonder, gaping with a great slack jaw as if he had just witnessed the visitation of a spirit."

"Perchance thee are the one that beheld a spirit," John said. He winked at the boy on the stool beside him. "Sarah always believes—" he began.

"Oh, marry!" a third child exclaimed, cutting John short. "Forget the spirits! Forget the visitor! Forget the sailing ship as well! Alas, we have been caught out of turn for certain this time! I doubt not we shall feel the rod this day, for yonder strides Mr. Flint and by his expression he is none too pleased with our gaming."

The child clutching the doll blanched. Lips quivering, she said, "I believed the sheriff to be away from Bay Colony on business. Thee assured me he was well away, John."

"Hush, Sarah. He is very nearly upon us," John said. He rose to stand beside Sarah. Almost as an afterthought, he reached down and grasped her small hand in his. The rest of the group rose in unison, stools toppling as they banded together.

Vivian Knight-Jenkins

Taylor stared at the grizzle-haired, black-garbed official bearing down on the children and shivered. With a face like a disgruntled thundercloud, he began yelling even before he reached them.

"No good Puritans today, I see!" he bellowed. Towering over the children, Taylor watched him brandish a leather-thonged stick in each of their faces by turn. She felt rather than saw them cringe.

The child called John dropped Sarah's hand and stepped forward as if to speak for the group, though Taylor believed he did so more to protect the little girl from Mr. Flint's wrath than anything else.

"We did not think a game of stoolball following the midday meal would be frowned upon, Mr. Flint. We have completed our chores, and there are to be no lessons this day since Goody Bradford is down with the ague."

"Thee possesses a most clever tongue, young John. But thy tongue will not talk thee free of my disappointment," Mr. Flint barked.

"We did not mean to offend," John stuttered.

"Silence! The frisking and gaming does not offend me as greatly as the singing I heard earlier on. Thee children must learn to abstain from immoral impulses."

"'Tis Christmastide," John responded in a low voice. He glanced down at the buckles on his shoes.

"Bah! There is no fast proof of the true date of the Nativity." Mr. Flint thumped John on the crown of his head with the knob of his stick. "Thee knows well enough 'tis for that very reason the General Court banned observance of Christmastide by abstinence from labor, or feast-

140

ing, or in any other manner."

"I did not think," John replied sullenly.

"Truly, thee did not! I shall need time to mull over a just and befitting punishment for your crime."

Mr. Flint bent down and scooped up the ball, then reached around John and snatched Sarah's doll from her hand.

"In the meanwhile, I shall keep these in my offices until a day appropriate to play arrives."

Taylor watched Sarah bite her lip to keep from crying out. The profound dismay in her tear-filled eyes tugged at Taylor's heartstrings as Sarah whispered brokenly, "He plans to take my poor poppet to jail. She will be so sad and lonely there without me to tend to her needs."

Taylor ran a gamut of emotions from fear, apprehension, and indignation, to pure outrage. Clenching and unclenching her fists, she struggled with the decision of whether, in her present predicament, she dared run interference for the children.

"I would refrain from interference if I were you," a deep, slightly gravelly voice cautioned.

Taylor whirled to discover a man standing in profile behind her. Though she judged him to be less than 15 feet away, he had remained so still and quiet she had failed to notice his presence earlier. She took a tentative step forward and peered into the smoky recesses of the smithy.

"What did you say?" Taylor asked.

The proprietor tossed the horseshoe he had been heating in the hearth into a wooden trough. The water sizzled and sputtered as he placed his pincers atop the anvil which rested on a maple trunk near the fireplace. When he finally turned to face her, Taylor stifled a gasp.

She found herself gazing into the placid face of the man of her dreams.

Well, not exactly, Taylor mused. His clothes were way off base. Her dream hunk had never appeared to her in a russet linen smock. Nor did he wear leather knee breeches, woolen socks, low black shoes, and a rough-cut cowhide apron.

His incredible cerulean eyes fit the bill, though, as did the sable hair teasing his shoulders. She liked his even white teeth and the slight cleft in his clean-shaven chin—she liked clean-shaven men over bearded men, period. His formidable physique wasn't bad either, though Taylor wondered how his skin came to be so bronzed in the dead of winter without the benefit of a tanning salon.

"Do not interfere," he repeated in a quiet, yet commanding tone that reverberated through Taylor like a minor earthquake. Though his stance was casual and his expression cool and reserved, interest in her, or perhaps concern for her, or maybe a combination of both, emanated from him.

"Are you a mind reader?" Taylor asked.

"Nay. The harsh frown upon your lips speaks louder than most words."

"But they're only children," Taylor said, marveling that she felt no fear of the stranger even though he wore a knife sheathed at his waist. If anything, his presence seemed comforting. Like solid ground at the end of a tumble.

"You possess a keen eye as well as an expressive mouth," he commented.

Taylor had a feeling he was making fun of her. The muscle in his jaw twitched as he fought to hold his lips compressed into a solemn line.

"The oldest child . . ." Taylor faltered.

"John Nash, Sarah's brother," he supplied.

"Yeah, that one. He can't be more than twelve," she stated, realizing the blacksmith had been listening to the children at play long before she'd arrived on the scene. That he'd probably overheard her arrival. And possibly witnessed her bizarre gymnastic exhibition as well.

His expression abruptly sobered. "Even children have an obligation to the law," he stated flatly.

Taylor cut her gaze away from his face. "It's an unreasonable law."

"For a newcomer, you speak your mind most freely. Among other things," he commented.

No doubt about it, Taylor decided. He'd seen her hurdle the fence.

Flustered, Taylor scanned the wall behind him, the unusual tools neatly ranging the wall, and the closed door in its center. She returned to his knock-me-over-with-a-feather-blue eyes only when she could no longer avoid them. "I call it being honest."

He raised a dark brow at her. "You are truly outspoken."

She felt her face grow warm. "Straightforward," Taylor bantered.

He considered her for a long moment. His gaze swept from her suede hood to her leather boots and back again to rest upon her mouth. Taylor absently licked her lips with the tip of her tongue.

"Perchance you think to change the ban against Christmastide single-handedly," he reflected in the same composed tone.

"Let's just say I have a chronic aversion to bullies. I can't stand to see someone intimidating a bunch of children like that."

"And?" he prompted.

Taylor wasn't about to explain that she suddenly felt compelled to stand up for Christmas—something she'd so recently taken for granted. *And dreaded for all it was worth,* her subconscious reminded her sternly.

"And the doll thing was out of line. Someone should tell Mr. Flint where the laws end and courtesy begins," she hedged.

His gaze veered from her mouth to scan her face, finally resting on her eyes.

"Suit yourself, but do not say I did not warn you."

His piercing eyes seemed to probe into her very soul and for a moment, Taylor thought he might say more. Instead he shrugged his broad shoulders and retrieved the horseshoe from the watering trough. She watched the rolled sleeves of his linen shirt tighten against his flexed biceps as he pumped the deerskin bellows and whipped up the flames in the hearth. He reheated the iron band to a red-hot glow and reached for his sledgehammer.

The sound of hammering told her in no uncertain terms that their conversation was at an end.

With a sigh of resignation, Taylor peeked outside the doorway, eyeing the cornhusk doll crushed in Mr. Flint *Scrooge's* cruel fingers. Marshaling her composure, she tilted her chin rebelliously and squared her shoulders.

"A person has to do what a person has to do," she muttered under her breath. Then more loudly, "Listen, I'm sorry I disturbed you. I didn't realize you were here or I wouldn't have barged in without knocking."

" 'Tis my shop, not my cottage," he said without looking up from his work.

Taylor had the feeling she'd been summarily dismissed. She frowned, feeling as if the good earth had been yanked from beneath her feet once again. Common sense told her to act accordingly, to backtrack to the edge of the village and search for the path back to the future. But her conscience argued that this was not the time to turn tail and run. That if she got home in one piece—and remembered this bizarre episode—she'd regret her inaction the rest of her natural life.

So you might as well go with the flow and do the right thing, Taylor told herself.

Combatting a sudden attack of nausea, she stepped from the relative safety of the blacksmith shop and out into the commons area. The ring of iron against iron punctuated her impending confrontation with Mr. Flint.

One-on-one, Mr. Flint was burlier and more craggy-faced than Taylor had anticipated. It took her a moment to find her voice—a "Lucille Ball-type-voice" her mother called it. She now used its commanding depth to advantage, though to her mortification it trembled ever so slightly.

"You can't do this. You can't intimidate children like this. Not for singing on public property. They have a right to sing Christmas carols anytime they feel like it . . . spring, summer, fall, or winter if the mood strikes them. It's known as freedom of speech." *Where I come from.*

Taylor took a deep, cleansing breath.

"And by the way, I'd like the doll back, please,"

she continued in a rush. She extended her hand, palm up, fingers slightly curled.

The children froze in place, much like the ice sculptures that had decorated the tabletops at her youngest sister's wedding, Taylor thought.

Mr. Flint flushed cranberry red from the collar of his coat to his hairline as he ignored the imperiously extended hand.

"And who might thee be, to question my official administration of justice?" he snapped. His narrowed eyes reminded Taylor of the incensed traffic cop who had written her first and only speeding ticket. She'd been 16 and the police siren had scared her out of her wits, so much so that she'd pulled off on the left-hand side of the highway.

"I asked who thee might be," Mr. Flint repeated impatiently.

"I—" Taylor began. What could she say? *I'm a kindergarten teacher. While en route to my parents' home for the holidays, I somehow overshot my target by about three hundred years.*

Taylor didn't think Mr. Flint would buy the truth. She could hardly believe it herself. As a matter of fact, if not for her stoic Dutch-American heritage, she might well have been tearing her hair out by now. It was a darn good thing resiliency was an intricate part of her character, Taylor decided, because this unscheduled side-trip was taxing her to the limits.

"Speak up," Mr. Flint demanded, shaking the doll at her so viciously she feared its head might fall off.

Taylor borrowed Sarah's scenario.

"I might be from a ship anchored in the harbor," she responded, wording the statement so it wasn't exactly an outright lie.

"That would account for thy unique accent and peculiar overgarments, but not for thy presence in Bay Colony," he said, suspicion rampant in his voice.

"I thought I might visit a while . . . rest, before finding the means to move on," Taylor responded, feeling her way along carefully.

"It seems logical enough after the months thee must have spent at sea. Does thee plan to travel as far as Virginia?"

"Something like that." *If I'm lucky, light years farther. Back home where I belong. In the twentieth century. Spending Christmas with my family.*

"That is a wise notion. The laws enacted by the General Court in Virginia are more tolerant of thy kind."

Taylor didn't care for Flint's acidic tone of voice. "My kind? What do you mean, my kind?" she demanded. She lowered her hand to her side.

"The devil's minions. Mischief makers. Imps."

Pride rushed to the forefront, beating out any fleeting sense of caution Taylor might have entertained.

"Now hold on a minute. You can't talk to me like that! That's . . . why, that's libel. Intentional defamation of character in front of witnesses."

Before Taylor knew what she was doing, she heard herself singing "The Twelve Days of Christmas" in a clear voice that wafted through the village as if carried on a capricious breeze. Doors flew open. Shopkeepers scurried out into the street. Homeowners threw open their shutters and gawked from their windows. And the ring of iron against iron emanating from the blacksmith's shop leveled off to silence.

Glancing around, Taylor soon realized she'd unwittingly rallied an audience with her vocalized defiance of Mr. Flint. That she had humiliated the sheriff before his peers and their children. And that by doing so, she had also sealed her fate.

"I take it that thee can afford the five shilling fine for celebrating Christmastide," Mister Flint growled at the conclusion of her song.

Taylor told herself she was going to see this thing through without bawling like a baby. After all, she'd chosen to stick her foot into it of her own free will.

"No. I'm afraid I don't have five shillings on me at the moment," she said. She wished her voice would stop crackling like crumpled plastic wrap.

"Then, young sir, thee must possess a dire need to observe the inner workings of my jail," Mr. Flint said, beaming her a satisfied smile. He stuck the doll Sarah called a poppet into the drawstring pouch at his waist, then reached for Taylor's hand. His fingers closed around her wrist in a viselike grip.

Dumbstruck, Taylor stumbled after Mr. Flint as he strutted down the street. Her bravado bagged around her ankles like cheap panty hose as he dragged her past the stocks to the steps of a plain, unadorned building in the center of town.

"Go home and study thy verses. Psalms are a far better manner in which to pass the daylight hours than gaming," the sheriff shouted over his shoulder.

Glad for the unexpected reprieve, the children thawed and scattered like dry leaves in a winter storm.

Taylor wished she could scatter with them, but she was trapped in the steel talons of Mr. Flint.

The Spirit of Things to Come

And not even the handsome blacksmith, leaning against the doorjamb of his smithy, arms folded across his magnificent chest, seemed inclined to assist her.

Chapter Two

"Good day to thee, Jared Branlyn," Mr. Flint said.

Jared nodded toward Mr. Flint, drawing his cape more snugly about his shoulders. For all the people milling around and despite the oak fire roaring in the fireplace, the main floor of the meeting house felt chilly. It was inevitable that the newcomer had spent a miserably cold night in the room below the bell tower. The lawbreaker's cell relied on only the feeble heat of a brazier for warmth, while providing nothing more than moth-eaten blankets and a hard seaman's cot in the way of comfort.

"I understand from my deputy that thee intends to take responsibility for Taylor Kendall," Mr. Flint said.

Jared Branlyn glanced up sharply. "Taylor Kendall?"

"To the best of my knowledge, that is the prisoner's name."

Jared counted out the five shillings, stacked, and pushed the coins across the pulpit toward Mr. Flint.

"I have need of an apprentice to operate the bellows and keep the charcoal fire going. Taylor Kendall will do as well as the next man," Jared said as he mentally chided himself for getting involved. He had fought the notion throughout the night and well into the wee hours of the morning—and finally succumbed to it against his better judgment.

Mr. Flint said to his deputy, "Thee may bring down the prisoner now."

The sheriff recounted Jared's coins and dropped them into a mounting heap in the strongbox resting on the pulpit.

"I see you have experienced a prosperous court day," Jared commented.

"Of a certainty," Mr. Flint said. He nodded toward a man sprawled on a front row pew. The prisoner wore the letter *D* draped around his neck.

"We discovered Goodman Horn drunk outside the tavern this morning. If not for the ale warming his innards, he might well have frozen to death. His drunkenness has cost him two shillings and an afternoon in the stocks."

Goodman Horn's body shivered so violently that Jared could hear his teeth chattering.

"And what of the young couple on the second row?"

Mr. Flint glanced at the woman dressed in a dove-gray gown and white neckerchief with her feet propped on a small metal foot warmer. The man seated beside her had his arm wrapped solicitously around her shoulder.

"Mistress Ann planned to wed Robert Gant yonder a month hence. But it seems they became more closely involved than the courting stick allows."

Jared frowned. "'Tis often difficult for a man to honor the distance of a broom handle when it separates him from the woman he loves."

"To be sure, I have been there myself. But 'tis neither here nor there. Ann's mother discovered her in a family way, and the law is specific in such cases. I have decreased their fine to one shilling since new couples have little enough money to squander, but I decreed two days in the pillory for each of them to allow them time to meditate on their promiscuous behavior. I shall lead them into wedded bliss the moment they are released."

"And Goodwife Simpson, huddled there in the corner? What is her offense?"

"The woman cannot hold her tongue! She has been gossiping again, and the other wives are complaining strongly of it."

"Which means?"

"Well thee knows 'tis the dunking stool for her. She cannot seem to get enough of the water."

"There is ice on the pond today," Jared commented dryly.

"Thee would imagine the coldness of a winter dunking would deter her from spreading tales. But she is like a cockerel—crowing day in and day out regardless of the weather."

Mr. Flint closed and locked his strongbox and tucked it under his arm.

"'Tis as well thee has bailed the prisoner from jail. I do not know from whence he hails, but his

152

hands are as tender as any woman's. I would say he is unaccustomed to hard labor. He will learn quickly enough under thy tutelage, however. And the wages he will earn at the smithy will see him well on his way to Virginia."

"Eventually," Jared said. "First, Taylor Kendall must work off the five shillings owed to me after today."

"Just so," Flint agreed. A pleased smile graced his lips. "Perchance the young troublemaker will think twice before opposing the law in Bay Colony again."

"Perchance," Jared said.

"I can see thee is pensive this day. 'Tis good for a man to be so, when he gazes upon his fellow man's wickedness," Mr. Flint commented.

"As you say," Jared responded. His tone was clipped, as he intended it to be. He had more important matters to attend to than Mr. Flint's philosophizing.

"By the by, are the firedogs I ordered nearing completion? My wife is anxious to put them to use," Flint said.

Jared smiled to himself. Dame Flint's affection for nice things cost the sheriff a sizable fortune yearly.

A sparkle lightened Jared's eyes as he asked, "Is not avarice a sin, Mr. Flint?"

"My wife assures me 'tis not greed that prompts her," Flint sputtered. "She says she can scarcely keep a proper fire going without them, and well I believe her."

"She explained as much to me when she placed the order," Jared said.

"Well, there thee has it. Thee should deign to sit down to board with us more often, Jared.

Thee would see for thyself she speaks the absolute truth."

Jared stifled his mirth. It was common knowledge Dame Flint's prowess did not pertain to cookery—she had wedded, bedded, and laid to rest three husbands prior to Mr. Flint.

"Never fear. The andirons will be finished within the week," Jared assured the sheriff.

"Does thee think I could take delivery of them on the evening of the feather-stripping party?"

"Do you plan to join us at Widow Nash's cottage?"

"My wife and I would not miss sharing in the activities. Laudable recreation is difficult to come by. And my wife does so love to dance."

"Then I shall deliver the andirons into your care at that time."

"Excellent! I shall convey thy message to my wife," the sheriff said.

Jared turned away from Mr. Flint and watched as the deputy weaved his way through the crowd, Taylor Kendall in tow.

He had pondered the newcomer's delicate features long after the initial sighting. The revelation that she was a woman in the guise of a man had come hours later—after Mr. Flint had arrested her. The knowledge had almost been a relief, for he had felt an overwhelming attraction for the newcomer.

His eyes connected with hers across the crowded room. For a long moment, he simply stared at her. How could he have mistaken the length of the lashes that shielded her steady brown eyes, the sweet curve of her jaw, the tempting softness of her throat, the way her hips swelled ever so gently beneath the hem of the hooded leather waistcoat with its unusual napped surface?

He had missed it at first because he had failed to look far enough beyond her overgarments, Jared told himself. The others had overlooked Taylor Kendall's gender because of the inconceivability of a female donning men's breeches.

Jared wanted to chastise Taylor for jeopardizing herself in such a way, but he would not. It served no purpose. The deed was already accomplished. Now she needed protection from the laws of the General Court. From Mr. Flint. And perchance from herself as well.

With a sigh of resignation and a self-derisive smile, he lifted his hand and motioned for her to attend him.

During her stint in jail, Taylor belatedly realized she wasn't about to walk out of the 17th century as easily as she'd strolled into it. Therefore, it was with immense relief that she saw the blacksmith wave to her. She recognized him immediately, even though he wore a broad-brimmed beaver hat and woolen cape. The warm sensation she experienced confused her even as the uncertainty of the last 24 hours drained from her. The sight of the blacksmith brought a lightness to her heart; she hadn't expected to see him again.

As the deputy shouldered a path for them, Taylor weaved her way along with him across the jam-packed room to the blacksmith's side. The deputy had explained that the blacksmith was a pillar of the community. That he had taken pity on her. And that she was being relinquished into his custody because he had taken it upon himself to pay her fine.

Taylor gazed up into the face of her better-late-than-never liberator.

"Why did you do that? Why bail me out after you warned me in no uncertain terms not to interfere? I don't understa—"

Jared interrupted her.

"Come. Let us speak of this beyond the walls of the meeting house. Three may keep counsel if one be away," he said in a brusque voice, nodding toward Mr. Flint.

Jared captured Taylor's elbow and maneuvered her toward the door. Once outside, he wasted no time in resuming their conversation.

"My hair is longer than yours," he said as he considered her bare head.

Taylor bristled at his off-the-wall comment.

"What has my hair got to do with anything?" she asked, allowing her eyes to adjust to the bright clearness of the winter day and the cloudless sky. In her time, it had been gray and snowy for weeks on end without a break in sight.

Absorbed in studying her hair, he ignored her question.

"Then again, perchance 'tis for the best. There are those who would consider its eloquent fairness a vice if it were longer," he said with a deep frown. He reached up and flipped her hood over her disheveled flaxen curls.

Taylor's eyes widened with surprise. "Pardon me," she said as she flicked the hood back off again.

"I suggest you wear the hood," he said tightly.

"Why?"

"Because you are a newcomer to the colony and you have much to learn concerning its ways. And because your hair attracts undue attention, Taylor Kendall."

"I'm not sure I want to learn any more than I already know," Taylor told him as she raised the hood and tied it in place. "That jail cell isn't the most comfortable place I've ever spent the night."

"You should have considered that before you introduced yourself to Mr. Flint's disagreeable side. Now, come along," he said grudgingly. "I have bailed you out to work as my apprentice until you accumulate money enough to move on to Virginia."

Taylor started to say something, which Jared promptly interrupted.

"I said, come along, Taylor Kendall. I have no wish to catch the ague by standing out-of-doors in the damp winter air conversing with a . . ."

"Convicted troublemaker," Taylor finished for him.

"I did not say that."

"But you thought it."

"Indeed, I did not, though it seems to be an accurate observation."

"If you feel that way, why bother with me?"

He glowered at her. "I did not think I could tolerate watching them press you to death." And with that, he started down the street.

Heart missing a beat, Taylor had no recourse but to stumble after him, barely keeping up with his ground-eating stride.

Struggling to remain shoulder-to-shoulder with him, she squeaked, "Pressed to death? Whoa. Wait a minute. What do you mean by that—pressed to death?"

"Covered with heavy rocks. Crushed in a most disagreeable manner. That is what will happen to you if Mr. Flint discovers this hidden whimsy of yours," he said.

Before Taylor realized it, they'd crossed the commons and were passing the general store.

An attractive, middle-aged woman dressed in a saffron skirt and jacket covered by a crisp apron and a becoming leaf-green cape stood out front with an armload of packages. Taylor entertained the fleeting impression the woman might have rushed over and grabbed Jared's arm if not for the precarious tilt of her purchases.

"May I depend on seeing thee at the feather-stripping party?" she called to Jared, momentarily distracting Taylor from their conversation.

"I fancy you will," he responded without slowing his pace.

"Then I will converse with thee there. Godspeed, Jared Branlyn," she said, obviously pleased by his announcement.

"Godspeed," he replied.

"Who was that?" Taylor asked when they were well out of hearing distance.

"Mary Nash, John and Sarah's mother."

Taylor frowned thoughtfully. "She's a widow, isn't she?"

Jared slowed to a brisk trot, a surprised expression on his face.

"How did you know that?"

"I overheard Sarah talking about her father yesterday. But even if I hadn't, I think I could have guessed Mary Nash was unattached by the way she looked at you."

"The dickens you say! And how is it that she looked at me, Taylor Kendall?"

"Like a flower thirsting for rain," Taylor said. She fought down an insane moment of jealousy. The man had rescued her; that didn't make him her exclusive personal property, Taylor reminded herself.

They had reached the door to his smithy. He paused to stare at her a moment. Taylor found his quiet regard infinitely unsettling.

In hopes of distracting him from his intense perusal, she asked, "Is that your name—Jared Branlyn?"

"That is my name," he said. His gaze never wavered from her face.

Taylor tried again. "I like it. It . . . has a pleasant ring to it."

"I fear I have strapped myself with a less than humble maiden," he muttered finally. He practically pushed her inside the smithy before continuing. "Besides which, you converse in riddles. I am scarce able to understand many of the things you say."

"You don't talk like everyone else, and yet you're accepted as one of the gang."

"One of the gang?"

"A member of the community."

Obviously unaccustomed to justifying himself, it took Jared a moment to answer.

"My father was a Puritan and a non-Separatist from the Church of England, my mother Cornish. She preferred 'you' over 'thee,' and since she taught me the fine art of conversation . . ."

"I see."

"No, I am afraid you do not. I was born in Bay Colony—the village has had thirty-odd summers to adjust to my little eccentricities."

I don't have thirty years! At least I hope I don't.

"You're trying to tell me in a nice way that they're slow to accommodate visitors."

"You have already experienced that for yourself."

Suddenly frightened of standing out in Bay Colony like a sore thumb, Taylor said hastily, "My great-grandparents were Dutch." She hated telling white lies. But she saw no way around it. Besides, her father's grandparents had been born and bred in Holland, though her mother's family was of German derivation.

"Perchance, as Flint mentioned, that accounts for your unique accent as well as your peculiar vocabulary."

"I suppose." It seemed as good a reason as anything Taylor could think up right offhand.

"A word of caution—if I were you, I would know my mind before I spoke out in Bay Colony. A certain wayward turn of phrase . . . a misplaced word . . . a misspoken thought can be easily misconstrued."

"This is the second time you've suggested I keep my nose clean." Bruised pride supplied Taylor's voice with a biting edge she couldn't quite suppress. "You're just full of helpful advice, aren't you?"

He stiffened. "Not advice, compassion for those unsettled in their judgment," Jared corrected.

His words smarting, Taylor asked, "Is that how you perceive me?"

"I know not yet how I perceive you, Taylor Kendall," he answered her with unabashed honesty. "Only time will tell. And by the by, I do not see that your nose is smudged. Your cheek, however, wants washing."

With that, he took her hand and guided her through the smithy to the door in the center of the back wall. His hand felt large and callused and marvelously masculine wrapped snugly around hers. Taylor couldn't remember the last time she'd held hands with a man.

Too soon Jared dropped her hand to open the door and usher her through it. With a curt nod, he directed her down the stable's wide hallway past a half-dozen stalls, and through a double door leading outside once again.

Across a narrow secondary avenue, Taylor spied an unpainted cottage with an arched roof, shuttered windows, and a huge brick chimney. He stepped to the threshold of the cottage and kicked open the door, beckoning her to follow.

Having no recourse, Taylor obliged Jared.

He guided her into the close quarters of the rectangular room, the palm of his hand strategically placed in the small of her back. He nudged the door shut and leaned back against it as if he expected her to attempt an escape.

In the privacy of the cottage, Taylor flipped her hood back.

Jared untied his cap and flung it along with his hat onto the high-backed maple settle postured before the fireplace. "Now, if you feel so disposed, pray tell me about this potentially dangerous deceit you have perpetrated."

Strings of dried apples hung from the rafters and Taylor had little doubt she smelled venison stew simmering in the iron kettle dangling on a hook over the fire. Her stomach growled and she swallowed heavily, darting a glance at the crock of maple syrup—a New England staple for countless centuries—squatting on the rough-hewn table.

The last thing she'd eaten was a sausage biscuit along with a carton of chocolate milk at a fast-food joint near her condo. That must have been about seven o'clock yesterday morning, Taylor calculated. She'd consumed nothing more since then, not even water, and was suddenly hard-pressed to keep her attention from straying to the food.

"You have cost me five shillings, a half a day's work, and a sleepless night in the bargain," he said. He pushed away from the door to light a sweetly fragrant bayberry candle in a saucerlike lamp. After that, he lit the candle set on the fire-place. Taylor knew it was a candle set, positioned on the fireplace so the smoke would exit up the chimney, because her parents had one just like it in their restored colonial.

"Through my decision to bail you from jail, I feel I have purchased the right to be privy to your thoughts. Answer me truly. Why masquerade in Bay Colony under the guise of a man?"

His voice sounded calm, smooth, and extremely sincere. Taylor couldn't have been more surprised if he'd demanded she disrobe.

"You've got to be kidding. I don't have the faintest idea what you're talking about!"

"You are a pure trial, Taylor Kendall. Come now, the truth."

Angry that he questioned her integrity, Taylor said stiffly, "I'm telling you the truth. I don't know what you're talking about. These are just regular—" Taylor stopped, her mouth dropping open.

Taylor felt his laserlike eyes on her as he attempted to drill peepholes into her brain and examine her thoughts. She forced herself to turn and face him head-on, and yet veil her inner turmoil with a faint smile.

"I've got the picture now. You're telling me that all this time, you, the children, and Mr. Flint too, thought I was a man," she stated more calmly than she felt.

"The children and Mr. Flint did—still do if luck is with us. From the moment you appeared on the edge of town, I suspected otherwise. When I saw you today in the meeting house and watched you walk toward me, my suspicions were confirmed."

It was all coming together for her now. Taylor stared at Jared in astonishment.

"That's what you meant when you said they'd press me to death. They . . . they wouldn't like it if they found out I was a woman underneath all this heavy winter gear, would they?"

"A woman in Bay Colony is not allowed to wear silk; 'tis considered vain and frivolous. She must not show her ankles; 'tis considered promiscuous. Her hair must be maintained beneath a coif; 'tis regarded as sinful to display it. She must wear an apron in public for propriety's sake or risk being fined."

Feeling suddenly warm and faint, Taylor slowly unbuttoned her parka. Jared frowned, watching her fingers as if they were suddenly the most fascinating thing about her.

"Why, the very buttons on your waistcoat are considered unnecessary adornment! You, Taylor Kendall, are scandalous from head to heel. Make no mistake about it."

Jared had a valid point, Taylor decided. She'd had so much on her mind lately, like the cold, the jail, being trapped in the past for good, and the odds for her prolonged survival in the wrong century, that concern for her clothes had never even occurred to her.

Taylor almost laughed aloud. And she might have, too, if she hadn't felt more like crying.

Who could have imagined the holidays would turn out to be so complicated? Being snatched up by fate like straw in a hurricane and tossed into a fanatical era that banned Christmas was bad enough without discovering her choice in wearing apparel might be construed as indecent exposure and therefore subject her to capital punishment. Thonged bathing suits were one thing; woolen slacks and sweaters were an entirely different matter!

With a sinking feeling, Taylor asked, "Do you mind if I sit down? I suddenly feel light-headed."

Jared almost reached out to her, until she paused to take off her waistcoat. As the over-garment slipped from her arms and joined his cape on the settle, Jared nearly choked on his own saliva.

The smock she wore was the most delicate shade of purple he had ever seen. It complimented her ivory skin and fair hair to perfection. It also displayed the proud posture of her breasts, mod-est though they were beneath the soft material, effectively proclaiming to an onlooker that if they were daft enough to mistake her for a man the first go-around, they had better take another long, hard look.

And then there was the way her gray woolen breeches clung to her gentle curves, emphasiz-ing the enticing length of her legs and the unquestionable firmness of her thighs. Jared's gaze skittered from Taylor's trim waist to her ankles as he tried his levelheaded best to overlook everything in between. He found only her boots to be satisfactory.

"We must do something about your overgarments," he said at last.

Taylor lowered herself into the settle before responding.

"My clothes?" she asked. She extended her hands toward the flames flickering in the fireplace, unable to disregard the musket and powder horn on the rack above the mantel. The apparent newness of what should have been an ancient weapon only reinforced the fact that she'd traveled through time.

"They are unsuitable without your waistcoat. And you cannot be expected to wear it all the time. It would appear odd. The consequences would be a drama that needs no playing out where we are concerned."

Taylor followed the direction of his eyes, glancing down at her chest. Without her concealing parka, the turtleneck sweater made the most of what she considered her meager assets. The lack of heat in the meeting house had most probably been a godsend, though she hadn't thought so at the time, Taylor surmised. Due to it, she had opted not to remove her parka. The cold had saved her from a faux pas from which she might never have recovered.

"I see what you mean," she said, imagining the feel of heavy rocks pressed against her breasts. Taylor shuddered. She'd read somewhere that the Puritans believed dinosaur tracks were witches' footprints. It wouldn't be out of the realm of possibility for them to decide she was one of the witches that had made the tracks.

"What do you propose I do about my clothes?"

"It would be simple for me to purchase something at the general store," he said.

"I've imposed on your charity enough as it is," Taylor said quickly. "I mean, there must be some other way. You've already paid my fine and all."

"'Tis not charity, Taylor. I expect you to pay me back out of the wages you earn at the smithy."

"I . . . I couldn't possibly pay you back before I—" Taylor paused. She searched for the right words to tell him she didn't plan to hang around long.

Eventually Taylor realized there was no way to tell Jared as much without also explaining that she was a time-traveler. A time-traveler who thoroughly expected at any moment for fate to recognize its bizarre mistake and snatch her back to the future—where she belonged.

At best, Jared would probably think her a liar. At worst, he might march her to the meeting house and hand her back over to Mr. Flint—which was the last thing she wanted.

"Please, don't spend any more money on me. I'll get by."

"I have a notion," Jared said slowly. He paused to listen to the bell tolling outside. "But we will speak of it later. For now, I believe we are being called to supper."

"I thought that bell meant someone was being punished," Taylor said. That was what she'd surmised as she'd sat alone in her dreary cell and listened to the sounds of the court proceedings which floated up to her from the meeting house below.

"Among other things. It calls us to rise and begin our day's work. It tolls out the meal hours. It tells us when there is a birth or a death in the community. Nine strokes means a man has passed on. Six a woman. Three a child. It can also signal danger, though I do not recall the last time it was used in that capacity. Did you not have a bell such as ours in the town from whence you came, Taylor Kendall?"

"We have church bells." *That chime a computerized tune. And electric alarm clocks that sometimes do, but more often don't.*

"Our meeting house bell is that too, on the Sabbath day," Jared said, using a long hook to swing the iron kettle from the fire. He settled the kettle on a block of wood in the center of the table and gathered two pewter dishes and a pair of spoons from a maple chest against the wall.

"I have prepared spoon meat and succotash, mashed turnips with parsley, and bread. You are welcome to join me."

He seated himself at the table and draped a large linen napkin over his shoulder. After wiping his hands on it, he broke a hunk of bread from the loaf he'd retrieved from the bake oven located on the side of the fireplace.

"Come, sit at the board and eat," he said. He motioned for Taylor to take the stool across from him.

Taylor rose from the settle and moved to the table.

He served their dishes, said a short prayer over the food, and dug in.

Taylor couldn't remember the last time she'd eaten a meal bereft of knives and forks. She also couldn't recall the last time food tasted so good.

Perhaps last Christmas at her mother's house. Her mother was a terrific cook. She made the most mouth-watering mincemeat pie in New England, rivaled only by her succulent goose with orange glaze.

Taylor experienced a pang of homesickness which she quickly quelled, looking toward Jared instead.

"Mmmmm. This is great—plain and simple, yet delicious. My compliments to the chef."

His spoon stopped midway to his mouth. "We do not ordinarily converse at the table."

"Is it against the law too?"

Jared's lips curved into an unexpected half-smile that Taylor found thoroughly captivating.

"Not that I know of," he said. "'Tis just not done."

"Three may keep counsel if one be away," Taylor mimicked.

To her surprise, Jared threw back his head and laughed. The sound was deep and rich and pleasing to the ear. It put Taylor more at ease than she'd been since the holidays began.

"As you wish, Taylor Kendall. Since there are some things I have been meaning to ask you, we shall converse over our meal."

"Ask away."

Jared had never felt quite so unrestrained in a woman's presence. The casual intimacy of the meal led him to ask the question foremost in his mind. "Are you wedded?"

This time, Taylor paused with the spoon midway to her mouth. "No. I'm not."

"Do not look so defensive."

Her eyes slid from his. "I don't look defensive."

"You do."

"Well, I don't mean to. And yes, I'm definitely single."

"You are a thornback, then."

"A thornback? That sounds like the name for a species of prickly toad."

Jared reached for his tankard, muffling his laughter behind a hefty swallow of mulled cider. He placed the wooden tankard on the table, saying, "A thornback is an unmarried woman of thirty."

"A spinster, you mean."

Jared nodded.

Taylor fought the frown threatening to wrinkle her brow. "Do I look thirty?"

"Yes."

So much for mud packs and night cream! Taylor thought in disgust.

Trying desperately not to be offended, she said, "You're right. I'm thirty. As thirty as thirty can be."

"Perchance we should move along to something else, something less inciting—do you have family, Taylor?"

"Yeah." *More family than a thornback can handle.*

"Did they sanctify you traveling so far from home alone?"

Not even in my mother's wildest dreams would she go along with this. "They didn't know I was coming here." *But then again, neither did I.*

Jared mopped the gravy from his plate with his last bite of bread, popped the soggy morsel into his mouth, and pushed his chair away from the table.

"In which case, I can understand why this must be a sensitive issue for you. No wonder you felt it necessary to travel to the New World in disguise. Crossing the Atlantic Ocean is a difficult proposition for a man, let alone a woman without a chaperon. Perchance your wisdom is keener than I thought. I admire your resourcefulness. The New World offers overwhelming civil liberties compared to the repression of the Old. 'Tis a mighty drawing card."

"I'm not so sure about that. Maybe in a couple of hundred years when the Flints of this world are overrun with Thomas Jeffersons, and Ben Franklins, and Patrick Henrys it will all make a lot more sense . . . when the laws like the ones banning Christmas celebrations are seen for what they are and repealed—"

"Taylor Kendall, you are a marvel. You simply do not comprehend that the Good Book does not ordain feast days or saints days and from there does the General Court make its rules," he interrupted.

Taylor silently berated herself for going off the deep end. She realized he couldn't possibly have the faintest idea what she was talking about. The American dream wasn't even formulated yet.

"I'm sorry, I was . . . rattling on. It's been a grueling day and I'm pooped." She pushed her chair away from the table and rose. "I don't even know what I'm saying anymore. I really need to get some rest."

"That is most probably wise." Jared glanced at the bed. "You may have the bed."

Taylor glanced at the bed as well.

"Where will you sleep?"

"There is a trundle beneath." He demonstrated by pulling it out. "I will make use of it."

170

The thing looked uncomfortable to Taylor. "I can't take your bed."

"I insist."

"But I—"

With a start, Jared acknowledged he had somehow allowed Taylor to touch him on a personal level, which was something he had never intended. He did not want her to sleep on the hard trundle bed. He wanted her to sleep in his bed. Even if he was not sharing it with her.

Jared knew he was allowing his heart to overrule his head, but avoided delving too deeply into his emotions. "You take the bed," he said as he prepared a warming pan and passed it between the sheets. "I will make do with the trundle. That is my final word. I will brook no opposition in the matter."

Taylor nodded. When she was in college, she'd lived in a coed dorm. During her first year as a teacher, she'd shared a house with three tenured teachers in Beacon Hills. One of them had been a single man in his mid-thirties. She had no problem sharing her living quarters with a man. Besides, Jared Branlyn had shown compassion toward her—a poor lost soul. She felt safe, warm, full, and protected in his company.

Taylor left the table, kicked off her shoes, and crawled into the platform bed fully clothed. She needed a bath, but Jared didn't offer and she didn't push.

Jared removed a homespun calico quilt from the same chest from which he'd retrieved the dinnerware. He tossed it to her.

"Thanks," she muttered sleepily, nestling into the welcoming warmth of the huge feather bed.

Tired beyond belief, Taylor closed her eyes. Her last coherent thoughts were of the pleasant male scent emanating from her soft pillow, and of the town crier calling out, "Nine o'clock and all is well!"

Jared reached for his clay pipe off the mantel. Plucking a hot ember from the fire with a set of smoking tongs, he ignited the tobacco in the bowl and clamped the pipe stem between his teeth. He banked the fire and covered it with a dome-shaped, perforated lid that allowed the fire to breathe and yet kept the precious embers smoldering throughout the night.

The final chore of the day done, Jared glanced toward Taylor, snoring softly in his bed as if she had not a care in the world. Absently, he pondered the fascinating woman he had taken into his care.

She possessed a comely smile, when she chose to bestow a smile. And mischievous brown eyes that spoke of hidden desires. And a body that intrigued him, triggered his imagination, and fanned his own fancy like the bellows in his blacksmith shop.

Jared squared his shoulders and puffed on his pipe. Somehow, he had to gain control of his wayward thoughts, he chided himself. But he could not. The harder he tried, the more vivid the image of the tempting curves molded beneath his bed linen became.

Jared tapped out his pipe and replaced it on the mantel.

He must get some sleep! All too soon the meeting house bell would usher in the dawn and he had a pair of andirons to complete for Mr. Flint, among other things.

Acutely aware of the woman in his bed, Jared snuffed the candles and stretched out on the trundle, leaving his breeches on for modesty's sake.

He closed his eyes only to find he could not rest. Taylor's image flitted across the backside of his eyelids, alternately bemusing and enticing him with her provocative antics.

Jared shifted from side to side as he sought a comfortable position. Sleep, like the reasoning behind Taylor's presence in Bay Colony, eluded him.

In the end, Jared spent the second night since her arrival wrestling with thoughts of how Taylor's tempting mouth might feel beneath the weight of his passion-starved lips.

Chapter Three

"Boy, you sure are grumpy this morning," Taylor commented sleepily. "Did you crawl out on the wrong side of the bed?"

"I was unaware there is a right and a wrong side to a bed. And 'tis no longer morning," Jared responded dryly. He stifled a yawn with the back of his hand and trundled the truckle beneath the platform bed with his foot. It wheeled into concealment, shaking the bed frame and Taylor along with it.

Her heart scampered with surprise.

"How long have you been up?" she asked.

"Since the bell tolled sunrise," he replied.

Taylor sat up and stretched, punching the pillow up behind her back. "What time is it?" she asked without bothering to hide her yawn.

"Noon."

Taylor blinked and rubbed the sleep from her

eyes. "No way! I never sleep in, not even on Saturdays."

She was a morning person—her internal clock was set on early to bed, early to rise. Each weekday morning she arrived at school by seven to plan her daily program. On Saturdays she jogged before breakfast. On Sundays she attended services in a redbrick church around the corner from her condo. And she was normally making Z's by ten P.M.

"Trust me, you did 'sleep in' this day," Jared countered.

Taylor glanced at the chafing dish in the center of the table. Ashen coals nestled in a basin beneath it, coals that she suspected no longer harbored any real warmth.

"You made breakfast."

"Yes. Mine, however, was tastier than yours promises to be."

Taylor wasn't quite ready for what happened next. She watched as Jared stalked to the settle. He reached over the back to retrieve a bundle of clothes from the seat, tossing them at her. Unprepared for a game of catch, the medicine-ball-like bundle hit Taylor full in the face before tumbling into her lap.

Bewilderment followed astonishment as she gazed down at the clothes.

"What's this?"

"Overgarments. And I did not mean to accost you with them."

"I can see that they're clothes. And I accept the apology. But what am I supposed to do with them?" she asked dubiously.

"Taylor Kendall, you would sorely test the patience of the most agreeable of gentlemen."

Though his voice was as bland and impassive as a news commentator's, his eyes related his growing annoyance with her. "What do people normally do with overgarments?"

"Wear them."

"Precisely."

She untied the bundle to examine the woolen breeches, purple smock, and sleeveless vest. "You're asking me to parade around town in these?"

"'Tis not a request."

Taylor scowled at Jared. She sort of liked being protected. She wasn't too keen on being ordered around, though. Obviously the man had never heard of equality of the sexes.

"And if I refuse?" She ran her fingertips along the inside of the breeches leg. She hated unlined wool. It made her skin itch to no end.

"You cannot risk going about in public in your own overgarments without covering them with your waistcoat. The smithy is too warm for such a heavy overgarment. Hence, the doublet and breeches are the only likely solution . . . more suitable than petticoats and garters, which would only serve to reveal our deception to prying eyes."

Taylor couldn't help but notice he lumped himself in with her.

"Mr. Flint would have you back in the lawbreaker's cell before you could defend yourself. In short, you must be made to see the precariousness of our position."

Taylor listened silently as he elaborated on the incentives for complying with his demands.

"A woman's garments would also make it impossible for you to remain under my care. You are an unwed woman, residing beneath my roof without benefit of a chaperon, and I am acting with scandalous disregard for your reputation in allowing it."

"What about the danger you've put yourself in by giving me sanctuary?"

"Allow me to concern myself with that."

A hard edge framed his words—whether for her or himself, she wasn't sure.

"You didn't . . . uh . . . buy the clothes, did you?" Taylor asked, trying to come to grips with fate's strange sense of humor. She'd never cared for dresses before. Now that she couldn't wear one, she wanted to.

"I told you I would not add another shilling against your indebtedness to me, and since I owned nothing to suit, I visited the widow Nash this morning. When I explained my new apprentice's need for fresh clothing, she generously donated the overgarments you see before you. Happily enough, Goodman Nash was a man of meager stature. . . ."

His voice trailed off.

"How kind of her." Her own voice sounded strange to her. Slightly choked up. And decidedly strained.

"Assuredly so," he agreed.

"And of you," Taylor said levelly.

Jared fell momentarily silent.

"I've put you in an awkward position, haven't I?" she asked in a low voice.

He shrugged. "I walked into the meeting house to fetch you with my eyes well open."

With a forced cheerfulness, Taylor abruptly relented, ending the contest of wills by saying, "Okay. I'll bow to your wisdom—this time."

Jared's cerulean orbs deepened to an ominous, storm-swept hue that fascinated Taylor. She'd never seen eyes that changed colors, like the iridescent stone mounted in a mood ring.

"The greater wisdom would have been to leave you to the frigid bed you made for yourself by waving your principles concerning civil liberty beneath Mr. Flint's nose."

Taylor lowered her gaze.

"But you didn't," she said.

"Indeed, I did not, and I know not why," he said, though his expression cleared somewhat.

"Do you regret it now?"

She felt his perusal. She glanced up, reading the answer to her question in his eyes even before he responded verbally.

"I do not come to decisions lightly, therefore I rarely repent of my actions."

"Is your decision concerning me the exception?" Taylor asked, forcing the issue. For some crazy reason, she needed to hear him confirm it aloud.

"I would do it over again if that is what you are asking, though I do not relish the notion," he stated solemnly.

Taylor smiled faintly, spreading out the clothes he'd given her on the bed. She smoothed the creases from the smock with the palm of her hand.

"I did pour it on a little thick with Mr. Flint, didn't I?"

"You did indeed."

"I thought for a minute he might blow a fuse."

"If you are alluding to his face, I agree. I have never seen the sheriff's color so high."

As if remembering and enjoying the scene, his

lips twitched slightly. Or at least Taylor thought they did. He recovered his sobriety so quickly, she decided she must have imagined it.

"Sometimes my convictions have a way of running away with me," she said.

Almost as if he was out to prove something to himself, he reached forward and tipped her chin up with his forefinger.

His voice took on a stern note as he told her, "It would be best for everyone concerned if you kept a tight rein on them during your stay in Bay Colony."

Taylor sighed. Few Americans realized that an old-fashioned New England Christmas meant no Christmas at all. If her convictions were tested again, she honestly couldn't say how she would react.

She'd like to promise him she'd behave. He deserved that much. But she had never been anything but straightforward. And now was not the time to try to change her stripes, Taylor decided. The man had risked too much for her to lie to him.

"I can't give you any assurances," she said truthfully. She mentally braced herself for his anger, wondering if he would physically throw her out into the snow and let nature take its course. Her bottom lip shook slightly as she sat in silent agony and awaited his response. Reluctant for him to witness her trepidation, Taylor bit down on the soft inner lining of her lip to control its telltale trembling.

He stared into her face, absently brushing her lower lip with his callused thumb as if measuring the fullness and shape of it while committing it to memory.

"I do not recall asking for any," he said rather hoarsely. He withdrew his hand slowly.

"There is water in the basin yonder if you feel the need to wash. And the dish on the board contains Indian pudding, though I doubt not it is stone-cold by now. You may reheat the porridge in the kettle on the hearth."

"Th-th-thank you," Taylor replied. She glanced at the chafing dish, experiencing a pang of homesickness. Her mother cooked cornmeal mush. It was one of her father's favorite hot cereals. It wasn't one of hers, however, but then beggars couldn't be choosers.

By now her parents had probably called out the National Guard, Taylor mused further. And since they weren't the kind of people to sit on their hands during a crisis, they'd be out searching for her too. She wondered if they had discovered her wrecked Jeep. Or the footprints in the snow she'd been unable to find.

Regardless, the episode would be heartbreaking for them, Taylor decided, feeling saddened that her disappearance had undoubtedly ruined her family's Christmas Day celebration. She wished she could send them a message to ease their minds—which she couldn't. Let them know she was all right—which she was; and she wasn't.

Taylor pursed her lips together.

She needed to get home. Besides her concern for her family, she had 23 kindergarten students depending on her return to class following vacation. She couldn't disappoint the kids. And last but not least, she had turned Jared Branlyn's life upside down without even trying. If she remained in Bay Colony, she might cause irreparable damage.

But the plain fact was, Taylor didn't know where to begin to look for the pathway home. She supposed she would simply have to bide her time, and at the first available opportunity, retrace her steps to the edge of the village. It was frustrating, but what else could she do?

"Might I trust seeing you in the smithy within a reasonable length of time?" Jared asked. He watched her closely. "I have need of an apprentice to assist me in finishing an order."

Taylor nodded. "I'll be there within the hour with bells on."

Jared frowned. "I could do without the addition of the bells, Taylor. They would be considered—"

"Unnecessary adornment, like buttons," she finished for him, not in the least bit surprised he'd taken her literally. "Don't worry. I'll leave off the bells."

"This time," he said, hand on the door handle.

"Yeah," she agreed. She flashed him a wry smile.

"'Tis as well. The items I intend to work on this afternoon are a pair of andirons for Mr. Flint. I would not put it beyond him to visit the smithy in order to gauge my progress. It would be devilish unkind of you to cause him to suffer an apoplexy in the middle of my smithy."

"Apoplexy?"

"A crisis within his brain."

Taylor shot Jared a perplexed look.

"Have you never seen the like?" he asked.

"I don't think so."

"It often cripples."

Taylor felt as if they were playing a modified version of charades.

"I'm sorry. I never have been very good at guessing games."

Jared offered her another clue. "Often people can neither converse nor walk after such an attack."

"Oh, you mean a stroke," Taylor said, thinking they really communicated pretty well, considering 300 years separated their speaking styles. "No, I don't think I'd want to be responsible for bringing on something like that. At least, not in the middle of your smithy. Now out in the street, that's another matter."

This time Jared bit his lip and hurriedly presented his back to Taylor, disappointing her. She'd hoped to once again see the captivating smile she'd glimpsed during yesterday's supper.

"Within the hour," he reminded her over his shoulder as he exited the cottage without turning around.

Released to her own reflections, she found esteem for Jared increased by leaps and bounds. The man was more accepting of her than anyone she'd ever met outside her family—and with more to lose than she could even begin to imagine. Her mother always said: "There's a silver lining to every cloud." If that was the case, then Jared represented the silver lining in hers.

Taylor reasoned if she hung around Bay Colony long enough, she could grow to like Jared Branlyn. A lot. More than she already did. Much more than was good for either of them, all things considered.

True to her word, Taylor met Jared in the smithy within the hour. He glanced up from his anvil when she entered, pausing to survey her critically.

"Well, how do I look?" Taylor prompted.

"The overgarments are . . . er . . . most adequate."

Taylor's face fell. Once she'd gotten them on, she'd decided the clothes weren't so bad after all. Purple was her color. And the breeches weren't as itchy as she'd imagined them. Besides that, everything fit remarkably well. And as an added boon, after sleeping in her own clothes for two nights in a row, they were a whole lot cleaner.

"It's my boots, isn't it? I thought they looked kind of funny with stockings, but I didn't have anything else to wear."

" 'Tis not the boots, Taylor. 'Tis your calves."

"What's wrong with them?"

"Absolutely nothing. Therein lies the rub. They are most . . . curvaceous."

Taylor squelched the urge to chuckle aloud somewhere between her Adam's apple and her teeth, because she didn't want Jared to think she was laughing at him. Which she wasn't. She was simply amused that the shapeliness of her legs made him uncomfortable. What would he think if he saw her in a miniskirt? Or better still, a pair of short shorts? Taylor wondered.

"I'm sorry, but there isn't a heck of a lot I can do about them. As for the rest of the clothes, I think they cover everything else up rather nicely. Don't you?"

Jared nodded crisply as he returned to his work.

Taylor spared a moment to glance around the fastidiously neat smithy, deciding Jared had been right about the warmth and humidity of the workshop. Her parka would have been too heavy to tolerate.

Her gaze eventually wandered to the broadness of Jared's shoulders. And then upward, along the strong, swarthy column of his throat to his square jawline. His face was turned away from her so that she was able to comfortably study him in profile without his knowledge. It struck Taylor afresh that Jared was an extremely handsome man. She'd seen hunks like him on the cover of *Gentleman's Quarterly*. But she had rarely met one in real life, at least not one as approachable as Jared.

She also noted that for some reason, he'd failed to shave that morning.

Because he was out on a mission of mercy, scavenging some suitable clothing for you, Taylor reminded herself.

The stubble added to rather than detracted from her attraction for Jared Branlyn, though she was normally put off by the devil-may-care connotations of a five o'clock shadow.

"So," Taylor said finally to combat the ever-increasing heat building within her body, a moist heat which had absolutely nothing to do with the atmospheric temperature of the smithy. "What can I do to help you around here, boss?"

Jared looked up. The woman intended to drive him to distraction! He was certain of it!

He had imagined it would be a simple matter to keep her at his side and out of harm's way, and yet at a safe personal distance. He had also envisioned the overgarments making their close association more tolerable. How could he have been so mistaken?

The purple smock mellowed her eyes to a more sultry brown and heightened her hair to a fairer fair. The vest emphasized the tantalizing trimness of her waist, while the stockings displayed her calves to excruciating advantage.

No one in the community would think to judge her as a woman. But since he knew her secret, he couldn't help himself. She possessed an indefinable quality that attracted him, and he wanted her as he had wanted nothing else in his lifetime. Perchance if he immersed himself in the work which he prided himself on, it would offset the latent desire churning within him. . . .

"As I told you earlier, I am in the process of forming Flint's andirons. Come and I will teach you to tend the bellows properly."

He demonstrated.

"I see," Taylor said after a moment's contemplation. "It's like a large set of lungs that breathe life into the hearth, at the same time regulating the flames."

"I could not have explained it better myself," he said.

"Here, let me try it," Taylor said, and Jared stepped aside. She squeezed the handles of the bellows, in and out, in and out, at a moderate speed.

"I am pleased by your immediate grasp of the work," Jared commented.

Utilizing a phrase her kindergarten students were fond of, Taylor replied, "I'm a super-fast learner."

"You may stop now," he instructed. "There is something else I would like you to see."

He showed her the andirons they would be working on. Taylor instantly recognized the quality craftsmanship.

"Now it's my turn to be impressed," she said. She reached for an andiron. He relinquished it to her without comment. She turned it over and over in her hand. "This is beautiful."

The firedog reminded Taylor of a life-size iron sculpture entitled *Minuteman At Parade Rest* that she'd recently seen at the Museum Of Fine Arts. It had been contemporary, ultra-conservative, and absolutely mesmerizing.

"You're an artisan. I hadn't thought about it before, but you produce everything around here that's made from iron, don't you?" She glanced around the shop again, seeing it in its real context for the first time. "The hinges. The nails. The hardware for the wagon wheels. Building tools like the ax on the wall. Cookware."

"Among other things. My knowledge of the craft is a legacy passed down from my father. Sadly enough, I was not 'a super-fast' learner. It took years for me to perfect my ability, though my father always insisted it came naturally to the men in our family."

No wonder the deputy had called Jared a pillar of the community. Without his expertise, the people of Bay Colony would all be lost. Or at the least, incredibly inconvenienced.

"And now, if you are so disposed, we will begin," he prompted. "We have much to accomplish before the bell tolls the supper hour."

Taylor nodded, anxious now to participate in the completion of the iron andirons.

All things considered, they worked rather companionably together throughout the afternoon, Taylor decided. It was hard, hot, painstaking work. But it kept her mind off other things. Like home. And the graceful way Jared's muscles flexed when he moved.

Besides, she was genuinely interested in Jared's work; he seemed absorbed by it.

As if a silent pact had been drafted between them, they avoided eye contact and concentrated on the andirons instead, each lost in his or her own thoughts. They shared a cold luncheon of flaky bakery squares Jared called marrow pastries. They drank cold milk dipped from a covered pail perched on a snowy ledge outside of the smithy—rich, thick milk which almost gagged her until she became accustomed to it. And according to his warnings, Taylor continued to expect Mr. Flint to pop in on them at any second.

In the end it was not one, but two guests that visited the smithy during the waning hours of the workday.

The boy spoke up first as he steered his sister into the blacksmith shop. "I fear Sarah has developed another inflammation on her eyelid. My good mother hoped she could come and watch thee for a short while."

Jared beckoned them to his side as he motioned for Taylor to take a break. "Did she now?" he asked.

"Aye, she did. She said as much to me as well," Sarah piped up.

"Hush, Sarah," John said. He nudged his little sister on the arm. "Mother told thee to remain silent and allow me to converse with Jared on this issue—man to man."

"But John, I only wished to ask him if he was hammering out something of interest yonder. I would much rather witness him fashion a fancy iron kettle with clawed feet and sloping handles than an ugly old horseshoe."

"Sarah! Thee was commanded not to say such

187

things! Mother will be disgraced when she hears of this."

"If thee does not run to her with tales of my misbehavior, she will not know to be disgraced," Sarah said in a small voice, gazing down at her folded hands.

Jared interceded.

"Perchance I *am* working upon something to capture your attention. And perchance 'tis unnecessary for John to tell your mother all he knows." Jared winked toward Taylor, and added, "This time."

Taylor suddenly felt as if she was being included in the group, and in Jared's life. It felt comfortable. Right.

Before she could stop herself, she winked back at him.

She watched as a startled expression skittered across his face, probably prompted by her bold response, she decided. Or the brief meeting of their eyes after a day of avoidance.

Jared led Sarah to the hearth and the evaporating steam which hovered above the watering trough.

"So you have another sty, Sarah. Here, sit beside me and let me have a peek at it."

"I would rather not. It pains me rather fearfully."

"I doubt not that it does," Jared said. "But if you will sit still and allow the steam to conjure up its magic, perchance I could see my way clear to pour some maple syrup out into the snow for you two ruffians."

Sarah laughed and clapped her hands. "Sugar candy?"

"You're bribing her, Jared," Taylor interjected

softly, though she cast him a supportive smile.

"I realize that, and so does Sarah," he said just as softly. "We have a mutual understanding."

"Which is?"

"That I will bribe her when she comes to me with one of her sties, and that she might come to depend on it so that the affliction does not seem so aggravating."

"You have a way with children," Taylor said, thinking Jared would make a good father, one that a brood of children could look up to and respect. A father like the one she'd grown up with.

"Mother says that very same thing. Often," Sarah said.

"I wouldn't doubt that a bit," Taylor responded. She shot Jared an I-told-you-so look.

"Let us not be bearing tales about things we have been told in passing, Sarah," Jared began.

"Such as the fact that the young sir yonder has spent time in the lawbreaker's cell. And that thee has apprenticed him, not because thee needs an extra hand, but because thee feels sorrow for him," Sarah said innocently.

"Who told you such a thing?" Jared asked.

"Why, no one. I overheard Goodwife Simpson conversing with Mother."

"Goodwife Simpson will find herself strapped to the dunking stool again if she is not more wary of her gossipy tongue."

"Mother warned her of that very thing on this morning," Sarah said.

Taylor raised her hand slightly as she'd taught her students to do, interrupting them. "Could I be excused for a few minutes? I have to run across to the cottage."

She realized her request sounded as if she

needed to make a trip to the outhouse. She didn't necessarily have to, but she allowed Jared to think she did because she was positive he wouldn't like what she was up to.

Involved with the kids, Jared simply nodded his approval.

Once outside, Taylor breathed deeply of the fresh, clean air, and for the span of a heartbeat thought about sprinting toward the edge of the village. But then Sarah's expression when Mr. Flint snatched the doll from her hands rose to taunt her. She couldn't even think about leaving Bay Colony until she set matters straight for the little girl.

Taylor crossed the street, detoured to the outhouse after all, then made a beeline for the cottage. She pushed open the heavy door and stepped inside, going straight for her parka.

Taylor dug deeply into the ample side pocket. She found what she sought, grabbed the maple syrup crock from the table, and returned to the smithy via the stable door.

Taylor handed Jared the crock without preamble. He immediately passed it on to John.

"Take this crock outdoors and spread a liberal amount of syrup upon the snow. Choose a spot that has been trampled by neither man nor beast," he told the boy.

John eagerly accepted the crock.

After John had scurried to do his bidding, Jared said, "Now, Taylor, you may explain what you fetched from the cottage and have hidden behind your back."

Taylor grimaced. "I don't think you're going to like it. As a matter of fact, I know you aren't."

"Allow me to be the judge of that."

Taylor turned toward Sarah, exposing the treasure she'd nabbed from Mr. Flint's desk as she followed the deputy sheriff from the lawbreaker's cell downstairs.

"This um . . . doll told me she'd had enough of Mr. Flint. She wanted to come home, so I gave her a lift. I believe she belongs to you," Taylor said. She extended the quaint, cornhusk doll toward Sarah.

Sarah's face lit up like a Christmas tree.

"My dear, dear poppet! Oh, however might I thank thee . . ."

"Taylor Kendall," Jared supplied dryly.

"How ever might I thank thee, Taylor Kendall?"

"Don't flash her around in front of the sheriff," Taylor said.

Brow puckered, Sarah questioned, "Flash her around?"

"Promise me you won't let him see her. It's far too cold in the big house for either your doll or me."

"Thee means the meeting house, doesn't thee, Taylor Kendall?"

"Right."

Sarah hugged the doll to her birdlike chest. "I vow I will not allow Mr. Flint even a glimpse of dearest poppet, for her sake as well as thine."

She blithely deposited the doll in the drawstring pocket tied at her waist, adequately concealing her from view. With a demure smile, Sarah told Jared, "The warmth of thy smithy has done me a world of good. My eye feels much improved."

"I am pleased to hear it," Jared said, though his gaze rested on her pocket.

Ten minutes later, John returned with the hardened maple sugar candy. The children said their good-byes and exited the smithy with their booty as quietly as they had entered it.

"You stole that poppet," Jared commented the instant the children were out of sight.

"No, I didn't. Flint had no right to take Sarah's doll from her."

"She was frolicking with the poppet when she should have been about her tasks."

"Playing can't and shouldn't be outlawed. No more than holiday celebrations."

Jared stepped within arm's reach of Taylor.

"Formality is a necessary evil, Taylor. For the adults as well as the children. 'Tis for the common good. Without it, anarchy would prevail."

Taylor cocked her head to one side. To a certain extent, she agreed with Jared. Without rules such as time in and time out, her kindergarten class would spend most of the day in chaos, which wasn't productive for either the children or her.

Taylor felt herself yielding to Jared's power of reasoning by degrees, like melting snow during the spring thaw.

"Okay. I admit it. I stole the doll from Flint's desk. So what can he do to me if he finds out. Cut my hand off?"

Jared raised a brow at Taylor, as if he seriously questioned her audaciousness.

She almost swallowed her tongue. "He can't do that! Can he? For snatching a doll?"

Jared's lips twitched, and this time Taylor had no doubt—she amused him, though he tried his darnedest to hide it. She watched him fight for control of the half-smile. And when he lost the tug-of-war, it was almost like an aphrodisiac to her. Her sensual response to the upward tilt of his lips caught Taylor entirely off-guard. It took her a full minute to recollect her composure.

Jared misread her reaction.

"Do not torment yourself," he said quickly. "As an elected official of the sovereign governing body, the sheriff could bring down such a verdict, but as contemptible as you perceive the man, I do not believe he would go to that extreme over a poppet."

Taylor wiggled her fingers, then clenched them into protective fists and lowered her hands to her sides.

"That's encouraging," she said. "I'm partial to my hands . . . had the both of 'em all my life. I'd hate to break up a perfectly matched set," she said.

"Then let us just hope Sarah keeps her word," he said.

"Cross your fingers."

Jared's partial smile grew into a full-blown grin.

"Now why ever would I want to do that?"

"Because it's for good luck," Taylor explained. "Like fine salt, a pinch of luck could do us no harm."

Deepened, darkened cerulean eyes met head-on with sultry whiskey-brown ones, and neither Taylor nor Jared looked away as they simultaneously crossed two fingers on each hand.

Chapter Four

"I thought celebrations were banned," Taylor said.

She stood with Jared outside the smithy, help-ing to load his sledge with special orders bound for the feather-stripping party.

"Unlaudable celebrations—like Christmastide," he explained.

"You're telling me the General Court allows feather-stripping parties, but not Christmas?"

"Precisely."

"It doesn't make a heck of a lot of sense to me," she muttered.

"It does not have to make sense to you, Taylor. Now stop dawdling or I shall be late."

Reacting like one of her kindergartners, Taylor stuck her tongue out at Jared when his back was turned.

"Pass me the trammel," he said over his shoul-der.

Taylor picked up the chain with a hook on the end which was used to hang kettles over the fire, relieved when he lifted the heavy item from her hands.

"And now the plow blade, and mind you do not cut yourself on the sharpened edge."

"One plow blade coming up."

"I believe the kettle should be next," he instructed as he stowed away the plow blade.

The iron kettle was intricately fashioned and quite lovely, with clawed feet and sloping handles.

"Who does this belong to?" Taylor asked.

"The widow Nash," Jared replied, placing the kettle near the chain trammel.

"I should have known."

He paused, glancing down at Taylor. "She pays well."

"I'll just bet she does."

His lips dipped into a frown. "You have never met Mary. Do not judge her so rashly."

"All right, already. I'm sorry. What next?"

Jared's expression cleared somewhat. "The toasting rack."

"Which one is that?"

"Taylor, you are astoun—"

"Never mind, I can figure it out myself." She handed him a gridlike contraption, along with a case of candle molds and Mr. Flint's andirons.

"And lastly, the sack of cornmeal," Jared said.

"Cornmeal?" Taylor asked.

"I fetched the meal from the gristmill for Mary . . . to save her a trip into the village."

Mary again. "Humph," Taylor said as she slung the sack over her shoulder.

Jared cocked his head to one side. "Why does my friendship with Mary Nash concern you so?"

I don't know. "You're imagining things."

"Am I?" he asked pointedly.

"Yes, you are."

Taylor glanced up expectantly, and when Jared failed to move fast enough for her, she said, "It wouldn't hurt my feelings if you took the cornmeal. I'm not a pack mule, you know." At least she hadn't resembled one the last time she'd looked in the mirror—mirrors, like Christmas, being something else she'd taken for granted.

Jared lifted the sack from her shoulders, asking, "What has angered you?"

Taylor brushed her hands off, one against the other.

"I'm not angry." *I'm hurt, and I don't know why.*

"Very well then, I shall not press you on the matter."

"I guess you'd better get going. You don't want to be late for your party," she said.

"As you say," Jared replied.

An awkward silence fell between them.

"Take care," Jared said finally.

"When will you be back?"

He hesitated. "Well after dark, I expect."

"How will you see to drive?" *Your sledge doesn't have headlights.*

"The feather-stripping was planned around a full moon. With the moonlight glinting off a base of white snow, I should have no trouble."

No matter how long I keep Jared talking, he isn't going to invite me to the party.

Taylor felt a little catch in her throat. She hadn't been left entirely alone since her stint in jail. It was slightly unnerving. Almost as unnerving as the knowledge that Jared would spend the next several hours in Mary Nash's company.

"I'll . . . um . . . wait up for you," she offered.

"You need not," he said, gathering the reins.

"Then I guess I won't," she said, thinking she could hardly go to sleep without Jared stretched in the truckle below her. She'd grown accustomed to the creaking of the bed when he shifted position. To his even breathing. To the way his thick lashes fanned his cheeks when his eyes were closed. To the knowledge that she need only reach out to him when the night magnified her fears for the future, and he would respond without question.

"Go to the cottage and rest. You deserve a reprieve from the smithy after the work you have assisted me in completing these last six days."

"*Great idea.*" *Twiddling my thumbs is one of my favorite pastimes.*

Jared clucked to the horse and steered the sledge away from the smithy.

Taylor watched Jared until the sledge disappeared from sight. Her eyes ached with unshed tears as she squared her shoulders and pivoted on her heels. *Stop feeling sorry for yourself! You're a big girl now*, she told herself as she went inside the cottage.

An empty sensation that had nothing to do with food gnawed at the pit of Taylor's stomach as she sprawled on the settle and gazed into the fire. She wasn't alone ten minutes before Jared barged into the cottage, almost scaring the life out of her.

"You did not bar the door," he accused.

"I didn't think about it."

"I suspected as much. That is the reason I returned. Your presence at the feather-stripping party disturbs me less than thoughts of leaving you alone to your own devices. Gather up your things. I have decided you shall accompany me to Mary Nash's home."

"But I wasn't invited." Her response sounded nonchalant enough, Taylor decided. As nonchalant as she could make it, considering her joy over his return.

"You are my apprentice; I am your teacher. Mary will not question your presence at my side. Remember only that you are considered a young man by the community and that you must behave accordingly."

It was all the prompting she needed. Taylor reached for her parka and mittens.

"I presume you have nothing hidden in your pockets today?" he said. He gave the parka a cursory once-over.

"You presume correctly," Taylor said, trying to walk sedately as she trailed him outside.

Taylor noticed he reached out to assist her into the sledge, but stopped himself just in time. She understood. He would not assist a man. Therefore, he could not assist her in public. Still, it surprised her that she liked the thought of his hand at her elbow.

"What's a feather-stripping party anyway?" she asked as she settled into the seat beside him, trying not to think of their intimate proximity.

"You do not know?"

"No."

"In the late summer the geese are dressed—"

Taylor interrupted. "Killed, you mean?"

"I know no other way to dress them."

"Neither do I. Go on."

"The feathers are plucked and sorted. The small ones are placed in pillowcases for use in the making of mattresses. The large quills are sacked. In the winter, members of the community gather together to strip off the down."

"I suppose it's used for quilts, like the one on your bed."

"Among other things."

"It doesn't sound like much fun to me."

"Trust me, it will be. More interesting activities will follow the stripping."

"I still don't see—"

Jared cut her short.

"The feather-stripping is a functional gathering, Taylor. Not only does it provide the down for warm winter bedding, it encourages bartering among the villagers. Goodwife Simpson is certain to bring a dozen maple syrup-filled crocks like the one you have enjoyed with your Indian pudding of a morning. I think perchance we could use a half-dozen ourselves," he teased.

Taylor blushed. The syrup made the Indian pudding more palatable.

"Flint's deputy is a furniture maker. I traded him an iron Betty lamp and a plow blade for my bed frame last year. Mary Nash spins and weaves the softest of wools and the finest quality linens in the colony—those are some of her fabrics you wear against your skin. There will be pewter plates, fishhooks, and spices to choose from."

"I get the picture."

Jared guided the sledge off the main street and onto a narrow secondary avenue where they passed a commotion in progress.

Pushing aside her questions concerning the feather-stripping party, Taylor asked, "What are those men doing?" She marveled at the squealing pig being dragged by its corkscrew tail backward into the pen.

"'Tis a newly purchased sow. 'Tis customary to back it into the pen to assure the animal a healthy life."

"Oh," Taylor said. She remained introspective for the remainder of their trip "over the river and through the woods," wondering if Jared would find the customs in her world as strange as she did those in his.

Mary Nash greeted Jared and Taylor at the door of her immaculate home. The house, sided with the unpainted boards so popular in New England, proved larger than Taylor had anticipated. Not only did it boast a spacious ground floor, it included an impressive second story that jutted out over the first.

Mary hooked her arm through Jared's and hustled him in with a flourish.

"I am so pleased thee has arrived. We were about to begin the feather-stripping contest without thee," Mary said.

Taylor followed quietly behind, listening to Jared and Mary exchange pleasantries. The room filled with people reminded her of the meeting house on court day—except here she saw only happy faces.

Almost immediately the married couples paired off for the feather-stripping. And then the singles—Sadie Hawkins style. Mary Nash chose Jared as her partner. Sarah Nash picked Taylor.

Holding the feathers by their tips, the couples ran them between their thumbs and forefingers while the sands of an hourglass sifted from one compartment to the next, and the elders recounted vivid tales of their voyages from England to the New World. Taylor almost got seasick. Or perhaps it was Mary's and Jared's easy rapport that made her sick to her stomach, she mused.

Jared and Mary won the contest. Taylor and Sarah came in last, much to Sarah's dismay.

Stomach still queasy, Taylor passed on the tray of taffy Mary offered around afterward, making up for it with a double helping of unbuttered, unsalted popcorn.

After the snack, Mary cajoled Jared into skating on the cranberry bog with her. Taylor owned no skates, which left her the odd *man* out.

Perched on a log like a bird on a wire, Taylor watched from the sidelines as Jared and Mary glided across the boglike pond amid the other skaters, his arm around her waist to protect her from falling over the cranberry branches sticking up through the ice.

Taylor wondered wistfully what it might be like to be in Jared's arms. On the tail of that thought followed another. In her time the farmers contracted to the juice companies would fill the skaters with shot pellet for trespassing on their bog.

Taylor smiled faintly. If she'd had a BB gun, she thought dejectedly, she might have been tempted to pop them one herself. But not for the same reasons as the farmers.

Later, everyone gathered back at the house to share in a hot supper of sourdough biscuits, baked beans, codfish, and blueberry tarts. Much to Taylor's chagrin, Mary proved to be a gracious hostess—warm, kind, and generous. She courteously served the meal with Sarah and John's assistance, administering to her guests' needs before her own. Taylor wanted very much to dislike her; she found she could only admire her.

Later, Mr. Flint's deputy offered Taylor a tankard of ale, along with the other gentlemen. She readily accepted it, blatantly ignoring Jared's scowl of disapproval. After witnessing his companionable interaction with Mary Nash, she needed something soothing.

By the time the deputy sheriff dragged out his fiddle, Taylor felt sufficiently recovered to tap her foot in time with the music. Mary noticed and asked between songs, "Do you dance, Taylor?"

Yes, she danced. But normally not with other women.

Fearful that Mary might ask her to accompany her onto the floor, Taylor fished for a means to deter her.

"No . . . I . . . uh . . . I play the violin, though."

She'd studied music since she was old enough to hold a bow. Her mother had hoped for a concert violinist. She'd gotten a teacher instead, then nurse, a chemist, and a stage actress, in that order.

"Pray, play something for us," Mary requested.

Tempted by a thoroughly disreputable ulterior motive, Taylor agreed. Mary commandeered the violin, and Taylor spent the next hour with the instrument tucked beneath her chin. The crowd seemed mesmerized by the sweet melodies, and not even Jared realized she'd opted for every Christmas carol she knew composed after the colonial period.

There was a downside to her silent protest, however. Jared danced every third dance with the widow.

The Spirit of Things to Come

She'd always enjoyed being a tomboy, Taylor thought as she coaxed the notes of "White Christmas" from the strings. Now she'd give anything to wear a dress like Mary's. One that fit tightly at the waist and twirled widely about her ankles as she danced. One that would force Jared to view her as a woman rather than a budding apprentice.

Similar thoughts swirled in Taylor's head as she daringly spliced the carol with scattered bars from "The Twelve Days of Christmas." In further protest against Flint, she told herself.

During intermission, Jared casually strolled to Taylor's side. Hand on her shoulder, he firmly maneuvered her to a private corner.

"You wanted my attention? Or perchance 'tis simply that you enjoy tripping along the edge," he hissed without preamble.

"What do you mean?" Taylor asked.

Mary smiled at Jared from across the room and Taylor's heart constricted. She tried to ignore the charming half-smile Jared so easily tossed back in Mary's direction. She failed. Her slight headache burgeoned into full-fledged drumroll in her brain.

Taylor squeezed her eyes shut and massaged her temples.

She felt Jared shift from foot to foot. "First the ale, and now this. Flint might have recognized the carol!"

"He didn't . . . not without the words."

"He might have, though! What are you thinking of, Taylor?" he asked, his mouth so close to her ear that she jumped.

Taylor opened her eyes. The look he wore said he'd guessed what she was up to with the violin solo long before the last song.

She shouldn't have underestimated him. From the beginning, their thoughts had sprinted hand in hand.

"I was thinking of the holidays back home, my family, our customs," Taylor improvised. "It just dawned on me that New Year's Day is just around the corner and I've hardly said hello to Christmas, much less good-bye. Call it sentimentality, but I've never been away from home during the holidays, never missed a family gathering, and it hurts."

Remarkably enough.

"I took evergreen garlands, the Yule log, and mincemeat pie for granted," she elaborated in a plaintive voice.

"A bit of caution, Taylor. It would not be to your advantage if Flint overheard us, since mincemeat is forbidden," Jared murmured.

"I suppose mistletoe balls are too," she said.

"Mistletoe balls?"

"Holly, evergreen, and mistletoe are gathered, tied with red and green satin ribbons, and suspended from the ceiling," Taylor explained. "It's a custom where I come from, like backing a pig into a pen is here. Men and women . . . they kiss beneath the ball in honor of the season. And if the man that kisses you plucks a berry and gives it to you, it's said you'll marry within the year. It's considered a crime to ignore a mistletoe ball—and I don't mean that literally."

"I see."

"What you can't seem to see is that laws are unreasonable when they spill over into the kinds of food you eat, the songs you sing, and the way you decorate your private property. You shouldn't be able to wake an entire town up with a bell, regardless of the kind of night some people might have had. The next thing you know, people will be burning books in Bay Colony's commons area! I'm not saying everyone should celebrate Christmas, Jared. I'm saying everyone has a natural right to freedom of choice."

Jared looked as if he might say more, but stopped when Mary sailed over to ask Taylor to play another song.

As they walked away together, it suddenly occurred to Taylor that Mary was a perfect match for Jared. And how entirely unsuitable *she* was for him. The knowledge slashed through her and she hit a sour note as she considered the incongruity of her situation.

Gazing deeply into her heart, Taylor also realized she was jealous of Mary Nash. And why. She didn't want to be Jared's apprentice, she wanted to be his friend, his helpmate . . . and yes, the love of his life. As he was hers.

Sawing away with a vengeance at the violin, Taylor didn't try to analyze her love for Jared Branlyn. It existed, and that was that.

Sometime later, Taylor saw Jared say something to Mary and slip quietly out the front door. He did not return until the party was nearly over. By that time, Taylor was more than ready to pack it in for the night. If she couldn't have Jared in reality, she could at least dream about him.

Chapter Five

Huddled in her parka, her thigh pressed against Jared's as he steered the sledge to the door of the stable, Taylor couldn't help herself. She didn't want to ask, because she didn't really want to know. But the old saying, what you didn't know couldn't hurt you, was a lie.

"They expect you to marry her, don't they?" Taylor asked tentatively.

It was the first complete sentence she'd spoken since they'd thanked their hostess and waved their good-byes.

Jared didn't ask who Taylor was talking about and for that she was grateful. As melancholy as she felt, Taylor wasn't sure she could utter Mary's name without bursting into tears.

"She will make a fine wife. She has a considerable fortune to recommend her. And she needs a strong hand to work the farm her husband bequeathed her, a father for John and Sarah . . . a man about the house."

Although it wasn't the answer Taylor had expected, it was more than enough to confirm her worst fears.

"So you'll marry her . . . because it's the 'laudable' choice."

"In Bay Colony, 'tis suspect to remain single."

Some things never changed. "That's not what I asked you, Jared."

"Of what possible importance could my decision be to you?" he asked, turning the tables on her.

Taylor felt as if she'd been punched in the stomach.

"I . . . I guess I want to know because I . . . wondered where I fit into the scheme of things. I mean, do I stay on at the smithy as an apprentice after the honeymoon, or what?" she added in a rush as she fought down her anguish.

"Mary and I grew up together," Jared said. He reined the horse to a stop, jumped from the sledge to open the stable's double door, then reascended to his seat. He clucked his tongue, guided the sledge into the stable's wide hallway, tied off the reins, and jumped to the ground.

Taylor wasn't sure what Jared meant by his comment and she didn't have time to ask, for the horse needed to be fed and bedded down for the night.

"Go on in ahead of me and build up the fire, Taylor. I will join you after I have seen to the animal," Jared said.

Taylor stood.

In the shelter of the stable, out of the view of the villagers, Jared spanned Taylor's waist with his strong hands, allowing her body to slide against his as he assisted her from the sledge. He held her for one breathless moment before depositing her on the ground.

Trembling from the inside out, she scurried toward the cottage without a backward glance.

What she saw when she reached the door astounded Taylor. Fresh garlands wreathed it in pungent evergreen—the symbol of constancy. But the garlands were nothing compared to what awaited her inside.

An apple wood Yule log burned in the fireplace, sweetly scenting the air, and from the ceiling hung a replica of the mistletoe ball she'd so recently described to Jared.

Now she knew why he'd left the party.

The door opened behind her. Taylor twirled on her heels, tears of joy burning her eyes.

"You set me up," she said in a choked whisper.

Jared nodded, a teasing glimmer in his intoxicating eyes. "Forgive me, Taylor. Truly, I could not resist the temptation."

"I don't know what to say."

Face suddenly solemn, his eyes probed hers. "Tell me that these things ease your heart."

"They ease my heart. Oh God, how they ease my heart."

They weren't gold or silver. They weren't expensive or awe-inspiring. And certainly not practical. Only plain and simple handcrafted items, and yet by far the most precious gifts she'd ever received.

"I have reflected upon your notion of Christmastide lo these many days, and have decided you are correct. A man possesses certain natural rights above and beyond the law. I admire and respect you for your single-minded determination. 'Tis easy to court peace; difficult to stand up for your beliefs."

Her gratitude was overwhelming, her love for Jared interminable.

"Your goodwill toward me—" she began.

He crossed the room in three easy strides.

"Do not mistake me," he said almost fiercely. "'Tis not a case of goodwill that has prompted this display. Consider it compensation for your care of Sarah Nash. Consider it a bonus for helping complete Flint's andirons. Consider it—"

He sucked in a deep breath, raking his hand through his hair. "The truth is that you have whittled my resistance down to nothing." He paused a moment as if weighing the possible repercussions of what he was about to tell her. "And you have whetted my appetite far beyond common endurance."

His admission was both a pleasure and a torment.

"Your first day in Bay Colony, you looked so incredibly lost. Even more so now. Perchance I have misread your feelings—pray, correct me if I have blundered."

The tortured expression on his face stabbed at her heart.

"The chemistry is there, but we have to be sensible about this. Look at all the trouble I've caused you . . . will continue to cause just because I'm . . ." Taylor faltered, fighting her acute longing for him.

Jared finished her sentence for her. "Impertinent, imprudent, impossible, and thoroughly disarming. When I am with you, my world fades to insignificance. The trouble is nothing compared to the delight. 'Tis simple—I love you, Taylor."

With a sense of wonder, she looked into his eyes and saw everything he wasn't saying: *It will be difficult, but we will make it work—somehow. I swear.*

And she believed him, because she wanted to so desperately.

Taylor didn't know who moved first, but before she realized what had happened, she was in Jared's arms—exactly where she'd craved to be from the first moment she'd met him.

"I love you, too," she said.

He ran his fingers through the curls at her temples, touching his lips to her forehead.

"You asked me if I planned to wed Mary Nash. I do not."

Taylor sagged against him, clinging to him for all she was worth. She felt rather than heard his indrawn breath as his chest swelled against her breasts. It was all the affirmation he seemed to need as his arms tightened around her.

"Look at me, Taylor."

She tossed back her head and gazed into his eyes.

"We were unable to dance at the feather-stripping party, though I could see you wanted to."

She nodded.

"Dance with me now," he said. He began to hum. His voice was low and melodious, like his laughter. It sounded better than a symphony. Better even than the warble of chickadees.

Cheek to cheek.

Sandpaper against silk.

Hard melting into soft, they swayed in a slow dance of leashed passion. Ebbing and flowing. Taking, giving. Willfully feeling their way along.

"Do you know how much I want you, Taylor?" he asked when their dance ended.

With a soft smile, she said, "It's fairly obvious."

Breathing heavily, his chest rose and fell rapidly beneath her hand. "Under the circumstances, I feel I have no time to woo you," he rasped in her ear.

A waterfall of desire washed over Taylor. "I don't need wooing," she moaned.

His blue eyes murky pools of need, he asked against her lips, "Should I trundle the truckle bed tonight, Taylor?"

"No way," she said, thinking how glad she was she'd worn her best teddy on the day she had appeared in Jared's time. She wanted this exquisite joining, this bonding of hearts and minds, bodies and souls. A sweet fever building within her, Taylor briefly touched her lips to his.

"You are irresistible," he said.

"Prove to me how irresistible I am," she said.

With a growl of pleasure, he lowered his mouth to hers. His eager lips claimed hers. His tongue probed the inner recesses of her mouth, engulfing her in a tempest of fluid sensation.

He withdrew a mere inch. "Proof enough?" he asked.

"I'm not sure I'm all that convinced. Not just yet, anyway," she said, her lips tingling with the moist heat of his bittersweet kiss.

"You need more."

"Much, much more."

"Never let it be said that I failed to oblige a lady," Jared said. His lips captured hers once again as his hands moved to the drawstrings of her smock.

With a shuddering sigh, Taylor shut out everything except the delicious sensation of his callused hands intimately stroking her bare skin. There were no inhibitions. No questions. No hesitation.

And no need for conversation. Actions spoke louder than words.

Taylor felt Jared spring from the bed like the deer that had bounded out in front of her Jeep. She watched through bleary eyes as he snatched up his clothes.

"Wake up, Taylor!" he hissed, as he hurriedly dressed. She noted the urgency in his movements, the way his eyes darted to the sunlight streaming through the shutters.

"What's wrong?"

"We have slept through the morning bell."

Taylor's heart almost leapt into her throat. "Oh, no!"

"I meant to take down the garlands before dawn. I suspect Mr. Flint has been apprised of them by now."

"Oh, no," Taylor moaned, tears gathering in her eyes as she frantically searched for the clothes Jared had supplied her. They were so tangled in the bed linens, she opted for her own neatly folded items instead. "What will he do?"

"To you, my love, nothing. Not while I live and breathe," Jared said grimly.

Taylor had no time to assimilate Jared's response into her groggy brain, for within seconds,

212

there came a sharp rapping on the cottage door.

Jared turned a critical eye Taylor's way, realized the manner in which she was dressed, and tossed her parka to her. The rapping grew louder as Jared yanked out the truckle and mussed the covers before he answered the door.

"Jared Branlyn, my deputy and I wish to converse with thee for a moment. I have a feeling thee already knows what it pertains to," Flint said through the door.

Jared glanced once around the room, then opened the door. Straddling the threshold in a protective stance, he blocked Taylor from Flint's view.

"Thee has not begun thy work in the smithy as yet. 'Tis late for thee, Jared. We were . . . concerned," Flint said.

"I missed the morning bell," Jared stated evenly.

"My wife and I had a like response after last night's revelry."

Flint loudly cleared his throat.

"'Tis not thy failure to rise on time that brings me to thy cottage, but the garlands Goodwife Simpson witnessed upon thy door and reported to me. Take them down, Jared." He glanced over Jared's head and through the door toward the mistletoe ball hanging from the ceiling. "Take that down as well and we will . . . we will overlook this slight indiscretion."

Jared stared the sheriff squarely in the eye, choosing his words carefully. "I think not."

Flint blinked.

Startled, Taylor blanched.

The deputy took a step backward.

Jared firmly stood his ground.

Flint cleared his throat again. "Thee knows the consequences of thy defiance—no less than a flogging."

Jared nodded.

"Then by order of a special morning session of the General Court of Bay Colony, I hearby sentence thee to eigh . . . nay . . . six . . . nay, let me think, five lashes. To be carried out by my deputy forthwith," Flint said as if genuinely sorry to be the one sentencing a friend and pillar of the community to a whipping. Or fearful of Jared's reaction. Or perhaps a bit of both.

Jared must have heard Taylor's muffled gasp, for he cast a warning glance over his shoulder, forbidding her interference. His eyes held hers possessively for a moment before he returned his attention to Mr. Flint.

"Give me a moment to apprise my apprentice of the situation."

"We will wait inside," Flint said.

"You will wait outside," Jared said sternly.

"But—"

"Do not be concerned, Flint. I do not harbor plans for escape. There is work to be done today. 'Tis obvious I shall be in no condition to carry it out. Therefore, there are things Taylor Kendall must know," he said.

Jared closed the door in Flint's face and dropped the bar in place.

As soon as they were alone, Taylor tumbled into Jared's arms. "Why didn't you just take the decorations down like Mr. Flint wanted you to do?"

"I have explained this to you before. I do not make decisions lightly."

Driven by love and the determination to save him from public humiliation, she whispered,

"If I reveal my identity, they'll forget all about the garlands and mistletoe. You could probably keep them up and they'd never even know the difference."

"Nay, Taylor, you are not thinking clearly," he said in a low voice that seemed reinforced with iron.

"But—"

"Listen to me," he said. He smoothed his hands up along her arms, reaching to twine a fair curl around his finger. "You, heart of my heart, are the epitome of everything my parents hoped to discover in the New World, and of my own hopes for the future. I cannot allow the General Court's prejudices to do you harm."

"I saw the stocks in the commons area when Flint arrested me. I saw the flogging post too, Jared. They'll tie you to it and . . ."

She couldn't say it, couldn't even think it.

"Shhh," he whispered.

Tears welled in her eyes. "I can't stand this, Jared."

"Do not dwell upon it, my love. It will be over almost before it begins." He relinquished the curl to caress her cheek with his knuckles. "Wait for me here in the safety of the cottage. As soon as the deed is done, as soon as we can travel, I intend to go to Virginia. As Flint said, the laws of the southern colonies are more lenient, more caring of a man's natural rights. Once Bay Colony is behind us, you can don more feminine overgarments if you so choose, can travel as the woman you are. As my wife, if you will have me."

Proud, terrified, and touched all at the same time, Taylor felt momentarily overwhelmed. Jared was willing to sacrifice everything, his social standing in the community, his livelihood, even his home and business, for her.

"There's something I've got to tell you," she said urgently. "Something you have to know." She took a deep breath. "I'm not who you think I am. I've come from another time, a different place. Not by choice, but by some glitch of fate. I know it sounds crazy, but—"

He stopped her by placing his forefinger gently against her lips.

"I know, Taylor."

She moved his hand from her lips to her cheek.

"You know? How?"

"When you were bone-weary and deeply troubled, you talked in your sleep."

"And you listened."

He smiled his most charming smile.

"I am not always the perfect gentleman."

"That's why you were so jumpy that first morning after you bailed me out of jail," Taylor surmised aloud.

"I realized there was something different about you the instant I spied you on the edge of the village. Not only your clothes and speech, but your hair, and lips, and skin. The sparkle in your lovely eyes. Your proud bearing. Later, I recalled John had called you a spirit. After listening to your late-night confessions, I had to see if you were indeed flesh and blood."

"You tipped my chin up and gazed into my eyes."

His chin atop her head, he held her close, rocking her as he spoke. "One touch and I knew I was lost because nothing else seemed important. Not who you were, or where you came from, or how you raced like a whirlwind into my life."

He gathered her more securely into his arms, guiding her beneath the mistletoe. "Now kiss me, Taylor, in the spirit of all the things to come. Send me off with a smile upon my lips."

With a sob, Taylor relented and gave him everything he would never see, could never know, all the wonderful innovation of her time. Music at the touch of a button. Microwavable food. Gasoline-powered engines. Television. And something else, something as old as time itself—the gift of all-consuming love.

When the kiss ended, he plucked a mistletoe berry from the ball. He pressed it into her palm, closing her fingers over it.

"Remember, Taylor. Wedded within the year," he said, tenderly sealing the vow of commitment with a moist kiss upon her knuckles.

He turned, unbarred the door, and stepped into Flint's custody.

Taylor resisted the urge to run after Jared, to beg him on bended knees not to go with them.

The tower bell pealed almost joyfully as it called the villagers to witness Jared's punishment. At least, it sounded so to Taylor. She covered her ears with her hands, but it didn't help. She could still hear the ringing.

Taylor busied herself with straightening the cottage. That didn't help either. Not only did the bell seem to grow louder, but the walls felt as if they were closing in on her. She couldn't stand being cooped up a minute longer! Not while Jared suffered such degradation on her account. . . .

Taylor stumbled from the cottage out into the gray winter day and circled around the side of the blacksmith shop, avoiding the commons. Dogged by the bell, she sprinted through a gate and across the empty enclosure of a nearby paddock, climbed the railed fence, and retraced her steps to the edge of the village, but to no avail. It seemed she couldn't escape the echoing voice of the meeting house bell.

Until the snow started falling around her.

And the sound suddenly transformed of its own accord.

From ringing to the muffled sound of knuckles rapping against glass.

Epilogue

Massachusetts, December 25, 1993

"Hey, lady! Are you okay in there?"

Taylor glanced out the front windshield of the Jeep. At least she tried to. A layer of snow covered the glass.

I'm back in 1993!

Taylor swallowed the lump in her throat and blinked at the middle-aged man who had scraped the driver's-side window clear and now rapped on it with his knuckles. With a tuft of red hair, a smattering of freckles, and a comical grin of relief on his face, he looked harmless enough. Still . . .

She rolled her window down halfway.

"I . . . I think so," Taylor answered. It was the biggest, most blatant, bold-faced lie she'd ever told. She might never be okay again. How could she be when she'd lost the man she loved? Taylor wondered, unfurling her fingers. She gazed down at the waxy-white mistletoe berry nestled in the hollow of her trembling hand.

It was real. I know it was. I hold the ever-loving proof!

Tears gathered in Taylor's eyes, tracking down her cold cheeks.

"Hey, you're crying. Jeez, please don't cry, lady! I don't mean any harm. I'm Tom Crenshaw. I work for the phone company. See?" He pointed to the logo embroidered above the pocket of his nylon uniform jacket.

Obviously he was uncomfortable being the first at the scene of an accident. Taylor might have felt compassion for him, if she hadn't been so wrapped up in feeling sorry for herself.

"We've got lines down in the area. I was riding along the shoulder checking the poles and saw your Jeep. Doesn't look like too much damage. Honest," he said. He hopped from foot to foot and rubbed his gloved hands together.

Taylor stared at his nose. It looked red, as if he'd been dancing around her Jeep, trying to gain her attention for a while.

His next statement confirmed her suppositions. "Listen, my truck's up there . . . nice and warm, too." He pointed toward the road.

Taylor sniffed, following the end of his finger to the red equipment truck with its flashing emergency lights parked atop the incline.

"Should I go up and radio for an ambulance?"

Taylor swiped at her tears with the back of her hand. With a final fond look at the berry, she placed the precious memento in her inner breast pocket, next to her heart.

"I'm fine," Taylor said. Maybe if she said it often enough, she'd believe it herself. Miracles did happen—sometimes. She was living proof.

Then again, how many miracles could one expect in a single day?

"My . . . um . . . family doesn't live far from here. If you could just give me a ride . . ." Taylor let her words trail off as she rolled up her window and unlocked her door.

She'd gladly go to her parents' house. She'd enjoy every minute of the family scene. She'd politely answer their questions concerning her dating status.

And she'd miss Jared Branlyn's arms until the last of her days.

"Ayup, I'd be more than happy to give you a lift," Tom said as Taylor pushed open the door and unfolded herself from the incapacitated Jeep's interior. He assisted her through the snow, up the hill, and into the passenger seat of his truck.

Once behind the wheel, he asked, "Which way?"

Taylor glanced down the road, seeing the telltale tracks where her Jeep had dived off the asphalt. She nodded in the opposite direction. "That way," she said woodenly.

"That's a dilly of a bruise on your chin," Tom commented. "Are you sure you don't need to see a doctor?" he asked, flipping the heater fan on high as he revved the engine and steered the truck off the shoulder and onto the road.

Taylor fastened her seat belt and reached up to test her chin with her fingertips. Yes, it was bruised. Yes, it hurt. And yes, she probably needed to see a doctor. A coronary specialist. Because she was positive her heart was on the verge of cleaving in two.

Common sense told her returning to the 20th century was probably for the best. That she wasn't suited for life in Bay Colony. And that because Jared was a pillar of the community and a law-abiding man, their love for each other had caused him nothing but trouble.

But oh, Jared! How in God's name am I supposed to make it without you?

"My father is a doctor," Taylor finally managed. "He'll take care of my chin." Falling silent, she withdrew inside herself, attempting to deal with the ache that had settled in her soul.

At four o'clock on Christmas afternoon, Taylor arrived on her parents' doorstep. Tom Crenshaw rang the doorbell. Wiping her hands on the hem of her Santa Claus apron, Mrs. Kendall answered the door. With a look of horror, she listened to Tom's hasty explanation. She thanked the lineman for his trouble and offered him a hot drink while ushering Taylor into the house.

Taylor barely heard Tom decline as she gratefully allowed her mother to take over.

After Tom left, her mother exclaimed, "I'm sorry about your car, honey, but it's you I'm worried about." Her mother draped her arm around her shoulder. "You look as if you've been through it and back."

Her mother stopped long enough to give her a hug. Hands at her sides, Taylor welcomed the soothing, maternal contact.

"I have been, Mom," she said. Her voice cracked as she tried hard not to cry. "The Jeep is down the road about three miles. I swerved to miss a deer and . . . and . . ." She faltered. What could she say? That fate had played a nasty trick on her? That she'd won and lost the man of her dreams, and she was more miserable than she'd ever thought possible? That she wasn't sure she could survive the knife-sharp pain?

"Well, it's a good thing that lineman found you." Her mother grimaced. "Of course, another hour and we'd have been out looking for you ourselves."

Taylor hadn't realized that all the time she was talking, her mother had been maneuvering her out of the drafty central hall and into the warmth of the spacious family room. A roaring fire crackled in the hearth, scenting the house with the pleasant aroma of a pine Yule log. A Christmas tree, like a fairy-tale princess decked out in all her finery, stood resplendent in the far corner of the room.

Taylor smelled the mouth-watering fragrance of mincemeat pie and roasting goose wafting from the kitchen. She listened to the Christmas music filtering throughout the house on her father's newly installed intercom system. Through the French doors of the dining room she saw her sisters laughing and talking as they set the table with her mother's best crystal and china. Taylor moved to the picture window and watched her nieces and nephews and their fathers laughing and frolicking as they built snowmen on the front lawn together.

She was relieved to be home, and yet devastated to be there without Jared.

"Honey, you stay right here and warm up. I'll go get Daddy. He needs to take a look at that chin. He's in the study with our special Christmas guest . . . purchased the Hanson farm . . . a contemporary sculptor . . . barn full of iron and welding equipment . . . such a nice young man . . . prosperous. Sit tight . . . won't be a minute."

Huddled in her parka, Taylor lowered herself into an upholstered wing chair and closed her eyes. Here she was with her family around her, and yet she felt more alone than ever before, she mused as she listened to her mother scurry down the hall and up the stairs toward her father's study.

One set of feet climbed the stairs; three sets hurried back down.

Mr. Kendall breezed into the room, flushed, concerned, and adjusting his reading glasses on the bridge of his nose. Mrs. Kendall followed closely behind. A tall, handsome man with sable hair brought up the rear. He teetered on the threshold, a funny expression marring his features, almost as if he had experienced a sudden flash of déjà vu.

Taylor wasted no time in checking him out.

He was dressed in a rust-colored chamois shirt, faded jeans, and white running shoes. His hair was short—shorter even than hers—and a neat mustache flattered his shapely lips.

Taylor's breath caught in her throat as his incredible cerulean eyes focused on her face.

"Taylor, what's all this about?" her father began. A worried frown furrowed his brow as he went down on one knee, switched on the lamp on the mahogany end table, and tipped her chin up to examine the discolored skin.

"I had a little accident," Taylor said numbly.

She stared beyond her father as the Christmas guest finally stepped into the room and advanced toward her.

"Does that hurt, sweetheart?" her father asked. He tested the area for swelling, running an expert finger along her jawbone.

Taylor shook her head as her eyes connected with the Christmas guest's over the top of her father's graying head.

"Move your jaw up and down for me, Taylor."

Taylor did as her father requested.

"Nothing seems broken," her father pronounced with satisfaction. "I think you'll live, though an X ray or two wouldn't hurt."

"Please, no X rays today, Dad," Taylor moaned. The hospital was the last place she wanted to spend Christmas Day. Before, she'd dreaded spending the holidays with her family. At the moment, she didn't want to be anywhere else.

Mr. Kendall rose, blocking Taylor's view as the Christmas guest sauntered to the center of the room and stopped.

"We'll see," her father said.

Taylor swiveled to the far left and gazed around her father, determined to get a good, long look at the man her parents had invited to dinner. When she finally did, she felt the blood drain from her face as simultaneously a tentative smile of welcome curved her lips.

"Taylor?" her mother asked in alarm, touching her daughter's arm.

"Uh, what, Mom?" She craned her head a little farther in the direction of the dinner guest.

"Nothing," her mother responded. A self-satisfied grin replaced her concerned expression.

Mrs. Kendall speculatively eyed her dinner guest. "You haven't been properly introduced to our oldest daughter—this is Taylor Louise," she said.

"Your parents have told me so much about you, I feel as if I already know you," the dinner guest responded. He leaned from the waist to see around Mr. Kendall and return Taylor's gaze.

"Do you? I mean, me too," Taylor said softly, acutely aware of the broadness of his shoulders, his formidable physique, of the way his presence filled the family room to bursting-at-the-seams.

"Henry," Taylor's mother said, glancing from her guest, to her daughter, to her husband. "Why don't you go outside and ask the boys if they will run down the road and see if we're going to need a wrecker for Taylor's Jeep?"

Mr. Kendall frowned, removing his glasses and slipping them into his dress shirt pocket. "We can do that after dinner, Winnie. There will be light for hours yet."

His wife raised her brows, her eyes communicating what she couldn't say in front of the others: *For heaven's sake! Don't be so dense, Henry. Can't you see your daughter has fallen head over heels?*

Glancing from their guest to Taylor, Mr. Kendall finally caught on.

"Oh, yeah, I uh . . . I'm sure Robert and Jack and Andrew would be . . . er . . . glad to trot on down and give the Jeep a look-see before dinner." He winked at his wife.

A pleased expression on her face, Taylor's mother said, "And I need to put the finishing touches on the meal, so I'll just scoot along and leave you young people to get better acquainted. Why don't you help Taylor with her coat," Mrs. Kendall suggested to her dinner guest. "I'll call you two when the food's ready."

The dinner guest nodded.

Mrs. Kendall glided over to the French doors and casually drew the lace curtains against the glass panes. "It will take a while, so just enjoy yourselves." She flipped off the lamp, flicked on the glimmering starlike Christmas tree lights, and poked the fire into a romantic orange glow.

Mrs. Kendall recrossed the room to hook her arm through her husband's and tug him to one side.

Taylor rose on unsteady legs. She stared at the man who had purchased the farm next door, afraid to take her eyes from him for fear he would disappear.

Taylor had no idea exactly when her parents filed from the room, though she heard her mother say quite distinctly as she herded her husband down the hall toward the kitchen, "I knew it was only a matter of time before we found the right one. I'm *so* glad we invited him to dinner."

And then suddenly, Taylor and the dinner guest were alone together.

His callused hands grazed Taylor's as she shrugged from her parka. He tossed it on a nearby chair, coming to stand so close she could smell his unique male scent and see the rise and fall of his muscular chest beneath the soft, pliant material of his chamois shirt.

He leaned down to whisper something in her ear. It was a conspiratorial whisper. A whisper meant for her, and her alone.

"I think it would be safe to say we've been set up."

A hint of laughter tinged his voice as he glanced pointedly at the ceiling.

Taylor's eyes followed his. Her mother had suspended the mistletoe ball smack-dab in the middle of the family room ceiling. Twined with evergreen garlands and tied with green and red satin ribbons, it was the second most beautiful sight she had ever seen, Taylor decided. The man standing beside her was the first.

"You could be right. I'm afraid Mom and Dad are . . . born matchmakers," Taylor stammered, her own voice only slightly above a whisper.

"Your brother-in-law already warned me they might have ulterior motives in extending my dinner invitation."

"Which brother-in-law?" Taylor asked, determined to keep him near her, to keep him talking because she felt so flustered she didn't know what else to do except make mundane conversation.

"Andrew," he said.

"Remind me to pinch Andrew at dinner," she said.

He threw back his head and laughed. His laughter had a melodious ring to it that rivaled the piped-in Christmas music.

"Andrew and I met through a mutual friend last summer," he continued. "He introduced me to your parents after I decided to buy the Hanson place. Andrew thought they might be able to give me some pointers on renovating the old colonial."

"And did they?" *Let this be real. And if I'm dreaming, please don't wake me up!*

"Yeah, among other things. You know, your mom bakes a mean Thanksgiving turkey. It's the first time I've tasted homemade cranberry sauce. And her mincemeat pie is out of this world."

Taylor's eyes widened.

"You ate Thanksgiving dinner here?"

"Yeah. My kitchen was a shambles at the time. Nothing but exposed studs and cracked linoleum. Besides that, my family is in Virginia and I had an exhibition in Boston that kept me in town through the holidays. Your parents were kind enough to ask me over, but now that I've met you, I think it was more or less a test run for Christmas—when they planned to officially introduce us."

Because I'd told them I couldn't make both Thanksgiving and Christmas this year, Taylor thought.

"Weren't you worried I'd resemble a . . . a prickly toad or something?" she asked.

"Along with the pumpkin pie, they shared the family album with me. I made sure they pointed you out . . . more than once. By the way, you look terrific in a baseball cap, tank top, and shorts," he said with a mischievous grin.

Taylor almost blushed.

"They might have been old pictures—high school or something from way back when."

He shook his head. "They're dated in ballpoint pen on the back. I sneaked one or two out of the plastic-covered slots just to make sure."

"Smart move. I'm . . . impressed."

"Forewarned is forearmed."

"I agree," Taylor said, loath to shake the apple cart. Waiting . . . wanting . . . hoping for him to make the first move.

He didn't disappoint her, leaning in so close that his breath tickled the side of her throat.

"I heard somewhere that it's a crime against fate to ignore a traditional mistletoe ball," he said. He smiled his most charming smile. Taylor's legs almost buckled.

"I've heard that too—somewhere."

"Then I suppose it would be wise if we followed through with a kiss," he said against her ear.

Taylor thought her heart would cease to beat as, hands behind his back, he touched her cheek with his warm lips. He drew back slowly. A puzzled expression shadowed his vibrant eyes.

His playful mood of moments earlier vanished as his face passed through a series of expressions. Like a roulette wheel, it finally landed on a compartment marked "downright serious business."

His face grew more somber, his tone grave.

"Do you believe in love at first touch, Taylor Kendall?" he asked in a low, carefully modulated voice. He silently searched her eyes for an answer.

"Yes, I most certainly do," she said truthfully, her own tone no less serious while her heart fluttered against the walls of her chest like a butterfly trapped in a bell jar.

Tentatively, he reached out to cup her face in his hands. He proceeded to lightly stroke her hair, fingering a springy curl, examining the color and texture and the way it naturally captured his finger.

Taylor smiled up into his eyes. "And I believe in Christmas miracles, too," she murmured.

She watched his Adam's apple bob as he swallowed. Twice.

Releasing the curl, his hands strayed from her hair to her shoulders, then down her arms to her hands. He gave them a hard squeeze.

"By the way, just in case it matters, my name is Jared Branlyn."

He gently kissed her bruised chin.

"I know," Taylor said simply, thinking she could grow accustomed to the mustache—given half a chance.

"Your parents must have told you about me as well," he said.

"Something like that," she said, adding, "Your name has a wonderful ring to it."

Fate, like coincidence, was a strange and miraculous thing, Taylor decided. She didn't know the rhymes or reasons behind her stint in Bay Colony. She knew only that her love for Jared Branlyn remained steadfast. That he stood in her parents' family room with her now, and nothing else mattered. Eventually she might question the mysteries of the universe, but for the time being she could only praise their glorious existence.

"I'm glad you like my name. And now, if you have no objections, I think I'm going to kiss you again," Jared advised her. Without waiting for her permission, he bent his head and brushed her lips with his.

Desire rose within her and Taylor realized she'd be all over Jared in another minute, initiating what she wanted most. To be entirely within the circle of his arms.

But she didn't have to worry, for he disentangled her fingers from his and slid his hands possessively around her waist instead. When he drew her against his aroused body, she felt her world finally and truly right itself for the first time in what seemed like eons.

Jared's chest rose against Taylor's as he inhaled deeply, then exhaled with a sigh. Her breasts tingled at the contact.

"It know it sounds crazy, but that mistletoe must have some sort of mystical quality. I can't seem to get enough of you," he growled.

"Me either. Not of you. Not ever," she responded. She gave a throaty sigh.

Eyes darkening with suppressed emotions, Jared admitted, "Ever since I saw your picture, you've haunted me."

"I have?"

"You bet. I thought Christmas Day would never arrive. And now here it is, and you want to know something?"

"What?" Taylor asked breathlessly. She felt happier than she could ever remember being—in the 20th century.

"You're everything I ever dreamed you'd be. In fact, Taylor Kendall, you're better than my fondest dreams. What do you think of that?"

She broke into a broad smile. "I think it's the best news I've heard in years."

Taylor slid more securely into Jared's embrace, fitting her body to his.

"We're perfect together," he marveled softly.

"Yeah, we were."

He looked at her quizzically.

"I . . . never mind," she said.

"Whatever you say, Taylor Kendall."

And then Jared kissed her deeply, in the spirit of all the things yet to come.

EUGENIA RILEY
"The Ghost of Christmas Past"

This story is dedicated, with love,
to our newest Riley, our own Christmas angel,
my precious niece—
     Sarah Carter Riley
     born December 22, 1992
and with special congratulations to
Mom and Dad, Philip and Cay.

Chapter One

*You are invited to meet
The ghost of Christmas past. . . .
"Through this portal, take your leave,
You'll come back on Christmas Eve. . . ."*

Sitting in a quaint café across from Piccadilly
Circus, Jason Burke sipped his cappuccino and
stared at the two cryptic messages inscribed on
the strange invitation that was included among a
stack of invitations given to him by his employer.
Of the half-dozen or so announcements for the
Christmas Candlelight Tours he was covering
here in London, this one was by far the oddest.
The peculiar notice was printed in old-fashioned
gold script, on ancient-looking yellow parchment
banded by red. Beneath the two messages was
written, "The Simmons Hotel," followed by an
address Jason had never heard of.

Not that he was that familiar with addresses here in London. An American, Jason was a reporter in England on assignment for a New York newspaper. Ever since Finias Fogg, an Englishman, had established the *Manhattan Chronicle* over 150 years ago, the paper had published an annual spread on Christmas traditions in England. As an added touch of whimsy, the series had always been run under Fogg's byline. This year, Jason had been awarded the dubious honor of becoming the sainted Mr. Fogg, and thus he was reluctantly writing the Yule spread.

Reluctantly. Now that was an understatement. Only a few months ago, Jason would have scoffed at taking on one of those softer, fluffier assignments for the women's pages or the Sunday supplements. Until recently, he had been a hard-edged news reporter who had covered trouble spots all over the globe.

But that was before he had lost his edge.

He sighed, wondering when he had lost his incisiveness, his vision. Had it been in Africa, when he had held in his arms that frail, pitiful child too weak to take the food he had offered? Or perhaps in the Middle East, when he had watched one of his best friends, a world-class photographer, lose his life when he had accidentally stepped on a land mine? Or maybe it had been the day a few months ago when he had returned to his Manhattan apartment, only to discover a note from Shelley breaking their engagement, telling him that he was too self-absorbed to make a good husband, and that she had gone off to "find herself" in L.A.

Whenever it had happened, at 29, Jason had become burned out. He had arrived at a point where he had ceased to care what he wrote—until his editor had yanked him off the fast track and had given him less-challenging assignments as a sort of enforced sabbatical. When Jason had revolted, refusing to cover whooping crane lectures or museum openings, his editor had given him an ultimatum: Prove yourself, or leave.

He hadn't left. He wasn't a quitter. He would prove himself and get his edge back, if only to escape the boredom of these frothy assignments.

Covering the West End Candlelight Tours here in London had to be the most frivolous so far, he mused. Over the next three nights, decked out in black tie and a forced smile, Jason would trudge through the formal, high-society affairs, going from one upscale London home or bed-and-breakfast establishment to another. The theme of the tours was "A Christmas Carol," and Jason presumed that there would be feasts, carolers, stuffed boars' heads and plum pudding ad nauseam. In fact, he understood that the homeowners or innkeepers were to dress in period costumes and to pose as citizens of Dickens's London.

He glanced again at the invitation from the Simmons Hotel and had to smile ironically. Now, it appeared that one of the tours was even to be led by an actual "ghost."

Hearing laughter at the table next to him, Jason turned to watch a large family group jovially toast a couple who were obviously celebrating an anniversary. He felt a sense of melancholy drift back over him. In truth, he rather disliked himself for greeting his current assignment here in England with such cynicism. After all, he had gotten to travel on expense account to London, and ordinarily he loved England. No doubt, too, the readers of the *Manhattan Chronicle* deserved far better than his world-weary approach to Yuletide.

Only, his life felt so empty at the moment. And thus he feared he would perform his current duties with all the enthusiasm of a true Ebenezer Scrooge.

"Will there be anything else, sir?"

Jason glanced up at the waiter, who stood in his apron and gartered shirt, with pad in hand.

"Do you know where this address is?" Jason asked, handing the man the invitation.

The waiter took it, turned it over, and frowned. "A very odd invitation, sir. Why, the paper looks almost as old as the address itself. Why the strange wording, do you suppose?"

"I'm covering the West End Candlelight Tours for the *Manhattan Chronicle*," Jason explained. "And it seems that the tour of the Simmons Hotel is to be led by a ghost."

The waiter broke into a grin. "Oh, yes, sir. You're referring to the annual wingding when all of London's high society dress up like they're straight out of Queen Victoria's time?"

"That's it."

The waiter handed the invitation back to Jason. "The address is off Belgrave Square, sir. I'm not really sure just where, but perhaps if you navigate over in that direction, you'll find it in good time."

"A comforting prospect," Jason quipped. "Now, if I can just remember to keep my rental car on the right side of the road—or rather, the left."

The waiter laughed and handed Jason the check. He paid the bill and left the cozy restaurant. Outside, the cold December air hit him, and he lifted the collar of his coat against the chill. Regent Street, with its three- and four-story classical facades, was jammed with cars and ablaze with lights. Mammoth glittering chandeliers hung suspended above the streets, and sprays of electric lights cascaded from one doorway to another. Late shoppers, diners, and theatergoers thronged the sidewalks, and the mood was one of holiday ebullience. Jason caught his reflection in the window of a china shop and saw a tall, black-haired man with cleanly cut features and shuttered dark eyes. He hurried on, feeling somehow uncomfortable to be looking at himself too closely. He arrived at his small rental car, unlocked it and ducked inside, groaning as he folded his tall form into the cramped driver's seat. He debated whether he should consult the map in the glove box, then decided that the waiter's advice would probably work just as well. He may as well begin his evening with a ghost or two, he mused ruefully as he started the car and ground the gearshift into first.

Jason followed the flow of traffic, eventually wending his way down through Trafalgar Square with its spectacular soaring Christmas tree next to the fountain and Nelson's Column. He maneuvered his way past the stately offices and clubs on Pall Mall, and finally out onto Knightsbridge near the park. He turned south into Belgravia and circled past the stuccoed embassies on Belgrave Square. He then began methodically following the side streets that fanned outward from each corner of the square. More than once, he got lost amid the endless rows of fashionable shops and elegant houses. At one point, he found himself out of Belgravia entirely, and inching his way through heavy traffic past the glittering spectacle of Harrod's on Brompton Road. At last, he wended his way back into the residential area, where the thickening fog and dimly lit streets further impeded his progress. He was to the point of giving up when, to his exasperation, he became even more hopelessly ensnared in the maze of streets, and couldn't even find his way back to the square!

At last, in disgust, Jason pulled up before a three-story Greek revival town house, hoping to ask for directions. He got out of his car and approached the steps to the pillared portico and suddenly, he was there! To his amazement, he looked up at the lettering over the door and read #10 Belgrave Lane—the very number on his invitation. And, on the frosted glass panel of the door was emblazoned, "The Simmons Hotel."

Looking up and down the stately three-story white brick structure, Jason frowned. He was at the right address, all right, but it looked as if no one was at home. The house had an eerie, near-deserted quality about it. Only the wannest light could be discerned glowing behind the yellowed window shades. And there were no trappings of Christmas to be seen at all—no wreath on the door, only a small sconce spilling out a dim puddle of light. Perhaps the owners had deliberately created this chilling ambiance for their "ghost tour"?

Hugging himself to ward off the cold, Jason sprinted up the steps and knocked on the door. He was half-expecting no response at all. But to his surprise, a moment later the door creaked open and a young woman stood before him, with a lit candle in her hand.

Unaccountably, a chill shook Jason, and for a moment he could only stare at her. Never had the sight of any woman so compelled or mesmerized him! She stood in a pool of light so dim that Jason could barely make out her features. A spooky feeling racked him as he realized that this lovely creature very much resembled a ghost.

She was quite beautiful, but also quite pale. There was something haunting, almost ethereal, about her countenance. She had a delicate face, eyes as light as honey, and lips as pale as faded rose petals. Her golden-brown hair was piled on top of her head. She wore an old-fashioned, brown velvet gown, with a skirt that swept wide and dragged the floor.

Jason smiled at her. "Hello," he murmured, in a voice that trembled oddly. "You must be the ghost of Christmas past—and I must say, a lovelier ghost I've never seen."

"Good evening, sir," the woman replied in a sweet, lyrical voice. She lowered her gaze self-consciously. "I am Annie Simmons, daughter of the hotel's owner, and your guide for this evening." She stepped back. "Won't you come in?"

"Thank you."

The disquieting feeling continued to grip Jason as he moved through the portal. Meanwhile, his ghostly tour guide moved farther away from him. Only when he was several feet beyond her did she turn to shut the door. He regarded her bemusedly.

"Follow me, sir," she murmured.

Jason glanced about in perplexity as they filed down the barren hallway with its high ceilings and carved frieze. The walls were darkly wainscoted, the faded wallpaper above hinting of a grander time.

"I take it I am the first to arrive on the tour tonight?" He laughed almost nervously. "If the others have the difficult time I did in finding you, Miss Annie Simmons, I'll wager they are all lost, just like I was."

She turned to stare at him. "You are not lost, sir."

Inexplicably, her statement—and the odd light in her eyes—unnerved Jason. She seemed to be talking about so much more than geography, and it suddenly struck him that he had felt lost, so lost, for such a long time.

He followed her into a large, barren room that obviously had once been a parlor. A crystal chandelier, unlit but still glorious, hung from a carved plaster medallion at the center of the room. The walls were papered in shades of faded, flocked rose damask.

At the fireplace, she turned. In a low, almost haunting voice, she said, "My father bought this hotel in 1832. I was born here the following year. My mother died that day, and my father raised me."

Jason regarded the woman with skepticism and uncertainty. While logic argued that she must be a member of a local historical society who was now merely reciting rehearsed lines, something about her visage almost had him believing this "ghost" was for real.

Trying to stave off the disquieting feelings she stirred in him, Jason took out his notebook and tried a stab at humor. "So, you really are up on your history, aren't you, miss?" He grinned. "Did it take you long to practice your role for tonight's tour?"

Again her pale, lovely gaze met his. "I am not playing a role, sir."

Jason forced a laugh that sounded oddly hollow. His guide turned to brush a bit of dust from the mantel of the fireplace.

"This room used to be our drawing room," she went on poignantly. "By the 1850s, our hotel was quite prosperous, the rooms always full. We would gather here with our guests each Christmas and sing carols and drink wassail."

"And did all the young men try their best to catch you beneath the mistletoe?" Jason teased.

For the first time, she smiled at him. "We called it the kissing bunch, sir."

"Ah, the kissing bunch," he replied approvingly, jotting down the term. "So you have done your homework. I'm impressed."

She did not comment, and the dimness of her visage, as well as the enigma of her shuttered expression, compelled him to study her at closer range. He edged toward her, but even as he moved, she was already sweeping away from him—as if she had read his thoughts! Feeling frustrated, he followed her out of the room.

In the hallway, she pointed toward another large, barren room where a bay window jutted out at the front. "This is where we all gathered for our meals. On Christmas Day our cook, Mrs. Chandler, would bring in the plum pudding aflame with brandy."

"Ah, the glories of Christmas Day," Jason murmured, unable to contain a hint of cynicism. "I do hope dear Mrs. Chandler didn't ignite the curtains when she set ablaze her culinary delights."

She stared at him sadly. "You don't much like Christmas, do you, sir?"

Again, the woman's uncanny insight knocked Jason off-balance. Before he could ponder a reply, the lovely "ghost" turned and started up the stairway. He followed her, wondering at the strange, spooky aura that radiated about her. Reason again argued that she was merely an actress playing a role—and yet his emotions were in turmoil, and he felt strangely drawn to her. Whatever he had expected on the Candlelight Tours tonight, it was definitely not this barren house and this sad, solitary "ghost."

Upstairs, his guide led him down a hallway, pausing at each doorway to tell him the history of each room: "This is where my Uncle Jed stayed, until he married a widow lady in 1848. . . ." "This is the room where Miss Media used to sit by the window and do her knitting. . . ." "In here, over against that wall, was the bed where I was born, and my mother died. . . ." "In this room, we had newlyweds—until the fever took them both. . . ."

With each step they took down the hallway, with each detail his tour guide uttered, Jason's feeling of unreality heightened. Annie Simmons— or whoever she was—made each statement with such conviction that it was becoming more and more difficult not to believe her!

Again, he wondered why he was the only person taking this bizarre "ghost tour." And why were there no furnishings, no Christmas decorations, no refreshments in sight? Somewhere along the way, Jason had even put away his notebook, and was now simply watching Annie, listening intently, fascinated, half-hypnotized.

She was now nodding toward the stairway that led to the third story. "Up there is where our servants used to sleep." Wistfully, she added, "But it's only storage now, with everyone gone."

Again, Jason tried to move closer to her, and again she glided away, elusive as a mist. He longed to touch her, but some instinct warned him not to. She led him back toward the stairs.

"If everyone is gone," he teased gently, "then who are you?"

She glanced at him over her shoulder. "I thought you knew, sir," she replied with a strange, almost chilling smile. "I am the ghost who haunts this hotel."

And, leaving him to reel in the wake of her eerie statement, she swept on.

Jason followed her downstairs. When she reached the first floor, she turned to stare at him, just a few steps above her. A haunting light played over her features as she murmured in a monotone, "I died on these steps on Christmas Eve in 1852, when I learned that my true love had deserted me."

Her words, her expression, sent a shudder through Jason. Intrigued and electrified, he hurried down to join her. It was uncanny as hell, he thought, but when she had just spoken, she actually had him believing she was a ghost!

"But why did you die?" he implored. "You must tell me more."

But again, she was already evading him, heading off toward the front door. "I'm sorry, sir. Your tour has ended now."

Jason felt strangely bereft. "Please," he murmured, "I'd really like to see you again. And I'd like to learn more about this hotel."

She smiled that same, eerie smile again. "Oh, but you will, sir."

She stood back so he could pass through the portal.

Taking one last, near-anguished look at the lovely, ethereal creature, Jason left. He headed back down the steps, feeling bemused and shaken by his "ghost tour."

When he turned back to look at the town house, all the lights were extinguished, and he could see only darkness.

Chapter Two

The next morning as he ate breakfast in his hotel room, Jason found himself endlessly reliving the moments he had spent on the "ghost tour" last night. It had undoubtedly been the strangest ten minutes of his entire life—and yet, on another level, the most compelling. His tour guide had in every way personified an actual ghost; indeed, when she had whispered, "I died on this staircase . . .", Jason had felt hard-pressed not to believe her.

And why had she been so careful never to let him venture too close to her, or to touch her? Her ethereal, elusive qualities fascinated him. Even though logic still argued that she had only been playing a role, he knew that he wanted to see Annie Simmons again, to get to know her better. He couldn't deny that something had sprung to life inside him during the brief moments they had shared. On some uncanny level, she seemed both to know and to understand him, to reach out to the emptiness in his heart and soul. Already he felt a deep bond with her.

Jason picked up the phone and called his editor in the States. He reached Bill Turner at home.

"Jason. How is it going?" Bill muttered, stifling a yawn.

"Okay. I'm working on the feature on the West End Candlelight Tours right now."

"Will you get the piece in by the deadline?"

"Don't I always?"

Bill chuckled. "What about the photos? Is Steve McCurdy on top of them?"

Jason groaned. "I'm afraid Steve has a touch of the flu."

"Oh, Lord."

"Don't despair. The tours are running for two more nights, and Steve has promised me he will play catch-up either tonight or tomorrow night."

"I love a photo finish," Bill quipped. "Listen, the spread is going to run in just over two weeks—"

"We'll get it in," Jason reiterated. He cleared his throat. "I do have a question for you, Bill."

"Shoot."

"Can you tell me anything about the Simmons Hotel? An invitation from them was included with the ones you gave me."

"Let me grab my briefcase and see if I can put my hands on the list of people and establishments we've been in contact with."

Jason waited, then heard Bill pick up the phone again and rustle through some papers.

After a moment, Bill said, "You know, this is odd. I don't see the Simmons Hotel on the list of homes and inns you are to cover."

Jason was mystified. "But I've got the invitation right here in my hand."

"Are you sure you didn't pick it up somewhere else?"

"Definitely not. It was in the envelope with the other info you gave me."

"I'll be damned," Bill muttered. "Maybe an invitation was sent, but the hotel wasn't included on the master list I was given. Tell you what—why don't you contact this Mrs. Jessica Fitzhugh? She's the chairman of the tours, and is serving as our London liaison."

Jason flipped through some of the papers Bill had given him. "Oh, yeah. Her number is right here with the other materials. Why didn't I think of that?"

"And you say you're on top of things?" Bill asked skeptically.

"You'll get your article on time," Jason said, and the two men hung up.

"Mrs. Fitzhugh?" Jason asked.

"Speaking," replied the elderly sounding, feminine voice at the other end of the line. "May I help you?"

"I'm Jason Burke, the reporter who is covering the West End Candlelight Tours for the *Manhattan Chronicle*."

"Ah, yes, Mr. Burke," the woman said eagerly. "I've been expecting to hear from you. Indeed, we were hoping that you would stop by our home last night."

"Oh, that's right," Jason muttered. "The Fitzhugh home in Mayfair is featured on the tour."

"You should have been here," Mrs. Fitzhugh related excitedly. "We had a crowd of hundreds, and carolers came by from our parish church. We couldn't have planned it any better."

"Sounds wonderful," Jason commented without enthusiasm. "I'll be sure to get by your home tonight. In the meantime, I have a question for you."

"Yes?"

"Can you tell me anything about the Simmons Hotel? An invitation for a tour of the inn was included in the package you sent my editor."

"Why, forevermore!" gasped Mrs. Fitzhugh. "I never mailed your editor any such invitation! And if that isn't the oddest thing I've ever heard of!"

"What do you mean, odd?" Jason asked.

Mrs. Fitzhugh laughed. "Why, the Simmons Hotel is not included in the West End tours. Indeed, during the forty years I've been chairman, the hotel has never been included in the tours."

A chill swept over Jason. "Then how can you explain my having the invitation?"

"I have no idea. A joke, perhaps?"

"If so, not a very funny one," Jason replied. Frowning to himself, he added, "But you do seem familiar with the hotel."

"Oh, yes," she replied. "However, you must be aware that there no longer is a Simmons Hotel as such—indeed, there hasn't been one for over fifty years."

Now Jason had to protest. "There, you are wrong. You see, I toured the hotel last night. The tour was led—"

"Yes?"

Reluctantly, Jason admitted, "By a young woman posing as a ghost."

He heard Mrs. Fitzhugh laugh. "Oh, Mr. Burke! Now you are pulling *my* leg!"

"Not at all," Jason argued. Feeling frustrated, he added, "What can you tell me about the hotel?"

"Well, as I recall, the Simmons was established in the nineteenth century. If memory serves, it closed down in the early 1940s, and thereafter was split up into flats or something. I believe it is now vacant and boarded up—if it hasn't been razed."

"But that makes no sense," Jason put in vehemently. "I tell you, I was there last night."

"Perhaps you were at a different address, and only thought you were there."

Jason frowned. "Do you know of any way I can find out additional information on this hotel?"

"Ah, yes. I believe the Simmons is included in a book on historic inns of the West End. You might ask for it at the library."

"Thanks."

"Oh, Mr. Burke?"

"Yes?"

Mrs. Fitzhugh paused for a moment, then related awkwardly, "I don't know quite how to tell you this, but the Simmons Hotel has always been rumored to be haunted."

The Simmons Hotel has always been rumored to be haunted.

That very statement was still haunting Jason Burke an hour later as he maneuvered his small car through the maze of streets in Belgravia. Navigating was somewhat easier by the light of day, and in due course, Jason managed to find his way back to Belgrave Lane—and to the town house he had toured last night.

What he saw astounded him. The candlelit inn was gone. In its place stood a crumbling edifice with soot-blackened brick, sagging roof, and boarded-up windows!

Jason left his car and strode onto the walkway, staring in disbelief at the derelict structure. The building standing before him had obviously been closed down for some time now—there was even graffiti decorating the graying boards.

Nothing made sense! Nothing made sense at all! There were no signs of life around the old edifice; in front of it, a sign proclaimed that the structure would shortly be renovated into an office building.

Feeling more bemused than ever, Jason got into his car and drove off. What on earth had happened to him last night? Had he gotten lost? Had someone truly played a joke on him? Had he been hallucinating? Or had his tour been led by an actual ghost?

Jason visited the renowned Guildhall Library not far from the London financial center. The librarian was very helpful, showing Jason to a table and bringing him the requested book on historic inns of the West End.

For a moment, he felt too unnerved to open the volume.

Five minutes later, Jason was staring at a faded daguerreotype of Annie Simmons and her father, both of whom were standing before the staircase at the Simmons Hotel in the year 1850.

Jason could not stop trembling. For he was staring at the very ghost who had guided his tour last night!

The Ghost of Christmas Past

To his deepening sense of amazement and mystification, the other details of the article confirmed just what Annie Simmons and Mrs. Fitzhugh had already told Jason—that the inn had known its heyday in the 1850s, that Annie Simmons had died there due to a tragic accident late in 1852, and that, for generations afterward, Annie's spirit had been rumored to haunt the hotel.

Jason buried his face in his hands and groaned. What was happening to him? Had he lost his mind? Was the woman he had met last night a descendant of Annie Simmons? But how could that be if Annie Simmons had died young and unmarried?

He was falling in love with a ghost!

That night as Jason drove his car through the zigzagging streets of Belgravia, he was still questioning his own sanity. Since the Candlelight Tours were to continue for two more nights, he had again donned his formal attire and had gone searching for the Simmons Hotel and Annie Simmons. He seemed compelled by forces too powerful and complex to understand.

Again, he got lost in the fog, in the maze of streets. He was growing intensely frustrated when some inner voice told him that perhaps he should give up his search for now and go visit the other homes on the tour. He suddenly felt a compelling need to conclude his business here in London.

Thus, Jason drove out of Belgravia and made the rounds of half a dozen homes on the tours, visiting a charming 18th century house in Queen Anne's Gate, a stunning Adamesque town house on Portland Square, a magnificent estate over-looking Regent's Park. Jason was warmly received at each home and, despite his impatience to locate the Simmons Hotel again, he enjoyed the lavish decorations and costumes, the wassail and hymn singing, much more than he would have thought. He visited the Fitzhugh home in Mayfair and at last met the charming Jessica Fitzhugh. When the elderly woman asked Jason if he had ever found the Simmons Hotel, he merely smiled enigmatically and said that perhaps he *had* gotten lost.

He did not finish with the tours until well past midnight, and when he returned to his hotel, he felt impelled to write the articles. He pulled out his laptop computer and worked feverishly through-out the night, completing all four features and then typing in his byline, "Finias Fogg." At dawn, he tumbled into bed and caught a few hours of sleep. At noon, he called Steve McCurdy and checked on how the photo shoot was coming along. Afterward, he went out and mailed the floppy disk with the articles to his editor in the States. He also mailed his parents a Christmas card, sending them his love.

That night, again in black tie, Jason drove back to Belgravia and circled through the darkened streets. A feeling of heightened tension gripped him as he realized that tonight would likely be his last opportunity to find the Simmons Hotel and Annie Simmons.

But this time, he found #10 Belgrave Lane much more easily than he would have thought—indeed, the structure appeared lit up like a beacon. "My God!" he cried as he braked his car to a halt.

Jason shut off the ignition and all but bolted out of his car. He stared in amazement at a far different Simmons Hotel that loomed before him tonight. Gone were the boards, the sagging structure he had seen yesterday. The Greek Revival facade now seemed perfect in every detail, and the windows sparkled like a Christmas tree! Indeed, the spirit of Yule was evident tonight in the garlands gracing the front steps and the freshly cut wreath on the door.

Jason bounded up the steps. He didn't know where he was headed, but he did know that he wanted with all his heart to be right here on this stoop!

He knocked, and this time—to his astonishment and delight—his knock was answered by a far different Annie Simmons, who swung open the door and regarded him with a friendly smile.

This woman, who so strikingly resembled his ghostly guide from two nights ago, was very much alive! Jason sensed that at once. She was dressed in a bright-red velvet gown, her cheeks were bright, and her eyes gleamed with merriment. Beyond her, the hallway was lavishly carpeted and furnished, as well as decorated in the spirit of Yule. He could hear the sounds of happy voices and soft music coming from the parlor. He could even smell the intoxicating aromas of Christmas— the spice of wassail, the crisp scents of cedar and pine. Indeed, he could see the "kissing bunch" she had mentioned two nights ago—a masterpiece of holly and mistletoe, pinecones and lit candles, hanging directly above her head.

Jason was tempted to pull this lovely vision into his arms and kiss her!

But she made the first move, reaching out to take his hand. Her flesh was warm and electric on his, and he felt suddenly as if he were hovering on the brink of some magical discovery.

"Hello, miss," he murmured.

"Good evening, sir," she murmured back. "You must be our expected guest from America. Won't you come in out of the cold and join us?"

Before Jason could think of a response, she tugged on his hand and pulled him through the portal. A sense of unreality swamped him, and he suddenly remembered the verse, "Through this portal, take your leave . . ."

For a moment, Jason felt genuinely disoriented, almost frightened. "Where am I?" he asked his hostess as she tugged him toward the parlor. "What is going on here?"

Her lyrical voice somehow soothed his fears. "Don't worry, sir. You are where you belong now."

Chapter Three

"Father, we have a guest," said Annie Simmons.

After taking Jason's overcoat, Annie led him into the drawing room. Jason could only glance about him in awe, and had to struggle not to gape at the astounding tableau unfolding before him.

Immediately, he sensed that this was hardly a scene enacted from the past, such as he had witnessed at several London homes last night. Instead, he was gripped by the intense, eerie feeling that he had stepped right into an actual Victorian parlor!

The same crystal chandelier he had spotted two nights ago gleamed overhead, casting about warm sprays of light. A vivid royal-blue-and-rose oriental rug covered the floor, and mauve-colored flocked wallpaper graced the walls. The furniture was fashioned of elegant carved rosewood, with silk damask coverings. Behind handsome brass andirons, a fire blazed in the grate. Everywhere were Christmas decorations, from the holly festooning the mantel to the Nativity scene on the tea table, to the Christmas tree in the front window, which gleamed with small lit candles, and was gaily decorated with everything from candied fruits, toys, and clocks, to sugarplums, doll furniture, and pieces of jewelry.

And the people! There seemed to be at least a dozen guests present, gaily visiting in the parlor—gentlemen in black tailcoats, matching trousers, ruffled shirts, and elaborate silk neckwear, ladies in sweeping floor-length gowns similar to Annie's. At the beautifully carved cabinet grand piano, an elderly woman was playing the sweet strains of "The Holly and the Ivy."

What on earth had happened to him? Jason wondered. He had the uncanny feeling that he had somehow arrived at the Simmons Hotel during its heyday—and that explanation could only make sense if he had somehow traveled through time! Such a possibility seemed preposterous.

Yet how else could he explain the resurrection of the hotel from the ramshackle structure he'd seen yesterday to the magnificent edifice in which he now stood? And how could he account for the transformation of Annie Simmons from the ghost who had mesmerized him two nights ago to the enchanting, beautiful, very much alive creature who now stood next to him?

A balding man with muttonchop whiskers now strode up to join them, glancing rather perplexedly at Jason. "Annie, who have we here?" he asked the woman.

"Father, our visitor from America has arrived," she explained.

"Ah, yes. We hadn't expected you for a few more days, sir." The man extended his hand toward Jason. "I am Oscar Simmons, proprietor of this inn. I see that you've already met my daughter."

Jason smiled at Annie. "Yes, I have."

As the two men shook hands, Oscar Simmons regarded Jason quizzically. "Then you are Finias Fogg, sir?"

"Finias Fogg?" Jason was amazed. "You mean the founder of the *Manhattan Chronicle*?"

"Why, yes. Mr. Fogg recently wrote us reserving a room for his stay in London." Scratching his jaw, Oscar Simmons appeared perplexed. "Are you saying you are not Mr. Fogg?"

"I'm afraid we have a misunderstanding here," Jason explained awkwardly. "I am definitely not Finias Fogg—except perhaps in a whimsical sense." As father and daughter exchanged bemused glances, he quickly added, "However, I suppose I am a representative of Mr. Fogg, since I do write for the *Manhattan Chronicle*. My name is Jason Burke."

"Ah, Mr. Burke," Simmons murmured.

"Then you have come to London in Mr. Fogg's stead?" Annie suggested with a puzzled smile.

Jason had to restrain a chuckle. "Perhaps in a manner of speaking, I have."

"And what is the purpose of your stay in our city, Mr. Burke?" Oscar Simmons asked.

Jason decided the truth might best suffice. "Actually, I am here gathering information to write a series of articles on Christmas traditions in Great Britain."

"Oh, how fascinating!" Annie cried with an expression of delight.

"Indeed," her father concurred. "As it happens, we are hosting a bit of a Yule gathering here tonight for our guests and a few friends. Won't you join us, Mr. Burke?"

"I wouldn't want to impose," he replied hesitantly.

"Nonsense," Annie said. "This gathering is for folks just like you. And you must stay here the night, as well."

"But if you were not expecting me—that is, Mr. Fogg—as yet—"

"Don't be silly," Annie cut in brightly. "At Christmastime, you will never see a sign at the Simmons Hotel reading No Room at the Inn."

"You must really like Christmas then, Miss Simmons," Jason felt compelled to murmur.

"It is my favorite time," she replied.

While Jason still felt highly confused and unsettled regarding his new surroundings, he managed to hold his own as Annie and her father took him about and introduced him to several of their guests. He met a farmer and his wife from Chiswick, as well as the owner of a nearby jewelry shop, and two elderly spinsters, sisters who shared a room at the hotel. When Jason learned that one of the spinsters was named "Media," he felt a chill grip him as he recalled Annie Simmons's "ghost" mentioning the same name two nights ago.

Although from their bemused expressions, it seemed the guests found both Jason's sudden appearance and his attire to be peculiar, all graciously made no comment to indicate that they found the newly arrived guest the least bit out of place here. Within minutes, Jason had a cup of warm wassail in one hand, a plate heaped with fruitcake and gingerbread cookies in the other. Annie had drifted off to visit with a couple of the women, and Jason hung about a small circle of men, which included Annie's father, and listened intently to their conversation.

"I hear Disraeli presented his new budget to the House of Commons today," the shop owner was saying.

"And an inspired proposition 'tis," said the farmer, "reducing the taxes that have so long burdened those of us who work the land."

"Ah, but with the increasing taxes on houses, innkeepers such as myself are bound to suffer," put in Oscar Simmons.

The shop owner turned to Jason. "What is your tax situation like in America, Mr. Burke?" He laughed. "Or are all of you too rich from mining gold out in your California to care?"

Jason smiled thinly. "Taxes do seem to be an eternal blight for us all."

"Aye," added another. "And I do wonder if the earl of Derby's regime will even survive the four weeks needed to see the year of our Lord 1853."

1853. This announcement of the coming New Year set Jason reeling. Feeling desperate to regain his equilibrium, he moved away from the group and headed toward the front window. What he saw as he moved aside the velvet drapery and glanced down at the street hardly comforted him.

Unfamiliar, ancient-looking three- and four-story houses lined the street, while on the corners, elegant gaslights spilled out their radiance. He noted that his car—indeed all the cars!—had disappeared. Gone was the asphalt street, replaced by time-worn cobblestones. As Jason watched, fascinated, a horse-drawn carriage rattled past, driven by a coachman who wore a heavy cloak and a top hat. Then, on the sidewalk, he observed a bedraggled woman in a long dress lumber by, pushing a flower cart.

So he had been thrust back in time to early December of 1852! His sense of amazement was overwhelming. And, if this were true, then—good heavens!—he had arrived at a juncture only a few weeks before Annie Simmons would die!

Jason was still reeling with this knowledge as he heard a lyrical voice murmur, "Mr. Burke, are you all right?"

He turned to see Annie Simmons standing beside him. He studied her delicately drawn face—the youthful skin, large, bright eyes, wide mouth, and charming dimples. A sudden anguish rent him. Oh, God, he thought, staring at her, she was so real, so lovely—

And in so much peril!

Jason managed a tremulous smile. "I suppose I'm feeling just a bit disoriented."

"When did you arrive here in London?"

"Only tonight."

She snapped her fingers. "And we didn't even ask about your luggage."

Jason coughed awkwardly. "It's a long story, but I'm afraid that I don't have any."

Annie was gazing at Jason in perplexity when a man stepped up to join them. He was blond, blue-eyed, tall, slender, and quite handsome.

"Annie, dear, you are ignoring me," he murmured. He glanced sharply at Jason. "Do I sense competition here?"

"Oh, Stephen, don't be silly," Annie scolded the gentleman. "This is our new guest, Mr. Jason

Burke, a newspaperman from America. I'm only trying to help him gather his bearings a bit." To Jason, she added, "Mr. Burke, this is a very special friend of mine, Stephen Prescott."

"How do you do?" Jason asked, shaking hands with Stephen.

"So you're a newspaperman—and an American." Stephen studied Jason's attire cynically. "Perhaps that is the reason for your rather eccentric garb?"

Before Jason could reply, Annie's father called out from near the piano, "You young people, come over here and join us! Miss Mary is going to play some carols, and let's all gather round the piano and sing."

Jason, Annie, and Stephen dutifully gathered with the others, singing several Yule hymns— "Deck the Halls," "God Rest Ye Merry Gentlemen," and "I Saw Three Ships." Watching Annie stand so close to Stephen, and observing the smug, self-satisfied grin on Prescott's face as he stood with his arm possessively at Annie's waist, Jason felt a strange sense of foreboding and powerlessness wash over him.

After the songs were completed, Oscar Simmons held up a hand. "Ladies and gentlemen," he began proudly, "I have an announcement to make." He smiled at Annie and Stephen. "It is my honor to inform you that my beautiful daughter Annie will shortly marry Mr. Stephen Prescott."

As a cheer went up from the guests, Annie and Stephen smiled happily. Jason felt a chill grip his very soul. He knew now that he had been thrust back in time to a period when Annie Simmons was still alive, albeit she might have only a few weeks left to live! Was he too late?

For Jason had the strong feeling that he had just met the very man who would be responsible for Annie Simmons's death! And yet there she stood, holding Stephen's hand, the very image of the blissful bride—totally oblivious to the disaster hurtling toward her!

Now, the guests swarmed around Annie and Stephen, offering congratulations and hugs. Jason walked over and dutifully extended to both Annie and Stephen his best wishes. Annie responded with a shy smile, Stephen with an indifferent handshake.

In the meantime, Oscar Simmons was making his rounds, handing out glasses of Madeira for a toast. Jason retreated toward a corner, where he could hear the farmer and the shop owner conversing quietly nearby.

"Looks like our dear Miss Annie has found herself a good match," he heard the farmer say.

"Oh, I'm not so sure," replied the shop owner. "When young Prescott came into my shop recently to buy Annie a brooch, he brought along a chap from his club who was giving him the very mischief over his plan to keep on his mistress after the wedding."

"Well, I'll be hanged!" said the farmer. "Prescott plans to philander following the nuptials? Do you suppose we should warn Annie or Oscar?"

"Nay, leave it be," advised the shop owner. "As our Mr. Bulwer-Lytton says, 'Boys will be boys.' Besides, it is not as if young Prescott's attitude toward wedded bliss is that unusual, now is it?"

As the two men chuckled behind him, Jason felt staggered by their disclosures. He again stared helplessly at Annie, who now kissed her father's cheek as he handed her a glass of wine, while

Stephen looked on approvingly. Again, he remembered her chilling words from the present, "I died on these steps on Christmas Eve in 1852, when I learned that my true love had deserted me."

Jason had been back in time for less than an hour, yet he already knew not only who would betray Annie Simmons—but also how and why.

Chapter Four

"If you'll just follow me, sir, the room is down here."

Two hours later, while Annie Simmons's father was downstairs bidding the remaining guests goodnight, Jason Burke was following Annie down the third-story corridor of the hotel. She strolled a few feet ahead of him, holding high a taper to light their way. With the long shadows spilling about them, their sojourn down the darkened hallway bore a spooky resemblance to Jason's "ghost tour" with Annie's spirit two nights ago—and almost a century and a half away! The very thought staggered him.

Not that he wasn't already reeling from his evident journey through time. He felt half-afraid that if he pinched himself, the entire fantastical world to which he had been whisked might simply disappear.

He wondered if Annie remembered taking him on the "ghost tour" two nights ago—and so far away! But, of course, she wouldn't, because he had returned to a period in time before she'd even become a ghost. That realization seemed mind-boggling. Was it then his mission to save her from the catastrophe that would all-too-soon spur her tormented spirit to haunt the Simmons Hotel for so many decades to come? If, indeed, he were even allowed to stay here that long?

Annie creaked open a door. "Ah, here we are."

Jason followed her inside a small, plain room that was furnished with little more than a narrow bed and a nondescript dresser. A couple of oil paintings of English pastoral scenes, as well as airy curtains at the window, lent a feeling of warmth.

Annie gestured toward the grate, where kindling had been laid out. "You can light a fire if you wish. I'm sorry we haven't a finer room available tonight."

"Don't apologize. This will do just fine."

Annie laughed, revealing her charming dimples. "You are very easy to please."

Jason couldn't resist winking at her. "But then, you please me so easily, Miss Simmons."

Jason could have sworn he watched her struggle to hide a guilty smile as she turned away to the dresser, using her taper to light the oil lamp. "We use this room for the occasional overflow of guests, when all our second-floor rooms are occupied." She turned to him. "You say you have no luggage?"

Jason suddenly felt very awkward, and shifted from foot to foot. "Actually, I have arrived not only without luggage, but also without appropriate funds to pay you for this room."

Although she appeared taken aback, she quickly protested, "Oh, please, you must not concern yourself about paying for the room just yet. But it does distress me that your employer, Mr. Fogg, did not adequately provide for you."

Jason grinned sheepishly as he improvised an explanation. "I must confess that I was not entirely truthful downstairs. Indeed, Mr. Finias Fogg may yet show up here."

"What do you mean?"

In a low, conspiratorial tone, he confided, "You see, I am not an actual employee of the newspaper in America. I'm what you might call a stringer. I've done assignments for the *Manhattan Chronicle* before, and I was simply hoping to sell them some articles on Christmas here in Great Britain."

"Oh, I see." Annie grew thoughtful, frowning as she placed a finger alongside her jaw. "Then perhaps—"

"Yes?"

"I do not mean to be presumptuous, but—"

"Please, feel free to speak."

"Would it be helpful if you could find employment here?"

"Indeed," Jason concurred with a dry laugh.

"You see, my father is good friends with a Mr. Spencer, who owns a local newspaper," she continued with some excitement. "Perhaps we could speak with him on your behalf—"

Jason held up a hand. "You are very kind, but I do feel that you've already done enough for me. Besides, even my staying here must be an imposition."

"Not at all. We want you to feel at home." She paused to study his formal black suit, then grinned almost impishly. "As for your clothing . . . I must say that styles seem to differ greatly in America these days."

"So they do," Jason concurred dryly.

"Across the hallway is a storage room where we keep items left behind by various guests. You're welcome to take anything you need, Mr. Burke." Again, she looked him over, her expression pensive. "As a matter of fact, a few months back, one of our boarders, a Mr. Haggarty, passed away of the fever, and he was about your size. I was going to include his things in the Christmas baskets my church is making up for the poor—but please feel free to claim anything you want first."

"You are far too generous."

"I'm just glad you can put the things to good use." She smiled rather shyly. "Well, is there anything else?"

A kiss, Jason thought suddenly, noting how adorable she looked, standing there and gazing at him so expectantly. *Yes, a kiss would do just fine.*

To her, he said reluctantly, "No, I have everything I need."

Appearing satisfied, she swept away toward the doorway, smiling at him over her shoulder. "Well, then, good night, Mr. Burke."

Watching her leave, Jason was rent by sudden anguish. He felt compelled to touch her again. He quickly closed the distance between them, took her free hand, and kissed it. "Good night, Miss Simmons. And thank you for all your kindnesses."

She blushed then, a look of delight spreading across her angelic face that almost had Jason pulling her into his arms—especially as he felt her fingers trembling in his.

Then, gently, she extricated her hand from his. "Good night, Mr. Burke."

Annie Simmons flashed Jason a happy smile as she left.

Jason lit the fire and, as the room warmed up, strode over to the window and gazed out. He studied a skyline that was curiously the same, yet vastly different from the world he had left behind. All modern structures were conspicuously absent. In the distance, he could spot the Belfry Tower of Westminster Abbey, the gothic spires of Parliament, the trees of St. James Park, and the solid outline of Buckingham Palace. Close by on the gaslit street, he watched smoke curl from tall chimneys, and observed another carriage clattering down the cobblestones. A fine powder of snow was beginning to flutter over the rooftops, and the glass of the windowpane felt cold against his fingertips.

Annie's hand had felt warm in his—so warm, he thought. Her flesh had felt so soft against his lips. The memory brought a stab of longing to his heart. Again he hungered to kiss that wide, sweet mouth that had smiled at him tonight with such joy, with such innocence. Annie—his enchanting, untouched 19th century lady. Though he had been with her only briefly, he already knew that she was like no one he had ever met before—a total departure from the worldly-wise girls he had dated back in the present. She was so young, so fresh, so beautiful.

So fragile. Remembering her with Stephen, he frowned darkly. Again, he wondered what he could do to stop the insidious catastrophe that might soon smash Annie's tender young heart to pieces—and end her very life! Protecting that precious life was much more important than his own budding feelings for her.

A weary sigh escaped him. Somehow, he must help Annie—but now, especially after last night's writing marathon, he knew he needed rest. He had definitely brought every bit of his exhaustion with him here to the 19th century.

Moving away from the window, he unbuttoned his jacket and automatically pulled out his wallet. In amazement, he stared at the leather billfold. Flipping it open, he examined his ID, credit cards, and traveler's checks. Everything was still there, intact. The contradiction of this reality astounded him. He was obviously now living in the year 1852—and yet he held in his hand proof that he had actually come from over 140 years in the future!

He laughed ironically. A lot of good these items would do him here now! He chuckled at the prospect of trying to cash one of his pound sterling traveler's checks, or of going to a restaurant and pulling out one of his credit cards. If he told anyone here where he had actually come from, he would likely be labeled a lunatic and carted off to Bedlam. He took his wallet, along with his wristwatch and keys, and placed the items at the back of the top bureau drawer.

Wondering what he might wear to bed, he took the oil lamp and crossed the hallway to the storage room Annie had mentioned. He sniffed at the unpleasant, dank air. Broken or worn furniture, as well as threadbare or patched linens, were stacked about.

Near the window, he examined two dusty, musty-smelling chests—one held women's clothing, the other held men's. Jason smiled at the sense of Victorian propriety that extended even to segregating old clothing in the storage room.

Turning to the collection of men's attire, Jason pulled out the items one by one. He could only shake his head at the curious contents—felt bowler hats, quaint men's coats with shawl collars, silk brocade vests with braided lapels, finely pleated linen shirts, white silk cravats, walking sticks, and boots. Concentrating on the least worn of the items, Jason selected a brown suit and hat, a white shirt, black cravat, a pair of boots, and a nightshirt. He took the items back to his room.

In bed, with the lamp extinguished, Jason found sleep elusive. His woolen nightshirt felt scratchy and the softness of the feather tick made him feel strangely adrift compared with the firm mattress he was accustomed to in the present.

He turned, punched down his pillow, stared at the dying fire, and wondered what tomorrow would bring. All his instincts told him that he had come here to 19th century London for a reason. Again, he remembered the rhyme on his invitation—"Through this portal take your leave; You'll come back on Christmas Eve."

He knew he had arrived here in early December 1852. Could it be that his time here would be limited, that he would be thrust back to the present on Christmas Eve—hopefully, after he had accomplished his purpose? Had he indeed been sent here as some sort of guardian angel or troubleshooter meant to save Annie Simmons from disaster?

He considered his flight through time from another perspective. Could it be that he had been sent here to learn something, just as Scrooge had experienced a spiritual awakening when he had taken his mystical journey with "the ghost of Christmas past"?

Then he groaned as he again remembered the feel of Annie's baby-soft flesh against his mouth. One thing he knew for a certainty—his first objective while he was here would be to remove Miss Annie Simmons from the clutches of Mr. Steven Prescott.

Downstairs, as she tiptoed about tidying up and snuffing out lamps, Annie Simmons found herself feeling consumed with thoughts of Jason Burke. She felt strangely drawn to the handsome, mysterious American who had appeared on their stoop tonight.

What an enigma he was—showing up here, so strangely yet elegantly attired, and yet arriving without appropriate funds or even luggage! Even his explanation about being sent by the newspaper had seemed odd as well as dubious.

Yet Annie couldn't deny that she found the American both interesting and intriguing. She considered his arresting face—the deep-set brown eyes, beautifully chiseled nose and firm mouth, the cleft in his strong chin. His physique was tall and trim, his hair thick and black as midnight.

There was a haunted, passionate quality about him that drew her most of all. Heretofore, the only man who had been important to her romantically was Stephen—and Jason Burke was all darkness, all intensity, to Stephen's lightness and charm.

She knew she had agreed to marry Stephen mostly to please her father. Oscar Simmons was getting along in years, and his heart was not as strong as it once had been. Annie knew her father wanted most of all to see his daughter happily settled with the successful haberdasher. She and Stephen had been friends for years, and she had found the prospect of marrying him to be pleasant enough.

Yet honesty compelled her to admit that, ever since she had set eyes on their dark, mysterious stranger who had arrived from America tonight, ever since he had pressed his warm, masterful lips to her flesh, she was having second thoughts about becoming Stephen Prescott's wife.

Chapter Five

"Did you sleep well, Mr. Burke?" Oscar Simmons asked.

Early the next morning, Jason, dressed in the quaint brown suit he had selected last night, sat in the dining room, eating breakfast with Annie Simmons and her father. Also present were the two spinsters, Miss Media and Miss Mary Craddock. The repast laid out on the lace-covered mahogany table was sumptuous—hot chocolate and coffee, scones and rolls, cranberry bread and cheese. A fire in the grate warmed the room, and the enticing aromas of the freshly baked goods filled the air. More than once during the meal, Jason had looked up in amazement as the pink-cheeked cook, Mrs. Chandler—the very servant Annie's ghost had told him about in the present!—lumbered in wearing her uniform, apron, and mobcap, and bearing a tray laden with more coffee, marmalade, or toast. With every moment that passed, it sank in upon Jason more that he was actually living in 19th century London—for whatever reason.

Now Jason glanced, smiling, from Annie, who sat across from him, to her father, who sat flanking him at the head of the table. "I slept splendidly, thank you, sir," he replied. "It was kind of you and your daughter to take me in on such short notice."

"And what are your plans now that you are settled?" Oscar asked. "Will you be pursuing your duties for your employer?"

When Jason, feeling at a loss, did not immediately reply, Annie filled the gap. "Father, I thought I might take Mr. Burke round to meet your friend Mr. Spencer, the newspaperman. You see, it seems that Mr. Burke is in need of a post during his stay in London."

Oscar Simmons scowled sharply at Jason. "I thought you said you were already employed by the American newspaper."

Jason coughed. "Our arrangement is an informal one."

"So it appears," Simmons murmured, an undercurrent of disapproval in his tone. He nodded toward his daughter. "Perhaps it would be best if I take Mr. Burke by to meet my friend Harley."

"But, Father," Annie protested, "you know the surgeon has cautioned you not to overdo in this weather. Besides, I must be out today, anyway. I had planned to go by Covent Garden to select the nuts and fruits for my Christmas baking." She smiled shyly at Jason. "I thought I might show Mr. Burke a bit of the town."

While Jason returned Annie's smile, Simmons slanted an admonishing glance toward his daughter. "My dear, may I have a word with you?"

"Of course, Father."

Simmons nodded to the others. "If you'll excuse us?"

Jason stood as Annie got to her feet. He watched the father and daughter leave the room together, then sat back down, nodding to the two spinsters—both of whom had been observing the exchange with expressions of fascination.

"Will you be staying in London long, Mr. Burke?" Media asked.

Jason mused that the old lady doubtless could not begin to understand the irony of her question. "I really have no idea."

Across the hallway in the drawing room, Annie and her father were talking in low, intent voices.

"Have you taken leave of your senses?" Oscar demanded of Annie.

She lifted her chin. "I really have no idea what you mean, Father."

He sighed in exasperation. "My dear, you are a promised woman. It is highly improper for you to be gadding about town with this stranger—a bachelor about whom we know nothing."

"But Mr. Burke is a newcomer to our country," Annie argued. "It is only common courtesy that we should help him get acclimated."

"You are letting your own benevolent nature rob you of all good sense!" Oscar declared. "It would be one thing if Stephen were accompanying you—"

"Stephen is quite busy at his shop, especially as it is the Christmas season," Annie pointed out. "Furthermore, are you saying that I am not trustworthy, Father?"

"Certainly not!" he said, flinging his hands wide. "I am simply trying to point out your error in judgment. You have always been far too generous for your own good, my dear. To become a mentor to this . . . newcomer—"

"Father, Mr. Burke is destitute," Annie cut in. "He arrived here without a farthing. He needs a post and a place to stay."

"But there are charitable institutions to see to his kind."

"Now you are sounding as dreadful as Mr. Dickens's Scrooge," Annie scolded. "And I must say that it is quite unlike you to be so stingy. Charity begins at home, Father. It is Christmastime—and I am going to help this man get on his feet."

"Very well," Oscar grumbled, realizing that he was defeated. "You may go out with this man. Just don't make a habit of it." He smiled gently at his only child. "You, I trust. But as for this American upstart—that's another matter altogether."

"Your father doesn't like me much, does he?" Jason asked.

Thirty minutes later, Jason and Annie were seated across from each other inside the family coach. They were headed out of Belgravia and toward Piccadilly. The day was quite chill, and Jason wore his wool overcoat over his suit. He noted that Annie looked simply adorable in her fur-trimmed pelisse over a carriage dress, and a feathered silk bonnet tied with a satin bow.

She smiled at him. "I'm all Father has. You see, Mother died when I was born—"

"I'm so sorry. Then you are an only child?"

"Yes. I suppose that is why Father is so protective of me. He won't be completely happy until I'm wed to Stephen."

"And what of you, Annie?" Jason asked, gazing into her eyes. "Will you be happy when you are wed to Stephen?"

She was pensively quiet for a long moment, avoiding his eye. At last, she said carefully, "Mr. Burke, I am glad to help you. But you must realize, as my father has just reminded me, that I am a promised woman."

Jason could not help himself. He reached out to touch her gloved hand—and again, her honey-gold gaze flicked up to his. "Should you need reminding, Annie?"

She did not reply, but Jason noted to his satisfaction a guilty blush staining her cheeks as she pulled away and turned to stare out the window. Jason also took in the passing sights. They were moving through Hyde Park Corner, with its view of the verdant park and the Corinthian columns of Apsley House. Jason stared at the Wellington Arch, complete with a statue of Wellington that had been absent in his own time. He was amazed. He watched a regiment of Royal Horse Guards trot past, on their way to exercises in the park. That particular London tradition had not changed, he mused.

As the coachman turned the conveyance onto Piccadilly, Jason marveled at the throng of coaches and omnibuses that had supplanted the usual cars and double-decker buses. In place of the usual shops and tourist bureaus, a polyglot of Italianate, Georgian, and Regency structures delighted his eyes. He recognized the familiar lines of Burlington House and the Adamesque façade of St. James Hall.

After a moment, Jason turned to see Annie regarding him with an expression of amusement. "What is so funny, Miss Simmons?"

"Your expression," she admitted. "I've never seen anyone so enthralled with the sights and sounds of London. Clearly, this is your first visit."

"In a manner of speaking, it certainly is," Jason concurred.

While she appeared bemused by his cryptic reply, she did not comment directly. "Tell me of your background, Mr. Burke," she suggested.

"Such as?"

"Your family."

He sighed, deciding the truth might best suffice. "They live in the American Midwest, on a farm in Missouri."

"Have you sisters and brothers?"

"Two sisters."

"And do you see your family often?"

"No," he replied almost curtly.

She at once picked up on the tension. "I'm sorry. I did not mean to broach a painful subject."

He flashed her a contrite smile. "I am the one who must apologize for almost biting your head off. It's just that my family and I, we've never thought much alike. My father wanted me to remain in Missouri and help him run the farm."

"While you wanted to seek your fortunes in the big city as a newspaperman?"

He grinned. "You are very perceptive."

"I think that it is often difficult simply to place oneself in a mold created by a parent. I do admire your courage in pursuing your own destiny, Mr. Burke."

"Perhaps you could use a little of that courage yourself, Miss Simmons?" Jason could not help but suggest wryly.

Again, she appeared reluctant to comment, and a new, awkward silence ensued. Glancing out the window, Jason noted that they had headed south, in the general direction of the Thames. They were now passing through Trafalgar Square with its dramatic statue of Nelson, the magnificence of the National Gallery serving as a backdrop, and the breathtaking spire of St. Martin-in-the-Fields just beyond.

Soon, they clattered along the stately Strand, with its three- and four-story Palladian and Tudor buildings, its lovely view of St. Mary-le-Strand to the east, and the panorama of the gleaming, vessel-jammed Thames running parallel to them to the south. The coachman pulled the conveyance to a halt in front of a storefront whose window was emblazoned with "The Bloomsbury Times."

Annie turned to Jason. "This is Mr. Spencer's newspaper."

As the coachman opened the door, Jason hopped out and escorted Annie out of the coach and into the office. They were greeted by a busy cacophony. Jason glanced in amazement at the old Hoe rotary press, which was whirring away, attended by a harried pressman. Various clerks were scribbling at their desks or scurrying about with papers.

Annie led Jason directly to the back office. "Mr. Spencer," she called out from the doorway.

An elderly, bespectacled gentleman with a balding head and a pleasant, round face looked up at them from his desk. "Why, Annie Simmons! Come right in here!"

Tugging Jason along by his sleeve, Annie stepped inside. Smiling brightly, she said, "Mr. Spencer, I'd like you to meet a guest from our hotel. Mr. Jason Burke is a journalist visiting here from America."

Mr. Spencer grinned in obvious approval and stepped forward, extending his hand. "How do you do, young man?"

"Fine, thank you. And I'm most pleased to meet you, sir," Jason replied, shaking Spencer's hand.

"What newspaper do you write for?" Spencer asked.

"I'm a stringer for the *Manhattan Chronicle.*"

Spencer scratched his jaw. "The *Manhattan Chronicle?* Strange, I've never heard of it."

"It's one of the newer—and smaller—newspapers in New York City."

Spencer nodded, then glanced from Jason to Annie. "So what may I do for you two today?"

Annie smiled. "Mr. Spencer, Jason needs a post while he is here in England, and I was wondering—"

"If I can use an extra newsman?" Spencer finished, winking at Annie.

"Yes."

Spencer chuckled, then turned to Jason. "How long are you planning to be in our country, young man?"

282

"I'm not sure—but probably at least through Christmas."

He scowled. "So you are really only looking for a temporary post here?"

Jason glanced at Annie. "It could work into something permanent."

"What kind of writing are you accustomed to doing?"

"All kinds," Jason replied. "Both current events, and lifestyle pieces."

"Lifestyle pieces?" Spencer repeated in confusion.

Realizing his foible in tossing out a decidedly 20th century buzzword, Jason quickly explained, "You know, articles on the way people live in various locales."

"Ah, yes," Spencer murmured.

"Jason is hoping to sell a series on English Christmas traditions to the New York newspaper."

"Hmmmmm." Spencer stroked his jaw thoughtfully. "You know, Charles Dickens has had such success with his *Household Words* magazine. I might also be interested in the type of pieces you are planning to do, Mr. Burke—that is, unless you are already committed on the series to the *Manhattan Chronicle*?"

"No, we have no formal commitment."

"But I think I would want a more personal slant," Spencer went on. "Say, what it feels like for an American to celebrate Christmas in England for the first time."

"I'd be delighted to give it a try, sir," Jason said sincerely.

"Then you are hiring Jason?" Annie cried with delight.

Spencer again winked at Annie, then turned
back to Jason. "Who could resist this Christmas
angel? Tell you what, young man. Come back
by tomorrow, and we shall discuss this matter
further."

"Thank you for helping me," Jason said.
"You are most welcome," Annie replied.

A few moments later, Annie and Jason stood
in the vast main arcade of Covent Garden, amid
stately pillars and high archways lit by gaslights.
They had paused at a fruit stand, where Annie
was selecting bright red apples from a cart piled
high with the gleaming fruit.

Jason was amazed by the sights and sounds
of the market. The huge building teemed with
noisy humanity, from the best-dressed gentleman
shopping to the most raggedy urchin begging
for coins. Shoppers haggled with fruit peddlers
and flower girls, while merchants waved their
wares and shouted to gain the attention of
passersby. Around them swarmed organ grind-
ers with their monkeys, vendors displaying the
newest toys, hawkers with squawking parrots
on their shoulders, pea-shuckers busily at work,
and porters dashing about with baskets on their
heads. Nearby, a group of children were gathered about a puppet show. The myriad booths
displayed everything from fresh and candied
fruits, nuts and spices, to flowers, cut holly,
and even the freshly cut Christmas trees that
Annie told Jason had been made popular by
Queen Victoria's husband, the German Prince
Albert. Despite the chill, a riot of smells laced
the air—everything from cedar and spice to smoke
and garbage.

Annie paid the vendor for her purchases. After the man wrapped the apples in brown paper and twine and handed them to Jason, they strolled on.

"You know, I've been thinking," Annie murmured.

"Yes?"

She flashed him a quick smile. "Well, if you are going to successfully write a series on Yule here in London, you will need to make the rounds and see how we celebrate. My father, Stephen, and I are invited to a number of Christmas gatherings and events—and we would be happy to have you accompany us."

Jason had to laugh. "You are too kind, Miss Annie Simmons," he chided gently. "You might be willing to have me tag along for the revelry—but don't speak for your father or Stephen."

That comment brought a frown to her lovely mouth. "But I cannot imagine either of them being anything but gentlemen about it, under the circumstances. After all, you are a guest who needs our assistance."

Before Jason could comment, Annie paused, smiling down at three ragtag street urchins who were crouched on their haunches, selling flowers. She handed each child tuppence, and the oldest boy popped up, bowing and presenting Annie with a nosegay of violets.

"Thank you dearly, miss," the lad cried in a heavy Cockney accent, a broad smile splitting his thin, smudged face.

Annie touched the boy's filthy hand. "Please, you must keep the flowers."

"Oh, no, miss," he protested. "They is already paid for, good and proper. You must take them."

"Very well, then. God bless you."

"And you, miss."

As Annie and Jason started on, she glanced over her shoulder at the tattered orphans. "It breaks my heart to see the young ones so," she murmured to Jason. "Of course, those stuck at the workhouses have an even worse lot in life. I'm hoping that the reform movement that is sweeping Parliament will help them all."

Jason stared at her for a long moment. "You know, you truly are a remarkable woman."

"Oh, I do not think so," she quickly denied.

"But you are. You think of others constantly, and never of yourself."

"You are exaggerating, I'm sure."

Jason lifted an eyebrow. "I am exaggerating? Let's see—giving money to orphans, inviting me along on your Yule activities." Gazing at her intently, he added meaningfully, "And marrying Stephen to please your father."

She glanced at him quickly. "Is that what you think, Mr. Burke?"

"You all but admitted it earlier."

She fingered the nosegay of flowers. "Well, I must confess that I've never tried to place my own needs first. That seems an exceedingly selfish way to live."

As Annie turned to select some spices at a stand, Jason pondered her reply. In the late 20th century, where selfishness was vogue, Annie's attitude might well be deemed foolish. Here, he found her outlook far too endearing. Again he reflected on how refreshing she was, how different from the self-absorbed women he had known in his time. She was truly an old-fashioned delight. Yet Jason was also left struggling with the reality that

Annie's very self-sacrifice might well prove her undoing—especially if she persisted in her plan to marry Stephen.

Annie made the rest of her purchases, and they left the marketplace together. They headed back toward the Strand, where the coach was parked.

Jason caught Annie's sleeve next to the doorway of a quaint shop with expensive cheeses and hams displayed behind leaded glass windows. "Annie?"

She regarded him shyly. "Yes?"

He smiled. "Thank you for today."

"You are most welcome."

He touched her hand. "Will you think about something for me?"

"What is that?"

Carefully, he said, "I think that sometimes, when we try so hard to please others, we may end up bringing unhappiness not only to ourselves, but to everyone. Do you understand what I'm trying to say?"

She chewed her lower lip. "I suppose."

"Then perhaps you could start thinking of yourself just a little more?"

All at once, Annie would not meet his gaze. She turned her head to watch an elderly couple, laden down with packages, emerge from the shop doorway.

Jason cupped her chin in his fingers, forcing her to look at him. "Annie? What is it?"

With a guilty smile, she admitted, "I'm not above thinking of myself."

"Oh, you're not?" he teased. "In what way?"

Her expression bordered on mischievous as she admitted, "Well, when I invited you to come along for the Yule activities, I was actually being—"

"Yes?"

She gazed up at him raptly and whispered, "Rather selfish."

"Oh, Annie."

Jason would not even notice until later that he had dropped all her packages. With a groan, he pulled her close and kissed her ardently. She did not resist; indeed, he heard a tiny sigh escape her as his mouth claimed hers. Her lips were warm and sweet, trustingly parted, on his. Her softness, her heat, seemed to seep into his very blood as he clutched her tightly and inhaled the heavenly essence of her—lavender and woman. Never had a woman thrilled him so, touched him so deeply, and he cherished her against his hammering heart.

After a moment, he could feel her hands reach around to stroke his back, caressing him, even as her lips eagerly moved against his. Her surrender ignited such a firestorm in his blood that he crushed her to him and thrust between her lips with his tongue. Even as he yearned to plunge deeply into the sweetness of her warm mouth, he felt a shudder rack her and he pulled back, afraid he had gone too far.

For a moment, they stared at each other, both breathless and wide-eyed following the moment of intimacy and discovery. Annie, too, had been left reeling. She felt vulnerable, bewildered, tremendously shaken. Never had any man stirred her as Jason just had with his kiss. She realized that her father had been right. She was behaving imprudently—and couldn't seem to stop herself!

At last, Jason said hoarsely, "I'm sorry. I was out of line, wasn't I?"

Annie didn't answer, but stared up at him with a tenderness and uncertainty that twisted his heart.

He stroked her flushed cheek. "Annie? I just feel you are selling yourself short. I want you to realize that there are other men in this world besides Stephen."

Then he saw the tears brim in her beautiful, golden eyes, and the sorrow and poignancy there lanced him like a knife in the heart.

"Unfortunately," she replied in a voice so low he could barely hear her, "at the moment, there is only one."

Chapter Six

Over the next ten days, Jason became better acclimated to 19th century London. He started his job at the *Bloomsbury Times*, writing nostalgic pieces about the city amidst Yule preparations. While it was an adjustment to write the stories by hand, without the aid of a modern computer, he did have Annie Simmons to thank for the wealth of material he was able to draw upon for his articles. She insisted that Jason be included in all the Yule events she attended with Stephen and her father—much to the exasperation of the two other men, Jason was certain. Yet both Annie's father and her fiancé were obviously consummate British gentlemen whose innate sense of good manners forbade them to exclude the American guest who so obviously needed assistance with his new duties. And Annie often invited along on the excursions an unmarried friend of hers,

Harriet Pierce, whose presence lent a more balanced effect—and no doubt somewhat appeased Stephen regarding Jason's continued presence.

Together, the five attended church, watched bell ringers and mummers perform in the London streets, and delighted at the colorful wares of the toy vendors, as well as the beautiful Christmas cards, greenery, and lovely gifts displayed in the various shop windows. They viewed a glorious pantomime of Aladdin at the Drury Lane Theater, as well as a *tableau vivant* at the Royal Opera House. Jason even helped Annie hand out small mince pies to the jolly carolers who seemed to appear nightly on the stoop of the hotel.

The highlight of the activities for Jason was an evening the five spent at St. James' Hall, hearing Charles Dickens perform a public reading from *A Christmas Carol*. For Jason, never had history so sprung to life before his very eyes than when he watched the stately, energetic author read his own brilliant descriptions of London at Yule. Jason could even feel something of Dickens's message of inspiration and hope seeping into his own blood.

Daily, Jason recorded his observations for the newspaper, in a manner Mr. Spencer found fresh and lively. Annie, too, was thrilled with Jason's progress. One morning at breakfast, with Jason, her father, and the two spinsters present, she read from his new column, "An American in London."

As the others listened and Jason sipped his tea self-consciously, Annie quoted, "This American sees in London a time of great misery, but also a time of great hope. A spirit of reform is sweeping the country, as evidenced by the many fine proposals being presented to Parliament. Yes, there are children slaving away in the factories, or selling flowers for pennies in the markets, but there is also concern and caring. An innkeeper and his daughter took in this stranger from America who arrived here without a farthing in his hand, and with no one to recommend him. Women such as the innkeeper's daughter are busy this season preparing baskets for the poor. This reporter finds here in London a very human time, compared with the impersonal world he left behind. Perhaps Charles Dickens summed it up best when he recently read publicly from *A Christmas Carol*, which is itself a tribute to the redemption of the human spirit. To quote Tiny Tim, 'God bless us, every one.'"

Annie finished her reading and flashed a bright smile at Jason. The two spinsters clapped and oohed and aahed with delight, while Jason tried to hide his embarrassment. Annie's father responded with a subdued nod toward the younger man.

"Your article is splendid, Mr. Burke," exclaimed Media.

"And do you indeed find America much more impersonal compared with Great Britain?" Mary added.

Jason nodded, turning to smile at Annie. "To tell you the truth, America seems a world away right now."

"A world that we are glad you left, so that you can bring us your beautiful insights, Mr. Burke," Annie replied sincerely.

"Well," Annie's father added, clearing his throat, "I am pleased to note that your employment is progressing so well, Mr. Burke."

With reluctance, Jason drew his gaze from Annie and nodded to her father. "And for that, I must thank you and your daughter."

Jason had not again kissed Annie, although he sensed that she felt the same tension and attraction that stirred him each time they were together. Being around her was, in so many ways, torture for him. She was so bright, so full of life and vitality. She seemed to take delight in every minute of the Yule activities. To Jason, she represented all the hope and optimism and zest for life that he himself had lost. He feared he was more than a little in love with her, and he had no way of knowing whether that love would ultimately save her or destroy her. He was frequently tortured by doubt. In wanting to rescue her from Stephen's clutches, was it possible that he was pushing her farther toward disaster—at his own hands?

While Annie was often nearby, she was also frustratingly untouchable. The solid barrier of her engagement to Stephen continued to loom between them. Watching Prescott perpetually hover about her, holding her hand or even kissing her cheek, was almost more than Jason could bear. He remained determined to disabuse Annie of her desire to wed Stephen, but he still wasn't completely sure just how he would accomplish his goal. If only he could arrange for more time alone with her—but, aside from the one excursion they'd taken together, her father, Stephen, or Harriet was always present.

At the same time, Christmas Eve—the very night on which Stephen would supposedly desert Annie, and she might well die—loomed ever closer. A sense of frustration bordering on desperation nagged Jason as he wondered if he could do anything at all to stop the coming disaster. Each time he glanced at the lovely Annie—watched her eyes sparkle with joy, her cheeks dimple with laughter—and then thought of her dead, his blood ran cold. And he could not even resolve to protect her on Christmas Eve, when he had no idea if he would still even be here in Victorian London then. He could not begin to understand the mystical forces that had brought him here—or to know whether, at any moment, he might be swept back to his own time again. Often, he remembered the ominous last line on his invitation, "You'll come back on Christmas Eve."

On an evening a week and a half before Christmas, Annie invited Jason and Harriet to accompany her, Stephen, and her father to a Christmas dinner given by her father's cousin. Using the better part of his weekly wages, Jason bought himself a new black suit for the occasion. Glancing at himself in the mirror, he had to admit that he looked rather dapper in the black cutaway, matching trousers, and ruffled linen shirt. Picking up his silk top hat and ebony walking stick, he felt like an authentic Victorian gentleman.

He went downstairs and paused outside the drawing room at the sound of voices. He could hear Annie and Stephen inside—and clearly, they were arguing.

"Must you drag along Burke again?" he heard Stephen ask irritably. "He is behaving rather like a stray dog who refuses to quit following us about."

"Why, Stephen, what a cruel thing to say!" Annie cried. "Mr. Burke is our guest. He is a newcomer from America, with no contacts in London, and he needs our help. Haven't you read his marvelous articles in the *Bloomsbury Times* each day? Why, if we hadn't taken him about with us, he never could have published those articles— or provided for his own livelihood."

"Why do I have the feeling that you are far more fascinated with the man than with his writing?"

"Stephen, that is simply not the case. And you are sounding jealous."

"I am jealous!"

"Mr. Burke may only be here for a fortnight longer. You and I will marry in the spring, and then we will be together. In the meantime—"

"In the meantime," Jason heard Stephen cut in, "I must remind you that I have no one else in my life—not even a casual lady friend. I'm simply asking the same level of devotion and commitment from you."

As Annie and Stephen continued to bicker, Jason silently seethed with anger. Oh, the cad, he thought, feeling incredulous over Stephen's lie. How could Prescott claim to Annie that he had "not even a lady friend," when the scoundrel kept a mistress on the side? How could he blatantly deceive Annie, then demand that she end her friendship with him?

Silence had fallen in the parlor, and Jason, fearing that Stephen was kissing Annie, felt jealousy shoot through him. He strode into the room, only to draw a breath of relief. The two were yards apart. Stephen stood scowling with his elbow resting on the fireplace mantel, while Annie had wandered over to pick up a small doll ornament that had fallen off the Christmas tree.

"Good evening," Jason said, flashing a cheery smile to both. "Are we ready to leave?"

Annie, looking gorgeous in a green silk evening dress with a low neckline and gigot sleeves, turned to smile a greeting at Jason. "Of course, Mr. Burke. And don't you look dashing. Father should be down any moment now, and then we shall all go pick up Harriet."

"Great," Jason said.

"Ah, yes, splendid," Stephen added with a sneer. "There is nothing I like better than courting my fiancée by committee."

The four left the hotel in Stephen's elegant custom coach. Heading into the city, they crossed London Bridge to the South Bank and picked up Harriet Pierce at her parents' charming Queen Anne town house on St. Thomas Street. Harriet, a vivacious creature with dark brown hair and green eyes, took the only remaining seat, next to Jason—and then greeted one and all with effusive hellos.

"Well, I must tell you, dears," Harriet said brightly as the carriage rattled off, "I have been running myself ragged today on Bond Street, trying to complete my Christmas shopping." She smiled at Stephen. "Mr. Prescott, I simply must get by your haberdashery to get Papa a new cravat."

"We have some very nice silks, just in from the Orient," Stephen replied.

"Oh, and Papa does so love those fancy things." She turned her glowing smile on Jason. "And what of you, Mr. Burke? Have you gotten around to Bond Street as yet? If you need more background material for your series of articles on our city, I should be delighted to assist you in any way."

Jason smiled at the young woman. Harriet was lively and pretty, and he suspected she was already rather enamored of him. The problem was, she wasn't Annie. He did often wonder why Annie so frequently included Harriet in their outings— and he fervently hoped it was to appease Stephen regarding his own presence, rather than to interest him romantically.

"You are very kind," Jason murmured.

"Why don't the three of us go over to Bond Street tomorrow afternoon?" Annie suggested. "I've shopping to complete myself—then we could go by Stephen's haberdashery, and perhaps the four of us could have tea together."

"Ah, a wonderful idea," agreed Harriet, clapping her hands.

Stephen, meanwhile, scowled darkly, but was evidently too much of a gentleman to veto Annie's suggestion.

They soon arrived at the home of Oscar Simmons's cousin, Catherine Holcomb, who lived with her husband, William, in a modest Georgian town home in the East End. Yet, while the Albert Gardens address was unpretentious, the cozy home was as festively decked out for Yule as the most lavish mansion in Regent's Park. As Catherine and her husband received Jason and the others, he glanced about the hallway, which was festooned with holly, and decorated with the traditional candlelit "kissing bunch" suspended over their heads, as well as angels, tambourines, trumpets, a gingerbread house, and a Nativity scene gracing the various tables.

Several other family friends, as well as Jason's employer, Mr. Spencer, had been invited for the dinner, which was held in the homey, paneled dining room. The table was set with the finest Irish linen and Paris china. A boar's head, stuffed with an orange, served as the centerpiece. The main course was roast turkey with chestnut stuffing, served with fresh vegetables, hot bread, and white wine. By each plate, the hostess had placed a "Christmas cracker" for the guests. The crackers were rolled cylinders of colorful paper cinched near each end. The cylinders made a loud popping sound when pulled apart, and the laughing guests cracked them open to find tiny treasures—toys, small bells, paper flowers, or hats. Annie exclaimed over the paper rose found in hers, while Jason was amused by the paper crown in his.

The conversation was convivial, several of the guests congratulating Annie and Stephen on their engagement. While Stephen and Annie accepted the fond wishes graciously, Jason noted a mood of tension between them that had been present ever since they had all left the house in Stephen's carriage. There was mention of the current clash in Parliament over Disraeli's new budget, and the rumors that even the queen and Prince Albert were growing concerned over the escalating crisis.

Several of the people complimented Jason on his recent articles. Their host, William Holcomb, said to Jason, "Mr. Spencer here tells me that you may not be staying long here in England."

Jason nodded. "That is true."

"But your pieces in the *Bloomsbury Times* are fascinating," put in Catherine, "and you seem to favor this country over your own. Have you not considered staying here permanently?"

298

Before Jason could answer, Stephen cut in rather sardonically, "Perhaps Mr. Burke might better seek his fortune back in his own country. It is not that easy making a life for oneself here on a newspaperman's salary." He glanced meaningfully at Harriet, then at Annie. "I should think that if Mr. Burke remained here, he could never hope to support a wife and children."

Harriet, not about to be baited, winked at Stephen and said, "I should wager that Mr. Burke feels as I do. Why worry about being rich if one can be happy?"

The guests seemed to agree. A couple even murmured, "Hear, hear," and raised their glasses.

Then, with a twinkle in his eye, Mr. Spencer spoke up to Stephen. "You know, you might be speaking precipitously, Mr. Prescott." He nodded proudly to Jason. "As talented as young Burke is, and as old as I'm getting, I wouldn't be at all surprised to see him running the *Bloomsbury Times* before too long."

At this pronouncement, both Annie and Harriet beamed at Jason, and he grinned back at both. As other appreciative murmurs drifted down the table, Jason could have sworn that he heard Stephen's jaw grinding.

After a lavish dessert of plum pudding served with hard sauce, the guests gathered in the parlor to sing the traditional carols—"The Holly and the Ivy" and "Silent Night"—while Catherine accompanied the hymns on the piano. Soon, Stephen suggested that their hostess play a few waltzes so the guests could dance. As the others looked on raptly, Stephen waltzed Annie about the parlor to the strains of a Chopin waltz. Old Mr. Spencer joined in with his wife, and Jason dutifully asked Harriet.

Staring at Stephen's smug smile as he held Annie close and whirled her about, Jason knew that Prescott was deliberately staging a scene, trying to prove a point. Meanwhile, Harriet tried to make pleasant conversation with Jason, but he responded in distracted monosyllables. When the music stopped, he muttered an apology to her, strode up to Annie, and bowed before her.

"May I have this dance?"

Annie glanced questioningly at Stephen.

"By all means," Stephen muttered less-than-graciously.

Jason was chuckling as he drew Annie in his arms and swept her about to a Strauss waltz. He felt deeply thrilled to be close to her—to watch the light play over the beautiful honey-brown curls piled on her head, to see her eyes sparkling with gaiety, her pink lips curving with happiness.

Jason glanced at Stephen, who stood scowling formidably at the side of the room. Teasingly, he confided to Annie, "Stephen was too much of a gentleman to refuse my request, but I'll bet he would like to call me out about now."

She dimpled. "Oh, he will get over it."

Jason felt a frown drift in. "I heard the two of you arguing earlier. It was over me, wasn't it?"

She shot a furtive glance at Stephen, then murmured, "Please, you must not concern yourself. It will pass."

"If I were truly unselfish," Jason admitted, "I would stop going out with all of you, in deference to Stephen." In a huskier tone, he finished, "But where you are concerned, my lovely Miss Simmons, I'm afraid I find myself feeling more selfish with each passing day."

Seemingly amazed, Annie stared up at him.

"I was wondering something earlier," Jason went on.

"And what is that?"

He nodded toward Harriet, who was laughing as she sipped eggnog with Oscar. "Do you keep inviting Harriet along for my sake, or to keep Stephen off-guard?"

She paled. "What do you mean?"

Jason pulled Annie slightly closer. Inhaling the sweet, feminine scent of her, he stared down into her wide, vibrant eyes. "Do you want Harriet along to distract me, or as a foil to distract Stephen from the fact that I'm interested in you?"

Appearing flustered, Annie responded, "I—I want Harriet along because she is my friend."

Her nearness, even her endearing confusion, were playing havoc with Jason's senses and his good judgment. Leaning toward Annie's ear, he whispered, "Do you want Harriet to distract me, Annie?"

Now she appeared adorably flustered, avoiding his gaze and stammering, "I—I'm not sure."

"Or is it you who is in need of a buffer?" he pressed on. "Do you like having your friend along because I make you feel things you'd rather not feel?"

"Perhaps," she admitted in a whisper.

"Doesn't that tell you something?"

She glanced up, frowning slightly. "What do you mean?"

"I don't think you should marry Stephen."

"And why not?"

"I just don't think he is right for you. I sense something false about him."

She smiled quizzically. "And are you offering an alternative, Mr. Burke?"

"Jason."

"Jason."

"Why must there be an alternative?" he argued. "Why should your life revolve around any man?"

She shook her head slowly. "Mr. Burke, now you are toying with me."

"In what way?"

"You want me to feel things, don't you?" she challenged passionately. "Feelings for you. But it is a game to you. You are hardly prepared to follow through with any kind of commitment, are you?"

Jason could only groan. "Annie, I'm sorry. There are complications—problems I can't tell you about. I don't know how long I'll be allowed to stay in England." With both fervor and uncertainty, he added, "But even if I were prepared to follow through, would you break things off with Stephen?"

"I—I don't know," she admitted honestly.

"I just don't want to see you selling yourself short for the sake of your father—or simply to have a home and security."

"Simply to have a home and security?" Her laugh was incredulous. "But Mr. Burke—"

"Jason."

"Jason." Earnestly, she said, "My purpose in life has always been to have a home and a husband—and children."

Jason stared at her—so determined, so naive, so beautiful. All at once, he desperately wanted to have all those things—with her.

It was hard for him to speak, but at last he said, "If such is your heart's desire, then I think you should pursue it. But with a finer man than Stephen."

She laughed. "You are saying I am too good for him?"

"Oh, yes."

"And what of you, Mr. Burke?" All at once, she took the offense, smiling and edging slightly closer to him. "Am I too good for you as well? Will you not be pleased until you see me canonized?"

Jason broke into a grin. "Miss Simmons—"

"Annie," she corrected.

"Annie, you are teasing me. That can be perilous."

"And I would like an answer."

As they spoke, Jason had maneuvered Annie out into the hallway. He glanced over their heads and pulled her to a halt, suddenly feeling quite devilish.

Nodding toward the ceiling, he murmured, "Isn't this the kissing bunch you once told me about?"

"Did I?" She stared up at him raptly.

He lowered his face toward hers and whispered, "What I have in mind for you, Miss Simmons, hardly involves canonization."

Jason pulled sweet Annie closer and kissed her. He moaned as the taste of her lips excited him unbearably. He crushed her to him and pressed his tongue hungrily against her wet, warm lips. She opened to him eagerly and Jason reeled with desire. She tasted so delicious, and felt so vital, so soft and warm in his arms. His heart pounded with the need to possess her. He could have devoured her on the spot. He realized she was perfect for him—his old-fashioned lady. He ached to make her his, forever.

Annie was equally mesmerized by Jason's kiss. It seemed like forever since he had held her thus, and his male strength, his scent, the heat of his mouth, set her senses aflame. She realized achingly that she had been deluding herself about Stephen. Never had any man excited her as Jason Burke did!

"What have we here?" demanded an angry voice.

At the sound of Stephen's harsh question, Annie and Jason sprang apart like lovers caught in the act. They turned to confront a furious Stephen, a scowling Oscar, and a white-faced Harriet, all of whom now stood beyond them in the hallway.

Not giving Jason a chance to reply, Stephen stepped forward and grabbed Annie's arm. "I think it is time for all of us to leave."

"But, Stephen," she protested, glancing helplessly from her fiancé to Jason, "you mustn't become angry at Jason. The kissing bunch is a Christmas tradition here in England—"

"That we'll all doubtless read about in Burke's article in the *Bloomsbury Times* tomorrow?" Stephen cut in furiously. He hurled a glare at Jason. "Mr. Burke, I think Miss Simmons has taught you quite enough about Yule customs here in England. Learn whatever else you need to know from someone else besides my fiancée!"

As Stephen led her off, Annie could not protest further. Jason helped Harriet into her cloak, and the five proceeded back to the Simmons Hotel in tense silence.

Half an hour later, after Stephen dropped Jason, Annie, and Oscar off at the Simmons

Hotel, Annie's father turned to Jason in the downstairs hallway.

"Mr. Burke," he said coldly, "you are no longer welcome to stay at this hotel."

Annie was aghast. "Father, how can you say such a thing?"

But Jason held up a hand. "Annie, it's all right." He turned to Oscar. "You are right, sir. I acted out of line tonight, and for that, I must apologize. I have also imposed on your family quite long enough. I will settle up accounts with you in the morning and seek lodgings elsewhere."

"Very good," Oscar said gruffly.

Meanwhile, Annie threw her father a look of confusion, hurt, and anger, and rushed off up the stairs.

Jason watched her helplessly, then turned to Oscar, who had also watched his daughter's flight with an expression of anguish.

"I didn't mean anything by my actions, sir," he reiterated. "I suppose I simply became caught up in the spirit."

"And in setting Prescott in his place after he insulted you at dinner?" Oscar finished with biting cynicism. "He was right, you know."

"What do you mean?"

Oscar regarded Jason with contempt. "You would never make my daughter a proper husband. You are an American upstart, a drifter. Stephen is a successful haberdasher, and well-established in this community."

"And you think he is what Annie needs?"

"Yes! Leave my daughter alone! You have taken advantage of her kindnesses quite long enough. Stephen Prescott is the right man for her."

Chapter Seven

The next morning, feeling dispirited, Jason packed his few meager belongings, settled up his account with Annie's father, and then left the Simmons Hotel. He let a room at a boarding house near St. James. He did not see Annie for several days, and he felt at something of a loss regarding her. He still very much wanted to protect her, but he did not want to cause her pain, or especially, to provoke an alienation between her and her father. Oscar Simmons obviously remained convinced that Stephen was the right man for Annie.

Jason sensed disaster hovering closer to Annie with each day that passed. He agonized about how he might help her in the scant days remaining before tragedy would surely strike her. Worse yet, he continued to experience the nagging fear that he might be snatched away from his new existence on Christmas Eve—and what would happen to Annie if he couldn't alter her destiny before then?

Then surprisingly, on a morning a week before Christmas, Annie appeared at the newspaper office. He glanced up to see her standing in front of his desk, dressed in a cloak, bonnet, and muffler, with her cheeks bright pink from the cold.

The sight of her filled him with both joy and relief. He stood and smiled. "Why, Annie. What a pleasant surprise."

"Are you doing well, Jason?" she asked awkwardly.

"Yes, of course."

"We haven't seen much of you since you moved out of the hotel."

He sighed. "Annie, you know how it has been with your father and Stephen."

"Are you getting settled in your new surroundings?"

"Yes—I like my room in the boarding house near St. James. I have a nice view of Westminster Abbey." Catching her dismayed expression, he quickly added, "Still, it is not the same as the Simmons Hotel."

She smiled. "Jason, I've come by to invite you to go on an excursion with me, my father, and Stephen tomorrow."

"Annie . . ." Helplessly, he shook his head. "I can't be responsible for causing any more bad feelings."

"But you must come along this time!" she protested. "You see, our friends the Youngbloods have invited us to a gathering at their farmhouse in the country. In her note, Mrs. Youngblood specifically urged us to bring you along as well. This would be the perfect opportunity for you to do research on how an English country Christmas is celebrated. Not only that, but Father has hired a sleigh and coachman for the occasion. It's a fairly long drive, so we'll be gone from before noon until the wee hours of the morning."

Jason felt very tempted, but he was also feeling skeptical. "What about your father and Stephen? What are their feelings on this?"

She lifted her chin. "They have both consented to your coming along."

Jason was astounded. "They have? But why?"

Annie glanced away, avoiding his probing gaze.

"Annie?" He grinned. "What did you do—apply the thumbscrews?"

She giggled, then flashed him a conspiratorial smile. "Really, Jason, such extreme measures were hardly necessary. I know Father feels badly for so precipitously banning you from the hotel following Cousin Catherine's dinner party, and I think I have managed to convince Stephen that he, too, overreacted to our kiss that night."

"You have?"

She flashed him a near-impish smirk. "And besides, I warned both Father and Stephen that I would not attend the Youngbloods' gathering unless you were included."

"Annie! You didn't!"

"I did," she admitted unrepentantly. "When I pointed out to them both that it would be the height of ill manners to exclude you when you could write about the occasion in the *Bloomsbury Times*, they both finally relented."

Jason shook his head. "My, you are determined. And count on a British gentleman ultimately to bow to good manners in all things." Rather hesitantly, he added, "What about Harriet?"

Annie sighed. "I invited her as well, but she claims to have a touch of the ague. However, I suspect that in reality—"

"Yes?"

She regarded him with mingled sadness and longing. "That Harriet is quite taken with you, Jason, and that she misinterpreted what she saw beneath the kissing bunch."

He felt a stab of regret. "Oh, Annie. I've been meaning to send her a note of apology." He reached out to stroke her soft cheek. "But was it a misinterpretation on Harriet's part, or did she simply view the truth, and find that too painful?"

Annie glanced away, obviously acutely discomfited.

"I'm sorry," Jason hastily added. "I didn't mean to put you on the spot. It's just that . . ." His voice trailed off as he stared at her wistfully. "I really can't offer Harriet any encouragement."

"Oh, Jason," Annie whispered, staring at him with equal yearning. Before he could comment further, she added quickly, "Will you come with us tomorrow?"

He frowned. "You are very kind-hearted, but I fear my being along will cast a pall over the entire occasion."

"Nonsense," Annie said briskly. She regarded him with touching tenderness. "Besides, I've missed you."

Jason felt bittersweet emotion twisting his own heart, and could not contain the fervency of his reply. "Oh, Annie. I've missed you, too."

*   *   *

The visit to the Youngbloods' farm did turn out to be a strained occasion in many ways. The sleigh ride saw the group divided into separate camps— Jason seated on one side, with Stephen, Oscar, and Annie on the other. Their journey passed mostly in silence.

Jason did enjoy the sights and sounds of the sleigh ride—the cold wind and the flakes of snow in his face, the jingling of the horse's harnesses and the sounds of the coachman's shouts to the team as they glided over the Great West Road toward Chiswick. The countryside was a fairyland—trees swathed with snow and dripping with icicles, farmhouses winking with warm, welcoming lights in their windows, smoke curling from their chimneys.

The Youngblood farmstead was equally picturesque. The roofs of the farmhouse, as well as the barn, well house, dairy, and dovecote, were caked with snow. The paths, corrals, and fields lay blanketed in deep drifts.

Jason and the others stamped their feet against the cold as they made their way to the door of the Tudor cottage with its high-pitched roof.

A smiling John Youngblood, with pipe in hand, greeted them and beckoned them inside. "Come in out of the cold, all of you."

Jason was amazed by the rustic farmhouse, with its soaring sawn timber roof, puncheon floor, and rustic country furnishings. The large main room swarmed with people, and the scene was one of near-chaotic revelry. John and Emma Youngblood had six children ranging in age from two to twelve, and the couple had also invited over friends from neighboring farms. At least a dozen youngsters scurried about, laughing and shouting, half of them playing a wild game of hoop-and-hide, while the others were chasing down a quartet of frisky kittens that bounded about everywhere, knocking over baskets of fruit, climbing the pants legs of guests, and chewing on the furniture. The smell of baking bread curled out from the bake oven, mingling with the aromas of spiced ham, sweet potatoes, steaming cabbage, and stewing pears that drifted out from the kitchen. On the open hearth, a crane supported a stock pot, steaming with mutton stew, and a whistling tea kettle.

Annie made a point of introducing Jason to everyone and explaining about the series of articles he was writing. A couple of the farmers really warmed to the subject, spinning yarns of Christmas memories from their childhood. Jason noted that Stephen made a point of trying to keep Annie out of reach of his American rival as much as possible. He also noticed Prescott drinking generous portions of the apple cider one of the farmers had brought along.

Dinner was a sumptuous feast. The adults were served at the large table before the blazing fire, while the children sat near the hearth with plates in their laps. Jason found the ham wonderfully spiced and flavored with oranges, the sweet potatoes delectable with their brandy glaze, the cabbage delicious with its tang of apples and thyme. The conversation was lively, especially when Oscar Simmons informed the others of the rumors of the pending resignation of the earl of Derby's ministry. There was much speculation regarding what coalition the queen might now form to run the country. Then the discussion turned more provincial, with the farmers voicing their hopes for an early spring, while the children down on the hearth whispered excitedly about the coming of Father Christmas. The kittens, meanwhile, were also feasting, having found their way back to their basket on the hearth, and to their mother's milk.

Throughout the meal, Jason had to struggle not to stare at Annie. She sat across from him next to Stephen, looking so beautiful with the fire dancing highlights in her hair and gleaming in her eyes. The shy smiles she occasionally cast his way made his heart ring with joy as he realized that she was indeed very happy that he had come along. Meanwhile, Stephen, seated beside her, looked on broodingly and paid much more attention to his cider than to the meal.

As Mrs. Youngblood was serving up the dessert of mince and pumpkin pie, the Youngblood baby awakened, wailing loudly in her cradle across the room. Annie hastened to go get the child and rock her. Jason could not take his eyes off her as she rocked the infant and hummed her the sweet, lulling strains of "The Coventry Carol." At that moment, watching Annie made him want desperately so many things that seemed forbidden to him here—a wife, a home, children of his own—the very things he had once scoffed back in the present. He realized that the spirit of Christmas, of family, hope, and joy, was in his soul tonight, even as his love for Annie was burning in his heart. And it seemed incredible to him that only two weeks past, he had been an unmitigated cynic who had greeted the 20th century Yule celebration with Ebenezer Scrooge's typical "Bah, humbug."

After the dishes had been cleared and the baby put back in her cradle, Mrs. Youngblood suggested that they all play games. The men arranged chairs in a circle, and adults and children alike played several riotous rounds of Hot Cockles and Hide the Slipper. The atmosphere grew really rowdy during the game of blindman's buff. Jason was even impelled to spring up and grab a rambunctious, blindfolded child who was charging about dangerously close to the fire.

As the guests were laughing, taking a break from the games to sip berry wine, John Youngblood glanced at Jason and said, "Perhaps our guest from America would like to suggest a game."

Jason pondered that a moment, then grinned and snapped his fingers. "How about charades?"

Several of the guests murmured their approval, while Stephen piped up in a slurred voice, "We do not play French games here, Mr. Burke."

Mr. Youngblood waved Stephen off. "Oh, nonsense, Mr. Prescott. I think we need not tremble in fear of Louis-Napoléon tonight. Indeed, England may prove the emperor's ally in his dispute with the Russians." He nodded to Jason. "A game of charades sounds splendid, Mr. Burke."

Oscar Simmons volunteered to be scorekeeper, and Jason suggested that the theme of the game be famous couples from history—an idea heralded with great enthusiasm by the others. Mr. Youngblood paired the guests off into two groups, and Jason was thrilled when he and Annie ended up on the same side, opposite the group that included Stephen.

Much fun followed. Two of the children did a splendid job of portraying Martha and George

Washington—the boy pretending to chop down a cherry tree while the girl went through the motions of washing. Mr. and Mrs. Youngblood sent the guests into gales of laughter as they portrayed Antony and Cleopatra, especially when Mrs. Youngblood performed a wildly histrionic version of the queen's death by an asp bite.

Jason's group selected him and Annie to do the next charade. He whispered a suggestion in her ear, and she nodded happily. Taking her hand, he led her across the room to the Youngbloods' candlelit Christmas tree, which sat resplendent on a small table near the window. He extended his arm as if to present the glittering, star-topped spruce to her. He then went down on one knee and kissed her hand, while she affected a pleased, if imperious, pose.

"Queen Victoria and Prince Albert!" one of the children cried.

Before Annie and Jason could even turn to confirm the correct guess, a red-faced Stephen came charging across the room and literally yanked Annie away from Jason.

"Keep your damned hands off my fiancée!" he blazed to Jason.

A collective gasp of horror rippled over the room, followed by a terrible silence. Jason shot to his feet and glowered at Stephen; this time the man had gone too far! When he glanced at Annie, he found to his dismay that she appeared mortified and very hurt.

Oscar Simmons rose and came over to join them. Seeming to recognize that Stephen was indeed out of control, he laid his hand on the younger man's shoulder and said quietly, "Stephen, you are letting the cider speak for you. This is only a game. Mr. Burke meant no harm."

Stephen hurled a contemptuous glance at Jason. "It is far more than a game to him and we all know it. He is playing for keeps!"

While Annie trembled with hurt and outrage, Oscar continued to speak to Stephen in low, firm tones. "This is not a matter to be settled here, in front of everyone. You will not embarrass us in front of our friends—nor will you humiliate my daughter this way."

Stephen seemed to remember himself then. He nodded resignedly to Oscar, then turned to Annie. "I'm sorry. Perhaps this time I overreacted."

Annie glared at Stephen and said nothing.

Oscar turned to address John Youngblood. "John, we've had a splendid evening, but we do have a long drive back to London."

"You could stay the night—we have plenty of room," Emma offered generously.

"Thank you, but we really must get back."

The foursome rode back to London, again divided into separate companies—Annie, Oscar, and Stephen sitting across from Jason. The night had grown bitterly cold, with a thousand bright stars glittering in the clear black skies above them. All four passengers were covered with many layers of quilts. Soon, both Stephen and Oscar drifted off to sleep, and Annie and Jason were the only ones awake. They stared at each other achingly, their stark faces illuminated by the silvery light of the moon.

To Jason, it was as if no one else in the world existed but the two of them. He watched in anguish as a tear trickled down Annie's cheek.

The sight of her sorrow seemed to drive a lance deep into his very heart.

"Sweetheart, please don't cry," he whispered tormentedly.

"I'm going to break off my engagement with Stephen," she whispered back, choking on a sob.

Jason could not help himself then. Staring at her with his heart in his eyes, he said, "Darling, come here."

Even as she was drawing back the quilts, Jason was reaching out for her, drawing her across the sleigh and into his lap. He covered her with the quilts, cuddled her close, and then his ravenous lips took hers.

Their kiss blazed like fire in the freezing cold night. Jason devoured Annie's mouth, plunging deep with his tongue, possessing and savoring her. She clung to him and kissed him back with equal ardor. To Annie, the moment was pure paradise—this man was everything she wanted, her destiny. She felt a part of him, as if they were truly one, inseparable. Jason, too, felt the love, the deep bond between them, and only wished he could hold her this way forever.

At last their lips parted on a sigh. He kissed away the tears on her cool cheek and slipped his gloved hand inside her cloak, pressing it to her slender waist.

"You were right about Stephen," she said brokenly. "He is shallow. He is a cad."

Jason felt guilt assailing him. "He is a man who feels threatened on a very basic level. He fears that another man is trying to steal his woman."

"Are you?" she asked achingly, lifting her brimming gaze to him.

"Oh, God, Annie, when you look at me that way . . ."

"Are you?"

A long, thorough kiss followed before he could answer. "I'm afraid I am," he admitted with a groan. "And I can't say I wouldn't react much the same as Stephen under similar circumstances."

"I know why Stephen got angry tonight," she said poignantly. "He saw the way I looked at you."

"Oh, Annie." Jason's voice was agonized. "Darling, you are making the right decision about Stephen. He is wrong for you. But please do not make this about me. It mustn't be because of me."

"But it is," she cried. "How can it be otherwise?"

"Annie, please, I could hurt you," he pleaded. "I may not be able to stay here—"

"I don't care! I want to be with you now, even if I must lose you later. I think I'm falling—"

"No, don't say it," Jason implored. "Please, you mustn't say it."

But she *would* say it—and thus Jason silenced her the only way he could, kissing her again and again and again, until both of them were feverish with desire.

Chapter Eight

A couple of days passed for Jason, and Christmas was now only five days away. Memories of the glorious time he and Annie had spent kissing and caressing in the sleigh continued to haunt him. He knew he was in love with her, and the anguish of his newfound love was tearing him apart. He kept telling himself that he had accomplished his purpose; he had convinced Annie to reject Stephen. Now he need not worry that Stephen might somehow hurt her on Christmas Eve, and thereby precipitate her death.

As for himself and Annie, as much as he missed her, he rationalized that it would be best if he put a halt to their budding relationship; otherwise, he might well risk becoming the man who would destroy her, especially if what he suspected came true, and he was somehow whisked back to the present on Christmas Eve. He had put into effect the delicate balance he had sought—now he had best leave well enough alone.

Only Annie would not give up on him. When she came by the newspaper office to invite him out for tea, it broke his heart to refuse her, to tell her that he was too busy. When she sent him a letter—a bewildered note asking him why he was avoiding her—he managed to restrain himself from rushing to her at once.

But then he came home from work one evening to find her sitting in his room!

Jason was mystified as he walked inside his room and saw Annie seated across from him in a chair by the window. A pale golden light spilled in from outside, outlining her lovely form. She had removed her cloak, bonnet, and gloves, and she looked so beautiful in her blue velvet dress, with her shining hair piled on top of her head. Her features mirrored a stark anguish that slashed at his heart, and it took all Jason's self-control not to rush over and pull her into his arms, crush her to his heart.

"What are you doing here?" he cried.

She rose and came over to stand before him. "I had to see you again, Jason."

"But how did you get in?"

She smiled. "I convinced the landlady that I am your cousin from Kent."

Jason clenched his fists helplessly. "Annie, you shouldn't have done that. You shouldn't be here."

An anguished cry escaped her. "Why are you treating me this way—so coldly, so cruelly? Ever since we went to the country, you've been like a stranger."

He avoided her bewildered gaze. "Annie, I'm sorry, but I just feel that it is best if we don't see each other."

"Then why have you stolen my heart as you have?" she cried.

"Oh, Annie." As much as Jason knew he was doing the right thing, the raw anguish on her face clawed at him and he could only hate himself in that moment.

"You have gotten your way now," she went on in a tortured voice. "I have broken things off with Stephen. Yet still you are holding yourself apart from me! Why, Jason? Is it because you know you must leave?"

"Yes, I doubt I can even stay beyond Christmas." He touched her cheek gently. "And I simply cannot face hurting you."

"But don't you know that you are hurting me terribly now, this very moment?"

When he saw her tears, it was more than Jason could bear. He pulled her into his arms. His lips took hers with ravenous need.

"Oh, Jason, Jason," she whispered, kissing his chin, his neck. "Please say you are mine. Please love me, if only for today."

Fighting for control, he broke away. "Annie . . . My God, we mustn't! You simply don't understand. What I feel for you could well doom you, destroy you."

"I don't believe that!" she cried, stepping forward and wrapping her arms about his waist. "I could never believe that your feelings could harm me in any way. And furthermore, I don't care."

He groaned in agony as her nearness battered his resolve. Helplessly, he stroked her hair. "You simply have no idea of the forces at work here.

Somehow, I must make you understand."

"Understand that you have my heart," she whispered, staring up at him with tear-filled eyes. "That is all that matters now."

When Annie stretched on tiptoe to kiss him so sweetly, so trustingly, Jason's control snapped. His mouth ravished hers and his fingers pulled the pins from her hair. At the back of his mind, he knew that he was surely giving in to madness, but he didn't care. All at once, nothing mattered to him but this moment, this woman he loved with all his heart. Surely what he felt could not hurt her—what he felt seemed so strong, so right. In his anguished soul, he knew that he would soon leave her, perhaps lose her forever. But they would be together now, today, in every way. And he would cherish that memory in his heart for the rest of his life.

He swept her up into his arms and carried her to the bed. He fell on her, covering her face with hot kisses, and she laughed with joy, kissing him back and hugging his neck.

"Oh, Jason! I knew you felt as I do! I just knew it!" she cried exultantly.

"Oh, Annie, Annie," he cried hoarsely, his lips against her lovely throat. "We really shouldn't. But you are right, my darling—you truly are in my heart, and I cannot resist you!"

Jason's mouth claimed hers voraciously, while his fingers worked at the tiny pearl buttons at her bodice, then undid the ties of her corset and camisole. She responded with equal fervor, pulling loose his cravat and undoing the studs on his shirt. He moaned as her warm fingertips caressed his muscled chest; she sighed as his hand cupped her firm, warm breast. When his lips and tongue followed to tease her nipple to unbearable tautness, she cried out with delight and dug her fingernails into his strong shoulders.

Again, they kissed ardently, making love with their lips and tongues until their mouths felt melded. Jason pulled off Annie's dress and petticoats, then pulled back to stare at her in her lacy camisole and bloomers. Desire roared through his veins, settling in his loins with tortured intensity. Never had she looked so irresistible, so adorable! Her honey-brown hair cascaded in lush waves about her face and shoulders. Her eyes were dark, large with passion, her cheeks hotly flushed, her lips wet and bruised by his kisses. Her breasts were bared, the beautifully rounded globes rising and falling so sweetly as she sucked in her breath in ragged gasps—gasps of desire for him!

The sight of her—wanting him, open to him—excited him beyond reason. "Oh, Annie," he whispered with rough ardor. "I wonder how I have ever managed to resist you!"

She smiled and stretched upward to press her lips to his chest, and violent spasms of need consumed him. He covered her breasts and her stomach with kisses, then raked his hungry gaze lower, reaching down to untie the ribbon at the waist of her bloomers. He felt her trembling and pressed his hand to her belly, caressing gently as he stared into her fevered eyes. He burned to join himself with her, but first took a moment to kiss her tenderly as he slipped his fingers inside her bloomers and stroked the warm center of her.

When he heard her soft cry of passion, when he felt her wetness, it was more than he could bear. His heart was pounding with his obsession to possess her, and he was aroused far past endurance. He positioned himself over her, pressing the heat of his chest to her warm breasts, and the hot steel of him to her tenderest parts. She moaned and arched against him eagerly.

Jason's control broke. His mouth took hers, smothering her low sob as he moved to embed his rigid length in the warm tightness of her. The fiery rapture of possessing her was like nothing he had ever felt before—exquisite pleasure. All of him became a building explosion centered in her heat. He felt her tense with pain as he broke through her maidenhead, and he murmured an apology into her mouth. When he felt her relax to take his deep thrust, he could have wept with joy.

Indeed, Annie was heedless of the pain as she felt Jason move deep to possess her. Her heart was brimming with the overwhelming joy that at last, he was hers. Never had she known such shattering, beauteous ecstasy as she did with his hard, hot body crushing into hers, his mouth fusing with hers, and the solid length of him at once tearing her apart and making them one. When he began to move gently within her, she encouraged him with wild, wanton kisses. He quickened his pace, impelling her to cry out and arch upward to meet him, until both of them were hurled into the searing cataclysm of rapture. They clung to each other as the powerful waves of ecstasy propelled them ever closer, ever deeper into each other's bodies and hearts.

A long moment later, Jason gently withdrew from Annie and stared down at her with concern. "Are you all right, darling?"

"Wonderful," came her joyous reply as she kissed him.

Though he kissed her back with equal fervor, inwardly, Jason was already feeling bedeviled by guilt and doubt, especially as Annie lay beneath him—so beautiful, so vulnerable, so fragile—and bound to him by the wondrous joining they had just known. Releasing her, he sat up in bed and raked his fingers through his hair.

Oh, Lord, what had he done? He had placed his own needs, his passion to possess her, over her best interests. He feared that Annie was falling in love with him. He knew he was in love with her, and he had no way of knowing whether that love would bless her or doom her. What if they did become involved in an intense love affair and then he was whisked back to the present on Christmas Eve? Would he be the one who would end up hurting her badly, and even causing her death? He had to consider what was best for her and act accordingly—as painful as it might be for him.

She sat up next to him, touching his shoulder. "Jason, what is it?" When he didn't answer, she added, "Don't tell me you already regret our lovemaking?"

At once he was contrite. He pulled her into his arms. "Of course not, darling. Get dressed now. We must talk."

After both were dressed, they sat down across from each other at the window, both wary as strangers.

Jason leaned toward Annie, lacing his fingers together. "Annie, this has to stop."

"Jason—"

He held up a hand and pinned her with his dark, tortured gaze. "Hear me out. We can't go on like this. Sooner or later, I'm bound to hurt you. I doubt I can even remain here in England,

324

or ever provide you with an adequate future."

"Do you think I care about money?" she cried. "And I think you are making excuses."

"Perhaps I am." He stared at her in anguish.

"But why?"

"I just . . ." He gestured helplessly. "There are complications. Forces that are too frightening, too dangerous, for us even to talk about. I . . . just can't give you what you need."

Her eyes flared with bitterness. "It sounds to me as if you won't."

"Perhaps so," he conceded.

"Then give me what you can," she pleaded.

"No!" he cried.

Jason stood and began to pace, staring at Annie in anguish. She regarded him with hurt and bewilderment.

"Don't you see?" he asked distraughtly. "We can't risk this happening ever again. In the end you'll only get hurt—and you could even become pregnant."

Listening to him, Annie was in torment herself as she realized at last that Jason could not possibly love her. If he did, how could he spurn her this way?

"Do you think I would try to trap you into marriage?" she asked angrily, getting to her feet. "Do you presume that this is why I came to you today?"

He stepped toward her. "Of course not, darling, but—"

"I came to you because I—"

He quickly crossed the distance between them and grasped her by the shoulders. "Don't say it!" he pleaded. "Please, you must never say it. You will only make things much worse in the end—for both me and you."

Now she shoved him away and regarded him with anger and disillusionment. "After what we just shared, you won't even hear my feelings?"

"I can't," he said hoarsely. Though it killed him to say these things, he knew he must bring her to her senses. "The truth is, I think we are wrong for each other and I can't ever marry you."

"Then what just happened between us?" she cried. "The passion of the moment?"

He could only groan.

Despite the tears now gleaming in her eyes, Annie drew herself up with pride. "I see that I have deluded myself about you, Jason. Perhaps Father was right. You and I are too different. I may have felt a certain passion for you, but that was only a fleeting thing. What I really need is someone trustworthy and solid—someone like Stephen."

"Annie! You can't mean that!"

"I do!" she flared. "With Stephen, I have elements in common, and we can build a good future together." Her expression was one of intense disillusionment. "You are not the man I thought you were, Jason. This was—only an infatuation."

"Annie—are you sure?" he asked in anguish.

"Yes. I am sure. After being with you today, I know now that it is Stephen I truly love."

Jason was in hell. He still did not trust Stephen with Annie—and yet how could he know that with him, she would fare any better? He seemed damned every way he turned!

"I—I'm sorry things turned out this way," he said helplessly.

"Of course you are." Her words were cutting as she headed for the door.

"Annie, please," he pleaded, following her. "I truly am sorry. Can't we at least try to part as friends?"

She turned to him, her face eloquent with her emotional struggle. At last she sighed and said, "You are right, Jason. After all, you never made me any promises. You never said you would stay. It is not your fault that I threw myself at you today."

"Annie, I'll not have you speaking of yourself in such a manner!"

Tears glistened in her eyes. "But it is the truth, isn't it? It is not your fault that you . . ." Brokenly, she finished, "Don't love me."

Jason almost lost all control then, almost cried out his love for her and rushed over to beg her forgiveness. In the nick of time, he managed to remind himself that such a reckless, selfish action might well cause her death.

"I—I don't know what to say," he murmured at last, clenching his fists.

"Will you be leaving for America soon?" she asked.

"Most likely, yes," he admitted.

"Will you at least come celebrate Christmas Eve with us at the hotel before you go?"

He was incredulous. "Annie, you must be joking. Your father and Stephen will roast me up with the Yule log."

"No, they won't," she insisted. "I won't allow it. And didn't you just say you wanted us to part as friends?" Thrusting her chin high, she added, "You *will* want to see how happy I'll be with Stephen, won't you?"

Jason could have died on the spot.

She stepped closer and spoke more gently. "At least drop by, so we shall both know that we part without ill will." Almost helplessly, she added, "Jason, it's Christmastime, and you mustn't be alone. And you can't simply disappear this way. Our boarders—particularly Miss Mary and Miss Media—keep asking about you. You must tell everyone good-bye."

Jason felt too defeated to protest. "Very well, Annie."

His heart felt broken as he watched her leave. He told himself that he had made the only right choice. Still, his agony brought him to his knees and tore an anguished sound from his lungs.

Annie, too, left Jason with a heavy heart. While she knew now that she would never have Jason's love, she could console herself with the remembrance of their glorious lovemaking, and the knowledge that she had acted in his best interests, that she had assured his happiness, even if at the loss of her own.

At least the two of them would get to spend Christmas Eve together. With that memory to treasure in her heart, perhaps she could get through the bleak years ahead.

And Annie couldn't deny that she had been just a little perverse, a little selfish, in her final invitation to Jason. She could not help but cling to the hope that, when he saw her with Stephen on Christmas Eve, he would have a change of heart and come back to her forever. . . .

Chapter Nine

Jason did not know which way to turn.

Following his emotional encounter with Annie, he was besieged by heartache and indecision. The memory of making love to her was so beautiful to him that he wanted nothing more than to rush to her and beg her forgiveness for his seemingly callous rejection of her afterward. Yet how could he know that such a move would not bring disaster hurtling down upon her?

On the other hand, she now seemed determined to wed Stephen, and this possibility filled him with equal fear and dread. If only he could know for certain whether it was to be himself or Stephen who was destined to hurt her on Christmas Eve! And that day was now almost here!

On the day before Christmas Eve, Jason decided to visit Stephen in his haberdashery in Mayfair. Sweeping through the front door of the elegant establishment, Jason noted that the gaily decorated shop swarmed with noisy customers and the air was redolent with the mingling smells of Christmas greenery, male toiletries, and new cloth. Both male and female customers were present, many of them sitting on plush ottomans sipping hot, spiced tea as clerks scurried about, showing the latest gentlemanly fashions.

Jason managed to flag down a clerk who was racing by, trying to juggle at least a dozen hats. The harried employee showed Jason to Stephen's office in the back. As expected, Jason's reception there was cold. On spotting Jason in the portal, Stephen arose from his desk and spoke with hostility.

"Burke—what are you doing here?"

Jason faced down the other man unflinchingly. "I came to speak with you because I am concerned about Annie."

"Hah!" Stephen scoffed. "That did not stop you from doing your best to put Annie and myself asunder."

Jason nodded grimly. "Obviously, that was a mistake on my part."

"Indeed!"

Jason offered a gesture of conciliation. "Please, can't we put aside our mutual antagonism for a moment and think instead about Annie's best interests?"

Now Stephen appeared both insulted and perplexed. "Of course, I am always solicitous of Annie's welfare. But what, specifically, is your concern?"

"Have you seen her?" Jason asked anxiously.

After hesitating a moment, Stephen admitted, "We have been very busy with the Christmas crush. But yes, I did see Annie briefly a few days ago when she stopped by the shop." He flashed Jason a triumphant smile. "She told me she is willing to renew our commitment."

Jason sighed. "She loves you, you know."

Stephen appeared pleasantly surprised. "She does?"

"That is what she told me."

Stephen frowned darkly. "Then it puzzles me that she would confide such intimate feelings to you, rather than speaking with me."

"Sometimes it is easier to confide in a friend," Jason stated carefully. "And what of your commitment to her, Prescott?"

"What do you mean?" Stephen countered defensively.

"Are you going to give up your mistress now?"

Stephen turned as white as some of the papers on his desk. "What makes you think I have a mistress?"

Jason laughed ruefully. "Don't be coy, Prescott. It's unbecoming. On the night we all met, I overheard some gossip in the hotel drawing room, and that's when I became aware of your shabby little affair. Have you never considered how hurt Annie may become if she ever learns of your betrayal? What if the next time, she is the one who overhears such a rumor?"

"Have you told her of your suspicions?" Stephen demanded angrily.

"Certainly not. Believe it or not, I want what is best for her. She loves you—and therefore, I would not deliberately try to sabotage her happiness."

Stephen nodded. With surprising humility, he said, "Listen, Burke, as much as I have resented your presence here, I must admit that your romantic competition has taught me a lesson."

"In what way?"

"I almost lost Annie. This is something I will never forget, for whether you believe it or not, I really do love her. As for my mistress—I have already ended the liaison. And I promise you that I will never again do anything to hurt Annie or compromise her happiness."

Jason regarded Stephen with surprise and some lingering doubt. "If what you say is true, then I must congratulate you on coming to your senses."

"You have my solemn word that I have."

"Are you willing to shake on that?"

"Of course."

After the two men shook hands, Stephen asked, "What of you, Burke? What are your plans?"

"I . . ." Awkwardly, Jason related, "I'll most likely be returning to America right after Christmas. In the meantime—I did want to warn you that Annie has invited me to attend the Christmas Eve gathering at the hotel. She wanted me to stop by and tell everyone good-bye—and I think it is also important to her that she and I part as friends."

"Burke . . ." Stephen shook his head resignedly. "Leave it alone, will you? Let her go. I assure you, she is in very good hands."

"I suppose she is," Jason felt impelled to admit as he left.

He had accomplished his purpose here. This realization brought Jason both joy and sorrow. He knew now that he must have been brought here to bring Annie and Stephen together, and especially, to make Stephen realize that he could never toy with Annie's affections, or betray her.

He realized, too, that Stephen was right that he needed to bow out now. Why prolong things by spending Christmas Eve with Annie when it was even possible that he might be whisked away to the present right before her very eyes? Again, he remembered the prophecy, "You'll come back on Christmas Eve." His mission here was completed, and he had the feeling that he might indeed soon return to his own world, his own time. He would have to cope with the heartache of losing Annie—but never would he lose the new hope and positive outlook on life she had given him.

But he also knew that he had to see Annie one last time to make certain that she was content in her decision to wed Stephen, and also to bid her good-bye.

Early on Christmas Eve morning he stopped by the Simmons Hotel, taking with him a Christmas present he had bought for Annie. In the downstairs hallway, he was greeted by a stern-faced Oscar Simmons.

"I am glad you've stopped in, Burke," Simmons greeted him coldly. "You have saved me a trip by the newspaper office."

"Sir, I would like to speak with Annie," Jason stated firmly.

"My daughter does not wish to see you," came the contemptuous reply. "If you will join me in my office, she asked me to give you something."

Bemused, Jason followed Oscar into the office. Oscar handed him an envelope. Jason opened it and, to his surprise and keen disappointment, he found inside a ticket for a steamer bound for New York.

The steamer was scheduled to depart the London docks tonight!

Jason glanced skeptically at Oscar. "Annie asked you to give me this?"

He nodded. "As I said, my daughter does not care to see you again. She is far too busy planning her wedding to Stephen."

"But—she asked me to spend this evening with all of you," Jason protested. "Indeed, she made me promise I would attend your Christmas Eve gathering."

Oscar gestured toward the ticket. "I think you have the answer to that right there." Vehemently, he added, "For God's sake, man, leave well enough alone! Haven't you done my daughter enough damage already? Let her enjoy Christmas Eve in peace—with her father and her fiancé."

"Will you at least give Annie my present?" Jason asked, extending the box.

Oscar Simmons took the gift without comment, and Jason left.

Jason went back by the newspaper office and handed Mr. Spencer both his final column and his resignation.

The old gentleman appeared keenly disappointed, saying, "I had such high hopes for your future here with us."

"I must apologize for leaving so suddenly," Jason replied. "But I've now finished my 'American in London' series, and I think it is time that I head back where I belong."

"If it is a matter of money," Spencer said, "I was already thinking of giving you an increase. Also,

I was not speaking idly at the Holcombs' dinner party when I said that one day you will likely be running this place."

"I know, Mr. Spencer, and I really appreciate your faith in me. I simply feel that my destiny lies elsewhere."

The two men said their good-byes, and Jason returned to his boarding house to pack.

That night, as Jason stood on the deck of the steamer looking out through the fog at the cluttered St. Katherine docks, he could hear the church bells tolling in the distance, their joyous tones seeming to mock him now.

Eight o'clock. Annie's gathering should be starting. Would she regret sending him away? Would she miss spending Christmas Eve with him, just as he was filled with anguish to be apart from her now?

He wondered idly what would happen to him. It didn't seem to matter that much, now that he knew he could never have Annie's love. Would he indeed travel on to America—where he might look up his ancestors, as well as the mysterious Finias Fogg—and start a new life there? Would he be whisked back to his own time before the steamer even left the London docks?

Did he care? What mattered was that Annie's happiness, her future, had been secured. He ached more than ever to go to her, yet he could not risk upsetting the delicate denouement he had established in her life.

Then, all at once, Jason was stunned to watch Stephen Prescott hurry up the gangplank!

Jason crossed the deck to confront the other man. "What in God's name are you doing here?

Why aren't you with Annie?"

"Burke." Stephen was huffing from the cold and exertion. "Thank God I've caught you in time. It was pure hell getting Oscar to tell me which steamer you were taking."

"But why did you wish to find me?" Jason asked incredulously.

Regret and anguish tightened Stephen's features. "I may be a cad, but I'm not that much of a cad. You must go to Annie immediately."

Jason remained flabbergasted. "And you must explain what you are talking about."

Stephen nodded. "As I told you yesterday, I've only seen Annie once during the past few days. I really had no idea the situation had gotten so grave. . . ."

"For heaven's sake, man!" Jason burst out impatiently. "Out with it!"

"I went by the Simmons Hotel two hours ago to ask Annie out for an early supper. That is when Oscar admitted to me that she has been crying in her room almost nonstop for days now—ever since you broke things off with her."

"What?" Jason cried.

"Oscar is furious at you for hurting Annie," Stephen continued in a rush. "He admitted to me that he bought the steamer ticket and gave it to you, claiming that it had actually come from Annie."

"You mean that—"

"Annie has no idea of what has truly transpired. And Oscar told me he cannot wait to tell her that you have left."

"Oh, my God," Jason muttered. "But why have you come to me now?"

Stephen drew a heavy breath. "Because, whether you believe it or not, I too want Annie to be happy. I've been deluding myself ever since you appeared here in London. I know now that it is you who she really loves. And when Oscar tells her that you have left her on Christmas Eve, without even saying good-bye, it is going to kill her."

It is going to kill her! Jason was left reeling as Stephen's ominous words reverberated through his brain, along with Annie's dire warning from the present: *I died on these steps on Christmas Eve in 1852, when I learned that my true love had deserted me.*

Oh, merciful heavens, what had he done? He realized that Stephen was right! Through trying to act in Annie's best interests, he had instead doomed her! He had brought about the very calamity that he had struggled so hard to prevent. For *he* was Annie's true love, and now he had deserted her—on Christmas Eve! And, when her father told her that he was gone, that he had broken his promise, she would die!

"Well?" Stephen prodded impatiently.

Jason was already bounding off for the gangplank, yelling over his shoulder to Stephen, "We must hurry to the Simmons Hotel at once—and pray that we are not too late!"

Chapter Ten

Let there be time. Please, God, let there be time.

This was Jason's fervent prayer as he and Stephen rushed in the doorway of the Simmons Hotel half an hour later.

At once, he spotted Annie conversing with her father at the top of the stairs. He saw the shattered look on her face, and his heart went cold. Oh, God, Oscar must be telling her that he had deserted her.

He saw her begin to collapse. Desperately, he bounded up the stairs.

"Annie!" he cried.

He watched her turn, saw the look of raw joy on her face as she spotted him. But it was too late, for she had already lost her balance. He saw her ashen-faced father reach for her, too late. . . .

With a strength that astounded him, Jason

sprinted upward and swept Annie up into his arms in the nick of time.

"Annie! Oh, Annie darling!" he cried, clutching her close.

"Jason—you have come back!"

You'll come back on Christmas Eve. All at once, Jason laughed aloud as at last, he realized the rhyme's meaning. He had come back—to save the woman he loved!

"Yes, I've come back—to stay, darling, if you'll have me," Jason said passionately. "Please, Annie, say you'll forgive me!"

Her reply could not have delighted him more. "I love you, Jason," she whispered.

"I love you, Annie," he said.

Followed by Stephen and Oscar, Jason carried Annie up to her room. Stephen bid her a happy Christmas and tactfully took his leave.

Jason sat in the chair next to Annie's bed, holding her hand. Oscar stood in the doorway, looking much sobered.

Annie glanced over at her father and smiled. "I'm going to marry Jason."

Oscar nodded and stepped inside. Torment twisted his voice. "Annie, I too must beg your forgiveness. Because I foolishly believed that marriage to Stephen was best for you, I interfered in your life and almost caused your death. Why, I wasn't even going to give you the Christmas present Jason brought you earlier today."

"Jason came by here—today?" Annie cried. "And you did not tell me?"

Oscar sighed heavily. "You see, my dear, Jason didn't desert you. I bought a steamer ticket and gave it to him, telling him that it came from you."

Shuddering, he glanced from Annie to Jason, then back to his daughter. "Then, moments ago, when I watched you almost tumble to your death—and even in the midst of that peril, saw you looking at Jason with such love . . ." His voice breaking, Oscar paused to wipe a tear. "Why, 'tis the same look that was on your dear mother's face the day she first told me she loved me."

"Oh, Father." Annie's face reflected her poignant joy.

"Can you ever forgive me?" he asked abjectly.

"Of course, Father." Annie held out her arms.

Oscar rushed to his daughter, and the two embraced for a long moment. Then a much-relieved Oscar stood, offering his hand to Jason.

"I'm trusting you with my daughter's future, you know," he said sternly, shaking the younger man's hand.

Jason nodded soberly. "I'll do my best to make her happy, sir—and to provide for her."

"Very good. I'm sure you will." Abruptly, he smiled. "Indeed, right before you arrived, I was speaking with Old Spencer downstairs. He's distraught over losing you. In due course, I'm sure you will be running the *Bloomsbury Times*."

An awkward silence ensued, and Annie caught her father's eye. "Could you leave Jason and me alone a moment?"

Oscar appeared taken aback. "But daughter, that would not be—"

"You may leave the door ajar. And I promise you that Jason and I will come down and join the rest of you in only a moment or two."

Oscar nodded. "Very well. But are you sure you are up to entertaining tonight?"

"Oh, yes."

340

Oscar left, and Jason sat down on the bed, hugging Annie tightly to him. "Darling, I'm so relieved that I arrived in time," he whispered against her hair.

She laughed. "Believe me, so am I."

He drew back to stare at her questioningly. "But I do wonder something. . . ."

"Yes?"

"Why did you tell me that you loved Stephen, that you wanted to marry him, when none of it was true?"

A guilty smile curved her lips. "Because I wanted to do what was best for you. I thought that if I could convince you that I truly was happy with Stephen, then you could return to America with a clear conscience and peace of mind."

"Oh, Annie!" Jason was shaking his head at the irony. "In wanting what was best for each other, we almost lost everything."

Annie regarded him with adoring eyes. "Still, in my heart, I always hoped that you did love me, that you would come back to me tonight. And I was convinced that you would at least stop by to say good-bye. That is why I was so stunned when Father told me . . ."

He kissed her hand. "I know, darling. And I'm so sorry for putting you through so much grief."

"We are together now, and that is all that matters." She regarded him curiously. "What changed your mind, Jason? What brought you to your senses—and back to me?"

There, Jason had to chuckle. "My darling, that is a very long story."

"But one you will tell me?"

"Oh, yes, when the time is right. However, for the moment, I think we had best join the others downstairs—before your justifiably irate father comes charging up here."

"Very well. Only, you've forgotten something."

"I have?"

Her smile was joyous as she curled her arms around his neck. "You have yet to give me a proper kiss."

He did.

A few minutes later, Jason and Annie joined the guests in the parlor. One and all were thrilled to see Annie and Jason there together, and Old Spencer in particular was delighted to hear that Jason was prepared to return to his post.

Jason helped Mr. Holcomb drag in from outside the giant Yule log, and a cheer went up from the guests as the two men dropped the huge chunk of wood into the fire. There followed wassail for all, served up with the traditional Christmas Eve "dumb cake" that the two spinsters, Miss Media and Miss Mary, had baked. The refreshments were accompanied by several rounds of "Merry Old Christmas."

Later that night, after the guests had departed, Oscar, Jason, and Annie left in the coach to go to midnight candlelight services together. The cold London night was ablaze with a million stars and alive with the sights and sounds of Christmas—pipers playing in the streets, carolers singing outside the ancient Tower of London, Christmas trees glowing in the windows of homes, and everywhere, the beautiful church bells tolling out the coming of Yule. Sitting close to Annie and holding her hand as they clattered through the streets, Jason had never felt happier or more filled with joy and hope.

At St. James Church, they listened with awe and reverence as the vicar read the story of the coming of the Christ child. Then the three held their candles high and sang together, "Joy to the World."

It was well past one when they returned to the hotel. A heavy snow was starting to fall. As the three navigated carefully up the slippery front steps, Oscar said to Jason, "Stay the night with us, why don't you? You must not head home in this blizzard."

Jason was only too eager to agree.

Inside the warmth of the hallway, Annie turned to her father and said, "I want to marry Jason right away."

Both Annie and Jason glanced at Oscar expectantly. Jason added, "Sir, I would be delighted to arrange for the license immediately after Christmas."

Oscar nodded. "Of course."

Then Oscar hugged them both. After Annie's father went upstairs, Jason pulled her close beneath the kissing bunch—and the two lovers long-savored that glorious tradition. . . .

Early on Christmas Day, Jason joined Annie, her father, and several of the hotel guests in the drawing room. A mood of great gaiety consumed all as they ripped open their presents. Jason was thrilled when Annie presented him with a blue sweater she had knitted—she was equally delighted with the fur muffler he had given her. Annie and her father were mystified to open a package from America which contained a fruitcake from none other than the mysterious Finias Fogg, who had also enclosed a brief note apologizing because neither he nor one of his representatives had been able to travel to London!

Her expression astonished, Annie turned to Jason. "Isn't it odd that Mr. Fogg never even mentioned you?" she whispered.

He leaned over and whispered back, "Don't worry, darling. One day, I'll explain all about how I got here—and we may even go to America to meet Mr. Fogg!"

At noon, Mrs. Chandler served up a sumptuous feast—roast turkey with sausage stuffing, candied sweet potatoes, English peas in cream sauce, and hot yeast rolls. Afterward, everyone clapped as the smiling cook brought in the flaming plum pudding. Everyone savored the rich, brandy-flavored dessert.

Following coffee, the yawning guests retired upstairs to nap off the feast. Jason left to go by his boarding house and pack his things.

That night, when all was quiet, Annie came to Jason in his third-floor room. He answered her knock to find her standing in the corridor in her gown and wrapper—and gazing at him with so much love!

"Annie, you shouldn't be here," he scolded in trembling tones.

Wordlessly, she shut the door and moved into his arms.

With a groan he clutched her close and kissed her. "Oh, Annie." He felt as if he held heaven itself in his arms.

"I wanted to wish my husband-to-be a proper Merry Christmas," she murmured, kissing his jaw.

The Ghost of Christmas Past

He stared down into her beautiful, golden eyes. "Oh, my darling! You've already given me the most joyous Christmas gifts ever. You've given me back hope—and joy, and love in my life."

Taking Annie's hand, Jason drew her over by the fire. They knelt together on the rug, kissing and caressing in the gilded light.

"Someday," he murmured, kissing her soft neck, "I shall tell you how a lovely ghost brought me to you."

"A ghost?" she retorted, dimpling adorably. "And a pretty one? Now I am jealous!"

"You shouldn't be, darling," he teased back tenderly, "for it was you. You are my beautiful ghost of Christmas past, Annie."

"I am?"

"Yes, indeed."

Annie regarded him with awe and delight. "And you are the light of my life—now and forever."

Soon their clothing lay discarded in a pile on the floor, and Jason carried Annie to his bed, pressing her beneath him. They lay with bodies tightly coiled, their fevered kiss burning with all the love they felt. Jason tenderly kissed Annie's breasts while she caressed him boldly, wrapping her fingers around the warm steel of him until he groaned with unbearable need. When he pressed to bring them together, she took him eagerly, deeply.

"Oh, Jason," Annie cried, feeling filled to her soul with ecstasy and love. Running her fingers through his hair, she murmured, "I want one more Christmas gift from you, my soon-to-be husband."

"And what is that, my soon-to-be wife?"

"I want your child."

"Oh, Annie."

There in the glow of the fire, the last Christmas gift was lovingly given—and, with love, was received.

FLORA SPEER
"Twelfth Night"

For all my readers,
a happy holiday season.

Chapter One

Farmington, Connecticut
December 23, 1992.

"Just where do you think you are going?" Lucinda Carstairs glared at her older sister. She kept her voice low, but Aline could tell Luce was angry. So was Luce's husband Bill, who pushed his bulk in front of Aline to block her exit from the dining room.

"Come on, now, Ally," Bill said. "You can't walk out on your own grandfather's funeral. It wouldn't look right."

"I am not walking out on the funeral," Aline replied. "I was there at the church and at the gravesite, and I have been here at your house for more than three hours. I've had enough of polite condolences and small talk—and entirely too much of dainty sandwiches and cookies and

349

tea. Gramps would have demanded a slice of roast beef on rye and a glass of good Scotch whiskey.

"Luce, it's nothing you've done, or you either, Bill. It's just that I need to be alone for a while," Aline added, feeling guilty for her imminent defection from the social duties her sister expected of her.

"But I have someone here I especially wanted you to meet," Lucinda protested. "A man I just know you will like."

"Not today," Aline cried. "Good God, Luce, can't you stop the matchmaking even for Gramps's funeral? I've told you at least a hundred times, I do not want to get married again. Once was more than enough."

"Ally, you don't understand."

"Let her go," Bill advised when Lucinda would have continued to argue. "Any man who meets her when she's in this mood will only turn tail and run the other way."

"Has anyone ever told you," Aline hissed, "that you are the most insensitive couple in the history of the entire world?"

"Aline!" Lucinda glanced around to see if any of her guests had noticed her dismayed exclamation. When she spoke again, she lowered her voice to a near whisper. "I don't understand why you are being so difficult. Gramps was almost ninety-three, he lived a full life, and he was ready to go. He told us so on the day he died. We all knew he couldn't live much longer. He—and I—accepted the inevitable. Why can't you?"

"You're right, Luce," Aline said. "You don't understand. You probably never will. Thanks for your efforts today. It has been a lovely party, but it's time for me to leave."

Twelfth Night

As Aline hurried out of the dining room she brushed against a man she had never seen before.

"Sorry," she muttered, assuming he was some friend of Bill's and unwilling to pause lest Luce or Bill should come after her.

"I say, aren't you—?"

But Aline was too eager to be gone from her sister's house to stop and chat. Grabbing her cape off the Victorian coatrack by the front door, she ran across the porch and down the steps. Only when she reached the street did she stand still long enough to put on the cape. Shivering in the cold December wind, she pulled the billowing folds of heavy gray wool around her, then fastened the silver clasp at her throat and drew up the hood.

Gramps had given the cape to her. Every time she enfolded herself in it, she felt as if his arms were circling her, holding her safe and warm. The cape was almost all she had left of him. Almost, but not quite all. For there was another legacy from Gramps that still survived: the illuminated Book of Hours he had purchased in Europe early in the century. Knowing he did not have long to live, Gramps had taken care that his most valuable worldly possession would be permanently kept in a safe place where others who cared about its beauty as he and Aline did could see it and use it for historical or art research.

As firmly as the gray wool of the cape sat upon Aline's shoulders, so the desire came over her to see the book again. If she could hold that beautiful object in her hands once more, perhaps she wouldn't feel so lost and alone. Perhaps some part of Gramps would cling to the book, too, and like the cape, it would comfort her.

She hurried to her car. Surprised to see a dusting of snow on it, she brushed the flakes off the windshield, then opened the door. Before getting into the car she glanced upward at the heavy gray clouds that seemed ready to open and engulf the world in white.

The Victorian Gothic architecture of the library remained unchanged since Aline's days as a college student. At the windows, pointed arches framed small diamond-shaped panes of glass. Overhead, dark wooden beams traced the higher arches that supported the ceiling. The oak cases holding the card catalog stood against one long wall, and two rows of oak tables with sturdy matching chairs marched down the length of the room.

"The architect tried to make this place look like the great hall of a medieval castle," Gramps had told Aline on one of their many visits. "He didn't succeed, though. There are too many windows and no big fireplaces." Personally, Aline had always thought the library more resembled a Gothic church.

There was nothing medieval about the young woman at the librarian's desk just inside the entrance. Perhaps in honor of the season, she was dressed in bright red from her turtleneck sweater to her miniskirt and opaque tights to her high-heeled suede shoes. She was also thoroughly modern in her abruptness.

"We're closing in one hour," she said to Aline.

"I don't intend to stay long," Aline replied. "I just want to see one of the rare books."

"You'll need permission from the head librarian."

"I have this." Aline presented the special library card Gramps had obtained for her when he donated the book to the library under the condition that Aline could have free access to it.

"I chose that particular library because it's close to where you live," Gramps had told her. "You'll be able to visit the book whenever you like, but you won't have to worry about keeping it clean and free from mildew or bookworms, and that new vault they've installed ought to be safe from thieves."

The librarian took the special card from Aline and looked closely at it. She seemed impressed by what she saw.

"The rare book room is through there," she said, indicating the door at the far end of the library, "or you can just use the big room. As you can see, there is no one else here this afternoon." She disappeared on her errand to retrieve the book from the basement vault.

Aline did not like the rare book room. It was small and dark, the walls filled with glass-enclosed, locked cases, the air heavy from constant recycling. She chose a table in the main room. After dumping her purse onto a chair and draping her cape over it, she glanced toward the windows. A few flakes of snow were drifting downward.

"You are supposed to wear gloves while you handle it." The librarian placed a box in front of Aline. On top of the box was a pair of thin white cotton gloves.

"I know. I won't forget." The librarian moved away toward her desk. Aline opened the box, then pulled on the gloves. The dirt and oils on human skin could damage the ancient vellum;

Gramps had never handled the book without clean gloves.

Aline lifted the book out of its acid-free nest, holding the medieval relic reverently in both hands. Originally created as a gift for a noble lady, the Book of Hours was intended as a guide during daily church services. It also contained prayers for private devotions. Every letter of each handwritten Latin word was gracefully formed, the ink still unfaded after almost 800 years. But though the lettering was beautiful, the illuminations were the true glory of the book. In addition to elaborately decorated capital letters and margins at the beginning of every prayer, the book contained a series of miniature paintings, each depicting a month. Aline had always loved the brilliant blues and greens and the tasteful accents of real gold on the robes of the painted nobles shown in the miniatures.

"Blue was the color of the Middle Ages." She could almost hear Gramps's voice at her shoulder, as if he were once more looking at the book with her. "Never before or since has there been a pigment so clear, so pure, so long-lasting. That blue makes my old eyes rejoice."

Rejoice. Spreading her hands, Aline let the book fall open where it would. *Rejoice*, she thought again, and began to smile, for she was looking at the scene for December.

Beneath an improbably blue sky, gaily dressed nobles and peasants together were dragging a Yule log across a snowy landscape toward the entrance to a great, turreted castle. The castle doors were open wide, and through the opening Aline could see a fireplace already blazing with orange and red flames. Beside the fire a noble lady sat, wearing a green gown and a crisp white headdress. In her hands she held a book. It was, of course, the very same book Aline was holding. She recognized the gold design on the cover. Behind her, Aline imagined she could hear Gramps's ghostly chuckle.

"Don't ever think the monks who made this book were all solemnity and prayers, Aline," he had told her once. "Those medieval folk had a fine sense of humor."

A chill draft blew across the back of Aline's neck. Setting the book into its box, she took up her cape and pulled it across her shoulders. Then she lifted the book again to examine the December page more closely. In the painting there was a figure following the men with the Yule log, a boy with his arms full of holly and evergreens.

"A medieval Christmas lasted for twelve days and twelve nights," Gramps's voice said in her memory. "Castles were decorated with greenery. There was usually plenty of food available. The harvest was over, the animals for whom there wouldn't be enough fodder to see them into spring had been slaughtered and the meat cut up and preserved by salting or drying. The sausages had all been made from the leftover scraps of meat and the innards. Work in the fields was finished until spring, so people had some free time and they were ready to celebrate. Even the worst winter weather didn't stop them. Being snowed in meant nothing to those hardy medieval folk. They had everything they needed to get through the winter, right there in the castle storerooms and cellars. They knew how to work hard and how to enjoy life."

Rejoice. Celebrate. Enjoy life. Gramps had gone on to describe the feasting, the riotous games and dancing, the hilarious foolishness of Twelfth

Night. Aline smiled again, recalling his stories.

"I remember, Gramps. How could I ever forget?" But the memory made her eyes misty. Fearing to allow a salty tear to drop onto the precious painting and damage it, Aline lifted her head to look up from the brilliantly colored December page to the window a few feet in front of her. Great, fat flakes of snow were coming down fast.

"I really ought to start home before the roads get too slippery for driving." But she did not move. She sat with the Book of Hours in her hands and her gaze on the falling snow. Her eyes were dry now, but the diamond-shaped outlines of the glass panes were blurring. Aline blinked once, twice. The pointed stone arch surrounding the window began to waver. She blinked again. The window, the arch—in fact, the entire row of stone arches and windows along that side of the library—began to dissolve.

The wind caught at her cape, nearly pulling it off her shoulders. Aline clutched at it. She was standing—*standing?*—beneath darkening gray skies in an open field and the wind was blowing hard. The library had disappeared, the Book of Hours was gone, and her hands were bare of the white cotton gloves she had been wearing.

"What is happening? Where am I?" A blast of wind nearly knocked her off her feet. Aline stumbled on uneven ground. She stared at the earth beneath her feet.

Ruts. Deep ruts frozen into a mud road.

She was so confused and the wind was blowing so hard that she did not hear the horses until they were almost upon her. Great, galloping beasts pounded down the sides of the road, avoiding the dangerous ruts that could trap and break a horse's leg. With a frightened scream Aline threw herself to one side. The dead grass at the edge of the road was slippery with frost and the first thin layer of snow. Aline almost slid under the hooves of the lead horse. Its rider pulled hard on the reins and the horse reared upward. Aline saw flashing hooves, bared equine teeth, and the shadow of a black mane.

"What the devil are you doing out here on the road?" demanded a hard, masculine voice.

"I don't know," Aline stammered. "I think I'm lost."

"You're no peasant, not with that voice, not with a silver clasp on your cloak. Where are your servants?"

"What servants?" Aline's teeth had begun to chatter. "It's freezing out here. Can you tell me where I might go to get warm?"

Behind the man who had spoken to her, a troop of horsemen now drew up to await the pleasure of their leader. Through the snow and the gathering darkness Aline could just barely see them. They were well muffled into their cloaks, but here and there she noted the gleam of metal.

They were wearing armor. The leader had a sword belted at his side. From his mounted height he looked down at Aline while his men waited and her confusion grew deeper.

"In this countryside, there is only one place for a lady to go," he said. "You will ride with us to Shotley Castle. Give me your hand and put your foot on mine." He edged his horse closer to Aline and bent toward her, extending his hand.

Aline had never been on a horse in her life and she was terrified of this particular huge, restless creature. Yet something in the man's voice made her obey his command. She put her hand into his, and when he lifted her upward she placed her foot on his mailed boot, momentarily resting her weight there. Then in a flurry of cape and skirt she was seated before him. The horse moved forward suddenly, and Aline thought she would fall to the ground. Her gasp of fear brought a pair of strong masculine arms around her.

"Have no fear, I'll keep you safe," the horseman told her.

"How far away is this Shotley Castle?" she asked, wondering if she would be able to stay on the horse for more than a few feet.

"It is not far."

"That's hardly an answer." Perhaps there would be a telephone at this so-called castle, and she could call Luce for directions on how to get home. Then Aline realized that she did not have her purse, and thus no money, no calling card, no identification. "When we get there, will they let me stay?"

"I have no doubt of it, my lady."

"Who are you?" she asked, struck by the term *my lady*. "Where am I?"

"I am Adam of Shotley, baron of that castle, returning from my forty days of service to my king. You are on my road. Now, my lady, tell me your name and what you are doing alone on such a night."

"I'm Aline Bennett. Where is Shotley Castle?"

"Just a short distance along this road," he answered. "We will be safe at home before the worst of the storm strikes."

"No, I mean, in what state are we? *Where* are we?" She couldn't remember leaving the library, but perhaps she had gotten lost in the snowstorm

and driven her car off an icy road. She could have
hit her head. She might have a concussion. That
would explain why she was so confused. But she
didn't have a headache and she wasn't thinking
in a confused way; it was just that her surroundings had shifted with a suddenness she couldn't
understand.

"State?" Adam of Shotley sounded puzzled by
her question. Aline wished she could see him
clearly but, like Aline and his men, he had raised
the hood of his cloak against the cold, and the
light was by now so dim that his face was only a
pale blur in the shadow of dark fabric.

"Do you mean, what country are you in? This
is England," he said. "How could you not know
that?"

"I guess I really am lost," she said, trying to
hide her growing fear with flippancy. "The last
time I checked, I was in Connecticut." How could
she have crossed the Atlantic without knowing it?
What in the name of heaven was going on?

"Were you set upon by thieves, here on my
land?" Adam of Shotley asked. "If you were, I
promise I'll find the brigands and see them publicly hanged."

"Hanged?" she repeated, stunned by this idea.

"I assure you, where a lady's safety is concerned,
I will not be remiss. Did they harm your servants,
or did the varlets run away, leaving you to the
mercy of outlaws?"

"Wait, please!" Aline cried. "I don't understand
what you are talking about."

"I am saying that in my barony I will have justice, and safety for all women."

"You needn't hang anyone on my account,"
Aline said, still trying to make sense of this

insane conversation. "I don't know exactly what happened, but whatever it was, I don't think it was a hanging offense." She paused a moment, trying to organize her thoughts. "I don't suppose you could tell me what day it is, could you?"

"Certainly. It is but two days before the holy Christ Mass, which is why we are in such a hurry to reach home."

"December twenty-third," she murmured. "Well, that's correct, at least. You mentioned a king you were serving?"

"King Henry," he replied.

"Which Henry?"

"He is the first of that name. Do you know another King Henry?"

"Eight of them, in England," she responded wryly, adding, "Forty days of service to King Henry I?"

"That is correct." He must have felt the way she was shaking, for he tightened his arms around her. "Lady Aline, what is wrong?"

"I can't explain it right now," she said in a tense voice. "Perhaps later."

"Are you running away from your husband?" he asked. "Or from your father? I cannot shelter for more than one night a woman who is fleeing her true lord and master. If this is your case, I am obliged to send notice to your lord at once."

"My grandfather was my only male blood relative," she said, choosing her words carefully, "and we buried him this morning."

"Well, then." He did not loosen his hold on her, but his grip changed in some subtle way, as if he would be more gentle with her. "If you are distraught from grief at your grandsire's death, then I will not tease you with more questions.

You may explain your unheralded presence on my land to me when you are ready."

I will explain it to you, Adam of Shotley, Aline thought, *when I understand it myself.*

Chapter Two

They found a lowered drawbridge awaiting them at Shotley Castle, and flaming torches set at either side of the portcullis. The horses clattered across the drawbridge and through a narrow, tunnel-like entrance into the outer bailey, which was well lit with odorous pitch torches, and crowded with folk in undyed woolen clothing who called out to Baron Adam and his men. Aline barely had time to note that the cheerfulness in their voices sounded genuine before they were riding through another gateway and into the inner bailey. Here Adam dismounted, tossed the reins to a lad who hurried up to take them, and then raised his arms to Aline.

"Come," he said. "I'll bear you safe to the ground."

If she wanted to get off the horse without breaking her neck in the process, Aline could

see no other choice but to do as he ordered. She
let herself fall downward into Adam's arms. She
was not graceful about it. She landed hard against
his chest and felt him rock back on his heels when
her full weight hit him before he steadied himself
and her.

"Lady," he said, releasing her from his embrace,
"I think you do not much care for horses."

"They are so big," she said. "They have such
large teeth." She heard him chuckle at that.

"I do believe you and my daughter-in-law will
find you have much in common," he told her.
"Constance rides but poorly, and she dislikes the
hunt."

"Does she?" Aline's response was absent-
minded, for she was looking around the inner
bailey. A few dogs were running loose, barking and
jumping up on some of the men, who bestowed
pats on the hounds or scratched their ears with
familiar affection. Off to the side of the bailey
several buildings had been constructed against
the castle wall. One of them was obviously a
stable; the horses were being led away toward
its wide doorway. By the armored men moving
in and out of another building, it seemed to be
a barracks. Aline discerned a small stone chapel
and a walled enclosure with a tree inside it.

"That will be the herb and kitchen garden," she
murmured, before she caught her breath and fell
silent.

It was real. The people and animals she saw
were alive, not phantoms from her imagination.
The narrow, unrailed stairway up which Adam
was leading her was real stone, as was the frame
of the doorway at the top of the steps. The guards
in the entry hall were wearing actual chain-mail

tunics. They all had swords. And when Adam doffed his hooded cloak and handed it to a waiting servant, Aline saw that he was wearing a full suit of chain-mail armor. A long sword hung from his gilded red leather belt.

"Come into the great hall," he said, taking her arm.

The entrance to the great hall was through a low, rounded arch. Stout wooden double doors had been flung wide, but Aline noticed the metal bolt that could secure the doors against invaders. Then she and Adam were inside the hall and she paused, surprised by its cleanliness and its grandeur.

The walls were gray stone, the high pitched roof was faced with wooden planks, and the massive roof beams looked as if they had been hacked from entire tree trunks. Banners hung from most of the beams, their tattered condition suggesting to Aline that they were either very old or else were battle trophies. A few bright tapestries decorated the walls, and wooden chests held a fine display of silver ewers, basins, or serving platters. At each end of the hall, flames roared in giant open fireplaces. At the far end of the room, close to one of the fireplaces, was a raised dais with several chairs and a long table.

"Welcome to Shotley, Lady Aline." Adam had pulled off his mail gloves. Now he pushed back his coif, letting the chain mail fall into a cowl around his neck. He took the two goblets a servant offered from a tray and turned to give one of the goblets to Aline. At last, in the firelight and the torchlight, she could see him clearly.

"This will warm you." Their fingers touched as she accepted the goblet from him. Most definitely, he was real, his hands strong and callused as befitted a warrior.

The wine was hot and well spiced with cinnamon and cloves. Aline sipped daintily, watching her host.

His hair must have been dark in his youth, but it was heavily threaded with gray. His features were rather plain, with a long nose and deep lines on either side of his mouth. His eyes were gray. He was not especially tall, but Aline was not surprised by this. In the museums she and Gramps had explored together, she had seen enough suits of armor to know the men of earlier times were not as tall as those of the 20th century.

She would guess his age to be somewhere in his early 40s. He had mentioned a daughter-in-law, which meant he had a grown son. Men were usually knighted at 21, and seldom married before that time. So, if he had married at 21, had a son at 22, and that son was old enough to marry, then Adam must be—

"Oh, dear heaven," she said, "I'm beginning to believe this is happening and that I am really here."

"You do appear to me to be here," Adam told her. When he smiled his face took on a virile warmth that had nothing to do with perfection of feature. Recalling the solid touch of his fingers against hers and the encircling strength of his arms, Aline felt her anxiety level rise by several degrees.

"Have I gone off the deep end?" she whispered, asking the question more of herself than of him. "Wouldn't you think a 34-year-old, supposedly intelligent and mature woman could handle her grandfather's death without this kind of extreme overreaction? But still, how can anyone ever be prepared to lose a loved one? He was father and mother to Luce and me since our parents died. I wish he were here now. He'd know what to do." Suddenly aware that she had been muttering beneath her breath and that Adam's smile had been replaced by a puzzled expression, Aline fell silent, with one hand at her mouth.

"My lady, I do not understand what you are saying." Adam's words raised an interesting question.

"But I understand every word *you* say. Why?" Aline stared at him. "I can only read a few words of modern French, let alone speak it well, so how can I be talking in perfect Norman French with you? That must be what we are speaking, since you claim to be a Norman baron. If what is happening to me is real and not a dream or a form of madness, then I ought not to understand you at all. Yet I do."

"I think you are frightened and overtired and deeply affected by grief. You need to rest." Adam looked around the hall, then motioned to a servant. "Where is Lady Constance? Send her to me at once."

"I'm either crazy or I'm dreaming," Aline decided. "Either way, I'm stuck in the twelfth century. I know what Gramps would do; he'd tell me to get into the spirit of the game. All right, I'll play along and see what happens."

"Come nearer to the fire." Adam's hand was at her elbow again. "Take off your cloak; you will warm faster without it."

She let him remove the cape from her shoulders, then stood close to the flames while she drank more of the spiced wine. She saw Adam looking at her clothing and was glad she was soberly dressed. Luce had criticized her dress as too long, but Aline had worn it anyway, saying it was appropriate for a funeral. Fortunately, it was not terribly wrong for the 12th century. The skirt of deep burgundy wool flared into folds at the belted waist and hung nearly to her ankles. She wore sheer black tights and low-heeled black pumps. The dress had long tight sleeves and a bodice that draped into a vee neckline. Adam looked her over quickly, not missing the long column of throat revealed by that neckline. When she lifted one hand to her throat, he raised his eyes to hers.

Aline knew masculine interest when she saw it. She had grown practiced at deflecting it. She did not want that kind of complication in her life. Not ever again. Yet, in the ordinary features and clear gray eyes of this stranger, she saw something that tugged at her heart. She longed to ask him if he could explain why she found herself so far removed from her own time and place. But she did not. She did not have the chance, for while she and Adam of Shotley stood by the fireplace gazing at each other a young woman came into the hall.

"My lord." The young woman hurried forward to kiss Adam on the cheek he presented to her. "Welcome home." She did not sound as though she meant the greeting.

"You should have been here when we arrived," Adam told her, rather too sternly in Aline's opinion.

"I did not know you were bringing a guest. You sent no word. I have not prepared a room. Oh, dear." The young woman fell silent, tears filling eyes already rimmed with red. She was a pale, thin girl, and she looked frightened. She bowed a head covered with a white linen coif, while her hands fumbled in the folds of her gray woolen skirt. "Forgive me, my lord."

"This," Adam said to Aline, "is my daughter-in-law, Lady Constance. Now, my dear girl, do stop your eternal worrying and have one of the guest rooms made ready. I feel certain you have been keeping the castle clean and the rooms aired as you ought to do, so there will be no great trouble needed to make Lady Aline comfortable. I assume you have ordered an adequate meal prepared for me and my men on our return, so you need only set an extra place at the high table. Now, I will want a bath in my chamber."

"Oh, dear." Constance looked so terrified by this stream of instructions that Aline took pity on her.

"There was no way you could have been prepared for my sudden appearance here," she said. "Lady Constance, let me help you. I can make up a bed. Just give me the sheets and I'll do it myself."

"I could not. It would not be fitting. Oh, my lord, I am sorry. Blaise will be angry with me, too. Oh, dear." Constance stood helplessly, still twisting her hands into her skirt and looking as if she did not know where to start her chores.

"And what do you imagine Blaise will be angry about now?" said a bold masculine voice. "I vow, Constance, you have compiled a total of at least a thousand reasons to fear me, and none of them matter a whit."

The young man who now joined them was tall, dark-haired, blue-eyed, and remarkably handsome. He shook his head in Constance's direction, the gesture causing that young lady to press her lips together as if to forestall a serious bout of tears. Then he looked at Aline—looked from head to toe and moved on with an expression that told her she was much too old to interest him. Aline received this assessment with good humor and no offense at all, for she had instantly seen in him the same male attitude that had once made her unhappy in the days when she had been married.

"Welcome home, my lord." With a slight swagger the young man went to Adam and embraced him warmly. At least he had an honest affection for his father, for this could only be the husband of timid Constance.

"My son, Blaise," Adam said, confirming Aline's supposition.

"Well, wife," said Blaise to Constance, "why are you standing there like a half-wit when there is work to be done?"

"Lady Constance, I do hope we can be friends." Aline linked her arm through the girl's, drawing her away from the fireplace. "Let us leave the men to their conversation while we speak of more interesting matters. Will you show me to the guest room you think will be best for me? Then perhaps I can help you with your duties, for I am certain the sudden appearance of an unexpected guest must upset your routine." As the two women went toward the archway and the entry hall, Aline overheard Adam speaking to his son.

"I wish you would treat her more courteously, especially in front of strangers," Adam said.

"How can you expect to be happy if your wife is miserable?"

"I do not expect ever to be happy with her," Blaise responded. "The girl is a bore, always weeping and afraid of everything."

Aline and Constance were by now out of the great hall and could hear no more. Aline was certain that Constance had also overheard her husband's contemptuous words and had been embarrassed by them for, as they mounted the stone staircase that wound toward the upper floors of the tower keep, she could hear Constance sniffling. By the time they reached a tiny guest chamber built into the thickness of the stone tower wall, Constance was weeping in earnest.

"Let me have that." Concerned that Constance would drop the oil lamp she was carrying and thus start a fire, Aline took the pottery dish from her and set it upon a wooden stool. The only other furniture in the room consisted of a narrow bed and a wooden chest that Aline guessed would hold linens or clothing. "Well, it's sure not the Ritz in Paris, but it will have to do."

"Have you been to Paris?" The question was so unexpected that Aline answered without considering the effect her words might have.

"I went there twice, with Gramps. We tramped through every museum in town and spent a whole day at the Louvre." Seeing the way Constance was looking at her, she muttered, "Whoops, another mistake. I don't think the Louvre I remember has been built yet. It may be just a small fort on the Seine."

"Have you traveled even farther than Paris?" asked Constance, forgetting to weep for a moment. "How I should like to travel."

This second unexpected remark left Aline gaping at her. When she found her voice again, Aline said, "Does Adam hold lands in Normandy as well as here at Shotley? I seem to recall that Norman barons frequently had estates on both sides of the Channel. Perhaps Blaise will take you to Normandy."

"I should like to see the Holy Land, but Blaise will not take me anywhere." The brief glow of animation faded from Constance's face, leaving it pinched with sadness. "My husband does not like me." She looked so dispirited that Aline forgot her own difficult situation and put an arm around her.

"I assume yours was an arranged marriage?" She could not imagine the vibrantly masculine Blaise voluntarily wedding this fearful girl.

"I brought a fine dowry to him," Constance said with a tiny flare of pride. "When I first met him on our wedding day I thought I had been greatly blessed because Blaise is so handsome, and at first he was polite to me. But when the celebrations were over and we were alone in our chamber, he changed most unexpectedly. Then he was cruel to me."

"Had no one told you what to expect on your wedding night?" It was a guess, but Aline thought it was probably a good one.

"My mother is dead, so I could not ask her. My maidservant said I would find pleasure in my husband's arms," Constance replied. "I had some idea of what he would do to me. It is impossible to grow up in a castle unaware of such things. But Blaise is so overpowering, so energetic, so impetuous, and he is so very *big*. He wounded me most painfully until I bled all over the sheets."

"I get the picture, Constance. You don't have to say anything more."

Great, Aline thought, *just great. Not only do I suddenly find myself living in the wrong century, but now I'm expected to be a sex counselor to a terrified teenage bride.*

"I am so sorry to trouble you with my problem," Constance went on, wiping her streaming eyes, "but there is no one at Shotley to whom I can talk. If I tell my servants about my unhappiness, they will only gossip and I feel certain Blaise would not want that."

"I think you are right there," Aline murmured.

"Nor can I confess to our castle priest. Father John is an old man and would not understand. He would very likely tell me that a good woman submits to her husband. But how can I submit to Blaise when I fear his touch?"

"In spite of your fear, I think you love him. If you were indifferent to him, he would not affect you this way." This was another guess, with the truth of it borne out by Constance's nod and a new flood of helpless tears.

Aline could understand the situation. A weepy, timid soul like Constance must be exasperating to a man of Blaise's temperament. Any regard he might have had for her, any sense of polite respect because of the dowry she brought him, would have quickly evaporated when Blaise realized he had a bride who cringed every time he walked into their bedroom. A man like Blaise needed a woman who was willing to risk direct confrontation when he became too overbearing. She could easily imagine Constance dissolving into tears instead of defending herself. All of this Aline understood because she had once been almost as shy as Constance and had married a handsome man much like Blaise.

At the moment, Constance had wiped away her tears and was looking at Aline as if she expected some wise advice that would instantly solve all her marital problems. Realizing that she could not avoid saying something, Aline began by asking what she thought was an obvious question.

"Have you talked to Blaise about this?"

"No, no, I could not. He would not listen. He would think I was criticizing him. A good wife does not criticize her husband."

"Oh, rubbish! If you don't tell him how you feel, how can he ever hope to please you?" Seeing that Constance was about to start crying again, Aline grabbed her by the shoulders and shook her. "Don't be like one of those people who occasionally sit beside me on airplanes and spend the entire flight spilling out all their problems, but they don't really want to *do* anything to help themselves, they just want someone new to complain to." Fortunately for Aline, Constance ignored the part of her speech about airplanes and fastened upon the words that most applied to herself.

"You are the first person I have ever complained to!"

"Oh, good grief!" She sounded so forlorn that Aline immediately regretted her outburst. "Connie, I'm sorry. May I call you Connie? Look, I've had a terrible day. If I told you just how terrible, you'd never believe me. The only advice I can give you is to stand up for yourself with Blaise. Do it politely but firmly. And, for heaven's sake, don't cry. A woman's tears always make a man feel guilty, and guilt makes a man angry. Trust me, it never fails. Don't—I repeat, *do not*—cry in front of Blaise."

Just listen to you, Aline, giving advice to this poor girl when you have made such a mess of your own romantic life.

"I will try to do as you suggest," Constance whispered. She paused, swallowing hard. Aline was pleased to see her straighten her thin shoulders. "I fear I am not a very good hostess, Lady Aline. I shall send a servant with fresh linens and a quilt for your bed. You will want a bath after your cold journey. I'll have hot water brought to you at once."

"It's a bit chilly in here for a bath," Aline said.

"You shall have a brazier for heat." Constance paused by the door. "Thank you for listening to me. My heart is lighter now."

"Remember what I said. Talk to Blaise. Tell him how you feel. And stand up for yourself."

"I will try."

When the door had closed behind Constance, Aline sank onto the bed, her face in her hands. How she wished there were someone to whom she could unburden herself as Constance had done. But there was no one. All she could do was sit on the edge of the straw mattress and try to figure out what had happened to her. She remembered looking at the Book of Hours . . . the painting of the Yule log . . . the snow outside the library windows. She could think of no rational explanation for her sudden presence in the 12th century. She pinched her arm hard, just to be sure she was awake, and then she tried to imagine what Gramps would do in her place.

Rejoice. Celebrate. Enjoy. She could almost hear him saying the words. Gramps had always seized every opportunity to enrich his own life and the lives of his granddaughters. He had tried to teach them to do the same.

"All right, Gramps," she said aloud. "I don't know if I will ever get home again, but while I'm here, I am going to participate in this life. If I get frightened, I'll just pretend I'm living out one of the stories you used to tell Luce and me. After all, this is like one of your medieval tales come true."

She went to the window to pull back the wooden shutter and look out at Shotley. It had stopped snowing. Through a jagged rent in the clouds she could see the night sky and a few stars. To her left rose the outer wall of Shotley Castle, with a heavily cloaked guard standing watch on the battlements. Directly below her and to her right lay open fields, silent beneath a smooth mantle of snow. Beyond the fields a forest extended as far as she could see. The road upon which she had come to Shotley was around the corner of the castle wall, out of sight to her left.

It was so quiet, so peaceful . . . a silent, holy night. With one hand still on the shutter latch, Aline rested her head against the stone window frame. There was no glass in the window, but she wasn't cold anymore, and she had not felt so relaxed in months. She heard the muffled voice of the guard behind the wall talking to someone, and then it was quiet again. Aline gradually became aware of a sense of deep contentment.

"My lady?" A maidservant came into the room, carrying a bundle of linens. She was followed by two boys lugging a wooden tub and a girl with a bucket of steaming water. Yet another boy carried a black metal brazier, which he set up on a tripod stand before dumping a basket of charcoal into the pan.

Then Constance was there, igniting the charcoal with a piece of braided straw that had been dipped into tallow, and tossing juniper branches into the brazier pan to sweeten the air. More buckets of water were brought in until the tub was full. Constance scattered dried rose petals and herbs onto the surface of the water.

"Now, bathe quickly," she bade her guest, "before the water cools. Here is a towel for you to use. Would you like to borrow one of my gowns, or will you prefer to wear your own tonight?"

"I'll wear my own dress. Perhaps tomorrow I'll ask for one of yours."

Aline could hardly believe the change in Constance, until she realized what had caused it. The girl had no doubt been raised to become the mistress of a castle, and must have been familiar with her duties long before she married. With the female or young male servants she seemed to have no trouble giving orders and behaving like the lady of the castle. It was her husband who terrified her and by extension, though to a lesser degree, her husband's father.

"Shall I help you, my lady?" the maid offered, reaching to unfasten Aline's belt.

"Thank you. I can manage by myself." She saw them to the door and then, seduced by the rosy fragrance rising from the tub, she stripped off her clothing to submerge herself in the hot, scented water. In addition to the towel, the maid had left a cloth for washing and a bowl of gelatinous stuff that she had called soap. It gave off a pleasant herbal scent, but Aline found it sticky on her skin. She used the extra bucket left for that purpose to rinse herself, then hurried to dress again. Constance had supplied a wooden comb, but there was no mirror so she had to fix her hair as best she could by touch. Lacking her purse, she had no makeup.

"No moisturizer, either," she noted. "I'll have to do something about that soon, or I'll begin to look like a chapped prune in this cold. Connie must have a recipe for some kind of potion for a lady's skin."

Fearing she might have taken too long at her toilette, she hurried down to the great hall only to discover that she was early. Blaise stood alone before the nearer fireplace, a silver goblet in his hand.

"Will you join me, my lady?" It was just a superficial politeness on his part and she knew it, but she saw an opening to praise his wife to him.

"I would like some wine, thank you." She watched him pour it from a silver pitcher. "How kindly Lady Constance has treated me. I feel like an honored invited guest instead of just a lost traveler." She had decided to use that excuse to explain her presence at Shotley.

"Constance but does her duty." As he was doing his, making conversation with a guest in whom he was not interested.

"How old is she?"

"She has sixteen summers." He looked mildly surprised by her question. "Why do you ask?"

"I am impressed that someone so young could be so competent a chatelaine. My room is spotless, the servants are well mannered and helpful, here in the hall the rushes on the floor are fresh and sweet smelling, and the silver sparkles. You are fortunate to have so industrious a wife, Sir Blaise."

Now he looked even more startled, but she could see him thinking about her remarks. Apparently it had never occurred to Blaise that Constance worked diligently to see to his comfort and his father's. Good, let him revise his opinion of his wife and understand that she was not the fool he took her to be.

Then Constance herself came into the hall from the screens passage. Busy directing a trio of servants in preparing the high table for the evening meal, she did not at first notice her husband, but concentrated on her work. Aline stole a sidelong glance at Blaise and was pleased to discover that he had a considering expression on his face, as though he had never really looked closely at his wife before.

A moment later Adam arrived in the great hall and Aline's full attention shifted to him. He had put off his armor in favor of a thigh-length tunic of dark green wool and a heavy gold chain with a large emblem hanging from it. His hair was still damp from his bath and he was freshly shaven. When he came toward her she felt the corners of her mouth lifting to match the smile on his face.

"I am glad to see Blaise has acted the host in my absence," Adam said. "Is the wine hot enough?"

"Indeed, yes. And wonderfully spiced. Is it Lady Constance's recipe?"

"It was her mother's." Blaise shot her a wondering look, and Aline decided she had said enough about Connie for one night. Any more compliments and Blaise would begin to question what she was trying to do.

"You must sit beside me at the table," Adam invited. Aline placed her fingers on his extended wrist and walked across the hall with him as if she did that sort of thing every day of her life.

He had the oddest effect on her. She had believed she was well past the age for trembling limbs and a palpitating heart in response to any man, but the warmth of Adam's wrist under her fingers made her feel positively dizzy. When he smiled into her eyes as he seated her next to the lord's chair, she thought of swooning. Smiling back at him, she saw that he was similarly affected. He hovered for a minute, bent toward her, one strong hand on the arm of her chair. She did not move. She could barely breathe. She noticed for the first time what a finely shaped mouth he had. It was a little too wide for the rest of his face, but his lips were nicely modeled and his teeth were white and even. Her own lips parted in silent invitation. She saw longing in his eyes and knew her own must hold the same message.

Still, he was lord of the castle and she but an unknown woman. He turned from her to sit in his own chair, leaving Aline shaken and wary. She did not want any kind of emotional involvement. Romance seldom ended happily in her experience, and it certainly could not when the lovers came from different centuries. It was ridiculous even to think of Adam in that way. She had defended her heart against better-looking men than Adam of Shotley. She would control her feelings and refuse to become attached to him. But she could not ignore him. He was, after all, her host.

"We will eat only fish today and tomorrow," he informed her. "We are fasting in preparation for the holy day. On Christmas we can offer you a grand feast."

"I am not sure I will still be here then," she said.

"I do not think you will be able to leave, even if we can discover where your servants have gone. The snow has stopped for now, but more will come tomorrow, and I believe it will be a great storm."

"How can you tell that?" she asked. If even the 20th century weather forecasters with their radar images and their satellite photos were unable to accurately predict the weather a day in advance, how could Adam be so sure?

"There is an old man who works in the stable," he said, "who an hour ago told me that all his joints are aching and his forehead, too, a combination that always presages snowfall. Then there is my leg. I have an old battle wound that sends me its own message of coming foul weather. These hints are to be disregarded at one's own peril."

"No wonder you were in such a hurry to reach home." She thought his method of forecasting was probably as good as any other. "I shall expect a heavy snow, then."

They broke off their conversation as the servants appeared and began to serve the meal. There were two main courses, both fish as promised. For the first dish, salted herring had been baked with bread and herbs and eggs and other ingredients Aline could only guess at, to make a tasty casserole. The second presentation was a large freshwater fish, poached and served up with an elaborate sauce. There was also a stew of boiled vegetables, and there was plenty of fresh bread and a wheel of cheese. Wanting to keep a clear head, Aline quickly switched from the hot spiced wine to homemade perry, a ciderlike beverage made from pears.

"This seems more a feast than a fast," she said to Adam.

"With no meats and wooden plates and cups instead of the silver, I would hardly call it a feast," he told her. "On Christmas, we will have oysters. I brought a barrel of them home with me." He paused, watching while Constance served poached fish to Blaise and ladled sauce for him. Dipping his spoon into his plate, Blaise tasted the dish.

"'Tis good," he said, nodding his approval. "I like the sauce."

"I am pleased, my lord. Cook will be happy." Constance began to blush.

"Sit with me," Blaise ordered, catching her wrist, "and eat from my plate."

"Oh, no, my lord, I cannot. I have so much to do. I beg you to excuse me." Her face now bright red, Constance pulled her wrist from Blaise's grasp and left the dais, heading toward the screens passage and the kitchen. Blaise sent a scowling look after her.

"Silly girl," Adam said beneath his breath. "Each time he tries to be kind to her, she runs away from him."

"She is shy." Aline felt compelled to speak, though she did not want to reveal what Connie had confided to her. "It is possible that she finds your son a bit intimidating."

"Well, she should not. She is his wife and lady of this castle, since I have no wife at present." Adam raised a spoon filled with fish to his mouth. Aline waited, sure he would have more to say on the subject of Blaise and Connie. She was right. Adam swallowed the fish, took a sip of wine, and went on. "For myself, I think people ought to have the good sense to make the best of the lives they have been given."

"Is that what you did?"

"Aye." He applied himself to the fish on his plate. "Lady Judith was a good woman. She managed my household well and never interfered with my duties as lord. She gave me my heir. We respected each other, and I grieved deeply at the loss when she died."

"Did you love her?" It was an impertinent question, but Aline had to know the answer.

"Love?" He stopped eating. "Of course not. I have observed that when nobles indulge in such passions, it always seems to end badly."

"So I have also observed," Aline said dryly, thinking of her own life. "Still, what we are talking about between Blaise and Constance is not desperate, soaring passion, but a degree of warmth that will allow them to live together in peace and contentment."

"It is perfectly obvious that they are not content now," Adam agreed. "I love Blaise well, and I wish him happy. I have advised him as best I can, but I am not skilled in dealing with a woman like Constance. My Judith would never let herself be cowed by me, and I respected her for it." Adam gave Aline a long, assessing look.

"My lady, would you think me presumptuous if I asked for your help? If you can think of a way to make that marriage a happier one, I will be forever grateful to you. Perhaps I should not speak so freely to one whom I do not know, and a woman at that. But then, perhaps a woman will know better than a man what ought to be done."

"I very much doubt that Blaise would listen to anything I have to say."

"Talk to me," Adam said, "and I will convey your thoughts to Blaise as if they were my own. Meanwhile, you could speak to Constance."

"I'm not sure this is a good idea."

"Lady Aline, you owe me a favor." His hand covering hers took the sting out of his insistent words. "Did I not this very day rescue you from death by freezing upon the open road? Have I not welcomed you into my home, fed you and offered you a bedchamber? Will you repay me by refusing to heed a simple request?"

It was on the tip of her tongue to tell him that she no longer responded to male manipulators and that he was taking unfair advantage of her situation, when it occurred to her that he did not intend manipulation. In the world in which he lived, what he had done for her deserved to be repaid as promptly and as cheerfully as she could possibly manage. In his world, which for the present was her world, too, it would be churlish of her to say no to what he was asking.

"I am not refusing you, my lord. I will do whatever I can to help, because I genuinely like Connie—er, Constance—and because I think she ought to be a lot happier than she is. Just don't expect too much of me—or of either of them."

"Any improvement would be a blessing." Adam sighed. "I hoped that in my absence they would find a way to grow closer. But I have been told since my return that Blaise's interest has lighted upon one of the maidservants. He needs children to carry on our line, and I would dearly love to see grandchildren before I die, but they must be legitimate."

"I understand." His hand was still on hers. Aline stared at it, large and hard and long-fingered, with a scar across the back of it. He might have lost the use of his hand from such a wound. Fighting the impulse to run her finger along the scar, she made herself imagine Lady Judith bandaging it. Then he let her hand go so he could raise his winecup and hold it out to the servant who moved along the table with a pitcher.

"I am a poor host," Adam said, "to speak only of my own troubles and press you for aid, and never ask how you came to be alone in the snow on my road. What happened to your attendants, Lady Aline? If you know where they have gone, I will send men after them tomorrow morning and have them returned to you."

"I didn't have any servants," she said, her words eliciting a hard look from him.

"Were you fleeing?" he asked. "You said you were not, but since you did not know me when first we met, perhaps you feared if you told the truth I would leave you there to die in the cold."

If I told you the truth, you wouldn't believe me.

"I was traveling alone," she said.

"No noblewoman travels alone," he responded, "nor on foot."

"Adam, I swear to you, I am not fleeing from anyone. I would return home at once if I could."

Or perhaps not immediately, she thought, looking into his eyes.

"Where is your home?"

"It doesn't matter. Can't you just accept that I'm here now, and let me stay for a while?"

"If you were a man, I would demand an answer of you."

"I'm not a man." She watched his gaze move from her eyes to her lips, and thence to her throat and the deep neckline of her dress.

"Most assuredly, you are female," he murmured. "Very well, my lady, I will agree to ask no more questions of you, thus putting you into my debt a second time."

"And what will you ask in payment for this new favor?" she whispered, knowing full well what it was he wanted. And, heaven help her, aching to give it to him despite her best resolutions.

"We shall see." A brief, teasing smile warmed his face. Then he looked over her shoulder and the smile faded. "We retire early at Shotley, my lady. I'll see you to your room."

When she rose, she saw what he had seen. Blaise had Constance by the arm and was leading her out of the hall toward the stairs. It was evident from the way she dragged her feet and hung back that Constance went unwillingly. Aline took a step in her direction. Adam put out a hand to prevent her from leaving the dais.

"We cannot stop that," he said. "It is her duty."

"She's afraid of him!"

"Then she must learn not to be afraid, but to accept her husband's embraces. Blaise does not beat her, and I am certain he is not rough with her."

"Did you ever—Forgive me, I should not have said that." But he answered her unspoken question anyway.

"No, Aline, I never forced my wife. Nor did she ever refuse me. She understood a wife's duty as

I understood a husband's. As Blaise understands his duty."

"You make it sound so tedious, so unemotional. Didn't you feel the least bit of passion, or love?" It was another question she should not have asked, but she could not seem to control her thoughts or her tongue. He did not appear to be offended.

"Love," Adam said, walking with her out of the great hall. "Passion. A young man's dreams. An old man's forgotten hopes."

"You are not old." She responded to the note of sadness in his voice. So Adam, bound in a loveless marriage, *had* dreamed of something more.

"I am forty-two, much too old to dream of love." Taking up an oil lamp from a table in the entry hall, he mounted the stairs behind her and followed her to her chamber door. Blaise and Constance had disappeared ahead of them, presumably to their own chamber. "How old are you, Aline? It's an impudent question, I know, but this evening you and I have spoken as if we were old and dear friends."

"I have just turned thirty-four," she said.

"And do you think you are too old for passion?" A faint smile curved his lips.

"I am convinced of it." She opened her door and would have entered her room, but he stopped her with a hand on her shoulder.

"You will want this," he said, giving her the oil lamp.

"Oh. Yes. Thank you." He put a finger under her chin, lifting the face she had bowed over the oil lamp. With the same finger he traced the outline of her lips while she held her breath.

"Are you absolutely certain you are too old?" he asked, and left her there.

386

Chapter Three

"I want the great hall decorated," Adam announced early the next morning. "If we are to bring in greenery, we will have to do it before midday, for I believe it will soon begin to snow again."

"We will need a Yule log," cried Blaise, entering into the spirit of his father's suggestion. "I know where the mistletoe grows. Let us ride into the forest as soon as we have broken our fast and see what we can find there."

"Constance, Lady Aline, you will join us." Adam commanded.

"Oh, no," Constance replied. "I cannot. The cold—and I would have to ride. Oh, no, my lord, I beg you, let me remain here and supervise the cooking. There is so much to be done before the holy day. Oh, my lord, do please allow me to stay behind."

"Nonsense, Connie." Aline broke into the stream

of protesting words. "It will be fun, and you deserve a break from your constant chores. The fresh air will make your cheeks pink and give you an appetite."

"Now, there you are right," said Blaise, who had given Aline a strange look upon hearing her nickname for his wife. "Constance is too pale, and much too thin for my liking."

"Oh, my lord Blaise, I am sorry I displease you." Constance began to apologize, but Adam stopped her.

"Lady Aline does not like to ride, either," Adam said. "Therefore, she will ride pillion behind me, and you, Constance, will ride in the same manner behind Blaise." He gave Aline a conspiratorial wink that she assumed meant she was to go along with this notion.

"What a good idea," she said bravely, trying to hide her own trepidation at the thought of riding on a horse. But perhaps there was a way to make the riding easier. The measuring look she cast upon Adam and then Blaise made each man shift position a bit uncomfortably. "Before I venture out-of-doors, however, I will need the right clothing. Those aren't trousers you are wearing, they are more like tights. I could probably roll a pair down at the top so they aren't too long, and tie them around my waist and keep them up that way."

"Do you mean our hose?" exclaimed Blaise.

"Yes, if that's what you call them," Aline responded. "I will also need a warm woolen tunic, and an undershirt, too. I can wear my own cape. Oh, and a pair of shoes or boots. These pumps aren't sturdy enough for tramping around in the snow."

"Do I understand," asked Adam, "that you are proposing to don men's clothing?"

"It's the sensible way to go." Seeing how horrified he was by the idea, she gave him a wink to match the one he had sent her.

"On second thought," Adam said, apparently deciding to go along with whatever Aline was trying to do, "it does sound like the best way for you to keep warm. I'll see that you have what you need."

"Thank you, my lord. Connie, what about you? If you wear a long skirt, it will only get wet and be uncomfortable."

"Oh, no, I could not." Constance began her usual deferential protest, but she was brought up short by Blaise's shout of laughter.

"Yes, *Connie*," he said. "A tunic and hose will make it easier for you to ride. Astride," he added, lowering his voice until only Constance and Aline, standing together near Blaise, could hear his next words. "You will have to spread your legs and grip your mount tightly to keep from falling off. Do you think you can do that?"

Aline put an arm around Constance, who was staring white-faced at Blaise. Aline looked at Blaise, *really* looked at him, in mingled fury and embarassment for Connie's sake. To her astonishment she saw in his countenance something other than the contempt and cruelty she had expected to find there. On Blaise's handsome face as he regarded his wife she saw a faint glimmer of hope.

"If I can do it, you can," she said to Connie.

"My lord," Connie whispered, still staring at Blaise, "are you giving me permission to wear men's clothing? But it would be most improper."

"Permission?" Blaise looked her up and down, then let his glance flicker toward Aline, still with an arm around his wife. "No, *Connie*, I do not give you permission. Nor do I command you. I challenge you. Will you accept the dare?"

"Oh, my lord, please—"

"Do it," Aline whispered softly into her ear. "Take a chance. Say yes." She could feel Connie sucking in a great gulp of air, felt the girl trembling and trying to control herself.

"Yes, my lord." Connie's voice was barely audible. "I will go in men's clothing."

"Well done, my dear." Blaise laid a hand on his wife's shoulder. Aline thought it might be the first time he had ever shown approval of any act of Connie's. "You cannot wear my clothes; I'm much too large for them to fit you, but I know a stable-boy who is about your size. Go to our chamber and undress. I'll be there shortly with your new costume, and I will help you to put it on."

"Do you really think you ought to?" Connie began. Blaise cut off her pleading words.

"Trust me, Connie. You cannot hope to fasten your hose alone."

"Go on," Aline urged, pushing Connie toward the hall doorway. "Do as he says. And don't forget to thank him for helping you. But not for allowing you to wear a tunic and hose. That was *your* decision, not his."

"My lady Aline," said Adam, coming up behind her, "your methods are positively scandalous."

She whirled around just in time to catch him laughing at her.

"If you will retire to your own chamber," he said, "I will shortly appear at your door with the garments you will need. Dare I hope that, like Constance, you will also require assistance to don them?"

"I'm sure I can figure things out by myself," she retorted.

"As you wish. However, should you discover that you cannot manage alone, do not hesitate to call for me, and I will rush to your aid."

"You are the perfect host, my lord." He bowed politely at that, but the look in his eyes was both dangerous and exciting.

"It is my intent to see you well served during your stay at Shotley," he replied.

In order to put on boys' clothing, Connie had been forced to remove her coif, revealing braids of a lovely golden-brown shade. She also had beautiful legs. The tan woolen hose Blaise had found for her were a little too small, so they fit snugly, outlining every feminine curve of her calf and thigh. The low brown leather boots and brown wool tunic only emphasized the fact that she possessed a slender, delicate figure. Her newly revealed charms were not lost upon her husband. When Blaise saw the other men surreptitiously looking in Connie's direction, he made haste to cover her with a voluminous cloak. But the point had been made, and frequently during their wood-land excursion that morning Aline noticed him regarding Connie with a smoldering gaze.

"I feel so wicked," Connie whispered to Aline as they stood in the inner bailey waiting for the horses to be brought out of the stable. "These hose are so unlike women's clothing. My own stockings are gartered just below the knee, but these go up to my waist. They touch my body in strange ways."

"Enjoy it," Aline whispered back, just before Blaise claimed his bride and bore her off to mount her behind him on his massive chestnut steed.

As for Aline, Adam's hose were far too large for her, so they hung wrinkled but warm about her legs. The shoes were also too big, but serviceable.

"I could have helped you to a smoother fit," Adam chided. "And a belt would nip in that too-large tunic."

"I'll be just fine this way, thank you. What have you done with my cape?"

"Exchanged it for this cloak," he told her. "It is shorter, and thus will be easier to manage after you are mounted." Once again he lifted her onto his black-maned horse, and with a small company of servants to help, they set off for the nearby forest.

It was a sparkling day with a deep blue sky, though Aline could see a line of clouds along the western horizon.

"Is that the storm you think will come tonight?" she asked Adam.

"Sooner than tonight," he replied, turning his head to look back at her. "Is it well with you, Lady Aline? I cannot see you when you sit behind me."

"No problem at all," she assured him.

"Your hands will be cold. I should have given you gloves."

"I think yours would be too large for me," she said, conscious of the way she was forced to sit with her arms wrapped around his waist.

"No matter. I'll keep you warm thusly." He covered her clasped hands with one of his, then drew a fold of his cloak around them, tucking in the fabric to keep her fingers warm.

They rode across the fields and a mile or more into the woods before Blaise called a halt.

"Here is holly and pine," he said to Adam, "and ivy on the ground there. Just ahead is a tree I marked earlier in the year for our Yule log. Come along, lads." Having dismounted and helped Connie to the ground, he led three young men armed with axes into the trees, leaving Adam to direct the rest of their party in gathering the necessary greenery. A large piece of heavy cloth had been brought along, and now this was spread out on the ground like a tarpaulin. Soon they were all piling branches of pine and holly onto the cloth.

"Here's the ivy." Connie grabbed a stem and pulled, her feet slipping in the snow. She went down face first. Aline expected her to dissolve into tears, but she got up laughing. There was a smudge of mud on her nose and her cheeks were as pink as Aline had predicted they would be. She looked surprisingly pretty.

"Blaise said he was glad I had come with him," Connie informed Aline, who was trying to remove some of the dirt from her tunic. "I expected to be cold and wet, but this is fun."

"Perhaps you should put on boys' clothing more often," Aline said.

"It is comfortable. But the hose produce the most unusual sensations." Connie's cheeks grew pinker still. In a moment she was back at work on the ivy, pulling up long strands of it. At the same time, the young men who had come with them began to move farther into the forest under Adam's direction, searching for more pine boughs and more red-berried holly. Aline stood alone, looking about the area where they had been working.

"We need mistletoe, too," Aline murmured, glancing upward to see if she could find any. She quickly located a tree bearing a growth of the parasitic plant, but there were no branches on the tree low enough to offer help in climbing it. There was a pine growing close to the host tree. "If I climb up that pine until I'm level with the mistletoe and then pull hard on it, I'll bet it would come down."

Standing underneath the pine tree she could see its branches spread out like steps, inviting her to climb them. It had been years since she had climbed a tree, but she worked out at a health club three times a week and did a lot of brisk walking. Deciding she was strong enough to do the job, she raised both hands over her head and grabbed a branch. Swinging her feet onto another branch, she began to work her way upward.

It wasn't a very hard tree to climb and soon she had reached the height of the mistletoe bush. She moved outward along a pine branch until she could reach over to the other tree and get a tight hold on the stuff. And then she pulled. The mistletoe would not come loose. She pulled again.

"Whoops!" She caught herself just in time to prevent a nasty fall, but she had the mistletoe, a fair-sized clump of it, the branches thick with waxy berries.

"You foolish woman," came a masculine voice. "What are you doing?"

"Hello, Adam," she called. "I'm up here."

"I can see where you are. Get down at once!"

"I've got the mistletoe. Here, catch." She tossed

it at him. "Watch the berries, you don't want to lose any. Someone ought to carry it home separately, instead of piling it in with the other greens."

"Will you get down before you fall!" It was not a question; it was an order.

"No problem. It's as easy as going down a ladder." Aline knew she was showing off. She liked teasing Adam, and she liked even better knowing he was concerned for her safety. "I shall now make an elegant descent."

Of course, she promptly lost her footing and nearly fell straight to the ground. She caught herself just in time, hanging by both hands from a branch until she could find a place to put her feet. After a pause until her heart had stopped thumping against her ribs, she then began to climb down more carefully.

"Jump," Adam called from directly below her. "Jump before you fall and break your neck."

"I do not intend to fall," she replied, still moving downward.

"You almost did. Why must you be so independent? You should have waited for me to send a man up the tree to get your confounded mistletoe for you."

"I learned a long time ago that if I wait for a man to do something for me, it will never be done," she said. "Independence feels great."

"Aline! This is not fitting behavior for a noblewoman." He sounded angry, or at least very annoyed. She turned herself around on the branches so she could look at him. He was only a couple of feet below her, with one arm stretched out to hold aside a low branch and thus make a space large enough for him to stand.

His face was turned upward and she thought he looked more worried than angry. Perhaps it was fear for her she had heard in his voice.

"Aline," he said more quietly.

"Oh, all right," she replied, and letting go of the branches, she launched herself into his arms.

He was not expecting her. She knocked him down and together they rolled over and over. First Adam was beneath her, then on top of her and their arms were around each other. They lay there in the snow with Adam's full weight pressing on her and his mouth less than an inch from hers.

"Aline." With a groan that came from somewhere deep inside him, he lowered his mouth to hers.

And Aline responded. With no pretense of resistance she gave herself up to his scalding kiss. It was what she wanted. Their mouths fit together perfectly, with a tenderness and a depth of emotion that shocked her. Where were all her carefully built defenses now, when she needed them? She who had vowed never to let herself be hurt by another man, she who refused to let any man get close enough for this heart-stopping, aching beauty? Melted, that was where the protective walls were—melted away in less than 24 hours in the fires generated by a middle-aged Norman baron.

She wanted him. Long-forgotten urgings of her body, deliberately repressed, forbidden admittance to her conscious mind, began to stir and awaken while Adam kissed her and she kissed him back. . . .

"Aline." His lips were on her throat.

"Too old for passion?" Gently she mocked him,

and herself, while she tried to get her feelings under control again. "I don't think you have finished with life yet, my lord."

"No more than you have." Briefly his lips touched hers once more.

"Aline, my lord Adam, are you injured?" Connie knelt beside them. "What are you doing here under the tree?"

"I thought it was obvious," Adam murmured into Aline's ear. "I must be doing it all wrong."

"Oh, no, my lord, it was very right." Aline began to laugh and Adam joined her. After a minute or two he helped her to stand and they tried to brush the pine needles and snow off each other, there beneath the tree with a bewildered Connie watching them.

"We are unhurt," Adam said to his daughter-in-law. "Lady Aline fell out of the tree and knocked me down. Here's the mistletoe she plucked. You carry it home, Constance, and be careful lest you lose any berries. I have a feeling we are going to use all of them before Twelfth Night ends."

"Out of the tree?" said Connie when the three of them were standing near the tarpaulin full of greenery. "Aline, did you climb into it, then? I would never think to do such a dangerous thing."

"Perhaps you should," Adam told her, but not unkindly. "Sometimes the reward is worth any risk."

The journey homeward was slowed by the need to carry the tarpaulin of greens slung between two horses, and by the effort of dragging the Yule log across the snow. It was too large and too heavy to carry.

"You don't think small, do you, Blaise?" remarked Aline when she first saw the log. "That thing must be six feet long and four feet in diameter. But will it burn if it's green wood?"

"Ah, there's the secret," said Blaise. "A year ago, the tree was alive, but it did not leaf last spring, so I noted it in my memory for Christmastime. It should be dry enough by now to burn easily."

"What a good idea," murmured Connie. "How clever you are, Blaise."

"I thought so," said Blaise. "Here, let me help you mount. How did you get so dirty?" With an amused smile he wiped a bit of mud off Connie's cheek.

"I'll tell you as we ride home," she replied. "And after, you must tell me how you cut down the tree."

"I am forced to confess, I did not do all the cutting myself," Blaise began.

"Aline, are you ready to mount?" Adam put his hands on her waist. "Will you ride before or behind me? You will be warmer in my arms."

"I will be safer riding behind you."

"There's naught to fear from me today, my lady. It's Christmas Eve and I am still fasting." He lifted her to sit in front of him, then mounted himself. "As for what I may do once the religious services are over, I make no promises."

They ate bread and cheese and drank cider at midday, finishing the sketchy meal quickly so they could start the decorating. Before long the great hall was festooned with evergreen and holly, and mistletoe hung at every doorway. Connie twisted branches of holly together with the ivy she had gathered, to lay along the tables as centerpieces.

Then it was time to drag in the Yule log. It was heavy work pulling it up the narrow outside stairs. Ropes were attached to it and while some men pulled, others pushed from below. It was considered good luck to help in this endeavor, so every person at Shotley Castle was eager to lend a hand. Having taken a tug or two at the rope, Aline stepped aside to let others pull the log up the last few steps.

Still garbed in hose and a tunic, she stood in the entry hall watching and thinking how closely the scene resembled the December painting in Gramps's Book of Hours. It needed only a lady in a green gown sitting by the nearer fireplace to duplicate the picture she remembered so vividly. She wondered if Lady Judith had ever sat there with her own Book of Hours.

Slowly, nobles and ordinary folk together dragged the log upward and into the entry hall. Even Connie took a turn, smiling prettily when Blaise warned her not to chafe her hands on the rope. Then the Yule log was pulled into the great hall. To Aline's surprise, it was not put into the fireplace at once, but only placed in front of it.

"Aren't you going to burn it?" she asked.

"Not yet," Adam told her. "Not until tomorrow."

Once the log was where Adam wanted it, a flurry of activity ensued. The mud and snow tracked in with the log was cleaned up. The tables were set for a feast with heavy linen cloths, Connie's holly garlands, and freshly polished silver plates, cups, and serving pieces. Folk who sat below the salt, who on other days had only a slice of day-old bread for a plate, tonight would eat from the wooden plates and drink from the wooden cups the nobles usually used.

Finally, it was time to prepare for the midnight church service. The men took themselves off to the bathhouse beside the bailey wall, while Connie and Aline were indulged with tubs of hot water in their own rooms. At Connie's insistence, Aline had accepted the loan of a dress. Of deep blue silk, and only a little too short for her, it was made with a plain rounded neckline and loose flowing sleeves. Beneath it she wore a thin white woolen underdress and a linen shift. There was a belt of jeweled, gilded leather to be worn about her hips.

"The color is beautiful with your black hair," Connie told her, offering a gold mesh net set with sparkling stones. "Let me help you to gather your hair into this."

Connie's own dress was bright green, with a narrow band of gold thread at the neckline. Her golden-brown braids were pinned earmuff style at the sides of her head; around her throat lay a gold chain set with amethysts.

"Blaise told me it was his mother's," Connie said. "He has never given me a gift before, not since our wedding day, but he was obliged to give me something then. This necklace he gave me because he wanted to please me."

"It's beautiful, and very becoming," Aline said, wondering why Connie did not look more happy. She soon learned why.

"I am afraid," Connie confided. "After giving me a gift of such value, Blaise will no doubt want to—I mean, he will expect—oh, dear."

"Connie, have you ever considered the possibility that if you were to show a little enthusiasm, what Blaise wants to do might turn out to be fun?"

"No." Connie was close to tears. "I have never thought of it as fun."

"Perhaps you should. After all, you didn't want to put on boys' clothing and go out into the forest today, but when you did, you admitted that you enjoyed it."

There was no time to say more. They were expected in the great hall. There, the assembled household awaited them. With Adam and Aline, Blaise and Connie leading the way, they marched in solemn procession out of the hall, down the outside steps and across the bailey in heavily falling snow to the chapel for the midnight Mass. Everyone who lived in or near the castle was there, the chapel so crowded that some latecomers had to stand outside the door and strain to hear Father John's words.

At first, Aline felt like an intruder. Then she told herself that since Gramps had been an Englishman, she was a direct spiritual descendant of these people. With a full heart and in sincere humility she stayed by Adam's side, where he had said he wanted her to be, kneeling when he knelt, standing when he stood, until the lengthy service was over.

But the festivities were just beginning. No one at Shotley had eaten or drunk a thing since the light repast at midday. Now it was time for the first of the Christmas feasts. It had all been prepared beforehand. They started with the oysters Adam had brought home from London. Then it was on to a roasted side of beef, cold meat pies, cakes dripping with honey and nuts, cheeses, beer, wine, cider, perry.

"Now do we light the Yule log?" Aline asked Adam.

"Not until later," he said. "First, we have another Mass at daylight."

Aline slept only an hour or two that night, and was up again in time for church at first light, which was not actually very early because of the late midwinter rising of the sun. There was no sun that Christmas Day, for a blizzard had begun. It mattered not at all to the inhabitants of Shotley Castle. Inside the stone walls all was torchlight and firelight and merriment.

In late morning the great Christmas feast began. There were so many courses of roasted meat, oblong meat pies, stewed meats with vegetables, fine white bread made especially for this day, wine, and sweets that Aline soon lost track of all she had eaten. There was even a whole roasted pig with an apple in its mouth. Connie had told her when she protested about the sheer volume of food that the scraps, along with extra food that Adam had ordered prepared for the purpose, would be handed out at the castle gate to any beggars who appeared there.

"But I do not think many souls will be abroad today," Connie added. "The weather is too bad."

When the long meal was over and the afternoon was drawing toward evening, Adam rose from the high table. With Blaise, Connie, and Aline following him, he went to the Yule log. Amid much laughter Adam sat down on the log. There he told a joke about a knight in battle that brought tears of laughter to everyone's eyes, except for Aline, who did not understand the punch line. But she laughed politely, and then applauded when Blaise took Adam's place sitting on the log and recited a story. Next it was Connie's turn. She sang a little song in a surprisingly sweet voice, and actually smiled at her husband when Blaise joined in the last line.

"Now you, Aline," Adam said, taking her hand and pulling her over to the log. "Before we can light it, everyone here must tell a story or a jest, or sing a song."

"But I don't know any stories. And I sing badly."

"You may not be excused," Adam told her with mock severity. "If you do not perform, you will bring bad luck upon our house."

"Well, I wouldn't want to do that after you have been so nice to me," she said. "Just remember, I did warn you about my voice." She launched into "The Twelve Days Of Christmas." By the time she got to the five golden rings, everyone was singing along with her, enjoying the repetition of verses. Her performance ended on a burst of applause.

"Next, the captain of the guard," Blaise called out, and a burly, bearded man took Aline's place on the log.

After everyone in the great hall had finally finished sitting on the Yule log, it was rolled into the fireplace where, at last, with a ceremonial flourish and shouted wishes for good fortune in the coming year for all who dwelt at Shotley Castle, Adam lit it. There was little question that it would burn, since there were already other, smaller logs ablaze in the fireplace, and a good supply of kindling had also been heaped around the Yule log to make certain it would catch fire.

A short time later, Adam pushed his way through the crowd to Aline's side.

"Look there," he said, turning Aline so she could

see Blaise and Connie standing under the arch at the entrance to the hall. As they watched, Blaise took his wife's face between his hands and kissed her. And, wonder of wonders, Connie's arms crept around his waist.

"Do you think it's aught we've done?" asked Adam. "Or is it just the spirit of the holiday? Or perhaps an excess of wine?"

"Does the cause matter?" She met his eyes. "So long as they are in agreement, let us not question why."

"And we?" he murmured. "Are we in agreement?"

"On what, my lord?"

"Aline, do not play the coy maiden with me. I am not a young knight, willing to sigh and smile and whisper sweet words and await a lady's beckoning. I am a grown man and I know what I want. I believe you also know what you want."

Unable to maintain such intense eye contact with him any longer, she looked away toward the arch.

"Where did Blaise and Connie go?" she asked. "I don't see them anywhere."

"No doubt they have gone where you and I should go," he said. "To bed. Together."

"That's certainly blunt," she said.

"I am no poet, to sing you pretty songs."

She had no answer for that. She saw the burning desire in his eyes. She wanted to respond to it. Before she could say anything, the castle folk surrounded them.

"Lord Adam, you have not yet kissed your guest," a woman cried. "Under the mistletoe with you!"

There was no way to escape the well-meaning

women who now pushed Aline toward the archway, nor the men who urged Adam to join her there. With servants and stableboys and men-at-arms looking on, Adam took Aline into his arms beneath the mistletoe . . . and bent his head to her . . . and kissed her quickly and sweetly.

An instant later, a young man trying to juggle five dirty wooden plates he had seized from the nearest table captured the fickle attention of the merry throng and all returned to the great hall, save for Adam and Aline, who remained beneath the arch.

"Lady?" His hands were still on her shoulders. The question in his eyes was unchanged. He must have seen the answer in Aline's gaze, for he swept her off her feet and into his arms and carried her up the curving stone staircase.

"Adam," she protested weakly, "everyone will know what we are doing."

"What do I care?" he murmured with all the fine disdain of the lord of the castle for lesser beings. "What do you care?

"Besides," he went on, kicking open a wooden door and then kicking it shut again behind them, "they will never notice we have gone. They have their food and drink and their games to entertain them. Here in my chamber, no one will disturb us."

"If I were one of them," she said as he laid her upon a huge, curtained bed, "I would notice if you were gone."

"Notice instead that we are here, alone together, and the door is now bolted." He suited action to his words before returning to the bed, pulling off his belt and his tunic on the way. Then his hands were in her hair, the golden net was cast aside, and a flood of dusky curls cascaded over his fingers.

"Yes," he murmured, "just as I imagined it." He pressed her backward until she was lying beneath him. His kiss was deep and demanding. Aline answered it with rapidly rising desire. When he had finished, he pulled away from her only long enough to remove her gown and underdress. Quickly his large hands traced the outline of her breasts against her shift. Through the sheer linen he kissed the tip of one breast. His hands moved lower, caught the hem of her shift, and began to pull it upward. She cried out at the roughness of his palms against the sensitive skin of her inner thigh.

"Aline," he groaned, "tell me true; are you yet a virgin?"

"No," she whispered. "I am so sorry, but no."

"Do not regret it. I only asked because I do not want to hurt you through ignorance. I have no taste for whimpering girls. I need a full-grown, hot-blooded woman to satisfy me."

"At the moment, Adam, I do feel hot-blooded." He moved away from her to divest himself of the last of his clothing while she watched him through half-lowered eyelids. He knelt above her, a broad-chested man with a mat of dark hair that narrowed across his flat belly. She saw the scar along his leg, the old battle wound he claimed warned him of coming bad weather. She did not have long to consider it, for she was immediately presented with the proud evidence of his need for her. She opened her arms to him and pulled him close, and when she felt him pushing against her she lifted her hips to meet and accept him. His cry of passionate pleasure was echoed by the sigh on her lips.

He grasped her tightly and pounded into her, shaking the bed with the force of his mighty thrusts. And Aline, having once sworn that she would never again lie with a man, now forgot all her previous resolutions and gave herself up completely to his desire and her own. For she did want him, had wanted him since the first moment when she had seen him clearly, standing in the great hall in his chain mail. He was all she had ever dreamed of in a lover, fierce and demanding, but tender, too, and he did not let her go until she lay sobbing in his arms, satisfied as she had never been satisfied before.

Sometime during the night Adam rose to pour wine for both of them, and to put more charcoal on the twin braziers that warmed his room, before he rejoined her under the quilts

"You claim to have no male relative," he said, sitting beside her with the winecup in his hand. "Is your mother still alive, or have you a guardian? Who shall I ask for your hand in marriage?"

Aline nearly dropped her winecup, until she realized it was inevitable that he should be curious about her. So far he had been remarkably forbearing, asking only a few questions about her origins and how she had come to Shotley. As for wanting to marry her, well, he would change his mind when he knew all there was to know. The thought made her sad.

"My only living relative is a married sister," she said.

"Then your brother-in-law is your guardian."

"I have no guardian." Trying to delay an explanation she thought he would not believe, she said, "Adam, I should have told you before we made love. This may make a difference to you. I am a divorced woman."

Now it was his turn to clutch at his winecup. His face grim, he drank deeply.

"For what reason were you divorced?" he asked. "I find it hard to believe that you would commit adultery. Are you barren, then? If that was the cause, it would not matter to me. I have no strong desire to see any small children in the nursery here except for grandchildren."

"I don't know if I can have a child or not. I never had the chance to find out. My husband did not want children." She had to say it. He deserved to be told. "He left me for a younger woman. He was generous about it; he let me divorce him."

"Generous? To hurt you so badly?" he shouted. "Desire for another woman is not an acceptable reason for divorce. Only adultery, or a too-close blood relationship that is not discovered until after the wedding has taken place, or—occasionally—barrenness, are reasons for so serious a step. Why did you not fight it through the church?"

"The church had nothing to do with it," she said. "It was a civil matter."

"I do not understand."

"Neither do I." She hesitated, then plunged on. "Adam, I know how Connie felt before I came here, because I don't have anyone to talk to, either. And, like Connie, I have to tell someone. I swear that what I am going to say is the truth. I am trusting you with my life."

"You can trust me," he said. "I will not reveal your confidences."

"First, I want you to know that I wouldn't believe what I am going to tell you if it hadn't happened to me. If it weren't still happening to me." She looked right into his eyes and said, "By a means I do not understand, I came here to Shotley from another time and another place. I was sitting in a library looking at a Book of Hours. I glanced up to the library window and saw the falling snow. Within the blink of an eye, I was standing on the road to Shotley Castle, and you and your men were about to ride me down."

"Some magic has been worked on you," he decided. He rose from the bed. Putting down his winecup he began to prowl about the room, a magnificent, firm-muscled man in the prime of life. "Do you know who would want to place you under an enchantment? Perhaps your former husband?"

"I would be very surprised if he ever thinks of me." She got out of bed, too. "Adam, where I come from, we don't believe in magic anymore."

"What other explanation can there be for what has happened to you?" he asked.

"I don't know." She ran her hands through her hair. "I've thought and thought, and I can't come up with any answers. All I remember is what I have just told you."

"You have acted as though you belong in this time." To Aline's dismay, he began to look doubtful. If Adam didn't believe her story, if he turned away from her, what would she do? Perhaps if she told him more about her background, that would help.

"If I seem to be in my natural time," she said, "it's Gramps's doing." She explained about the museums Gramps had taken her to and the books he had read to her and her sister. "Luce never cared much about history, but I devoured everything Gramps said and every book he wanted me to read. He even talked about medieval Christmas customs, though I didn't know you waited so long to light the Yule log."

"I think I am no coward," Adam said, "but what you have just told me frightens me."

"It frightens me, too," she admitted. Still unclothed, she began to shiver. "Please tell me you believe me."

"I believe that *you* believe what you have said." He put his arms around her, holding her close. "I know an honest woman when I meet one. There is no guile in you. There must be some other explanation than deceit for what you have told me."

"Thank you. It's so good to tell someone about this." Afraid she would begin to cry, she broke away from him to stand facing a corner of the room, with one hand over her mouth. There was a wooden chest in the corner, the kind used in the 12th century to store clothing. Adam's tunics and extra hose were probably in there. The chest had a finely carved front panel; on top of it sat a branched candlestick—and a Book of Hours. Aline let out a wild cry.

"Adam!" Seizing the book, she held it out to him. "Whose book is this?"

"It was Judith's." He took it from her.

"I have not opened it, have I? And I have not been in this room until you brought me here."

"That's true."

"Take the book to the candle there, where you can see it better, and open it to the December page. I will describe the painting to you."

"Are you saying this is the same Book of Hours?"

"It's a test for me, Adam. Open it!"

Sitting down upon the bed, he did as she commanded and she gave him every detail of the December painting. When she was done she was shivering so hard she could not stand. She knelt in front of him, both of them naked, the book in Adam's hand.

"This is the book you were reading in the library," he said. "The very same book. What can it mean?"

"Perhaps it means that there is some reason why I was sent backward in time," she suggested. "Some purpose. To bring Blaise and Connie together?"

"Or were you sent to comfort me in my loneliness?" he asked. "Am I important enough to deserve such a benediction? No, I do not think so."

"Perhaps we will never know," she said. "Perhaps my being here is a Christmas blessing and nothing more."

"A blessing is not nothing. Will you stay with me?" he asked. "Or will a day come when you must return to your own time?"

They gazed at each other wordlessly, until Adam put down the book and lifted Aline off her knees and into his arms to make love to her again. Afterward she slept upon his broad chest and did not dream at all.

Chapter Four

"Aline, I have made a decision," Adam said. They were still in his room, drinking hot spiced wine and eating bread and cheese that he had commanded be brought to them. "I will not delay as I otherwise might have done. I will reject caution and say what is in my heart and I ask you to do the same, for if we wait, we may not have the chance again. We have known each other but a few days, yet in that short time you have stormed the ramparts of a heart I thought safe against passion. You have given me new hope. You have made me feel young again. Last night we asked what your presence at Shotley, in a time not your own, could mean. Perhaps it was for this that you came."

He approached Aline where she stood by the brazier in her borrowed blue gown, with her hair down around her shoulders. Outside the snowstorm still raged, but in his chamber it was warm.

"I love you, Aline. In proof, I give you this ring." He took it off his hand and held it out to her, a gold band with the carved design of a flower on it, centered with a small red stone. "I had a sister once, who died in childbirth when she was but fifteen. This was hers. I had it stretched to fit my little finger and I have worn it since that time. Now, I want you to have it."

His hands were larger than Aline's, so she put the ring on the index finger of her left hand.

"I will treasure it," she said. "Adam, I have nothing to give you in return."

"Did you not hear what I just said?" he asked. "You have made me laugh again. You have shown me that I am not too old to love. With you I have found a tenderness and passion unlike anything I have ever known before. What greater gifts could there be than those?"

"But you have done the same for me, so it's a fair exchange, and I am still in your debt," she murmured, wishing she could promise to remain with him forever and be certain the promise could be kept.

"Give me your heart," he said, "as I have given you mine, and we'll be even."

"You have it." She looked into his eyes. "I once swore I would never again take the chance of being hurt by love, but I do love you, Adam. My heart is yours."

The kiss he gave her in response to this declaration was long and deep, and when it was over she clung to him.

"Adam, if I am taken away from you," she began, then paused at the tightening of his arms.

"No, listen to me. Let me say it. If I am taken from you, I want you to find someone else to love."

"I could not," he declared. "In all my life, you are the only woman I have ever loved."

"But don't you see, it would give me pain to think of you left here alone, grieving for me. More than anything else, I want you to be happy, Adam."

"I will promise this only if you swear to do the same," he said. "You are made for love. If we are separated, do not live out your life alone."

They were both in tears. Surely, never had two lovers found themselves in such a situation, intoxicated with newly discovered love, yet knowing that at any moment more than eight centuries might separate them forever. She could not bear to think of never seeing him again. How quickly he had become an integral part of her heart—and how he had lightened that heart, until old and recent griefs alike had begun to loosen their grip on her, leaving her free to love Adam completely and joyfully—and unselfishly.

"I swear that I will love you until I die," she said. "But if we are parted, I will do as you wish. But, Adam, even if I learn to love another, I will never forget you and what we share here and now."

"So do I also swear." He took both her hands in his and, leaning forward, kissed her full on the mouth. "Thus do I seal my pledge to you.

"And now, my dear lady, let us go from this room to greet this new day as if we had the hope of many happy years together, for I hope and pray we have."

She sensed that he could not tolerate much more emotional talk about their possible parting or he would forget his position as strong lord of the castle and battle-hardened knight. She did not want to see his pride so broken, nor could she endure the thought of separation from him. Together they would pretend that she was at Shotley for an extended visit and thus maintain their composure. She took the hand he held out to her and answered him as lightly as she could.

"Indeed, my dearest lord, let us discover what this day holds for us."

They found the great hall nearly empty. A few maidservants were there, shaking crumbs off the tablecloths into the rushes on the floor and then replacing the cloths so the tables could be set for the midday feast.

"We will keep holiday state until Twelfth Night," Adam told Aline, "with a great feast each midday that will last until evening, and whatever entertainment we can make for ourselves. Some years we have a minstrel to sing for us or tell stories, but the bad weather has kept such wanderers away this season. Still, we can rely on Blaise to sing for us."

Blaise did not look as if he would care to sing anytime soon. He stood before the nearer fireplace with a flagon of beer in one hand and a sullen look on his face. For Adam he had a brief greeting, for Aline a glare and an accusation.

"What right have you to interfere in my marriage?" he demanded. "You have been filling my wife's head with nonsense."

"You will speak more politely to our guest," Adam commanded. "I asked Aline to speak to Connie—er, Constance—to try to discover why she is so unhappy and if there is some way to help her, and you, to be more contented."

Blaise fell silent. Aline knew he loved and respected his father, so she did not think he would take offense at what Adam had just said. With Adam backing her, she dared to speak what was on her own mind.

"It is not just *your* marriage, Blaise. It's Connie's marriage, too, and if either of you is unhappy, the other partner will also be unhappy. Notice, I said *partner*. I know the law says your wife belongs to you, but Connie is something more than chattel. She is a person, with hopes and dreams of her own."

"How dare you?" Blaise began. Aline gave him no chance to go further with what, from the look on his face, might become a blistering attack.

"Have you ever taken Connie to Normandy?" she asked.

"Why should I?" demanded Blaise. "She would only weep and complain, and I shudder to think what crossing the Narrow Sea would be like with her. She'd be seasick all the way."

"You won't know that for sure until you give her the chance to be sick, or not be sick," Aline told him. "Did you know that Connie longs to travel?"

"She does?" Blaise looked baffled. "No, I did not know that."

"Did you ever ask her about it? Or ask her opinion on any other subject?"

"I did, at first, but she only stammered and got confused, so I stopped."

"She wants to please you," Aline said. "She's afraid to voice her own opinions for fear you won't approve of them."

"She was not afraid last night." Blaise looked sullen again. "She told me exactly what she

416

thought of what I was doing."

"Did she?" Aline smiled at him. "I'm glad to hear it. You are making progress, then."

"Aline is right," Adam said. "In my opinion, you have been too high-handed in your treatment of your wife. Be kinder to her, speak more gently. She's like a skittish foal who needs a gentle hand to reassure her that you won't hurt her."

"As you were gentle with my mother?" said Blaise in a sarcastic tone.

"Judith was a different kind of woman. We understood each other well." Adam took a deep breath, glanced at Aline, and went on. "A man can learn from his mistakes, Blaise, and the wisest man of all learns from the mistakes of others. Connie loves you. Could you not learn to love her?"

With an angry exclamation Blaise tossed the remains of his beer into the fireplace. Throwing the flagon to a nearby servant, he stalked out of the hall without another word.

"My efforts to help seem only to cause more dissension," Aline said to Adam.

"*Our* efforts, my dear. Blaise will calm down and think on what we have said. You may have done more good than you know."

"We," she reminded him.

"Aye, sweet lady." He pulled her into his arms, heedless of the knowing glances of the servants. "You and I, together."

At this point, Connie came into the hall from the kitchen entrance. She was wearing her plain gray wool dress and her linen coif. Her eyes were swollen and red as if she had been weeping.

"Talk to her," Adam urged. "Try to encourage her."

Flora Speer

"Adam, perhaps Blaise is right and we are interfering too much."

"I cannot live in a household where there is such unhappiness. Aline, if you would not see me driven from my own home to find peace elsewhere, then help me to help them."

"All right. For your sake, I'll try." Aline fell silent. Connie had seen her and came rushing across the hall to her. Adam discreetly moved away to talk to the captain of the guard, who had just appeared, all covered with snow.

"I told Blaise how I feel about his too-impetuous lovemaking," Connie whispered to Aline. "And he tried to please me. I know he did, but his need was so urgent that I became frightened and began to cry, which made him angry. Oh, Aline, I have failed him again." She burst into tears on Aline's shoulder. Aline provided the only comfort she could think of at the moment.

"It was just one night, Connie. Try again. You will have to teach Blaise how to please you. From what I saw of him on Christmas Eve and yesterday, I think he does want to make you happy."

Aline could hardly believe she was giving marital advice as if she knew what she was talking about. Although, after her night with Adam, she did feel much more competent on the subject of lovemaking. Recalling the bold way in which he had taken possession of her body and her own eager response to him, she felt herself grow warm. She glanced across the room to where Adam was listening to the captain of the guard. Over the shorter man's head, Adam's eyes met hers. She could see the banked passion in his gaze and knew his thoughts were similar to hers. He, too, remembered their night together

418

with pleasure and looked forward to the coming night with burning anticipation. And this—this remembered joy and hope for its renewal—was what he wanted for his son and daughter-in-law. Aline tore her eyes from his face to take Connie by the shoulders and hold her at arm's length.

"Why are you wearing this dull mourning gown when today is a holiday? Come with me, Connie. We are going to dress you in something more suitable."

When they returned to the hall an hour later, Connie was once more gowned in bright green silk with the necklace Blaise had given her adorning her slender throat.

"Now remember," Aline told her, "don't give up. Keep trying. Sooner or later, you will get it right."

She watched Connie walk up to Blaise and take his arm and smile at him. She saw Blaise look down at his wife with some surprise before he spoke to her. And then Aline turned her full attention to Adam.

The days of feasting and reveling and nights of passionate love flew by. As soon as the heavy snow ended, beggars appeared at the castle gates, for word of a generous lord traveled fast among the folk who lived along the roads. There were some who came to ask for work as well as food, and those whom he could use, Adam accepted into his household.

"I trust this problem has been alleviated in your time?" he said to Aline one day when she had accompanied him on his morning visit to the outer gate.

"I am ashamed to say that in the treatment of such unfortunate souls I see little difference between your time and mine," she admitted. "If you were to walk down any city street in my country you would see homeless beggars with their bowls, and many of them with their children."

"Some of these are ill or maimed," Adam said. "Father John and our barber-surgeon will help as best they can."

"It's the same in my time," she responded. "Churches, hospitals, various charitable organizations try to help, but the supply of poor seems endless."

"The scripture says we will always have the poor with us. Perhaps they are sent to us to test the degree of our charity. I try not to fail in my duty to them. We are especially bidden to help at this holy season. Even at castles where beggars are turned away at other times, they are given food and a night's lodging at Christmastide."

She watched him squat down to wrap a shawl around a little boy in tattered rags, watched him hand an apple to the boy and send him off with a pat on the head to where his mother was feeding her other children from a large bowl of hot vegetable stew.

"You are a good man, Adam of Shotley," she said, taking his arm with pride.

"I do what I can," he replied humbly, "but it is never enough." His somber mood lightened when they returned to the great hall, where he saw Blaise and Connie talking to each other with unusual animation.

"I see some hope there," he said to Aline. "Connie grows warmer by the day."

They feasted again all that afternoon and into the evening. And when night had come, Adam took Aline to his bedchamber, where he made love to her until it was almost daylight.

She had kept her original guest room as a place to which she could retreat for privacy when Adam was occupied in his chamber with Blaise or the captain of the guard, or with any of the other men of the castle who came to him to discuss its administration. Adam was on good terms with the priest, Father John, and he also had a cleric, Robert, who acted as his secretary. In addition, Adam and Blaise spent a lot of time together each day, Adam having given his son a fair amount of responsibility for the castle defenses. Somehow, Adam managed to stay up-to-date with all of his lordly duties and still have the afternoons free for the feasts his people expected of him. The nights he kept for Aline.

She made no secret of her feelings for Adam. She was deeply and passionately in love with him and she would not allow herself to think of being parted from him. Having arrived in the 12th century, and having made a reasonable adjustment to her new life, she prayed daily to be allowed to remain where she was.

Her days were busy. She had begun to help Connie with the domestic chores, which during this season consisted mainly of supervising the cooking and serving of enormous amounts of food for each day's banquet, and the cleaning of the resulting mess in the kitchen and great hall so preparations could begin for the next feast. As Aline had noticed soon after her arrival at Shotley, for all her timidity with Blaise, Connie was a competent chatelaine and the servants willingly obeyed her. Only the temperamental cook occasionally challenged Connie's authority in the matter of food, but even she accepted offers of help with peeling or chopping or the apparently endless grinding of ingredients with mortar and pestle. Aline learned quickly how to be helpful, for she did not find this kitchen greatly different from the old-fashioned one she remembered in her grandparents' house when she was a girl.

The differences, of course, were in the areas of refrigeration and cooking method. At Shotley, all the cooking was done in a huge open fireplace fitted with iron hooks so kettles could be hung over the flames. There were what looked like large trivets on long legs, on which iron pots were set for slower cooking. There was also a system of spits of varying sizes, and a young boy whose chief duty was to keep the spits turning so the meat would roast evenly.

Next to the fireplace an oven had been built into the wall, and in it bread, meat pies, and pastries were baked. A heavy wooden table sat in the center of the kitchen, a chopping block off to one side. The storage cellars where the fruits and grains of the harvest were kept were directly below the kitchen. Just outside the kitchen door was a smokehouse for meats, and a coldhouse for cream and eggs and butter. Aline found the kitchen a most efficient arrangement. Working there and talking with Connie, the cook, the spitboy, or the other servants, she felt a warm sense of belonging. Since Connie and Adam accepted her, no one else questioned her presence at Shotley.

The servants did think she was peculiar for insisting upon a bath every day. When she offered to go to the bathhouse, Connie was horrified.

"Oh, no," she cried. "Aline, you cannot. All the men of the castle go there, and sometimes a woman who lives in the outer bailey joins them. Adam says it was different in the days when Lady Judith was alive, but I have not had the courage to try to change the bathhouse. When I wish to bathe, I do it in my own chamber, and so should you."

Thus admonished, Aline allowed herself the luxury of hot baths in her private chamber, and afterward annointed herself with the rose-scented lotion Connie had given her. She now used a concoction of rosemary and mint to clean her teeth, and after washing her hair she rinsed it with chamomile water. Adam had commented several times on how sweetly her hair and skin smelled, so she spared no effort to make herself attractive to him. She noted that, following her example, he came to each day's feast freshly scrubbed and shaved and emitting the piney tang of rosemary. She loved him all the more for his decision to please her in this way.

So quickly that she scarcely noted the passing of time, the holiday season slipped by until it was the early morning before the Twelfth Night celebration that would bring Christmas to an end. Aline and Adam entered the great hall together as usual, only to discover that Blaise and Connie had not yet appeared.

"How glad I am that you are here, Mistress Aline," called a maidservant. "There is a crisis in the kitchen. The cream has curdled and Cook threatens to leave. Lady Constance is still in her chamber. Will you come and see to it?"

"At once," Aline said, "though I believe Lady Constance would advise Cook to put mint into the cream to sweeten it again, and tell her she ought to know that without making such a great fuss." As she left Adam's side, he caught her chin in one hand and gave her a quick kiss.

"You see," he said, "neither they nor I can get along without you. How quickly you have learned to sweeten both the cream and our lives."

Laughing, she hurried to the kitchen to find the tearful cook threatening not only to leave the castle forever, but to beat the spitboy with a large wooden spoon. It took her a while to settle their dispute and to determine that the cream was not curdled at all, but only needed more whipping.

"I know you are weary," she said to the cook. "You are perhaps the person in this castle who has worked the hardest during these last two weeks, and I know you are anxious about completing all of today's chores before noontime. If you can work long enough to produce just one more of your marvelous feasts, then tomorrow you may take a well-earned rest."

"Someone forgot to put a bowl of milk and scrap of bread out for the fairies last night," sniffed the cook, with one eye on the spitboy, whose duty this was. "The fairies were annoyed and placed a spell on the cream so it would curdle and not whip properly."

"My grandfather once told me that fairies cannot work their enchantments during the blessed Christmas season," Aline said, silently blessing Gramps for relating this particular bit of folklore to her. She knew better than to try to argue about this superstition, or any other for that matter. She had seen enough food left for the fairies, or salt thrown over Cook's left shoulder when it was spilled, had heard enough special prayers and whispered graces to know the kitchen ran on magical belief as well as on practical common sense and tasty recipes. Her comment about the sacred season apparently pacified the cook, who sent the spitboy back to his work of turning a haunch of venison.

"And you," the cook said to one of the kitchen wenches, "do not let your basting brush rest, or the meat will be dry and not to Lord Adam's liking. Oh! Good day to you, my lord." The cook broke off, staring toward the door.

Adam stood there, surveying the busy scene. At the cook's exclamation, all work stopped, for Adam never came to the kitchen. This was the domestic side of the castle and thus the province of the lady of the castle.

"Forgive the intrusion," Adam said, treating the cook with the respect she considered her due from her master. "Lady Aline, are you able to leave your work? There is something I want you to see."

"I think all is well here." Aline smiled at the cook. "The feast is in excellent hands." She followed Adam through the screens passage from the kitchen to the great hall. They came out beside the dais and the high table.

"Look there." Adam pointed toward the other end of the hall where Blaise and Connie stood together before the fire. Connie was just giving her husband a cup of wine and a plate containing bread and cheese. The grin on Blaise's face could have warmed the entire hall. He put Connie's food offerings down on a nearby bench, then drew his wife into his arms for a long kiss.

"They came in together just a few moments ago," Adam said. "We need not ask what has caused Connie's face to glow as though a hundred candles were shining in her eyes, nor why Blaise looks like a proud conqueror."

"I am so happy for them." Aline turned her head to look at Adam. "And for you. Now you will have the peaceful home you want."

"And I have you." Adam wound his arms around her from behind, pulling her back against his chest. "You have brought blessings beyond measure into my life, Aline." His lips brushed her ear and then her throat. "Dear lady, might I coax you upstairs for an hour or two?"

Aline was tempted. The touch of Adam's mouth on her skin, his one arm around her waist and other arm sliding upward to press against her breasts, all made her heart beat faster. She felt the melting warmth begin deep inside her. She opened her lips to whisper that she would, indeed, escape with him to his chamber, and do it gladly.

But their swiftly rising desire was not to be fulfilled just yet, for Connie had seen them.

"Aline! I am sorry to be late and leave all the morning's work to you, but it was so—I mean, we were—oh, dear. Oh, dear." The stream of words stopped abruptly, with both of Connie's hands against her flaming cheeks. But she was not crying. As Adam had noted, her eyes were shining.

"Good day to you, daughter." Releasing Aline, Adam kissed Connie on the cheek.

"Good morning, my lord. I am sorry to be tardy. Truly, I did not mean—" Connie's face was now bright red. Adam wagged a finger at her.

"Enough. You need not apologize if your husband has kept you long abed. It is his privilege. And, Connie, I have asked you many times to call me Father, as Blaise does. Since you never knew your own father, I thought you would be glad to find one in me, but if you cannot bring yourself to call me as I wish, then Adam will do. 'My lord' is much too formal between close family members."

"I think I could call you Father now," Connie whispered with a tremulous smile. "Now I feel worthy to do so—Father."

"Thank you. It means much to me. Aline, I believe Connie wishes to speak with you in private, so you and I will finish our discussion later."

"Yes, my lord," Aline replied demurely, and had in return a quick wink from her love before he took himself off to join his son. In the manner of men in any period of history, they did not talk about what had happened between Blaise and Connie. Adam merely clapped his still-grinning son on the shoulder and said something about seeing to an ailing horse, and off they went together to the stables.

Connie was much more verbose than the men. She threw herself into Aline's arms, hugging her hard.

"Oh, Aline, it was so wonderful! Blaise was marvelous, so tender and gentle at first, and this time I was not frightened when he became fierce. It was like sailing to the stars! And he cares for me. He said he does. He said I have changed from a silly fool into an interesting young woman. He even promised to take me to Normandy when spring comes. I am so happy!" She stopped, looking hard at Aline. "Why did no one ever tell me it could be like that? If I had known, I would not have been so frightened these past months. I would not have refused Blaise so often nor believed that I must only endure what was pleasure for him."

"Love is something each woman must discover for herself, in her own way," Aline said.

"I have watched you and Adam together." Connie sounded just the slightest bit resentful.

"It has been so easy for you."

"No, it has not," Aline told her. "You do not know this, Connie, but many years ago I was married. I was even more unhappy than you and Blaise were. With Adam, I also had to learn to set aside my own fears and trust him."

"You are happy now?" Connie cried. "I want you to be happy with Adam."

"I am," Aline said. "I have never been so happy before."

"So it is with me." Connie hugged her again. "This morning, for the very first time, I feel like a true woman."

Chapter Five

Twelfth Night was different from the other days of Christmas. On this last day of the holiday season, the servants ruled the castle from midday to midnight, while all those usually in authority acted as servants. On the morrow the castle would return to sobriety once more and all the festive greenery would be removed and burned, but for this one afternoon and night a hilarious madness reigned.

Displaying a fine sense of the ludicrous, the servants chose the spitboy to be their Lord of Misrule during the festivities. In an uproariously foolish ceremony they crowned him with a lopsided homemade circlet of leather trimmed with pieces of multicolored glass for jewels. They then installed him at the high table in the lord's chair and placed the cook on the lady's chair beside him as his consort. To her credit, the cook accepted this accolade with a graciousness worthy of a true queen. Servants and ordinary men-at-arms filled the other chairs along the high table and at the upper ends of the two lower tables. Adam, his family, the priest, secretary, the captain of the guard, and officers of the men-at-arms, along with a few others who held important offices at the castle, were relegated to places below the salt—but they were not allowed to sit down until after they had served the dinner.

Adam himself carried in the haunch of venison and carved it up and presented it to his people. Blaise passed meat pies, Connie poured wine, and Aline had a huge bowl of vegetable stew and a ladle with which to serve it. The brawny captain of the guard was delegated to carry the silver tray containing dainty sweetmeats, which he did with good humor. Several barrels of wine were broached, and there was plenty of beer, cider, and perry.

During the afternoon rowdy games were played in the spaces between the tables. A group of men-at-arms sang a series of funny, if somewhat off-color ditties about the castle's inhabitants. Adam's usually solemn secretary engaged in a game of leapfrog with two kitchen maids and one of the stableboys. The mistletoe was all but denuded of its remaining berries, as one was plucked for each kiss stolen beneath it.

"Come and dance with me." Adam pulled her into a group of people.

"I don't know the steps," she protested.

"You will soon learn them." He caught her hands and swung her out, then back into the pattern of the dance while her new friends laughed and clapped and cheered her on. Before long she had discerned what the pattern was and found she could keep up with the others.

Aline noticed that never did the servants carry their merriment too far. They enjoyed a noisy, cheerful day and made a few observant comments about Blaise and Connie, or Adam and Aline, but they did nothing that might offend their noble masters. And when midnight came, like Cinderella after the ball with her coach and horses and footmen, they would all resume their ordinary lives. Aline thought this night was a wonderful idea, a time for masters and servants alike to let off steam and release a few discontents that might otherwise fester through the long winter months yet to come. In a place so closed in upon itself by cold and snow and ice, this celebration was needed. For it had begun to snow again, the second blizzard in 12 days.

"My lady." Adam interrupted her musings by putting an arm around her waist. "I believe you and I have an interesting conversation yet to finish."

"I do seem to remember something begun this morning and left uncompleted," she murmured. "But dare we leave the party?"

"It is almost over," he said. "Here comes Father John with my secretary Robert, to tell us when it is midnight."

"If you think either of them will be accurate timekeepers, you are much mistaken," she informed him. "They have both had too much wine and may well imagine it is still Christmas when February comes."

When Adam burst into laughter at this remark, she added, "Don't be surprised if Robert asks your permission to marry Connie's personal maid. If he doesn't, he ought to, after what I caught them doing an hour ago when I went into the coldhouse to get more butter."

Adam's renewed laughter was drowned out by the sudden noisy appearance of Connie, who came from the kitchen with Blaise behind her. Flushed and with her hair pulling loose from her braided earmuffs, Connie was banging on a pan with a rolling pin while her husband cried loudly that midnight was nigh.

"There's another who has had too much wine in celebration," Adam observed. "Ah, well, Blaise can hold her head when morning comes. It will make him a better husband."

"Listen, one and all," cried Father John, supporting himself with a hand on Robert's shoulder. " 'Tis midnight, 'tis time to end the feasting and revels. Go ye to your beds now, and rise early to the profitable performance of your duties with hearts grateful to Lord Adam, who has allowed you to make so merry this night, and all the other nights of Christmas." He concluded with a loud hiccup that brought a murmur of quiet laughter as those in the great hall began to disband. Calling their good nights to Adam, they filed out to the barracks, or the loft above the stable, or the kitchen hearth, to seek their pallets.

"There is a major cleanup job needed here," Aline noted, looking about the suddenly empty hall.

"Tomorrow," Adam said. "For now, my lady, I am taking you to bed. I have a few important things to say to you."

"And some interesting things to show me, too, I am sure," Aline teased.

"Always," he whispered, urging her up the curving staircase. When they had almost reached the top, Aline looked back to see Blaise and Connie climbing up behind them.

"Good night," Connie called out. "Sleep well."

"And you, my dear." Obeying an impulse, Aline went down a few steps to meet Connie so she could hug her and kiss her cheek. "Be happy always, Connie. And you, too, Blaise. Treasure what you have found in each other." She touched Blaise's face lightly with one hand. He caught it, holding her where she was for a moment.

"Thank you, Lady Aline. I regret those harsh words I spoke to you a few days ago. You are a wonderfully wise woman."

She stood watching them hurry along the short corridor to their bedroom, until Adam caught her at the waist again, drawing her upward toward the lord's chamber at the top of the stairs.

"What a day it has been," he said, taking her into his arms. "No man on earth is more blessed than I am tonight. My people sleep safe and secure, healthy and well fed, so I need not worry about them. My son is happy in his marriage at last, and I believe he will continue that way. And I have in my heart and in my bed the most wonderful woman in all the world."

When he kissed her, Aline wound her fingers through his gray-streaked hair and pressed herself against his strength. She felt his hands along her spine and then upon her hips, where they worked to free the knotted sash that rested there.

"I love you, Adam."

"I love you, with all my heart."

Swiftly he undressed her and then himself before he lifted her into his arms to kiss her again. With his mouth still on hers he carried her to the bed. There, slowly and tenderly, he aroused her to a state of desperate need until she wept for the aching emptiness he had created and pleaded with him to take her.

"If you are half-mad with longing," he muttered, "then I am completely mad. Only with you do I feel such passion, Aline. Only with you."

He knelt between her thighs and with one hard thrust buried himself in her. Aline received him with a wild cry of joy, giving herself up to his hot, driving passion, responding eagerly to his ever-deepening movements. She loved his complete lack of inhibition when he was inside her, loved the way he stayed with her, no matter how long it took, until she shuddered and gasped and cried out his name over and over in a strangled voice. But with Adam it never took very long; with Adam her fulfillment was easy and natural, and always, always, exquisitely tender in spite of his forcefulness. She loved most of all the moment when he went rigid and caught his breath, and then relaxed and moved more slowly in her, for she knew in that instant she was giving him what no one else could: his own fulfillment with a woman who loved him deeply and completely.

Only slightly less sublime was the time immediately afterward, when he gazed at her in the candlelight as though she were some incredible miracle of womanhood, when he told her he loved her and would never stop loving her, no matter what might happen in the future.

When he slept, with his hand on her breast and her head on his shoulder, Aline lay quietly so as not to disturb him. She did not feel like sleeping. She was too happy. She lay warm in his arms, listening to his breath and feeling his heart beat, and knowing that in Adam she had found the love she had always wanted.

Outside Shotley Castle the snow fell steadily and the wind blew, shaking the shutters in the lord's chamber. Adam stirred and turned over on his back, releasing Aline from his embrace. She tucked the quilt in around his shoulders and kissed him lightly.

"Hmm. Love," he murmured, and drifted off to sleep again.

A fresh blast of wind blew the shutter open, letting in cold air and a shower of snow. Aline leapt out of bed to close and latch the shutter. She paused with one hand on the latch, looking at the snow. Through a thick haze of white she could just barely see the castle walls. The wind had stopped for a moment, and in the stillness big, fat flakes floated gently downward across the window opening, just like the flakes she had noticed from the library on the day when she had first come to Shotley.

A slight stirring of air blew flakes against her face and bare shoulders. She was standing in the wet melted snow that had come in already and now more was drifting into the room through the unglazed window. Shivering violently, she began to push the shutter closed. . . .

The stone window frame began to dissolve. The latch and shutter vanished. Around her there was only white . . . snow . . . cold . . .

"Adam!" Aline turned toward him. She saw his bed, saw Adam sit up and throw back the quilt.

435

"Aline!" He was on his feet, trying to get to her, but his figure began to waver and blur before her eyes.

"Adam, I love you!" She knew what was happening. She prayed he had heard her last cry. She had heard his, in her heart if not actually in her ears.

"Aline . . . love . . ."

Then all was white and cold and silent.

Chapter Six

"Excuse me, Miss Bennett. Miss Bennett? Are you sick?" The voice was deeply masculine, with a cultivated English accent.

"What did you say?" Aline took her eyes from the falling snow beyond the library window to stare at the man in the chair next to hers.

"Are you all right? You have been sitting so still. You didn't answer when I called to you."

"I must have been dreaming," she said, looking around in wonder. "What a strange dream. It was so real. I was speaking Norman French."

"Dreams can be like that," he said. "You *are* Aline Bennett, aren't you? I'm Phillip Mallory. I was at your grandfather's funeral. We nearly collided when you left your sister's house in some haste."

"Oh?" Aline was having trouble adjusting to being back in the library. How could she have

437

had so long and so vivid a dream?

"I volunteered to follow you," Phillip Mallory said. "Your sister thought you would come here. She is worried about you because you have been so upset over your grandfather's death."

"That seems a long time ago now," Aline murmured. Then she remembered what Luce had said. "You are the man she wanted me to meet. Luce never stops her matchmaking efforts."

"This time it wasn't matchmaking," he told her. "She wanted us to meet because I called her this morning, not knowing your grandfather had died and hoping to visit him. He and my grandfather were boyhood friends. I met him once. I met you that day, too. You were just a little girl, and I was all of fourteen."

"You knew Gramps?" She looked at him with more interest after hearing that. Even sitting in a big library chair he looked tall, and a bit too thin, as if he didn't eat regularly. His hair was dark with gray streaks in it. His eyes were dark, too. On his ordinary face an indefinable sadness lay. Until he smiled. The corners of his eyes crinkled and his entire face was lit with pleasure. But he wasn't looking at Aline.

"I also remember this, and how beautiful the illuminations were," he said, indicating the Book of Hours that still lay open in front of Aline. There was the December page, with the painted castle gate under a blue, blue sky, with the men straining to pull the Yule log across the snow and, in the great hall, the lady sitting by the fire. Aline pushed the book along the table toward him so he could look at it more closely.

"If you want to touch it, you'll have to wear these," she said, pulling off the white cotton gloves.

She went absolutely still from shock. On the index finger of her left hand was a golden ring with a flower carved into its surface. At the center of the flower was a small red stone. Aline turned her hand over to stare at the smooth back of the ring where the metal had been heated and stretched to fit Adam's hand.

Adam! He had not been a dream. She did not know what had happened to her in the library that afternoon, but whatever it was, the ring was proof that she had not imagined it. Adam, Connie, Blaise, all of the folk of Shotley Castle were real, and she had walked among them, had talked, and laughed, and loved. . . . *Oh, Adam, my dear, lost love.*

"This book is still as wonderful as I remembered." Once more Phillip Mallory's accented voice recalled Aline to the present. "No wonder your grandfather treasured it. I'm glad he gave it to a library where others can see and appreciate it, instead of selling it to a private collector. Do you come here often?"

"Today is the first time."

"Ah, of course. You are here because of the funeral. It must have been comforting to hold something he loved."

"Actually . . ." She paused. If she told him where she had been during that snowy afternoon, and what she had done there, and how the first bitter grief of her grandfather's death had left her because she had spent a holiday with a Norman baron, he would think she was crazy. She said something else instead. "The book once belonged to a woman named Judith."

"Yes, I do recall your grandfather saying something about the names at the end. I'm afraid I was so bowled over by the glorious paintings that I didn't really pay much attention to his account of the history of the book."

"Oh, my God!" She gaped at him, memory flooding over her. "For all the times I looked at the book when Gramps had it, I always looked at the paintings, too, and the illuminated capital letters and the margins. But you are right, there is something written at the back." She would have seized the book had he not lifted a white-gloved finger to stop her from touching it. Carefully he opened the book to the last page. Unlike the illuminated pages of the body of the book where the words were still sharp and black, on this one page the ink had faded until it was so pale she could barely read the words written there.

Adam, Baron of Shotley, to Judith his wife. Squeezed in between that first line and the next was a note in someone else's hand. *Maud, his second wife, wed in the year of our Lord 1126.* Below, in the first handwriting again, was a neat list, each name on its own line.

Blaise of Shotley.

Constance his wife.

Adam their son, born October in the year of our Lord 1122.

Aline their daughter, born Christmas Day in the year of our Lord 1125.

Beneath this last notation was a single line, by the same hand that had written the note about Maud. Directly below the baby Aline's name and birth date were the words *A Christmas Blessing.*

"Adam." Aline could not stop herself. She put her bare finger on the words she believed he had written as a message to her across the centuries. Adam had known that she would look at the Book of Hours after returning to her own time. He had made Robert write the list of names in his neat clerical hand and then had added his own notes. "I am so glad you married again. I hope you were happy with her."

Phillip Mallory was looking at her strangely. She removed her finger from the book and sat with her head down, her hands clasped together in her lap.

"It is always hard to lose someone you love," he said. "However, I know from personal experience that time does ease the pain. And you do have the book to remember him by. You can come here to the library and look at it when you feel the need to be close to him again."

"Yes." Her voice was low. Phillip Mallory had no way of knowing that they were talking about two different men. "Time. It's already centuries away, and it can never return once it's gone. It is going to take me a long time to recover from what happened today."

"I understand. I do think you ought to return to your sister's house now," he said. Glancing toward the desk by the entrance, he added, "I can see by her frequent looks in our direction that the librarian would like to close up shop and go home."

"I can't go to Luce's house. I don't want to see a lot of people. Not tonight, not until I've had time to get used to what has happened."

"I rather think all the mourners will have left by now. Lucinda was extremely concerned about

441

your state of mind. It would reassure her if you were to stop by for a little while. I don't mean to interfere, but it seems to me your sister loves you very much."

"I know. I love her, too, in spite of our occasional misunderstandings. I said some nasty things to her earlier today. I ought to apologize. All right." Aline unclasped her hands and stood up. "Since you are wearing the gloves, would you mind packing the book into the box?"

"A favor for a favor," he said, smiling a little. "Might I drive to Lucinda's house with you? I came to the library in a taxi, and I fear I would have a difficult time finding another on such a night."

"Certainly. I think I owe you that much." Aline stopped, reminded of the lighthearted bargaining she had once done with a certain Norman knight. She said nothing more while Phillip Mallory took care of the Book of Hours with a skill that made her believe he was not unfamiliar with rare or ancient books.

They emerged from the library into a heavy snowfall. From somewhere in the direction of the college dormitories came the sound of recorded Christmas carols.

"It's the night before Christmas Eve," Aline said, still trying to reorient herself in the 20th century. "So much has happened, yet it's still only the 23rd day of December."

"So it is. I expect this has seemed a never-ending day to you." Phillip Mallory took her arm to guide her down the icy library steps and along the unshoveled walk to where her car was parked under a streetlamp. "It can scarcely be a joyous and carefree holiday for you this year. Still, no matter how sad one may be, each Christmas brings its own blessings. You have only to look for them."

"There was a time long ago," she said, clinging to his strong arm when she slipped on a patch of ice, "a time when Christmas lasted for twelve days and twelve nights."

"There are places where it still does." She could tell by his voice that he was smiling again. "Remember, Aline, when Twelfth Night is over and gone, there will be a bright and hopeful new year ahead for you. Now, give me your car keys."

"Why?"

"Because I am going to open the door for you." The smile was still in his voice, along with a teasing note. Aline found herself smiling in response to it.

"It's this key." She handed him her key ring. When he took it, his fingers closed around hers.

They stood there beneath the streetlamp, with the snow falling softly upon them, looking into each other's eyes. And in the distance, the recorded music began to play "The Twelve Days Of Christmas."

BLUE CHRISTMAS

Sandra Hill, Linda Jones, Sharon Pisacreta, Amy Elizabeth Saunders

The ghost of Elvis returns in all of his rhinestone splendor to make sure that this Christmas is anything but blue for four Memphis couples. Put on your blue suede shoes for these holiday stories by four of romance's hottest writers.

___4447-1 $5.50 US/$6.50 CAN

Dorchester Publishing Co., Inc.
P.O. Box 6640
Wayne, PA 19087-8640

Please add $1.75 for shipping and handling for the first book and $.50 for each book thereafter. NY, NYC, and PA residents, please add appropriate sales tax. No cash, stamps, or C.O.D.s. All orders shipped within 6 weeks via postal service book rate. Canadian orders require $2.00 extra postage and must be paid in U.S. dollars through a U.S. banking facility.

Name_____
Address_____
City_____State_____Zip_____
I have enclosed $_____ in payment for the checked book(s).
Payment <u>must</u> accompany all orders. ❑ Please send a free catalog.

Three Heartwarming Tales of Romance and Holiday Cheer

Bah Humbug! by Leigh Greenwood. Nate wants to go somewhere hot, but when his neighbor offers holiday cheer, their passion makes the tropics look like the arctic.

Christmas Present by Elaine Fox. When Susannah returns home, a late-night savior teaches her the secret to happiness. But is this fate, or something more wonderful?

Blue Christmas by Linda Winstead. Jess doesn't date musicians, especially handsome, up-and-coming ones. But she has a ghost of a chance to realize that Jimmy Blue is a heavenly gift.

___4320-3 $5.50 US/$6.50 CAN

Dorchester Publishing Co., Inc.
P.O. Box 6640
Wayne, PA 19087-8640

Please add $1.75 for shipping and handling for the first book and $.50 for each book thereafter. NY, NYC, and PA residents, please add appropriate sales tax. No cash, stamps, or C.O.D.s. All orders shipped within 6 weeks via postal service book rate. Canadian orders require $2.00 extra postage and must be paid in U.S. dollars through a U.S. banking facility.

Name_____
Address_____
City_____State_____Zip_____
I have enclosed $_____ in payment for the checked book(s).
Payment <u>must</u> accompany all orders. ❑ Please send a free catalog.

Enchanted Christmas
Emma Craig

Noah Partridge has a cold, cold heart. Honey-haired Grace Richardson has heart to spare. Despite her husband's death, she and her young daughter have hung on to life in the Southwestern desert, as well as to a piece of land just outside the settlement of Rio Hondo. Although she does not live on it, Grace clings to that land like a memory, unwilling to give it up even to Noah Partridge, who is determined to buy it out from under her. But something like magic is at work in this desert land: a magic that makes Noah wonder if it is Grace's land he lusts after, or the sweetness of her body and soul. For he longs to believe that her touch holds the warmth that will melt his icy heart.

___52287-X $5.99 US/$6.99 CAN

Dorchester Publishing Co., Inc.
P.O. Box 6640
Wayne, PA 19087-8640

Please add $1.75 for shipping and handling for the first book and $.50 for each book thereafter. NY, NYC, and PA residents, please add appropriate sales tax. No cash, stamps, or C.O.D.s. All orders shipped within 6 weeks via postal service book rate. Canadian orders require $2.00 extra postage and must be paid in U.S. dollars through a U.S. banking facility.

Name_____
Address_____
City_____ State _____ Zip _____
I have enclosed $ _____ in payment for the checked book(s).
Payment <u>must</u> accompany all orders. ❏ Please send a free catalog.